MW00948423

The Crafter's Defense

A Dungeon Core Novel

Dungeon Crafting – Book 2

Jonathan Brooks

Cover Design: Yvonne Less, Art 4 Artists

Edited by: Celestian Rince

Acknowledgements

I would like to thank all my friends and family who have supported me on my writer's journey, as well as providing much-needed encouragement. You're the best!

This book wouldn't be as wonderful as it is without the support and assistance of my beta-readers, in addition to Patreon comments as it was being written. Your feedback and comments helped to develop and shape the story to where it is today!

Aaron Wiley

Alexander Canavan

Brian O'Neil

Dakota Lee Manchette

Damion Spearman

Dann Douglas

Emerald

Emma Baker

Gary York

Grant Harrell

James Carter

Kelly Padgett

Michael Harrington

Michael Katz

Nate Martin

Neil Stalker

Ryan Adams

Sean Hall

Steven Genskay

Table of Contents

Recap

Sandra was born a merchant and died a merchant – but that wasn't the end of her existence. She was born with crippled hands that prevented her from crafting all but the most basic materials; because of this – and the ability to *see* but not *manipulate* all of the elements – she spent most of her life learning everything she could about her fascination with crafting. After indulging in her hobby a little too much, she over-reached and ended up being sacrificed to fuel an enchantment from the very person she was hoping to learn it from.

Reborn as a Dungeon Core – centuries in the future – in a place uninhabited by Humans, Sandra was thrust into an underground space without a clue of what she was and why she was there. With the help of a Dungeon Fairy named Winxa, however, she was able to learn how to create Monster Seeds, Dungeon Monsters, rooms, tunnels, and even traps.

Her new incarnation wasn't without its own dangers, however. Soon after she started to increase her Core Size, she was incessantly attacked by Territory Ants that tried to destroy her Core. Without another option, she was forced to use her Constructs-based Dungeon Monsters to completely eliminate the threat.

From then on, though, Sandra was able to expand her dungeon all the way to the surface, filling a dozen rooms with traps and increasingly powerful Dungeon Monsters to protect herself from the outside world. Not only that, but she was able to finally do what she had never been able to do when she was a Human: Craft. Using her abilities as a Dungeon Core, she created multiple rooms for different crafting trades, including a forge, a textile shop, leatherworking workshop, and even a jeweler's station. Unfortunately, she didn't have the correct materials to make many of the things she wanted, but she had plenty to occupy her time.

Although, that time rapidly disappeared when a Half-Orc/Half-Dwarf named Kelerim appeared at her entrance chased by huge Bearlings. Sandra ended up killing a few of the monstrous beasts before they retreated, and she saved the person who had inadvertently brought them inside. With some application of her Core abilities, she was able to designate Kelerim as a "Visitor" and started to teach him the correct way to blacksmith, fixing and improving his meager skills so that he could go back and help the land of Orcrim against the pervasive attacks of the nearby "normal" dungeons.

Fate had other plans as Kelerim's previously unknown half-brother Razochek Bloodskull stumbled upon Sandra's dungeon while hunting the Bearlings. Not willing to risk letting the new dungeon expand and threaten the village of Grongbak and – eventually – the entire Orc homeland of Orcrim, the Warband Leader fought his way through the dungeon with the intent to destroy Sandra's Dungeon Core. Kelerim wouldn't allow his half-brother to destroy what he saw as Orcrim's salvation, however, and fought against Razochek, killing him with some help from more of Sandra's Dungeon Monsters.

Affected by the slaying of his own flesh and blood, Kelerim set off to find his father and to start his own smithy, bringing much-needed quality to the progressively poor work done by the existing Orcish blacksmiths. This, of course, left Sandra all alone – with just Winxa as company...

Chapter 1

Saving the world not only takes work, but it's rather boring, too, Sandra thought.

It had only been a couple of hours since Kelerim had left, and the loneliness brought on by his absence was in no way filled by Winxa, her Dungeon Fairy. It was nothing against her frequently absent friend who was forbidden to give her advice for some reason by The Creator; on the contrary, Winxa was a vital reason Sandra hadn't gone crazy from her new existence as a Dungeon Core over the last few months. In fact, she didn't know what would've happened if the diminutive fairy *hadn't* been there; she thought it likely that she'd be as crazy and murderous as the other dungeon cores in the world without Winxa's help to keep her sane.

Crushing loneliness was nothing new to her, however. Growing up constantly on the move and possessing her crippled, disfigured hands hadn't lent to having many friends (none, really) – so she should have been used to it by then. Of course, it was the fact that she had a real-life person as a friend and then lost him that hurt the most; she almost regretted letting him walk away, but she realized that if she forced him to stay against his wishes, she would be just as bad – or worse – as the other Dungeon Cores in the world. They only wanted to *kill* people; if she gave into her selfishness and kept him there, it would've been akin to *slavery* – which was somehow a whole lot worse in her opinion.

Therefore, she loaded him up with some of the things that he might need on his journey and let him go. It was necessary, but that didn't mean she didn't wish it were otherwise.

Shortly after the fight through her dungeon and the consequential deaths of the Orcs – including Razochek, Kelerim's previously unknown half-brother – Sandra let the Half-Orc/Half-Dwarf figure himself out while she did what she could to return her dungeon to the way it was before the attack against her Dungeon Monsters. *Massacre* would probably be more accurate, as most of her defending Monsters had been utterly destroyed. In fact, the only ones left in her dungeon at all were most of the smaller ones she had roaming through her workrooms absorbing ambient energy. She still had her Mechanical Wolf and Jaguar outside roaming around, of course, but she didn't really count those – especially when she was considering her defense.

Sandra had cancelled her flame wall trap in the Home room where her Core was located, before she sent as many of the smaller constructs as she could spare to gather up all of the left-behind Monster Seeds dropped by her slain defenders. When they were brought back to her Core, she had absorbed the corpses of the Orcs for Raw Materials and used the massive amounts of Mana they dropped upon their deaths to rebuild her small army of Dungeon Monsters. There was so much Mana, though, that she ended up adding in four extra Ironclad Apes *and* Steel Pythons to her defense in the first few rooms; it was a bit of a stopgap measure until she figured something else out, of course – because it was obvious that her current setup wasn't quite prepared to withstand an assault by a determined group of Heroes. Or an Orcish Warband for that matter.

In the end, all of that Mana had been enough to complete everything she needed to replenish her Monster room defenders, as well as providing six more Mechanical Wolves and 6 additional Jaguars that could roam around aboveground, collecting ambient Mana. She had found that those two constructs were the most agile and fastest over rough terrain, which the wastelands surrounding her dungeon had plenty of. That wasn't the only benefit, however; they were her eyes and ears in that dry, blasted land – which was desperately needed so that there weren't any more surprises.

They were, in fact, what had let her know far in advance that the Warband came back after Razochek and the others disappeared – but they had fortunately not seen the faint tracks leading to her dungeon entrance. Sandra kept them roaming around as they wished, only stressing upon them the importance that they stay as hidden as possible if they sensed a living being nearby – be it an Orc or otherwise. And, if they *were* spotted, they were to run in the complete opposite direction of her dungeon entrance; she would gladly take their loss if they were caught or left her Area of Influence altogether, rather than lead whatever it was to her dungeon again. Being invaded by something else right then was the last thing she needed.

Sandra had managed to use all but the tiniest amount of Mana that was provided from the deaths of the Orcs inside her dungeon before it faded away, which she still felt somewhat bad about. Although she had been justified in defending herself, she wished that Kelerim had been successful in convincing them to leave without more bloodshed; barring that, she had hoped that – after a few of them had died – they would've left and never come back. It was only with a heavy reluctance that she acknowledged the best outcome (in her own case) had actually occurred; if they had left, they might've come back with even more Warriors – which may have spelled her doom.

She had held off on upgrading her Core Size until Kelerim left, because he had been acting very strange – which she later found was because he wanted to leave. Only a few hours after he had left, however, she used her full Mana to finish off the last of her stages to become Core Size 17. The same reduced awareness affected her like it did with every upgrade, but fortunately Winxa was there to help keep her company – like usual. The Dungeon Fairy offered tentative suggestions on how to improve her traps – cautious all the while because she didn't want to end up being punished by The Creator for "giving advice" – and also evaluated how well her Dungeon Monsters worked against the Orcs.

It was enlightening, to say the least, because it just emphasized the point that her dungeon had been *barely* adequate in her defense. As much as Sandra didn't like killing living beings, she now knew that it was inevitable if someone or something decided they wanted to destroy her Core. She resolved to greatly improve her defenses; to do that, though, she was going to need a lot more Mana.

Winxa— Sandra thought towards the Dungeon Fairy, as soon as her Core Size upgrade was complete— *what's the **best** way to increase my Mana flow?* She was pretty sure she knew the answer, but she wanted to see if there were any other options.

Winxa jumped in surprise as that was the first thing Sandra had said for almost a day and a half. "Are you talking about the *fastest* way, or just the most *efficient* way?" the Dungeon Fairy asked with a little wariness in her voice.

Uh...the most efficient way. I can guess that the fastest way is what I've just experienced, but I would like to avoid that if possible.

The diminutive Fairy breathed a sigh of relief. "Thank the Creator; I was worried that a taste of the Mana you can get from killing sentients had turned you into the same bloodthirsty murderers that the other Cores always seem to be," she said as she smiled. "To answer your question, though, the most efficient – but more time-consuming – method of increasing the amount of Mana you're acquiring is to do the same thing *outside*

14

that you're doing *inside*. What that essentially means is to blanket everything aboveground with Dungeon Monsters, which will absorb and funnel the ambient Mana to you. It will take a hefty initial investment, but it will pay off in the long run.

"If you're efficient enough, and avoid detection for a long period of time, your Monsters can eventually absorb every available drop of Mana out there. This rarely happens with other dungeons, however, because all they are concerned about is expanding as quickly as they can so that they can reach their victims. Which, to be fair, is essentially what The Creator had envisioned for them, but their crazed single-mindedness doesn't often lend itself to strategic planning."

I can only imagine. So, does the ambient Mana extend...upwards?

Winxa looked confused for a moment, before comprehension dawned on her. "Yes, your Area of Influence extends as far up above the ground as it does belowground, though the concentration of ambient Mana tends to reduce dramatically the farther up you go. Up to approximately 200 feet above the surface, the intake of ambient Mana is essentially the same as ground level, which gives any Cores that have flying Dungeon Monsters a bit of an advantage – because there is a whole lot more that they can absorb—" the Dungeon Fairy said, before muttering under her breath— "though it's not like they take advantage of it."

That was exactly what Sandra was hoping for. She was reluctant to "blanket" the wasteland with Dungeon Monsters, especially since it would cause way too much attention. Other dungeons didn't care about being seen, as they *wanted* people to come attack them – so that they could acquire the Mana from the sentients' deaths. Sandra, on the other hand, wanted to stay as hidden as possible – at least for the time being. The less people who knew about her presence and location, the better.

With a potential solution to her ambient Mana acquisition problem rolling around in her mind, Sandra finally concentrated on the screens that had popped up in her vision.

Core Size Upgrade Stage complete!
9/9 Completed

Your Core has grown!
Current Size: 17

Mana Capacity increased!
Ambient Mana Absorption increased!
Raw Material Capacity increased!

New Constructs option!

Core Selection Menu	
Dungeon Classification:	Constructs
Core Size:	17
Available Mana:	32/10014
Ambient Mana Absorption:	10/hour
Available Raw Material (RM):	16500/28895
Convert Raw Material to Mana?	16500 RM -- > 660 Mana
Current Dungeon Monsters:	684
Constructs Creation Options:	16
Monster Seed Schematics:	70 (18)
Current Traps:	27

Trap Construction Options:	All
Core-specific Skills:	4
Current Visitors:	1

All in all, Sandra had ended up using 72,000 Mana in order to upgrade her Core Size. It didn't seem like that much, though, because more than half of it had been supplied to her within a couple of minutes from the deaths of the Orcs fighting the Bearlings almost a week before. In order for her to continue to grow, however, she was going to have to concentrate on the other methods at her disposal.

She was currently up to 684 Dungeon Monsters, although 60% of them were the smaller constructs that roamed through the lower rooms absorbing the ambient Mana inside her dungeon. The rest were comprised of the hundreds filling up her uppermost rooms, defending her entrance from any invaders that might come along. To add to that number, however, she had acquired a brand-new Construct with her Core Size upgrade – but it was going to be extremely expensive to produce.

Constructs Creation Options	
Name:	Mana Cost:
Clockwork Spider	5
Small Animated Shears	10
Tiny Automaton	20
Rolling Force	25
Segmented Centipede	100
Articulated Clockwork Golem	150
Singing Blademaster	300
Small Armored Sentinel	400

Mechanical Jaguar	800
Mechanical Wolf	1000
Basher Totem	2000
Automated Digger	2500
Repair Drone	4000
Ironclad Ape	6000
Steel Python	8000
Iron-plated Behemoth	10000

Not only did the Iron-plated Behemoth cost 10,000 Mana – which was almost the maximum she could hold in the first place – but the only Monster Seed she could produce and use to create it was the Tiny Dragon Glass Flake.

Monster Seed Origination				
Name:	Raw Material Cost:	Mana Cost:	Min. Mana:	Max. Mana:
Tiny Dragon Glass Flake	20000	7000	5000	10000
Large Steel Orb	32000	3200	5000	16000

In all, she would have to provide 20,000 Raw Materials and 17,000 Mana to produce the construct; to top it off, with the *Behemoth* name, she was a little worried that it wouldn't even fit in her Home room. At Core Size 18, she predicted that she would have a large enough Raw Material maximum to produce a Large Steel Orb – which would cost half as much Mana; she technically still had one of the Large Steel Orbs from unlocking the use of it in the first place, but she decided against producing her newest construct until she had both made room for it and used her slowly accumulating Mana on something more productive.

There is just so much I want to do, and never enough
Mana to do it.

With that thought, she mentally sighed and got to work.

Chapter 2

As much as she wanted to start crafting again – especially with the new materials that Kelerim had acquired from the nearby Orc village – she decided to put her Mana absorption plan into place. To that effect, Sandra started to produce Small Animated Shears one after another, using up many of the extra Tiny and Small Copper Orbs she had stacked up around her Core. As soon as they were created, she sent them down the hallway and into the Vertical Air-trap Transportation System (VATS) to get to the top of her dungeon rather quickly. As soon as they got to the entrance, she sent them outside into the bright sunlight and had them shoot straight up into the wide-open air.

At first, the ambient Mana she had been receiving from her constructs inside her dungeon had capped out at around 10 per minute, which would allow her to create a single Small Animated Shears and the accompanying Tiny Copper Orb (when she ran out of her stockpile). The 14 Mechanical Wolves and Jaguars (7 of each) that were roaming around outside weren't affected by the ambient Mana cap that her dungeon seemed to have, so they were providing even more. Although the Mana wasn't as concentrated outside of her dungeon – and from what Winxa had told her a few weeks before, would continue to thin out the further she went from her entrance – there was *much more* to explore. In the beginning, she calculated that she was receiving a little less than a single Mana every minute from her outdoor constructs.

While that didn't seem like that much, she also had to consider that her Wolves and Jaguars also moved slowly and cautiously through the wasteland above; again, that was to make sure they were safe and unspotted (hopefully) by anything else roaming around up there. When they crept around instead of running full out, they could accumulate less of the ambient Mana that was available and just sitting there waiting for them to gather it up.

After the first dozen Shears floated through the air at about 200 feet, however, she could feel even more start to funnel into her. She was able to spread them out into 20-foot-long cubes, where they would slowly – but continuously – move in their designated space and soak up all the Mana in the air. They were angled so that their points were facing towards the Orcish village of Grongbak, presenting as little profile as possible to avoid detection.

Using the vision that they afforded her with a figurative "bird's-eye view", she was easily able to see the village on the horizon but couldn't make out many details. All she knew, though, was that the village – in addition to about 600 feet beyond from what she could "feel", due to her recent Core Size upgrade – was now thoroughly within her Area of Influence. She couldn't actually see that far yet with her Shears because she didn't dare get too close to people, so she was basing the distance on what she could envision underground.

Although that somewhat limited the space to the northwest where she could expand her ever-widening net of Shears in the air, she still had literal miles of air to fill up with her constructs in other directions. In fact, since she could see a bit farther away now, she could see that she wasn't quite in the *middle* of the wasteland – as she had first supposed. Instead, it appeared that her dungeon and her Core were located somewhat closer to the Orcish lands than the other three lands – owned by the other races – that were reportedly out there somewhere.

To the north, south, east, and west, she could see the unmistakable sight of trees in the distance, though they were still a bit too far for her Area of Influence to reach yet. The northern and western forests were the closest, however, which was how Sandra knew she was closer to the Orcish lands than the others. She couldn't quite see anything to the southwest, but she saw a small break in the tree line where she supposed the Elvish lands were located – at least according to what Winxa had told her. It was hard to make out, but she thought she saw similar breaks to the northeast and southeast, where the Dwarves and Gnomes lived, respectively.

She recounted what she saw to her Dungeon Fairy friend, who looked sadder and sadder at the descriptions Sandra supplied to her.

Winxa seemed lost in her memories for a moment, before she volunteered some information. "From what you describe, it sounds like nearly 100 square miles of land was destroyed and turned into these wastelands. I've only really had second-hand knowledge of what was going on up there from others, so I wasn't completely sure how much had actually been devastated.

"Those forests you see used to extend and meet in the middle of this area, almost like a crossroads. It was here that Wester had his dungeon, and at the end of his existence, his Area of Influence had extended for hundreds of miles in every direction. Most of the wreckage of the land was concentrated here, though, where his actual Core was located; it's almost like the combined armies of Elves, Orcs, Dwarves, and Gnomes were determined to eliminate every trace of his dungeon, so they probably overdid it a little here. I can't blame them, however, as he was quite...dangerous and ruthless." Winxa seemed to shiver at the mention of her former Core.

Well, let's hope I don't make the same sort of mistakes and ruin the land even more, Sandra sent her thoughts towards the melancholy Fairy.

"From what I've seen of your actions so far, I wholeheartedly believe that's the last thing that you want – and I'll do whatever I can to help you stay away from that outcome."

Thanks, Winxa – I appreciate your confidence in me.

Sandra really did appreciate the confidence Winxa showed towards her. She *wanted* to be different than the other Dungeon Cores out there; sometimes it was hard, though, not to think about how much Mana she could acquire from the deaths of living beings. Fortunately, she wasn't comfortable with the thought of murder and killing, so whenever thoughts of taking a shortcut to expansion entered her mind, they were almost instantly snuffed out.

After over 100 Small Animated Shears were sent aboveground and into the air above her dungeon, Sandra noticed a significant uptick in how much Mana was being funneled to her. She was still getting approximately 10 Mana per minute from the constructs inside her dungeon, but the amount she was receiving from outside was already just over 3 Mana per minute.

And that had only been a little less than an hour's work.

Encouraged by the increase, Sandra continued to create more of her small flying constructs over the next 24 hours, until she was to the point where she was starting to make 2 of them a minute...and then 3...and then 5... By the time she was done, the sky was blanketed with Shears over much of her Area of Influence – barring the area around the Orc Village, of course. The ambient Mana absorption increase was exponential as time went on; a steady stream of Shears flowed out of her dungeon in a seemingly never-ending parade of metallic objects. As she neared the 6-hour mark, she was able to produce 19 or 20 constructs *a minute* to send out to join the others in the sky.

All told, she had just over 9,000 of her Small Animated Shears covering 180,000 square feet of airspace. From the ground, they appeared very small and hard to spot, though if you knew what you were looking for you could see them; regardless, unless someone was specifically looking for them, they were practically invisible, being only 3 inches long.

She could've kept going, but she had already had to split her concentration during the whole process and dug out a massive room connecting to her boiling vats (previously used for tanning) room in order to supply enough Raw Materials for the Tiny Copper Orbs the Shears needed; she placed it there because she had a plan to use it for something when she was finished with her current project. The cost to excavate the room and acquire the RM was fairly low, but if she hadn't had to use some of the incoming Mana to do that, she thought she could've had another three or four hundred of her small constructs.

Again, she theoretically could've kept going, but the whole process was very repetitive, monotonous, and extremely *boring.* And yet, when she finally stopped, took a mental step back, and calculated what she was bringing in every *minute,* she could see that the entire day spent on her project had been completely worth it.

Previous Mana Intake

> *Core Absorption: 10 Mana/hour*
>
> *Dungeon Absorption: 10 Mana/min*
>
> *Aboveground Absorption: >1/min*
>
> *Daily Intake: ~15,000*

Current Mana Intake

> *Core Absorption: 10 Mana/hour*
>
> *Dungeon Absorption: 10 Mana/min*
>
> *Aboveground Absorption: 260/min*
>
> *Daily Intake: ~390,000*

Before she started her Shears-blanket project, Sandra had been accumulating just under 15,000 Mana a day – which wasn't a small amount, but not nearly enough to satisfy her need for it; especially when she considered her new construct, which would take more than a full day to supply enough Mana for it – not to mention the Raw Materials needed for its Monster Seed. Now, however, with just a day's worth of work – boring, monotonous work, of course – she was acquiring 270 Mana per minute, or a little under *400,000 a day*!

Sandra had noticed that the farther she placed her Shears from her dungeon, the less her constructs had started to return. They were still plenty effective, but they had diminishing returns as her blanket extended over the wasteland. She was almost tempted to do another round of creating thousands more Small Animated Shears, but she decided that she needed a break from the monotony of it – and her intake had increased by 2,600%...so, not a bad day's work.

"I've...never even heard of something like what you've done here before," Winxa remarked, after Sandra finally told her the results of what she had done. The Dungeon Core didn't really have the opportunity to split her attention enough to carry a conversation while she had been working on her project, so it was the first Winxa had gotten any information from Sandra. "The closest I can think of was when a Natural-element Core created a swarm of toxic small mobile mushrooms that covered about a half-mile of ground before they were sent against a nearby village. Almost every other Dungeon Core thinks more in terms of 'bigger is better', so they rarely use their smallest Dungeon Monsters after they unlock access to larger ones," the Dungeon Fairy explained.

It doesn't sound like they employ much strategic thinking in their actions, do they?

"Very rarely. In fact, the last time any of them really used their Dungeon Monsters with any type of strategy like the way you have...well...you can see the result up there for yourself."

Don't worry, Winxa – I'm not planning on trying to take over the world; I'm trying to save it.

"I hope so...Creator help us if you're not."

Chapter 3

Now that she had a workable amount of Mana coming in at a fairly rapid pace, Sandra could finally concentrate on other matters. There were three things she needed to do: upgrade her Core Size, improve her defenses, and – of course – get back to crafting. Somehow, she needed to figure out how to both divide her concentration and her available Mana in order to do all three; which was imperative that she do, because it would further the progress of her purpose – to save the world...or at least the people in this corner of the world.

The first one was easy enough to do; currently, upgrading her Core to Size 18 was going to require 10 stages, each consisting of 10,014 Mana, for a total of just over 100,000 Mana. Theoretically, her dungeon and her "Airborne Mana Absorption Net of Shears" (or AMANS for short) could supply that amount in about 6 hours, but she was reluctant to go back into that helpless space again so soon after her last Core Upgrade. It needed to be done, however, so she still needed to apply some of her incoming Mana to complete the stages, but she was planning on putting it off for at least a couple of days – preferably more – before she completed the entire process.

The second action she needed to complete was to improve her defenses; they were woefully inadequate to properly defend herself from any other incursions. Before she did that, however, she needed some pertinent information from her resident Dungeon Fairy.

Winxa? I want to expand my dungeon some more to improve my defenses, but I'm not sure how to go about that. And, added to that, I don't want my various workshops to be destroyed if more people try to come in and harm me.

"Oh, that's easy. You can just branch off from one of your established rooms and add some more passageways. For instance, you can seal off the tunnel leading from the eleventh room down from the surface to Kelerim's old forge, as long as you still have access to your Core – or Home – Room down here. Dungeon Cores do it all the time; expanding a dungeon to make more rooms is a common practice to make it harder to reach their Cores. You just have to make sure that there is always a route throughout the entire dungeon, otherwise you won't be able to fill in a tunnel – which would essentially block you off from everything."

Seems simple enough. As long as she had some sort of access to her Home room, she could do whatever she wanted. Looking at her underground dungeon with a bit of a faraway view, she saw what she remembered: a downward spiral of rooms leading from the entrance to her Core far down below, with her extensive VATS column filling up the previously empty middle of the spiral. But now that her Area of Influence had greatly expanded, as well as the influx of Mana from her AMANS above, she could add much more around her central spiral.

The first eight rooms that had proven at least moderately successful against the Orcs she left alone for the moment; she was planning on upgrading the traps inside of them since she had a greater maximum Mana, which would increase their deadliness even more. As much as she hated the thought that what she was doing was to *kill*, she knew it was unfortunately necessary for her own survival – and what she was hoping was the survival of the other races...as confusing as that thought was.

Therefore, Sandra started on the 9th, 10th, and 11th rooms, which were essentially empty and had acted as a kind of buffer between the trapped rooms and her workshops. For these rooms – and a few more that she was planning on digging out and filling with traps and Dungeon Monsters – she adapted her new technique of multi-element traps that she had discovered after Kelerim had arrived in her dungeon. Since the first eight rooms had a single-element trap – Nether, Holy, Water, Fire, Nature, Air, Spirit, and Earth (in order from the entrance on down) – she thought it was only fitting that she would have some dual-element traps to slow down any invaders. In the future, when she was able to successfully adapt three elements into a single trap, Sandra planned on expanding even further, but that was going to have to wait for now.

In the ninth room down from the entrance, she expanded the previously 30-foot by 30-foot room with 10-foot ceilings outward from the downward dungeon spiral by a hundred feet. She then used the Raw Materials from excavating the now 30X130X10-foot space by creating curved walls inside the room; these walls led from the entrance to the room into small little 3-foot-wide hallways that led every which way, with dead ends, various twists and turns, and eventually led to the exit to the tenth room.

The walls themselves were made from a core of pure shiny Steel that she was able to manipulate enough with her Mana to produce a mirror-like surface. This was for two purposes; one, the Steel would add a lot of stability since she sunk it deep into the floor, as well as the strength to withstand repeated blows if someone tried to break it down to avoid the little maze she had made. Second, the metal would be hot to the touch from the intense heat that Sandra was planning on pumping into the entire room.

Because she now had much more maximum Mana than the traps she had set previously – just over 10,000 – her traps were much deadlier. With a combination of Air and Fire, Sandra set up a room-sized trap that would heat up the ambient temperature in the room to nearly 250 degrees – hot enough to set some cloth on fire, but not nearly enough to ignite wood. Given that powerful heat, anyone entering the room for more than a few moments would start to suffer greatly from the oven-like environment. The trigger point for the trap was only a few steps into the room, which would last for a little over 5 minutes before the Mana ran out and had to recharge for a lengthy period of time.

Learning from the previous incursions, she also placed a second trigger on the threshold to the room that would deactivate the trap if every person who had crossed it exited the room. That way, they couldn't just activate it and run out, waiting for it to expend all its Mana before entering again; well, they *could* just do it multiple times in a row and slowly deplete the Mana inside of the trap, but she was hoping that no one would know enough about how it worked to realize that.

There was one other way someone could deactivate the trap, however. Inside the small corridors of the maze, there was a Steel Python located in the room towards the exit, which was the catalyst for the trap. Every room that had more than one element in its trap needed a catalyst to maintain its presence within the room; in this case, it was the Python, and destroying it would deactivate the trap. Through some experimentation, she found that she could retie the trap – with a comparatively small application of Mana – to another Python if the original was lost, so replacing it in the future didn't mean she would lose the trap for good. Of course, getting to the Python was going to be difficult, as one would need to traverse the entire maze in order to get there.

In the tenth room – if anyone managed to get that far – she flipped some things around. Previously, when she applied the Spirit element to a trap, she had caused those affected by it to imagine they were trapped inside a large spider's web and attacked by multitudes of spiders, which also had the benefit of ramping up their Fear quite a bit. When she combined Spirit with Holy in this next room, however, she went in the opposite direction.

Dozens of large, densely packed, and bright floating lights would hover throughout the room – which she didn't change from its previous 30X30X10 size – when the trigger was activated by someone crossing the threshold. The trap would last for a little more than 20 minutes, which was plenty of time for the 30 Singing Blademasters she had placed along the rear of the room – because those who touched one of the bright floating lights likely wouldn't even know they were there.

The lights weren't harmful by themselves, however – just the opposite; if someone allowed a portion of their skin to come in contact with the floating light, they would experience the greatest euphoria they could ever imagine as long as they stayed touching her Bliss Globes. Or, that's what she decided to call them, because pure bliss was what she was hoping people would "suffer" from. When they were incapacitated and in their joyful, introspective world, her Singing Blademasters would attack when they weren't prepared for them. Simple, and yet – hopefully – effective.

She had tried to make the entire room one whole euphoric experience, but the effects would only last for about 20 seconds; as soon as it was activated, the timer started, so that if only one person walked in and was caught by it, the others outside in the tunnel leading inside would be completely unaffected – not the ideal situation.

In the eleventh room, Sandra combined the Natural and Earth elements to design something that she thought was going to be extraordinarily lethal. First, she expanded the room to be about the same size as the ninth room with the maze, but instead of walls – she built pits. A narrow, 2-foot-wide, zig-zagging walkway wound through the room, with a deep, 30-foot pit filled with extremely sharp jagged rocks tipped with Dragon Glass (for extra penetration). The walkways actually came fairly close to each other as they crossed through the room, but to avoid the chance that anyone could just hop over the pit to another walkway, there were Natural-element-created vines hanging down from the ceiling. Normally, this would probably look like a way to swing across, but the vines were connected to a very lightly wedged piece of heavy stone created by her Earth element; if the vines were pulled on even slightly, the stone would plummet down from the ceiling and impact anyone nearby.

Sandra even placed a few vines in the middle of the walkways, which were difficult – but not impossible – to pass by. To make it harder, she placed over 100 Rolling Forces along the walkway and created small ramps that pointed at anyone walking towards the exit. Her constructs could pick up speed and either run into someone's foot or propel themselves through the air via the ramps, where they would – hopefully –

hit them when they were least expecting it. The traps were tied to the very last Rolling Force in the room, which acted as the catalyst, and if it were destroyed, the vines and the falling rocks would disappear; if anyone managed to survive more than 15 minutes the trap would disappear as well, but she didn't think anyone would last that long.

The next room down was technically Kelerim's old Forge and workshop, but she branched off and made the real exit to the walkways on the wall adjacent to the tunnel leading there. She couldn't seal it off yet because then there wouldn't be access to her Core and her Home room, but she was planning on that to happen in the future when she was done.

Sandra started to hollow out the thirteenth room down, when she took a mental step back and evaluated where she was at. She now had three more fairly deadly rooms to add to her defense, and though she knew that likely wasn't enough, she felt it was time she worked on the third thing she needed to do to ensure she succeeded in her future enterprise of saving all of the people nearby: crafting.

Chapter 4

It had only been about 24 hours since Sandra had completed her AMANS project, and she had used all but 10% of the Mana she had accumulated on constructing her new rooms, the traps located therein, and the Dungeon Monsters that populated them. She also completed four of the ten stages needed to progress to the next Core Size, and she thought that was fairly good progress. Although she still didn't like the experience of losing control of her dungeon and constructs – as well as "the trapped in her head" feeling – that upgrading her Core brought with it, she knew it was necessary...but she was just fine leaving it for later.

With a little better defense in place, Sandra split her concentration between hollowing out more rooms to help with that defense as well as working on her new crafting project. Before she found out that Kelerim had been followed, she had been excited to start working with the new materials he had brought back with him. First, though, she wanted to unlock their larger forms to be of use as Monster Seeds, which – due to her increased Mana intake – didn't take as long as she feared.

Monster Seed Origination				
Name:	Raw Material Cost:	Mana Cost:	Min. Mana:	Max. Mana:
Tiny Salt Cube	20	5	5	10
Tiny Clay Cube	80	15	15	150
Tiny Nickel Orb	200	20	20	200

Locked Seeds:	Unlock Requirements:	Mana Cost to Unlock:	Min. Mana:	Max. Mana:
Tiny Silver Orb	3000	300	40	400
Tiny Gold Orb	4000	400	50	500
Small Salt Cube	2 Tiny Salt Cubes	10	5	20
Average Salt Cube	4 Small Salt Cubes	40	5	80
Large Salt Cube	2 Average Salt Cubes	80	5	160
Small Clay Cube	2 Tiny Clay Cubes	30	15	300
Average Clay Cube	4 Small Clay Cubes	120	15	1200
Large Clay Cube	2 Average Clay Cubes	240	15	2400
Small Nickel Orb	2 Tiny Nickel Orbs	40	20	400
Average Nickel Orb	4 Small Nickel Orbs	160	20	1600
Large Nickel Orb	2 Average Nickel Orbs	320	20	3200
Small Silver Orb	2 Tiny Silver Orbs	600	40	800
Average Silver Orb	4 Small Silver Orbs	2400	40	3200
Large Silver Orb	2 Average Silver Orbs	4800	40	6400
Small Gold Orb	2 Tiny Gold Orbs	800	50	1000
Average Gold Orb	4 Small Gold Orbs	3200	50	4000
Large Gold Orb	2 Average Gold Orbs	6400	50	8000

Sandra now had access to Salt, Clay, Nickel, Silver, and Gold as both seeds and materials; the wood that he had brought back, she belatedly remembered, didn't work out. What she did have, however, was Flax Seed as a material, which she could grow and eventually turn into linen. She knew there were other types of cloth out there that could be – and were – made from plants, but she didn't have the seed available to make them; she was hoping more would become available to her soon – or else she might have to start looking for some on her own.

While she wanted to use the Nickel, Silver, and Gold to start working on some jewelry, she held off for the moment for a few reasons; for one, the fine art of crafting and perfecting rings, necklaces, pendants, earrings, chains, bracelets, circlets, brooches, hairpins, torcs, armlets, and even hairpins took a steady hand that could do delicate work – which none of her constructs could quite accomplish. While her Tiny Automaton was actually a great size for the smaller, more precise work that required a keen eye, it didn't have any type of dexterity to accomplish more than the most basic of tasks.

Secondly, most of the jewelry she had seen being crafted in her former life usually had some sort of gemstone accompanying it. These gems were the material of choice for enchanting, because the runes involved in the process could be created directly into the harder stone without as much fear of it being destroyed. Since most – but not all – of the jewelry she had seen made over the years were primarily to enhance some aspect of the Heroes battling against the dungeons, it only made sense for the runes and enchantments in general to be as durable as possible. And since she hadn't found any gemstones yet in all of her excavations, she was out of luck when it came to those.

Granted, she could theoretically practice making some of the bulkier jewelry items that didn't take as much finesse, but she still decided to hold off on that for the third reason: there were plenty of other things she could do. For instance, the clay that she received as both a Monster Seed and a material could be used for all sorts of different pottery crafts. The salt she received was an additional component to improve the tanning process; it could be used to improve her cooking skills (though she really didn't have a way to test it out), and also during some simple paper-making processes.

But those weren't what she wanted to craft; some of those different crafts were missing materials that she didn't have access to, or she couldn't easily perform the actions that were needed (such as jewelry making and even pottery). Instead, she wanted to work on something that she had already partially started on earlier while she was excavating Raw Material for her Small Animated Shears dotting the sky outside her dungeon.

She had ended up clearing a room that branched off of the room with her boiling vats, where she had previously used them for cleaning off raw Bearling skins for tanning purposes. Now, however, it would serve another purpose – cleaning the bark off of Flax plants. Well, she hoped it would if she could get everything to work properly in her new room.

Sandra couldn't produce cloth as a material at the moment, because she thought that it was technically a finished product that could be used for clothing and protective defensive purposes – just like leather and metal armors. Therefore, she had to start from scratch...which meant growing Flax plants from the Flax Seeds she had received approximately a week ago from Kelerim's foray into the nearby village. He had brought back some linen cloth, which she assumed was why she had received the seed – because it was needed to produce it from the very beginning.

To this end, Sandra filled the bottom of her new 100X100X40-foot crafting room with 5 feet of plain old dirt. Then, with an extra application of Mana, she created very narrow walkways leading through the room by turning the dirt into stone, separating long 10-foot-wide plots of dirt from the others. The walkways were going to be useful in moving some smaller constructs she was planning on using to seed the ground with her Flax seeds – and for harvesting afterward.

So, she had dirt and seeds – but there were three other issues that she had to address. One, the dirt she had supplied had very little in the way of nutrients that plants needed to survive, grow, and thrive. Two, there was no sunlight in the room to help them grow – the ambient light provided by her construction of the room wasn't nearly enough. And three, they needed water – and most likely lots of it.

The easiest solution would be to create a trap that combined three different elements: Natural (substituting for the nutrients the plants needed and to speed up growth), Holy (for the light needed by the plants to grow), and Water (for...water, obviously). She attempted to do this by placing a Natural-based trap inside the dirt, which would supply what was needed there; she placed another Holy-based trap in the ceiling, which would shine light down on the growing plots; and lastly, she placed a Water-based trap on the walls, which would spray out water when it was activated.

And every time she tried to tie it to a catalyst, it completely failed.

Sandra even sent one of every construct she had access to (other than her Iron-plated Behemoth), and every single one of them had no luck. She tried to tie multiple constructs together as a catalyst without success; trying to tie it to a stationary object didn't seem to work, either. She wasn't sure what was going on or what she was missing in the whole process, and neither did Winxa.

"Using multiple elements in a trap is a little beyond my knowledge. If I hadn't seen you do it already with two elements already, I would've said it was impossible." The Dungeon Fairy shrugged in apology. "It's just unfortunate that you have to place them all in the same room, otherwise I think you have a good idea."

Yes, that ***is*** *unfortunate—but wait...do they all have to be in the same room?* That really got her to thinking. After running a few scenarios through her head, she thought she might have a solution. *Thanks, Winxa – you figured it out!*

The Dungeon Fairy looked confused but pleased at the same time. "Um...you're welcome?"

Sandra had been thinking that she had to have everything in the same room to get it to work, but that wasn't necessarily the case; ironically, she could split things up to make it all come together. With this new thought in mind, she began excavating a room *above* her growing room. It didn't have to be very large, fortunately; in fact, while it was the same length and width as the one below, it was only 6 feet tall – just enough to be classified as a room and have a trap installed into it.

She created a steep tunnel that curved sharply up to the new space to make it an "official" room in her dungeon, and then she added some more stone dividers so that it looked like a replica of the growing plots down below – minus the dirt. Instead, she created a Rolling Force construct and sent it up to her newly built room and created a stone pathway that led across the separated plots. Lastly, she drilled multiple holes in the floor per plot equidistant from each other, so that they led directly down to the growing room.

Going back to the dirt-filled plots, she created and brought in a veritable army of 50 Articulated Clockwork Golems, created a big pile of Flax seeds on either side of one of the 10-foot-wide plots, and set her constructs to work digging holes and transporting seeds. Their clamp-hands worked just fine digging through the dirt and even clamping onto seeds, and they were able to cover the seeds back up once they were planted without difficulty. Once they were done, she picked a single Golem for a catalyst and began her trap preparation.

First, Sandra infused the dirt in the planted plot with the Natural element, which would locate, sustain, and enhance the growing speed of the seeds planted there. Next, along the ceiling she placed large orbs of the Holy element that would shine brightly down and illuminate just the plot of dirt that had

42

been planted; she wanted to concentrate on just the single 10X100-foot section of the room to make sure her experiment was working.

Unsurprisingly, since there wasn't really anything too Mana-intensive with the trap she was making, it only required about 500 Mana for the entire dual-element trap to be placed and tied to the Golem – which meant that it would be easy enough to fill the entire room later...if it worked. She also placed an activation trigger at a central point in the room where her construct could turn the trap on and off as necessary.

Next, in the upper room, she placed a simple water-producing Water trap in the corresponding plot above the planted dirt. It would fill slowly, however, because she didn't want to flood the ground below; while plants needed water, there were only a few that she personally knew of that could grow while they were drowned underwater. She also placed an activation trigger on the "walkway" where her Rolling Force was located, so that she could activate it when it was needed.

With everything in place, she had her constructs activate her two traps...and multiple events started to happen at the same time. Water filled up the reservoir above and started to pour down in great streams, light bathed the dirt below in a bright steady flash, and shoots of green growth sprouted from the ground – but only in certain places. Some of the plants grew at a rapid pace but were quickly drowned out by the quantity of water pouring down on them, while some grew slowly or not at all because the water didn't get to them.

Sandra deactivated both traps and rethought the process. It seemed like the Natural and Holy traps were working fine, but the water was the issue. She briefly thought about just adding a bunch more holes to the ceiling and making them smaller, but she thought she would have the same issue as before – flooding. She wracked her mind for a few minutes trying to think of a solution; she needed to both control how much came down from the room above and find a way to disperse it evenly over all the dirt.

Eventually, she thought she had an unconventional solution, but a solution, nonetheless. Over the next few minutes, she created a dozen Singing Blademasters and sent them up to the growing room; once they were all in place, Sandra altered the water trap above so that the water level would rise even slower than it had been previously, to reduce the flow of the pressure pushing the water downwards. With that changed, she activated both traps again and positioned her Blademasters underneath the holes about halfway in between the dirt and the ceiling.

The light turned on and the growing activated; the water flowed down slower than it had before and hit the quickly spinning constructs in the middle of the air, and the water was flung out in a circular spray, liberally covering half of the room. Acting quickly, she lowered the Singing Blademasters until they were only a few feet above the plots of dirt, and their flung-out spray was limited – mostly – to where she wanted the water. Within minutes, the Flax plants had grown out of the ground in beautiful green shoots, reaching three feet in height before stopping and starting to turn yellow. As soon as she saw it start to turn colors, she deactivated both traps and sent her Golems back in to work.

The best way to harvest Flax was to pull it up by the roots to extend the amount of fibers that would be found inside – so that was what her constructs did. Snapping off the seed pods from the end and placing them in a pile, the Golems then brought the stalks of flax to the vats of water in the next room and placed them inside. Sandra had already removed the boiling water traps from inside the large vats and instead replaced them with warm, but not hot, water that would continuously churn. When the flax stems were placed inside and a very thin stone cover was placed on top to contain it all, the retting (or removal of the tough bark on the outside) would commence.

There was a bit more that needed to be done to turn the fibers inside the Flax stalks into linen thread and then into cloth, but the retting was going to take a few days to break down the fibers enough to be useful. In the meantime, she had the hard seed pods that were produced by the plants broken open and reused for replanting the rest of the room. The seeds themselves could be used in different applications as well, including cooking, but it wasn't something that she wanted to do anything with at the moment.

Since the growing room had been a success, she got rid of the current traps and set it up so that there were traps that covered both rooms – which ended up taking approximately 4,500 Mana for the actual growing room and another 2,000 for the Water trap. She also placed trigger switches for each plot of land, where her Golem and Rolling Force could dictate which plot of dirt they wanted to focus on; when they would activate each trigger, the Singing Blademasters would move over and provide the water spraying system she had developed.

She thought about doing the entire room at once, but she thought about the future; if she eventually obtained different seeds, then she would want to be able to grow different plants – and hopefully even trees – at different times and different growing periods. After working out a few kinks with the new system that were easily fixed, the growing room was working as perfectly as she could get it.

Now all she needed was more seeds or other growing materials.

To get that, however, she thought she was going to need to be able to reach the forests she saw in every direction, and to do that, she was going to have to give in and upgrade her Core Size. Anxiety rippled through her mind at the thought, so she turned back to her blacksmithing for a little while. She reset the catalyst in Kelerim's Forge to an Ironclad Ape and used it to start churning out steel swords and knives by the dozens.

There's nothing like banging away with a hammer to settle the nerves.

Chapter 5

Crafting didn't take a lot of Mana, and neither did expanding her dungeon to include new defensive rooms, so most of her Mana was used to finish up the rest of her upgrade stages – and to create more Shears for the air aboveground. Sandra also created more constructs for her new rooms, though she hadn't placed any traps in them quite yet. What she did do, though, was expand her Home room where her Core was located, because she finally decided to check out the new construct she had received when she upgraded to Core Size 17.

Now that she didn't have to worry about any Territory Ants discovering her and attacking, it was easy enough to expand her room upwards and outwards – to the point where her ceilings were 50 feet high and her ovoid-shaped room was now over 100 feet at its longest. Her Core was now floating 25 feet above the floor – right in the middle of the room – so she figured it was safe enough to create her newest Dungeon Monster: the Iron-plated Behemoth.

She created a Tiny Dragon Glass Flake, which was actually about half the size of a Tiny Copper Orb – a very strange Monster Seed for something that could contain so much Mana in a construct. When it was ready, she selected it and infused 10,000 Mana into it to create her new Dungeon Monster...and found that she was very glad that she had expanded her room.

The Behemoth was a monstrous 15-foot-tall, 30-foot-long, and 6-foot-wide construct that appeared beneath her Core; it reminded her of stories about an animal called an elephant that was found far to the south of Muriel – the Human lands where she grew up. Its main body was completely covered with Iron-plate scales that draped off its back to the ground, and four tree-trunk-like legs supported the massive frame with additional iron plates.

The strangest thing about it, however, was the fact that it had two heads – one on each side of its body. Though, "heads" was a bit of a misnomer; on each end there was a long chain attached near the top that had a large spiked ball attached to it, kind of like a strange flail-like weapon. She directed her new construct to walk away from her and she watched it ponderously move forward – it was extremely slow in comparison to any of her other constructs. When it turned, however, it could turn quickly, and the spiked balls were flung outwards at tremendous speed; anything that they ended up hitting was not going to have a very nice day.

Rather than have it wait in her Home room where it might inadvertently damage her core if it was forced to fight, she started to create a massive room that branched off from it. She had to make the tunnel leading to it quite large to fit her new Behemoth, but she had plenty of Mana to spare in the construction process – so it was no big hardship. In fact, she almost had *too much* Mana still coming in and she couldn't spend it fast enough.

Splitting her concentration between new room construction, producing more constructs to fill those rooms, blacksmithing, producing more Shears for aboveground, and trying to automate the growing process (all of the extra Flax produced was actually a good source of Raw Materials) was time-consuming and kept her thoroughly occupied. By the time an additional five defensive rooms and one extra-large room (for her Behemoth) were connected together and were complete, she had added an additional 1,000 Small Animated Shears to her AMANS outside, bringing it to a total of 10,000 and bringing in an additional 25 Mana per minute. She spent almost a full day filling in the rooms that were just made with more constructs, but she held off on adding any traps to them until she had upgraded her Core at least one more time – so she could make them extra powerful.

Once that was done, she cautiously filled in the tunnel leading from the eleventh room down to Kelerim's old Forge room with stone and found that there was no issue with sealing it back up. There was now a route from the entrance through the original eight trapped rooms, leading to nine partially trapped constructed rooms filled with her Dungeon Monsters, which led to her Home room. From where her Core resided, another tunnel branched off to her various crafting workshops, her growing room, and the VATS system that would allow for rapid transportation up and down her dungeon.

That was about all that Sandra could reasonably do for the moment; she knew she could continue to craft and even attempt a few of her other crafting options, but she realized that she was just putting off the inevitable. *Might as well just do it to get it over with...besides, the retting of the Flax might be done by the time my upgrade is complete.*

"Don't worry, it won't be that bad – I'll be right here keeping you company."

Thanks, Winxa – you're one of the only things keeping me sane during those times. It didn't take long for her Mana to fill up completely again, so within a few minutes she had activated her Core Size Upgrade.

Sandra was doubly glad that the Dungeon Fairy was there to keep her company – even with her talking about nonsense that didn't really interest her – because the change in her elevation meant that she couldn't hear or see any of her little constructs roaming around her Core. She technically didn't even need them anymore because she had more than enough constructs throughout her dungeon absorbing and funneling the maximum amount of ambient Mana that she could get from it, but she had kept them around because they were her...companions, of a sort.

Most of them had been there from the very beginning and it felt comforting hearing the clomp-clomping of her Tiny

Automatons moving around, or watching her Shears floating by in their now-unnecessary absorption routes. Because her Home room was bigger, though, her awareness didn't cover the entire small room anymore, and she couldn't hear or see anything. Winxa – sitting on top of her Core, which she realized now almost dwarfed the little Fairy – was the only connection she had to the world, and Sandra grasped on to her incessant prattling like a lifeline.

An inconceivable amount of time later when she thought it would never end, her Core Size Upgrade finished, and she breathed a mental sigh of relief. *Thank you for being there for me, Winxa – that was a tough one. How long was I out this time?*

"No problem, Sandra. That's what I'm here for, you know. Oh, and I estimate that you were down for almost two days this time."

Thanking her again, Sandra checked on her dungeon and what she could see aboveground with her extensive AMANS setup. Everything looked fairly similar to how it was before and nothing jumped out needing her attention. She let go of the anxiety that she always seemed to have coming out of her Upgrade when it all looked normal – but then she could feel that her Area of Influence had expanded again. When she looked underground and estimated how far it extended, she realized that it was likely able to reach the trees dividing the Orcish and

Elven territories; not only that, but Sandra thought she could reach the forest dividing the Elven and Gnomish lands.

Putting aside the excitement of potentially getting access to wood, she double-checked everything and finally pulled her attention back to her Core, where her Upgrade screen was waiting patiently for her.

Core Size Upgrade Stage complete!
10/10 Completed

Your Core has grown!
Current Size: 18

Mana Capacity increased!
Raw Material Capacity increased!

Through your use of the intuitive Dungeon Core interface, your current Mana intake, and your unique dungeon fixtures, you have also learned the ***Organic/Inorganic Material Elemental Transmutation*** *skill!*

Now, that was a surprise. While she hadn't received any more constructs as part of upgrading her Core Size, she received another skill.

| Organic/Inorganic Material Elemental Transmutation (Core-specific Skill) | Organic/Inorganic Material Elemental Transmutation allows the Dungeon Core to use various Elemental Orbs to have a chance to transmute Organic and Inorganic material into similar-type materials. Once transmuted, those materials can then be used by the Core as usual, and even new Monster Seeds can be created by this method. Elemental transmutation can only be used when no invaders are present. The larger the Elemental Orb and Mana used in the process, the higher the likelihood of success. Does not work on biological-based materials. Requirements: Mana, |

Raw Materials, specific materials to transmute, and Elemental Orbs. (Skills are permanent and remain even after a Classification change)

Uh...what? Does this mean what I think it means?

"What's wrong? Did something happen?" Winxa asked as she overheard Sandra's confusion.

No, no...nothing's wrong – at least I don't think so. She explained what her new Core-Specific skill was to the Dungeon Fairy, and for once Winxa seemed to have an idea what it meant.

"Ah, that sounds like some of the skills I've heard Dungeon Cores received in the past, though this one seems not to be as limited in its scope. Basically – at least from my knowledge of similar skills – you can 'transmute' one of your materials into something different but adjacent in type."

That...didn't help explain all that much.

Winxa thought about it for a second, before she tried to explain it a little more. "So, yours is a bit different from the others with the use of your Elemental Orbs, but I'll try to explain it from the perspective of other Dungeon Cores that have something at least *similar*, if not exactly the same.

"These skills were usually given to Dungeon Cores who would have difficulty obtaining many Monster Seeds on their own for some reason or another, so this was to help them acquire different – and higher-quality – Seeds so that they could grow. Basically, instead of Elemental Orbs, they would have to save up enough Mana to unlock another variation of a material or Monster Seed they already had; for instance, if they had Copper as a material but couldn't acquire any Iron, let alone anything higher/more powerful than that.

"They would then have some sort of skill menu that they could access to select what they could 'transmute', as well as seeing what it would cost in terms of Mana. Normally, it would only be confined to a specific type of material, such as Copper could transmute into Iron for say...40,000 accumulated Mana – and then perhaps Steel for 400,000 accumulated Mana. They were outrageously expensive, but it would also allow the Cores to diversify their Seeds so that they could produce larger Dungeon Monsters. If you think about it, if you weren't able to produce Steel and how you unknowingly created of Dragon Glass, it's not likely that you'd be able to create some of your more powerful constructs."

You have a point there. In fact, looking at her available Monster Seeds, if she discounted Steel and Dragon Glass (and the Silver and Gold she had just acquired from Kelerim), the most she could fit into a Large Iron Orb (her biggest Seed) would be 3,200 Mana. That meant that she wouldn't have been able to produce her Repair Drones, Ironclad Apes, Steel Pythons, and certainly not her new Ironclad Behemoth.

"But your skill seems different, somehow. The others had limits on what they could produce – such as only metallic orbs or types of wood – though there was no limit on how powerful the material they wanted to produce could be. Of course, something like Mithril or Elderwood were very, very expensive Mana-wise – and wouldn't do much good to a fledgling Dungeon Core anyway. And your skill also seems to need Elemental Orbs instead of just straight Mana to 'transmute' the materials, so that could change some things as well." Winxa shrugged in a gesture that portrayed her confusion and lack of knowledge.

Thanks – I'll have to play with it a little and see what I can find out.

Before she did that, however, she checked her Core Selection Menu to find out what else had changed.

Core Selection Menu	
Dungeon Classification:	Constructs
Core Size:	18
Available Mana:	943/12517
Ambient Mana Absorption:	10/hour
Available Raw Material (RM):	12500/34674
Convert Raw Material to Mana?	12500 RM -- > 500 Mana
Current Dungeon Monsters:	11252
Constructs Creation Options:	16
Monster Seed Schematics:	85 (3)
Current Traps:	30
Trap Construction Options:	All
Core-specific Skills:	5
Current Visitors:	1

Other than an increase in her maximum Available Mana and Raw Material, nothing much had changed. It was strange seeing that she had over 11,000 Dungeon Monsters, but when she considered that 10,000 of them were Shears floating 200 feet above the wasteland, it wasn't so hard to comprehend. The rest were filling up various workshops, her Home room, and of course the trapped (and currently non-trapped) defensive rooms. The one thing that didn't change like it normally did was her Ambient Mana Absorption, which looked like it had completely maxed out at 10 Mana per hour.

Sandra took control of her Golems near her churning water vats to check on the progress of the Flax retting and saw that it was still going to take a couple of days for it to complete. With that still for the future, and with no other crafts calling out to her for attention, she turned to her waiting defensive rooms and decided to fill another couple of them with strong traps now that she had a greater amount of maximum Mana at her disposal.

But the whole time she was thinking about what she could do with her new skill.

Chapter 6

Crouching down behind some brush near one of the giant trees that marked the boundary between the Elven and Gnomish lands, Echo took careful aim at the small boar shuffling noisily through the dead leaves carpeting the forest floor. It appeared to be just wandering aimlessly around, without any particular purpose; it was that reason – along with the blank-seeming consciousness behind the eyes – that clued the young Elf Ranger into what she was hunting.

She let the fingertips of her right hand release her arrow, while at the same time using a small application of her Air Element on her projectile. While she didn't have great strength in Air as opposed to her Holy element, it was more than enough to correct the slight imperfection in her aim for her arrow to slam right into the boar's dead-looking eye, driving straight into its brain. A small squeal escaped its mouth before it collapsed to the ground as its legs folded under it, the critically shot Ironwood arrow vibrating slowly as it buried itself so deep it likely impacted the rear inside of its skull.

I hope that didn't chip the arrowhead; I must've put too much into that draw. Within seconds, the boar stopped twitching and...disappeared, leaving behind her arrow and something else on the ground. While her perfect shot through its eye was ideal when she was hunting natural game – thereby not damaging its hide or ruining any of its meat – it didn't really matter that much when killing the dungeon's nearby monsters. It helped with killing the boar quickly and efficiently, however; she wasn't real adept at fighting up-close and if she had missed, she wasn't sure if she'd be able to kill it with the long knife that was strapped to her right thigh.

Echo froze and looked and listened around her for almost five minutes before she stood up and dropped her active camouflage. She only felt a little drained from the use of the Holy element to bend the light around her, causing her to be cloaked in a near-invisibility that gained her the name everyone knew her as now; while she wasn't completely invisible, there were only faint "echoes" of her form left behind when she moved at more than a snail's pace through the forest.

She slipped her artfully crafted bow over her shoulder, resting it against the supple brown and dark-green-accented leather jerkin she was wearing, which matched her tight-fitting bottoms; the last thing she wanted while sneaking through the underbrush of the forest was to have her clothing snag on something and give her away. Her arms and hands were also covered up – as well as a hood covering her fine, waist-length silver hair – because anything that caused her to stand out amongst the trees in the few times that she didn't have her active camouflage working could be deadly.

It was hot back in the village of Avensglen, where there weren't towering trees blocking the sunlight and gifting her with the cool air that she reveled in when she went hunting. From the elder's stories, their race used to live primarily amongst the trees, but ever since the dungeons along their border started to become more and more dangerous, they had taken to living in the wide-open plains of Symenora, their Elvish homeland. Only Lyringlade – their capital city in the middle of Symenora – had the towering trees that were representative of their people. Which was probably why there were so many of their dwindling race living there now.

There were only a few villages and towns located around the border of their land that were still inhabited and that hadn't been overrun by dungeon monsters. The village of Avensglen – where she was based out of – and the others were vital to maintain because they provided much-needed dungeon loot that wasn't readily available anywhere else. While the Elites working out of the capital were keeping back the dungeon monsters from encroaching on the city's boundaries and surrounding area, these satellite "outposts" provided the raw materials required for weapon and armor production that were used to arm those premier fighters.

Echo turned 50 later this year, which meant that she was finally eligible to apply for a position in the Elites; although their numbers had steadily declined over the years, they still held with the tradition of only accepting those with a bit of "experience" to their name. While 50 might seem old to some of the shorter-lived races like the Orcs and even the fabled

Humans she'd heard about before but never seen, in comparison she was barely even a teenager by Elvish standards – and a young teenager, at that.

Echo bent down to retrieve her Ironwood arrow and winced as she looked at the blunted tip of the thin iron arrowhead. She was glad that it hadn't chipped, at least, because that would've been almost unsalvageable; as it was, with a little work and manual labor she could fix it until it was as good as new. Checking over the shaft of the arrow, she smiled when she saw that the Ironwood had held up quite handily even through all of the abuse that she had put it through over the last couple of weeks. She knew it would eventually start to crack from the strong impacts it had to endure, but it had been proving its worth ever since she picked it up from their village fletcher about a month ago.

Not that she had any problems using arrows made from Ash wood, but they tended to break at the most inopportune times. Which meant, obviously, that she went through more of them on a daily basis – thereby decreasing what she could earn by culling the nearby dungeon monsters and hunting the normal beasts in the forest. *Although, now that I think about it, it's getting harder and harder to find any "real" animals out here.* She was beginning to suspect that the dungeon had expanded its range again and was wiping out the competition.

It might be about time to call up another Elite squad from Lyringlade to cull the dungeon again. She hated when that happened, because it seemed to take months or years for more monsters to appear aboveground in any large numbers, but it was a necessary precaution to prevent their village from eventually being overrun. Well, that, and it allowed the local wildlife to flourish again. The last time it had been needed had been around 6 years ago, and she was forced to travel to the northwest forest that divided their lands from the Orcish land of Orcrim to hunt; she didn't like going there, because she wasn't quite suited to kill the various slimes that inhabited the trees – and who could sense her better than beasts that relied on actual eyesight.

At least this is better than fighting off hordes of monsters near the capital. Sometimes she was almost tempted to forget her dream of joining the Elites and just stay where she was; however, she knew it was important that any Elf that could join the Elites actually did – they couldn't afford for someone who could fight to sit on the sidelines. It wasn't just the elders that could see that their race was in a bit of a decline right now, and the only way to fight against their eventual demise was to do just that – fight.

She didn't really want to think about that, though. She shook her head free of the depressing thoughts and bent down again near where she had retrieved her arrow. A 2-foot-long dark-brown branch was lying on the forest floor, dropped by the monster as loot; she picked it up and immediately recognized it as yew wood, which made her smile in satisfaction. The dungeon had been stingy lately when it came to wood drops, as she had primarily been getting iron, copper, tin, or even a tiny amount of steel in the last few days. That was all well and good for those Elites that liked to get up close and personal to kill the monsters, but it didn't really help her kind – hunters and Rangers.

They specialized in long-range attacks and that made it extremely important that they had the best-quality equipment. She brushed her fingertips against her own yew bow, which wasn't mastercraft work – by any means – but she had lovingly crafted it herself...with a little help by another Ranger that had a bit of the Natural element to fuse the quantity of pure, pristine yew wood drops she had stashed away for her own use. It was to help her with her hunting, so she didn't feel bad about not providing it above her normal quota.

Her work done for the day and with dusk soon approaching, Echo turned to head back towards the village. However, rather than taking a direct line there to the west, she instead turned north; she knew she was rather close to the border with the wastelands and she didn't want to run into any beasts or monsters on the way back. It was much easier to journey the small distance to the north and walk around the forest to the village – because nothing ever traveled into or out of the dry, barren lands. It would be a little hotter, but the season was starting to turn a little more towards fall so she didn't think it would be that bad.

She carefully picked her way through the brush, making as little noise as possible; just because she couldn't see or hear anything around her didn't mean that an animal or beast couldn't hear *her*. Because she was being careful, by the time she reached the edge of the forest the sky had begun to darken, and the sun was just barely touching the horizon. She had been half-crouched in her walk so she was glad that she could finally straighten up and travel normally, now that she didn't have to worry about being seen.

Echo was just about to stand up and walk out of the trees when she saw something out of the corner of her eye. About 100 feet away, a glint of metal reflected off the weak setting sun and caught her attention; instead of it being on ground level, however, it was nearly 30 feet up in the air next to the spreading branches of the oak tree that comprised that section of the forest.

She froze and used her Holy element to activate her active camouflage while she tried to find what had caused the glint...and struggled to see anything out of the ordinary. She was beginning to think that it was just a trick of her mind after a lengthy day of hunting, when she saw a branch near where she had thought she saw the light sway a little in the relatively windless day. The next thing she knew, one acorn dropped down to the ground, followed a few seconds later by another. A third dropped to the ground almost 20 seconds later and then all was still...for about a minute. The branch she was staring at intently started to violently jostle back and forth for a short time – and then a small branch broke off from the tree seemingly all by itself. Echo watched in confusion and astonishment as it flew off into the distance.

But it wasn't heading toward Avensglen or anywhere else in Symenora; no, it was flying straight into the wastelands.

As much as practicality and prudence warred with her now-insatiable curiosity, she knew that playing it safe in this case had no chance against the need to *know*. This was a completely new development and she knew she had to check it out; only the slightest hesitation made her pause as she followed the direction that she saw the branch flying.

Besides, everyone knew there wasn't anything too dangerous in the wasteland – or at least nothing that could see her. *Right?*

Chapter 7

The twelfth room down from the entrance – the one
right after the room with the vines and stone blocks in the
ceiling – was one of the easiest traps she had created for
defense; upon reflection, it was probably one of the more
devious ones as well. She combined Water and Nether elements
together to create a dark, sludgy, swampish bog that had thick
fog drifting through the air above it. She pumped enough Mana
inside the trap that it didn't even need to be triggered – it was
always on and wouldn't disappear.

On the surface, all it really did was make it difficult to
move through the room, because the likelihood of being sucked
beneath the surface and drowning was very low. Of course, the
dozen Steel Pythons hidden underneath the sludgy water didn't
allow anyone passing through to do so unscathed, nor did the
thirty Shears hiding in the fog waiting for an opportune moment
to glide down and attack.

Overall, though, if whoever was passing through was
careful and could avoid being killed by vicious Pythons, then
they would move on to the thirteenth room – which was where
the deviousness came in. She created a narrow pathway very
similar to the one in the room with the vines and stone blocks;
instead of stone spikes at the bottom of a pit, however, she
filled it with lava using Earth and Fire elements in a trap. It took

all 12,517 of her maximum Mana to maintain the large pools of lava for all of 5 minutes and 13 seconds, but it was more than worth it – especially when it was so close to the edge of the pathway.

She had to coat the whole pit and even the narrow pathway with Dragon Glass, which took quite a bit of Mana to do – over 180,000 all told – but it ensured that the intense heat wouldn't damage her dungeon while the lava was active. She added some Blademasters to the room to add some obstacles to getting across, but that wasn't the deviousness she was so excited about!

Since the lava was so close to the pathway, even a small disturbance in the pool would cause it to flow over and cover anything in its way – including anyone trying to pass by. She left the ceiling of the room relatively unfinished and placed an Automated Digger up there – which she also used as a catalyst for the room's trap; when someone entered, it would start to dig out more of the dirt and rocks above and drop it down into the lava pool, causing it to splash and overflow onto the pathway.

And best of all – the sludgy Nether-Water residue from the previous room was highly flammable. Anyone getting any type of flame or heat on them if they were still covered in the sludge would go up like a torch. She'd like to see someone get past *that!*

The intense satisfaction and desire to see someone die to her traps and Dungeon Monsters running through the dungeon made her take a mental step back in horrified shock when she realized what she was doing. *Where did all of these feelings come from, I wonder?* Sandra hadn't been as consumed with perfecting her traps and making them as lethal as possible before, but then again, she hadn't been so directly threatened with complete destruction by people, either. The Territory Ants and even the Bearlings she could kind of understand – it was in their nature and they couldn't really help themselves. But the Orcs...the Orcs had made a conscious choice to come after her.

And that scared her – badly.

She knew that she would try to avoid conflict when it arrived so that it didn't result in the deaths of *anyone*, but she now also knew that sometimes it was unavoidable. She had traveled and seen enough when she was Human not to be *completely* naïve about the way the world worked, after all; that didn't mean she couldn't try to stop death and destruction before it happened. And if it did...well, what she was doing with her defensive rooms was likely to be more than enough to ensure her own safety.

Not wanting to create anything specifically designed to kill something, she left off finishing the traps in rooms 14-17 (though they still had plenty of constructs inside them) and turned back to something a little more therapeutic: crafting. However, blacksmithing didn't really appeal to her at the moment because of the association with death it had, so she turned her attention to her new skill. Sandra had to admit, she had been wanting to play around with her new skill but wanted to make sure nothing else needed her attention before she really investigated what she could do with it.

Organic/Inorganic Material Elemental Transmutation Menu				
Transmutation Options	Elemental Orb Required (Size/Qty)	Mana Required	Additional Seed Material (Size/Qty)	Unlocked (Y/N)
Metals				
Copper	N/A	N/A	N/A	Y
Nickel	N/A	N/A	N/A	Y
Tin	N/A	N/A	N/A	Y
Lead	Earth (Large/5), Fire (Tiny/2)	0/25000	Earthenware Clay (Large/4)	N
Bronze	N/A	N/A	N/A	Y
Iron	N/A	N/A	N/A	Y
Steel	N/A	N/A	N/A	Y
Titanium	?????	0/1000000	?????	N
Platinum	?????	0/5000000	?????	N
Orichalcum	?????	0/20000000	?????	N
Mithril	?????	0/50000000	?????	N
Fibrous Plant Seeds				
Jute Seed	Natural (Average/2)	0/20000	Oak (Average/2)	N
Flax Seed	N/A	N/A	N/A	Y
Cotton Seed	Natural (Large/3)	0/30000	Maple (Large/3)	N
Bamboo Seed	?????	?????	?????	N
Ramie Seed	?????	?????	?????	N
Clays				
Earthenware Clay	Earth (Average/2)	0/5000	Iron (Average/2)	N
Stoneware Clay	Earth (Large/4)	0/15000	Iron (Large/4)	N
Ball Clay	?????	?????	?????	N
Fire Clay	?????	?????	?????	N
Kaolin Clay	?????	?????	?????	N

That...is enlightening. After she had thought about her skill, a menu had popped up describing the different types of materials she could unlock with the use of Elemental Orbs, copious amounts of Mana, and a surprise additional material that was needed from another type of material. For instance, to unlock Lead, she needed Earthenware Clay as a material, which she could unlock with two Average Earth Elemental Orbs, 5,000 Mana, and two Average Iron Orbs.

69

There were also many unknowns on the menu, though everything still had a Mana cost; however, the Elemental Orbs needed for them – as well as the additional materials – all had question marks, which indicated to her that she was going to have to experiment with different combinations of things to achieve success. She didn't mind experimenting a little, especially if it meant unlocking some of the higher-quality metals like Titanium and Platinum, but the Mana cost for those were quite expensive. For instance, at her current intake of Mana – which was now quite considerable – it would still take nearly four months of saving up every drop to afford Mithril.

Regardless, what Sandra was currently excited about were the different "Fibrous Plant Seeds" like her Flax Seed she already had; it ultimately meant there were other plants that she could use to make cloth with – ones that were much more durable and easier to work with than Flax and the Linen that was produced from it. The only problem, however, was that she needed an additional material that wasn't something she previously had access to: wood. Now, however, her Area of Influence had expanded enough to include the nearby forests – prime locations for acquiring samples of trees that she could grow in her dungeon.

Sandra started to use her incoming Mana to finish off some of the 11 stages of her next Core Size Upgrade, even though she wasn't planning on doing it any time in the next couple of days. She mainly did it because she didn't want it to go to waste, and her concentration was going to be elsewhere for a while – miles away, in fact.

As soon as that was taken care of, Sandra took control of one of her slowly moving Small Animated Shears in her AMANS and made it head towards the South and a little east. "Control" was a strong word for what she did because she couldn't really understand how it floated through the air, nor how it directed how it moved in different directions, so it was more like she gave it an order and watched through its...eyes? Again, there wasn't really a comparison to a person's body that she could focus on, so she just went with it.

She chose to go a little further out of her way to the land of the Elves and then to the forest border between the Elves and Gnomes for two reasons. One, she wanted to avoid calling any attention to herself from the Orcs – because it had already been proven that they didn't take kindly to a dungeon on their doorstep, so to say – and going to the western border forest between the Orcs and Elves was inviting too much trouble her way. And two, she was curious about how the Elves were doing in their village that she could see as a tiny point in the distance from her AMANS.

The sun was heading towards the horizon when Sandra's construct neared the Elven village on the edge of the wastelands. She was astonished at how fast a pair of shears could move through the air when there wasn't any reason to impede its speed; she kept that in mind for future improvements to her dungeon's defenses – if any were needed, of course.

Before it arrived within 1,000 feet of the village, she sent it shooting up into the air so that it wouldn't be observed very easily. When she estimated that it was about twice the height that it had been earlier, she slowed it down and looked down on a small village made up of only about two dozen smallish buildings in the middle of a grassland far away from the nearest forests. They appeared strange-looking to her and she risked getting closer to see why; instead of cut planks of wood, or even whole logs from nearby trees, it appeared as though the homes and other buildings she could see were *grown*. They weren't full-on trees reaching for the sky, however – they appeared as though they were trees that ballooned outwards when they started to grow and then just stopped when they were as large as they needed to be.

There were a few tall people walking in between the buildings that had silver, gold, and even deep-bronze-colored hair; most of them were wearing clothes or leathers that reflected the brown and green colors of nature, which blended perfectly even in their current village environment. In fact, if the squat tree-buildings were in the middle of a forest, she might've passed them by without a second glance; as it was, though, they kind of stood out as the only real structures around.

Although she wasn't close enough to see their faces – or their pointed ears that they were famous for – she assumed they were Elves, since they definitely weren't Orcs, Dwarves, or Gnomes. And, although things might've changed in the 200+ years she was "dead", she didn't think Humans had the metallic-looking sheen of hair she saw on so many of them below.

Out of the corner of her vision, Sandra saw two figures run across the grasslands from the direction of the forest to the east, though it looked almost leisurely instead of with any type of alarm. They slowed as they got close, and a few others went out to greet them as they neared the outskirts of the village; she could see them exchange greetings and say something else, but she was nowhere near being able to hear more than a faint sound so high up. As much as she wanted to hear them talking – and relieve a little of the loneliness that still affected her after Kelerim left her dungeon – she didn't dare get any closer for fear of discovery. What she was doing was reckless enough and she didn't want to push it any more than that.

The sun was starting to finally touch the horizon when Sandra watched most of the people enter the "houses" and disappear, and she was left without anything to really see. Knowing that most people didn't leave the safety of a village at night – at least, she assumed that Elves took the same precautions as did Humans – she took off towards the trees to the east to complete the mission she had assigned herself.

Within minutes her construct was there on the edge of the forest bordering the wastelands where her Dungeon Core made its home. Before she had the Shears descend, she looked

73

around and searched for anyone nearby for almost a minute; when she didn't see anything out of the ordinary, she had it slowly approach the nearest tree and aimed the construct for one of the small branches near the edge. If she was correct, the closest tree was an Oak tree, and it would have some acorns that would work excellently for a seed to grow the tree from.

Finding an acorn was easy; keeping ahold of it with a pair of scissors was much harder. The first one fell before her construct could try to catch it; the second was temporarily caught by its handles before it could fall, but a slight jostling caused the acorn to plummet to the ground anyway; she had slightly more success with the third by using the actual shears part to grab ahold of the acorn, but it soon cut into the Oak seed and it slid out and onto the ground below.

It was time to rethink her plan.

Fortunately, she knew that cuttings from most trees could be re-planted to grow a new tree, though there was some difficulty if there wasn't already a root system in place. Luckily for her, she had her Natural-element trap to help with that back in her growing room, so she wasn't too worried about it.

Her Small Animated Shears, while relatively sharp on their cutting edges, weren't quite suited to sawing off a small-sized branch. With a little cutting work, and more than a little tugging at the small branch, she was able to free it from the tree. Before it could fall to the forest floor, she instructed her construct to quickly slide its open ovoid handle along the bottom of the branch, where it slid down and stuck in place when the smaller offshoots snuggled up against it.

After she was sure it was secure, Sandra instructed it to fly back to her dungeon, though she made sure it moved much slower because she didn't want to drop the branch along the way. Satisfied that she was successful – and without alerting anyone else to her presence – she started moving her Golems around in her growing room, making room for her new acquisition. If everything worked out the way she hoped, she'd soon have access to the Oak tree she had snagged the branch from.

Which was just another step in the direction of crafting with an even greater assortment of materials.

Chapter 8

Despite going slow, it still didn't take more than 15 minutes for her Shears to return to the dungeon, fly inside, enter her VATS, and make its way down to her growing room. The branch was almost lost when the powerful air-traps blew the relatively lightweight Shears upwards because of the extra surface area, but she saved it by getting rid of the traps in the whole transportation system before they could destroy it. As soon as it was through, she reinstalled the traps, which was fortunately easy because she was already practically full of Mana again.

Without wasting any time, her Golems delicately took the Oak tree branch from her Shears and she sent it back out of the dungeon to join into the AMANS again. Planting it deep into the spot she had them clear earlier, they arranged the dirt around it to keep it upright and stepped back. A quick activation of the two rooms' traps and the placement of her Singing Blademasters started the growing process; almost instantly, she could see the tree jiggle a little as it settled more firmly into the ground and the Natural-element trap forced roots to grow out from below the cut portion of the branch.

From there, it grew much slower than the Flax plants from before (which grew to maturity within a matter of minutes), but it was barely a fraction of the time it would normally need to grow in the wild. Sandra wasn't exactly sure how large it needed to grow to in order to have enough viable wood to become something she could use as a material – or provide the acorn seeds for that matter; regardless, by the speed of which it was growing, she estimated that it was going to take three or four hours for it to become large enough to fill the space in her room up to the ceiling. If it needed to be larger, she'd probably have to expand the room again – but this time *down*.

The roots of her Oak tree were getting quite large as well, but as soon they reached the stone walls separating the plots they immediately expanded where they could – down the dirt plots instead of out. Sandra never realized the sheer quantity of the roots system underneath a tree before; while she knew they were extensive she didn't realize that it was as large or even larger than the tree aboveground.

After about 10 minutes, Sandra decided to remove portions of the walkway to let some of the roots expand into another plot, just to see if having a little more room would allow it to grow a little faster; although she didn't mind waiting, if she was growing other trees in the future she wanted to do it as efficiently as possible. However, when she went to remove some of the stone, she got an unexpected warning.

Uh…what? Winxa, what's wrong? Why is it saying there is an invader in my dungeon? The Mechanical Wolves and Jaguars – not to mention her extensive AMANS net above the ground – hadn't seen anything, otherwise they would've alerted her. At least she hoped they would; it hadn't really been tested with something small trying to get into her dungeon's entrance. The only time it had really worked was when the Orcs were seen following her Ironclad Apes' tracks, but they were loud, obvious, and not trying to hide their presence.

"I'm not sure – it shouldn't say that unless there is an actual invader inside. I've never heard of it being wrong before – but there's always a first time, I guess," the Dungeon Fairy replied with equal confusion. "Maybe there are more Territory Ants that you hadn't seen before now; I'd check around every part of your dungeon just in case."

Sandra was pretty sure she would've seen something get close to her dungeon underground, but she made sure to check anyways. It didn't take long for her to find nothing in all of her rooms, nor were any of her constructs attacking anything. She expanded her search farther out to see if there was anything threatening nearby underground; she hadn't been paying attention to it before, since it was relatively far away, but she did end up finding a dozen other Territory Ant nests scattered across the wasteland. Fortunately, none of them were closer than 1,200 feet away from her nearest room, so they weren't alerted to her presence in the slightest and didn't even seem to know she was there.

She also found two other lairs of Bearlings to the northeast and farther east, but there were only about a half-dozen in each one and they also didn't seem to be aware of her presence. Well, that wasn't precisely true; when her vision traveled over them, they seemed to tense up momentarily, but other than that they ignored her Area of Influence completely. If there were any other insects, beasts, or other creatures in the wasteland, they weren't part of the underground system, so she couldn't see them.

Suddenly, Sandra's attention was pulled back to the first room near the entrance when her Nether trap was triggered unexpectedly. Even in the darkness brought on by the trap she could see inside the room perfectly and saw...nothing. And neither did her Basher Totems and two Ironclad Apes she had stationed in there, as they were completely frozen, waiting for an enemy to attack.

It was only when she took control of one of the Apes and had it walk towards the tunnel entrance when she finally saw the barest hint of something. It was like a flicker of a shadow in the darkness – almost imperceptible – and she only saw it because she was looking for any evidence of why the trap had triggered. She moved her construct quickly toward where she saw the flicker – which was when Sandra heard a *thwack* and an arrow shot out of seemingly nowhere to impact her Ape's head with a bright flash of light, though the wooden projectile shattered as a result and left a large dent and scratch on her construct's face.

Of course, that didn't stop her construct in the least, as it moved toward where the sound and arrow came from. That appeared to be enough to arouse some more movement, as a blur that was hard to pinpoint moved very quickly out of her dungeon entrance and back out into the wasteland. The sun was still a slight sliver on the horizon, so it wasn't hard to see what seemed like a blurry shadow streak away towards the southwest, leaving a sort of echo of its form in its wake. She immediately dispatched one of her Shears to follow overhead, though she made sure to stay far above, which made it nearly imperceptible to anyone on the ground at that distance.

The shadowy echoes were easy to follow because her floating Shears were quite fast and the form – while quick – had virtually no chance to outrun it. Two-thirds of the distance to the Elven lands, the echoes started to become less frequent and closer together, almost as if whatever it was had been slowing down; another 500 feet passed, and the flicker was almost non-existent. Eventually, it stopped altogether, and Sandra thought she had lost track of whatever or *whoever* had entered her dungeon.

Her construct continued along the same route the echoey shadows had been heading for a while, which seemed to be aiming in the general direction of the Elven village along the wasteland's border. Sandra was about to give up when at the edge of her Shears' vision she saw a form pop out from seemingly nowhere. The faint remnants of Holy elemental energy faded away from around the form in a matter of seconds, and the person wearing the same type of brown and dark-green leathers turned around while walking backwards and looked off toward her dungeon – and then into the air.

I think they can see me. She was worried for a moment that her construct had been spotted, but the figure below didn't look right at it; instead, the Elf – for that was likely who it was – just let their vision pass over the sky without stopping on anything in particular. The Elf turned away after a moment and crossed the distance to the village within a matter of minutes, moving at a fairly quick and alarmed pace.

This isn't good...

"What isn't good?" Winxa asked, and Sandra realized that she hadn't communicated what had happened. With as quick an explanation as possible, the Dungeon Core got the Fairy up to speed.

"It looks like you've been found out, alright. You should get your construct in closer so that you can listen in; even if they see you, it's likely not going to matter."

Good point. With only a slight hesitation, Sandra brought her Shears down closer to the village, making sure to stay out of the line of sight of the figure walking towards the village. Sandra was even bold enough to go drop down completely, where her construct was able to touch and hide flat against the roof of one of the village's outermost "houses".

And then she just waited, curious at what was going to happen.

*   *   *

Echo pushed back her hood, the sweat running down her back in rivulets – and it wasn't just from the exertion of running through the wastelands. What she had seen there scared her more than she wanted to admit.

It was almost impossible to keep up with the floating branch as it flew into the wasteland, but there was plenty of light to see where it went. She let her active camouflage drop while she ran at a full sprint toward the unknown, using her Air element to speed her on her way. Slightly reducing the air resistance in front of her running body while gently pushing from behind was all she could really do with it, but it helped to speed her up until she was almost flying through the dry, broken land. She envied the Elite practitioners back in the capital that had a greater Air affinity than she did – they could *literally* fly…though only for short distances at a time.

About 20 minutes and nearly 4 miles later, she slowed down as she started to near where she thought the branch had gone. As usual, she hadn't seen anything in the wasteland – there were occasionally some random beasts that roamed around it at night, but rarely during the day – but she was too experienced to go into an unknown situation without caution. Using her Holy element again, she wrapped it around her body, where it would bend the light and make her essentially invisible to the naked eye. With her active camouflage in place, Echo walked – crouch-walked, rather – toward the spot where she had seen the branch descend and disappear.

Within 100 paces, she was extraordinarily glad that she had hidden herself again, because there were strange creatures roaming slowly around the landscape. They were hard to spot at first because they actively worked to conceal themselves behind outcroppings and small hills, but she had been hunting for decades – not much escaped her notice nowadays. She froze for almost a minute while she stared at the spot where she had seen the closest one; she was soon rewarded when what looked like some sort of creature made up of shiny bones came stalking out from behind a large upright rock about 15 paces away.

Echo tensed up and slowly – but expertly – slipped her bow off her shoulder and nocked an arrow in one smooth motion. The bony...wolf?...looked right past her location without seeing her, fortunately, and then ambled off in the opposite direction. She released the tension on the bow's string but kept the arrow in position as she kept walking.

Is that wolf an undead? I've never seen any undead like that, but I can't think of another explanation. While she had never actually been inside a Nether dungeon, she had fought against undead a few times when she was younger. Her manipulation of her Holy element was extremely useful fighting against its opposite; while she wasn't adept at many of the more offensive casts that the Elites could perform, she had fairly balanced control and could use it effectively against most Nether-based monsters. The most useful attack she could perform was to charge her arrowheads with Holy energy, where the energy would release upon impact and doing quite disproportionally explosive damage to the undead.

As she cautiously walked toward where she thought the branch had disappeared, she saw another few figures of shiny undead wolves and what she could've sworn was a large cat — but, luckily, none of them saw her. At one point, however, she almost lost her concentration and dropped her camouflage when she inadvertently saw a glimmer in the air above her. As she stared upwards to see what had captured her attention, she saw something that finally started to blunt the curiosity that had driven her.

While she couldn't make them out precisely, she could see small metallic specks nearly 200 feet above her spread out in a large...*net*, was probably the best word. As she looked at them, the setting sun reflected off of them all at once as they moved at precisely the same time, drifting in one direction to another. There were entirely too many to count, but she estimated that there were hundreds, if not thousands, of the objects floating above her head.

Wh-what is going on here?

Echo almost turned back, but something drove her on to discover what she was dealing with. She was fairly confident in her active camouflage, so she pushed on and tried to ignore the metallic-looking objects poised above her head. While she didn't know what they were, she could almost guarantee they didn't bode well.

Another few minutes later led her to the approximate location where the oak branch had disappeared, and she looked around the area cautiously. Years of tracking and hunting had let her read the environment well enough for it to tell her a story – and the location she found herself in told an interesting one.

What appeared to be Orc tracks led all around the area; Echo could tell they were Orc by their large size and lack of anything resembling caution – they were more likely to run in yelling than try to sneak up on something. They seemed to be following some other tracks she didn't recognize at all, though whatever made them was *heavy*; deep impressions in the dry, cracked dirt was evidence enough of that. She also saw what appeared to be Bearling tracks – almost two dozen different sets – that led to an area where some sort of battle had taken place. Dried blood stained the ground in multiple areas; some of it was the slightly greenish-tinted red blood of Orcs, but most of it was the pure-red blood of the Bearlings.

It looks like a Warband tracked something out here and found a lair of Bearlings. Looking around further, she couldn't see much evidence of anything else, though she saw plenty of prints made from the shiny undead wolves scattered about. It was when she looked to see where the Orcs had gone after they had obviously defeated the Bearlings that she saw the hard-to-spot cave entrance in the nearby hill. As she approached, she could see different tracks leading *out* of the cave; they appeared to be a person's because they only had two feet, but they weren't familiar to her in size.

Letting that mystery go for the moment, she herself approached the cave cautiously and peered inside – but it was too dark to see much. *I...have to go inside, just to see...* In her head, her mind kept telling her it wasn't a good idea and for her to just leave, but she had already gone this far – she couldn't turn back now. Before she stepped inside, she noticed for the first time the scratches along the edges of the opening; based on what she had seen so far, she assumed they were made by the Bearlings, though why they were trying to get *in* the cave was a mystery.

Taking a deep – but silent – breath, Echo took a step inside the cave and she instantly knew where she was: a dungeon. The walls of what was now obviously a tunnel were uniformly cut – unlike a natural cave – and down the tunnel she could, for the first time, see a room beyond the passageway. It was lit up – not brightly, but with more than enough light to see by – in some unseen and unknown manner, which was another indication that where she traveled was unnatural.

From what Echo could see of the room from her position just inside the entrance, it looked fairly plain, empty even; if she hadn't seen the shiny undead monsters outside – as well as the floating net of metallic objects in the air – she would've guessed that the dungeon was old and abandoned. She knew better, though – but she also needed to see *more*; she wasn't going to run back to the village without getting a little more information. If this was indeed a dungeon, they couldn't allow it to survive and thrive out in the wastelands; with nothing stopping it, the dungeon could grow out of control and threaten not only her people, but the other races living nearby.

She wasn't old enough to have experienced the brutal war against the dungeon that had been in the wastelands before it was destroyed, when it was still healthy land – but there were plenty of her race that remembered it with horror. If this was something that could threaten them all again, her people needed to know; in fact, *all* of the races should know, but she would leave that communication to those in charge.

A dozen short paces was all it took to arrive at the threshold of the first room, and she got a better look at it. Not that it helped, because she still couldn't see anything – it looked just as empty as it had from the entrance. While Echo had only been in a single dungeon before – albeit briefly in a quick training mission decades ago – she had heard that they were generally all the same. Monsters would be filling the rooms, traps would be laid for the unwary, and death awaited around every corner. The room she stared at for almost a minute, however, looked quite unlike what she remembered – or had heard – about.

With her bow still out in front of her waiting for an attack, she took a single cautious step inside the room and everything abruptly went dark. She almost yelped at the sudden loss of light, but her Ranger training had drilled into her the need to be unseen and unheard – so she held it back. Besides, the darkness was only temporary as she used the dwindling supply of Holy elemental energy she currently possessed and wrapped a band across her eyes. The darkness lit up in her vision a bit; it wasn't quite what it was before the darkness descended, but she could at least see an outline of the room again.

A sound off from the left of the room caught her attention, and she jumped in astonishment when a big, heavy form stomped its way from around the corner and slowly headed in her direction. A quick look with her eyes around the corner showed other forms, though with the very low light and lack of movement, she couldn't really tell what she was looking at. Either way, her twitch must've been enough to show some of her *own* form, because the big heavy *thing* walked faster.

Before she could think, her fingers pulled back her bowstring and released her arrow. A split second before it left the string, she pumped a little bit of Holy elemental energy into the arrowhead – not as much as she wanted, but some – and it flew toward where she thought the head of the creature was. If it was an undead like she was now suspecting – given the darkness and obvious Nether-element-based trap – then even that much would do a bit of damage. She nocked another arrow even as the previous one flew and watched it hit, creating a brief flash of light as the Holy energy discharged...and it didn't seem to have any effect.

In fact, it almost sounded like her iron arrowhead smacked right into a metal wall, for all the effect it had; Echo also heard the shaft snap into pieces, and she lamented the loss of one of her newish Ironwood arrows. Rather than stick around however, she turned around and ran; she ran faster than she ever had before, pushing all of her energy to speed her along as fast as she could. She left up her active camouflage as long as she could, but three-quarters of the way back to the village she had exhausted her capacity for the moment. That was fine, though, because she was pretty sure she was out of direct danger from the dungeon and its strange monsters outside. She turned around and walked backwards to see if any were following her, but she didn't see anything; she glanced upwards to see if there were any of the metallic objects, but either there weren't any there or it was now too dark to see.

She was exhausted, but she needed to get back to warn everyone about the threat out in the wasteland, so she pushed herself to run as much as she could. As she got closer, she could see Wyrlin – one of her fellow Rangers – on the outside border of their arborents, the dwellings that were quickly grown from a small brown Boren seed with Natural elemental energy.

"You're late – I was starting to get worried about you; though, I guess I shouldn't worry since none of those monsters can see you enough to hurt you," said the bronze-haired Ranger good-naturedly.

Her breathing had returned to normal by that time and the panic she had experienced had died to a small simmer, so she was able to respond to him without sounding like she was in pain while she closed the distance between them. "That's a good point, though that's not why I was late...is Elder Herrlot still up?"

He looked confused at her question. "Of course she is – you know she doesn't sleep nearly as much as she used to; besides, it's barely dark out here. Do you want me to go get her?"

She was finally close enough that she didn't have to speak loudly to be heard. "Yes, but while you're at it, bring everyone you see to the gathering circle – I have some grave news," she told him seriously. "I'll help, but hurry – this can't wait." All sense of joviality that Wyrlin possessed before she spoke was gone as he turned to go fetch the Elder.

There wasn't an arborent large enough to contain every villager, so when they had to have a meeting with everyone in attendance, they used the open circular center left for that purpose in the middle of the village. As much as she wanted to run shouting in a panic about what she had seen, Echo helped to quickly round up the rest of the village inhabitants – which didn't take long. The commotion of her arrival had caused most of them to emerge from their dwellings, anyway, so within minutes everyone was present and accounted for – including the leader of their little village, Elder Herrlot.

The rest of the villagers were, for the most part, hunters or Rangers, tasked with culling the nearby dungeon monsters or gathering meat from the wild beasts still alive out in the forest. There were a few that helped supplement their diet with grown foodstuffs using their Natural-element-based energy, but for the most part everyone was there for their singular purpose: culling and collecting dungeon loot to send back to the capital.

"What is it, Echo? What did you see out in the forest that's got you so worried?" the Elder asked, though "Elder" was only based on her age in comparison to those around her. She still likely looked the same as she did centuries ago, with only the barest wrinkles around her eyes betraying her age. Or, more likely, they were worry lines from the decline of their people she had seen over the years.

"It wasn't in the forest, Honored Elder. It was in the wastelands..." Echo proceeded to tell them what she had seen on her way out of the forest earlier, her journey into the wastelands, the strange "net" of metallic objects floating above the ground, and finally the discovery of the dungeon out in the middle of the dry, barren landscape.

Horror suffused the Elder's face as she described what she had seen and the strange monster that had attacked her; out of everyone there, Elder Herrlot knew first-hand how dangerous an unchecked dungeon in the wasteland area could be. "...and so, I turned to run, keeping my camouflage up as long as possible to make it back here safely. I'm not sure what to do now though; based on my futile attack against that monster, I doubt I could do any serious harm to it. Perhaps if we all joined together to attack the dungeon, we would be more successful, but if that was just the first room, I dread to see what else is in there."

Everyone was quiet for a while as they took in the information, their faces a mixture of fear and determination; while the knowledge of the new dungeon's existence couldn't come at a worse time, her people weren't going to turn over and let it destroy them. "No...we can't take the chance that the dungeon is already powerful enough to stop all of us. I'm going to send a runner back to Lyringlade for some expert help, and permission to send envoys to the other races nearby. For now, there isn't anything we can do to stop the dungeon, but we can definitely keep an eye on it; Echo, since you're the only one it would have difficulty seeing, I want you to keep an eye on it. Your knowledge of it will help you see if anything changes in its methods and be able to warn us if it is going to attack here."

As much as she wanted to protest and insist that they strike *now*, she held back when she considered the consequences of that some more. The Elder was correct, she reluctantly agreed; if they went in without knowing more information, they could all end up getting killed and accomplish nothing in the end. If that happened, the village of Avensglen would likely be abandoned and cease to exist – which would only hasten the decline of their people.

"Yes, Elder – I can do that," she responded tiredly.

"The rest of you, it's business as usual until Echo tells us differently. Hopefully we get help back from the capital in time to stop whatever this dungeon is up to; if not, I can only pray to the Creator that our people are spared the coming catastrophe." And with that, the Elder went back to her personal arborent.

"You should get some sleep, Echo," Wyrlin said from her side. "You have some long days ahead, if I'm not mistaken, and it sounds like you really need to recharge your spent elemental energy."

She couldn't help but agree, so she headed for the arborent she shared with two other Rangers and collapsed on her mat. She briefly thought about changing out of her leathers...but that idea went by the wayside as she was asleep within moments.

Chapter 9

Sandra waited until most of the people in the meeting had gone back to their treehouses and it was fully dark outside. Well, the sky was dark, but the village wasn't quite bathed in shadow; light orbs that were enchanted with Holy-energy-fueled runes were suspended from poles in strategic locations around the perimeter of the village. Two Elves were also stationed just outside the village, facing towards the two distant forests in the distance; she assumed they were some sort of night guard to warn everyone in case there was a surprise attack when everyone else was sleeping.

After instructing her construct to go back to its place in her AMANS, she turned her attention back to her dungeon and her Home room, where she had been relaying the entire village meeting to Winxa.

"So…it appears you have a minder, now. At least you don't have to worry about them attacking tomorrow, but if they send some of their Elites from the Capital – if they are anything like how they used to be – you could be in trouble. Despite the excellent defenses you have in your dungeon so far, it's doubtful that it would stop even a small group of them if they had an elemental specialist or two in their party. Though…" Winxa trailed off as she cocked her head to the side in apparent thought.

What? Though what?

"Well, I was thinking that you might get lucky if they only send a Holy elemental specialist; if they think you're a Nether dungeon, like that 'Echo' woman thought, then they might not send anyone else — because that would probably be all they would need," Winxa said absently, still lost in contemplation.

I don't understand — why would that be all they would need?

"Huh? Oh, well, it's because Elves are rightfully recognized throughout the world to be the masters of elemental manipulation; humans can probably match that prowess when it comes to enchanting and rune creation, but as far as simple — and not so simple — manipulation of the elements for the casting of what they term 'spells' in various useful ways, no one can beat the Elves. And going up against a dungeon filled with Nether-based traps and monsters, they could potentially pick apart the defenses like they were nothing."

So why are they in danger of being wiped out if they're so powerful?

"Don't you remember what I told you? They don't reproduce very often, and though they are long-lived, each time one of them dies it's almost a tragedy to the Elven nation. Their decline mainly comes from the inability to replenish their numbers, not through something as simple as the inability to craft better weapons like the Orcs suffer from."

Ah, that's right. If that's the case, then what do you think I should do about—wait, don't try to answer that. I don't want you to inadvertently say something you shouldn't.

"Thanks," Winxa said with relief. "I probably would've said something out of reflex, and I really don't want to experience that again. What you do is up to you, but now you're on a time limit. I'd give you...two weeks or so."

Sandra thought the same thing, though apparently unlike Winxa, she hadn't a clue of what to do about it. She had been hoping to help the Elves out in the future – somehow – but things with them hadn't really gotten off to a good start. Though, she had to admit, it was a much better start than the one with the Orcs had been – Kelerim notwithstanding. The problem with the Elves didn't sound like it could really be solved by anything she could craft, either, because it sounded more of a "manpower" issue than not having the best weapons or even enchantments.

One more question for you, Winxa – and hopefully it won't be classified as advice; if you think it is, then don't answer it.

"Okay...there's no harm in hearing it, I guess."

Why aren't the different races working together to fight against the dungeons? It seems like that would be an ideal solution to the problem.

"That's something I can answer without too much difficulty, though the answer is technically a long one – I'll try to

97

shorten it for you," Winxa said happily, after hearing that it was something she could safely answer. "Now, this is some of the information that I learned after I became assigned to be your Dungeon Fairy," she warned.

In the beginning, Sandra remembered Winxa leaving the dungeon quite a bit more looking for information than she had lately, though Sandra was never precisely sure what the Fairy had found out – but some of it she was likely to learn now.

"Basically, after the races came together to defeat Wester—" Winxa looked sad at the mention of her former Dungeon Core's name, though whether it was because she was sorry for what he did or because she was sorry he was destroyed, Sandra couldn't tell— "they retreated back to their respective homelands. Things were a little tense despite the cooperation, because even after the success here, they were forced to defend their respective nations against their "native" dungeons; since most of their concentration was on destroying the hugely powerful Dungeon Core that was threatening *everyone*, their local dungeons had also become relatively powerful as a result of inattention.

"This led to squabbling between the races as fault was passed back and forth, with accusations of the others not contributing enough to the war against Wester, and even to blaming the other races for destroying what was once a vital area of international trade and access between the different racial nations – namely, the wasteland you now find yourself in.

Normally, this place had been a kind of "off-limits" area for dungeons, which fostered many to travel between the different lands – which was actually the opposite of what the Creator had planned when the Dungeon system was put into place. If you remember, it was developed to curb the conquering impulses of the races so that they would stick to and protect their own lands.

"Anyway, in comes Wester to upset the entire thing, and the resulting destruction of the area was – as crazy as it sounds – exactly what the Creator wanted, though the consequences of those decisions are still being felt today. I would never say that the Creator made a mistake—" Winxa looked up as she said this for some reason— "but some choices weren't exactly...the best. Which was why I said that you're likely here to fix some of that.

"So...years went by and more disagreements were had between the races, leading to a few fights, which then led to an increase in the number of dungeons bordering their lands. This led each race to concentrate on their own people rather than trying to foster any type of discourse between themselves, and so now you can see where that got them."

That...was the short version? Sandra asked humorously at the long discourse.

"Well, yes...I could've added another couple hours' worth of information, like specific information on the disagreements between the Orcs and the Elves, and the Dwarves and the Gnomes, and—well, you get the idea."

99

Thank you, Winxa – I was just messing with you.

"I figured."

Getting the races to work together didn't seem feasible at this point, so there didn't seem to be a solution to help the Elves right then. That didn't mean she couldn't still help the Orcs and the others, though to do that she was going to have to communicate with them somehow; in addition, communication might aid in convincing the Elves not to come after her – she could dream, right? Nevertheless, opening up some sort of dialogue before things escalated too far was a bit of a priority now.

The only way she could think to do that reliably, however, was if Kelerim came back to her dungeon; since she had no idea where he even was at that point – or whether he really would come back – she was at a loss of what to do. With that not an option, she tried to think of other methods of communication.

Writing out some sort of message came to mind. She thought she could eventually make some rudimentary paper from the tree that was almost done growing with a bit of work, as well as some sort of writing instrument, but Winxa shut that down immediately.

"While you can understand and even speak any language due to your status as a Dungeon Core, the system set up in place for that doesn't extend to the written word. You could write in your common Human tongue, but it's unlikely anyone would be able to read it."

Sandra hadn't really thought about being able to understand the speech of both the Orcs and the Elves – it just sounded..."normal" to her. That it was some sort of Core-based ability was news to her; regardless of the new information, she was glad that she could understand everyone – otherwise things so far might've gone far worse than it had already. Not being able to communicate with Kelerim or learning that her time was limited from the Elven village meeting would've had much different results.

So, writing a message was out, so that left...what? Pantomime? Attempt to convey her non-threatening nature by having her constructs allow themselves to be destroyed? Have them put their hands (or other appendages) up in the air in surrender? Make her Mechanical Wolves outside roll on their back in submission? None of that seemed like it would work, plus it would likely only convey that she was weak and easily taken advantage of; she had seen that kind of attitude entirely too much when she was alive as a Human to know that wasn't a good idea. She needed to put forth a position of non-threatening strength, but with also a warning that she would defend herself lethally if she was forced to that point.

Other types of non-verbal communication through the use of body language was also out, as her constructs had relatively expressionless faces (if they had faces at all) and she didn't know any way to convey meaning through subtle shifts in their hands, arms, legs, or bodies. That also went along with oral communication, as none of her constructs – despite a few having mouths – had any type of way to speak; that was actually one of the first things she tried when Kelerim had been in her dungeon and had been slightly disappointed when it seemed impossible. Fortunately, she had been able to mentally communicate with him through the Visitor's Bond, so it became a non-issue.

At least, it was a non-issue until Razochek invaded with a portion of his Warband. If she had been able to actually communicate with him at the start, she might not have had to kill them all; there was nothing she could do about that now, though, but the non-communication problem was still present.

Another type of visual communication she could reasonably see being effective was through some type of artwork or even a mural that could somehow portray her desire for peace and wish to help the other races. She didn't really have the materials for any type of painting or drawing, and even if she did, she had nothing to paint or draw *on*. The stone walls were a possibility, but she didn't know if that would convey her message well enough; carving into the walls themselves was another idea, which could definitely work. It was something that she would have to consider for the future and with a bit of practice, because she had never "sculpted" anything before, and wasn't even sure if she could do it with any type of skill.

While she had learned many of the techniques used by painters, sculptors, and other artisans, their individual strengths didn't lie in recipes and doing things by a specific formula over and over. True, there was some improvisation needed every once in a while – when crafting metal weapons and armor, cooking a meal, or even carving a wooden table – but it wasn't the same as what true artists did every time that they created something. Their whole purpose was to create something new and never seen before, using their imagination and own creative mindset to do it. That was something she needed to discover if she could apply that same creative thinking to a piece.

Or, she could always make rudimentary stick figures and hope someone understood the meaning she was trying to get across. That would be a last resort, however, and she wanted to practice first – later, though.

Do any of the Dungeon Monsters from the other Classifications have the ability to speak? That was the last idea she had, though she didn't put much hope in the question she asked her Dungeon Fairy friend.

"Hmm...I'm not actually sure – I don't think any Dungeon Cores have ever *wanted* to talk to their victims before. It's possible some of the Bipedals or even the Goblinoids might be able to, but I can't guarantee that," Winxa told her without much confidence.

Better than nothing, I suppose. Essentially, what that meant was that she was going to have to speed up her upgrading of her Core Size; however, the mere thought of being trapped inside her Core again – for who knew how long – gave her intense anxiety. It hadn't really even been that long since she had increased her Size and she was hoping to have at least another week or so before she had to do it.

She had already accumulated more than enough Mana to finish all of her stages, however, and in fact her Mana was completely full after she had let it fill up while she was looking into the Elven issue. Since Winxa was fairly confident that Sandra had at least two weeks before she was threatened with destruction by a party of Elven Elites, she decided to finish some projects for a day or two before she went under again. The delay shouldn't matter that much in the long run, and it also allowed her mind to process the upcoming shut-in experience enough that she thought she could handle it.

While she was observing the Elven village and the meeting, her Oak tree had grown tremendously. Looking at its root system, it had spread them out all along the dirt it had access to, without caring about the stone walls separating the different plots. Her plan – that was interrupted by the appearance of that Elven woman, Echo – to remove the stone so that the roots could expand was unnecessary, as it had done just fine. As for the tree itself, it was now over 20 feet tall and still growing; Sandra thought it was reaching the stage where it could be harvested for wood – because she could see some acorns growing along its branches. While it could keep growing for quite a while before it got too big for the space, she didn't think there was any need.

Without waiting too much longer, she sent a few of her Small Animated Shears from her Home up to the growing room, where they immediately cut the acorns off the Oak tree and dropped them down to the floor. Sandra's Golems quickly picked them up and put them into a small pile; it was still a relatively young tree in comparison to the large ones in the forest outside, which meant that it only had a small number of acorns growing on the tree at that time. As she watched, she could see a few budding up and starting to grow, but she thought she had more than enough for now.

Sandra "ate" one of the acorns and she got a satisfying Dungeon Core system message in response.

New Origination Material found!

Oak Tree Seed
While the Oak Tree Seed cannot be used directly as a Monster Seed, it can be used in specific applications to create a whole new Monster Seed.

That was the same sort of response she had gotten when she had obtained the Flax Seed by consuming some linen cloth; she assumed at the time that – because the cloth was a finished product – she had only gotten the base component and nothing else. Now, however, she was beginning to think there was some other sort of material and Monster Seed she could obtain from the Flax plant. Her suspicions were confirmed when she took a chunk out of the growing Oak tree.

New Monster Seed and Origination Material found!

Oak Wood
While Oak Wood can be directly used as a Monster Seed, it can also be used as a material for use in the dungeon or other purposes.

You now have access to:
Tiny Oak Wood Chip
Origination Raw Material Cost: 50
Origination Mana Cost: 10
Monster Min. Mana: 10
Monster Max. Mana: 50

I did it! I finally have access to wood! While Oak wasn't necessarily the best material for certain crafts, the fact that she finally had some sort of wood that she could use was spectacular.

And it opened up a whole new level of crafting that she had been waiting for.

Chapter 10

Having access to wood of *any* type opened up a world of possibilities, though there were some crafts that required a certain type of wood to be more effective. For instance, Oak didn't work too well as components for melee weapons – because they tended to be heavier than others – but they worked...fine for bows; they made a heavier bow which wasn't always great trying to steady if you didn't have the strength for it, and the draw was usually more – which could be a good or bad thing. For other woods such as Pine, they were almost useless because they weren't quite strong enough and you had to make them much thicker if you didn't want them to snap in your hands.

For making the shafts for the arrows, however, Oak was far from ideal. They were rarely straight-grained and were hard to straighten without some sort of elemental energy assistance – which wasn't always available when crafting. Cedar or Ironwood were the ideal candidates for arrow shafts, and even Pine was acceptable if you could find it in enough straight quantities to be effective, because it was also difficult to straighten.

Fortunately, Sandra didn't really have to worry about that; after easily unlocking the larger sizes of Monster Seeds, she found that she could create the wood in any basic shape that she needed.

Monster Seed Origination				
Name:	Raw Material Cost:	Mana Cost:	Min. Mana:	Max. Mana:
Tiny Oak Wood Chip	50	10	10	50
Small Oak Wood Block	100	20	10	100
Average Oak Wood Stick	400	80	10	400
Large Oak Wood Plank	800	160	10	800
Locked Seeds:	Unlock Requirements:	Mana Cost to Unlock:	Min. Mana:	Max. Mana:
Small Dragon Glass Sliver	2 Tiny Dragon Glass Flakes	14000	5000	20000
Average Dragon Glass Shard	4 Small Dragon Glass Slivers	56000	5000	80000
Large Dragon Glass Chunk	2 Average Dragon Glass Shards	112000	5000	160000

And by "basic", that was essentially what it was. While she could use the materials in which she had access to create normal objects through her use of her Mundane Object Creation skill – like some tools, tableware, and even furniture – when it came to using it to craft, it only came in pre-arranged shapes. The same thing essentially happened during blacksmithing; she could create different-sized ingots of metal and even longer bars – in addition to the orb-like shapes that her Monster Seeds looked like – but anything other than that didn't really work.

So, with her Oak Wood, Sandra could create similar things as her Monster Seeds; tiny little wood chips, wooden cube blocks, rounded sticks, and flat boards. She had the ability to change the size – like the thickness and length of the material – but the general shape was essentially stuck in those forms.

Which was fine, because when she looked at the quality of the wood – she was again struck at how pristine it was.

She had become accustomed to the "pure" form of the metals she had created for her blacksmithing; sometimes it was difficult to imagine what having impurities in them again would mean for the crafting work she did. With the wood she was able to create, however, it was obvious how different it was compared to the tree that was still growing and repairing the chunk she had taken out of it.

First of all, the graining inside was perfectly straight, which was essential to maintaining strength while granting a little bit of flexibility. There were also no flaws or cracks, no knots in the wood, and it appeared extremely smooth – as if it had been sanded with the finest sandstone wheel. She couldn't actually "feel" it to tell, of course, because her Ironclad Ape only had so much tactile response in its form; she longed to run her fingers over the grain to feel the utter perfection the wood she created represented. It was just another reason to see what other kind of Dungeon Monster from another Classification could do for her – one that hopefully had some sort of responsive skin to it.

In her woodworking workshop, she had used an Earth trap to set up a moving bladed saw that was similar in form to a grindstone. Instead of stone, however, it was a circular piece of Steel that had little teeth cut into it like a handsaw, and it was connected to a central shaft that would turn very quickly through the use of the trap's function. She had it sticking up from the center of a flat stone table, in which she could use her Ironclad Ape to feed and cut her wood into whatever shape she desired.

Deciding to start with something simple, she created a dozen Oak wood boards that were 3 inches wide, 2 feet long, and an inch thick. Activating the trap via standing in a particular spot near her saw table, she had her Ape lay the wood flat against the stone and push it into the quickly rotating metal saw – and wood chips started to fly and the board was almost ripped out of her Ape's hands.

Whoops – pushed it in on the wrong side. Realizing what she did, Sandra had to correct the trap activation placement and moved it to the other side of the table, so that instead of cutting in an *upwards* motion, the saw was cutting *downwards*. With that fixed, she had her Ape try again and succeeded in cutting the board with precision. Buoyed by her success, she brought her boards up to Kelerim's old Forge and used her blacksmithing skills to craft a simple flat Steel band 2 inches wide that would stretch and wrap across all 12 boards in their center.

While it was still relatively hot and malleable, she placed the boards next to each other and quickly wrapped the Steel band around them; when it was in place, a few quick hammer strikes allowed her to seal the ends of the bands together in a relatively crude weld, but it was enough to hold it in place. The metal was still hot enough to start to burn the wood, so she brought the whole board and band combo to a small trough she had filled up nearby with cool water from the Kitchen/Dining Room. Steam rose up as the metal rapidly cooled, but the Steel was of such purity that even rapid cooling couldn't cause it to weaken from the extreme change in temperature.

When it was cool enough, she brought the now-wrapped bundle of boards to the woodworking workshop again. Laying it flat on the saw table, she used the rapidly rotating circular saw to trim and shape the outside of the boards into a rough circular shape. Her Ape didn't really have as fine of control as she would've liked; subtle movements of the entire bundle was difficult with its sausage-like iron fingers. As a result, it looked more like someone had taken an axe and inexpertly cut around the edges of it, but it would work.

Fortunately, blacksmithing for the Ironclad Ape was much easier. Once the shape was achieved, she brought it back to the blacksmithing shop and created another quantity of Steel to make another flat band; this time, however, it was shaped to cover the *outside* circular shape of the wood bundle. It would also cover the previous Steel band, keeping it in place and extremely secure. When the still hot and malleable Steel was ready, her Ape used its bare hands to shape it along the edge, allowing it to wrap the wood and then welded the end together when it had made a full circuit. It was a little too long, however, so she had to cut the end of the band off when she was done using a hammer and a sharp chisel that could cut through the still-slightly soft metal.

Another bath in the water prevented it from burning up and catching fire, and when it was cool, she brought it back out. Now was time for a dozen rivets to hold it in place; using a center punch tool – which was essentially a long spike with a sharp point – she hammered a hole into the edge of the outer band, through the wood, and then created another hole on the other side. Directing her Ape exactly where to place the 11 other holes she wanted along the outside rim and four along the band in the middle, she then used a second Ape she had nearby to start making rivets in the forge. They were essentially long slender cylinders that had one end flat and spread out; when they were ready, she would heat up the other end just enough to make it slightly malleable, hammer it straight through the holes made previously, and then finish it up by hammering the softer, heated side – so that it would be flush against the metal rim.

Using another rounded bar of Steel, she controlled one of her Apes at the forge and heated and shaped it until it looked like a wide U with flattened ends. On those flattened ends, she punched another hole for another rivet, which would correspond to the holes previously made on the center Steel band. Attaching the U-shaped Steel to the back side of the project she was working on, she pounded more heated rivets into the ends to secure it in place and then stepped back to look at her creation.

It wasn't the best Steel-banded Oak shield in the world, but it wasn't the worst either. She could already see where she could improve her riveting to make it cleaner, work on the spacing between the holes, and smooth over the hastily welded parts; all in all, though, it appeared at least serviceable. The wood grain was superb and unnaturally straight, which gave the shield an almost-striped appearance, which she thought was a neat addition to the otherwise relatively crude crafting job. Though, it wasn't exactly "crude" – not like the junk swords she had seen the Orcs wielding – but she knew she could do much better with practice.

Just like she had needed to practice with metal and improve her blacksmithing, she needed to practice with wood. Back when she was alive in the land of Muriel, wooden "dungeon loot" drops weren't very common. In some areas, the higher-quality woods like Magewood and Elderoak were present – but they were few and far between. Humans tended to like more of their premium crafted weapons made from dungeon-looted metal, as opposed to wood; bows and a few staves that were enchanted from some special woods were about all she saw used for weapons or armor, so working with such pristine "common" woods like Oak – as she now possessed – was fairly new to her.

In order to become a little better at working with the wood, over the next day she practiced creating more of the same shield she had just produced, as well as adding wooden components – like lightweight handles – to weapons such as swords, knives, axes, and even some short spears to help with balancing issues. Since what she had produced before had been made entirely of metal, it was also the first time she had to really utilize some of the leather she had made shortly after Kelerim had arrived; when wrapped around handles – and even things like where an axe head joins the haft – it helped to hold everything together and even supplied a better grip for a person's hands.

Sandra spent so much time utilizing her new material that she barely had time for anything else. Crafting only took up a fraction of her incoming Mana, however, and since she had already completed the stages toward the next Core Size Upgrade, she spent everything she had on producing more Monster Seeds. In an area past her Home where her core was located, she started hollowing out a massive room and used the Raw Materials from that excavation and her available Mana to fill it with…"loot", essentially. She didn't want everything she was taking in to go to waste, so she filled up what she was now calling her treasury with various Orbs and other seeds of every size she had access to.

There were Copper Orbs, Tin Orbs, Nickel Orbs, Bronze Orbs, Iron Orbs, Steel Orbs, Silver Orbs, Gold Orbs, elemental

Orbs from every element, Cubes of Salt, a small pile of Dragon Glass Flakes, stacks of Oak wood Planks, and even a small castle of Clay Cubes that she had her Tiny Automatons build as they transported them from her Home room. She wasn't exactly sure what she wanted to do with all of the Seeds she accumulated, but she didn't want all of those resources to go to waste.

She was about to start work on trying to create a bow – which would take a little bit, as she needed the normally straight wood she could create to soak in a tub, making it slightly more flexible so that she could bend it into shape – when she realized she hadn't checked on her Flax in a while. She ate away the covering of the warm churning-water tub where her flax stems were retting and found that they were finally ready for the next step in the lengthy process.

The next step required the bark on the outside of the fibers inside to be scraped away – which was made much easier and prevented overall breakage from the retting process – and then the water squeezed out and dried. Placing them on the heated tanning racks was the most efficient process, and within an hour they were dry and ready for the next step. Normally, special tools that looked like a long thin grouping of spikes were used to break up the stalks and separate the fibers, but Sandra had something more efficient – or at least more fun. Dozens of Segmented Centipedes crawled all over the dried Flax and used their mandibles to delicately separate the fibers until they were placed into a large pile for further work.

The next step required melding the fibers together to form one giant "rope", which she accomplished by making a series of rollers inside her Textile Workshop that were essentially two large grooved stone pillars laid horizontally and angled to produce a thinner rope toward the end. Essentially, placing the long Flax fibers on one end mashed and spun them together so that they formed one giant strand, and adding more fibers as the grooved rollers moved them up, it would continue the rope chain. When it was all done with that step, it moved on to the spinning part, where she had her Ape use a spinning wheel to turn the Flax rope into Linen Thread.

Sandra absorbed the first bit of thread that emerged...and that's when it happened.

New Monster Seed and Origination Material found!

Linen Thread
While Linen Thread can be directly used as a Monster Seed, it can also be used as a material for use in the dungeon or other purposes.

You now have access to:
Tiny Linen Thread Bobbin
Origination Raw Material Cost: 10
Origination Mana Cost: 5
Monster Min. Mana: 5
Monster Max. Mana: 10

She couldn't absorb and gain access to the Linen cloth that Kelerim had brought back from the village, but that was because she needed to "craft" the base components herself. She doubted it would be the same with a piece of cloth made

116

from the thread – though to make sure, she quickly spun enough for two small spools of thread and placed them on the loom she had created weeks ago. Within 15 minutes of having her Ape fumbling around with it for a while, she had created a small length of Linen Cloth – which, admittedly wasn't the best quality, as she was anxious to see it complete – and nothing happened when she "ate" it with her Dungeon Core ability.

She never remembered Linen Thread *or* Cloth being something ever dropped as dungeon loot – or any other type of textile, for that matter. Though, she doubted that any other dungeon had taken the time to actually craft it, so unless they acquired it from someone who just happened to have a bobbin or spool of thread on them and dropped it in one of the dungeons, it wasn't likely that they ever would. And even *if* they acquired it, they probably wouldn't use it as a Monster Seed unless it was really valuable.

With the knowledge of being able to unlock materials like the Linen Thread in the future, Sandra was excited for what was to come.

Now all she needed to do was survive to see it.

Chapter 11

Before succumbing to the inevitable feeling of being
thrown down a hole without being able to move or speak that
came along with upgrading her Core Size, Sandra started to
investigate the options again with her newest Core-specific skill,
Organic/Inorganic Material Elemental Transmutation, or OMET
for short. In addition to what was on there before with Metals,
Fibrous Plant Seeds, and Clays, she now had an additional
category: Non-Fruit-Producing Tree Seeds.

Organic/Inorganic Material Elemental Transmutation Menu				
Transmutation Options	Elemental Orb Required (Size/Qty)	Mana Required	Additional Seed Material (Size/Qty)	Unlocked (Y/N)
Non-Fruit-Producing Tree Seeds				
Oak Seed	N/A	N/A	N/A	Y
Maple Seed	Natural (Average/3)	0/5000	Tin (Average/2)	N
Cedar Seed	Natural (Large/2)	0/10000	Nickel (Average/3)	N
Ash Seed	Natural (Large/2), Fire (Tiny/2)	0/15000	Lead (Large/2)	N
Pine Seed	Natural (Large/4), Water (Small/2)	0/20000	Bronze (Large/3)	N
Birch Seed	Natural (Large/5), Earth (Tiny/2)	0/25000	Silver (Large/4)	N
Redwood Seed	Natural (Large/6), Fire (Large/2)	0/50000	Iron (Large/5)	N
Yew Seed	Natural (Large/12), Air (Small/2)	0/100000	Gold (Large/10)	N
Ironwood Seed	?????	0/500000	?????	N
Elderoak Seed	?????	0/1500000	?????	N
Magewood Seed	?????	0/5000000	?????	N
Ancient Silverpine Seed	?????	0/10000000	?????	N

Sandra was a little disappointed not to see the presence
of actual Wood and Thread on there, but she supposed she
needed to grow and make them first before she could use them
as material and as a Seed. Still, the fact that she could unlock

those new seeds made her excited – and it was entirely possible that she could figure out some of the mysterious "unknown" requirements for the more powerful Tree Seeds. She also took special notice of the fact that the new category said "Non-Fruit-Producing", which meant that she could theoretically find fruit-producing trees later – where some of the wood off of them were useful in special cases.

Because she had all of the components to finally unlock some of the new materials through the use of her new skill, that was exactly what she wanted to do. How exactly she was supposed to actually use her skill, though, was another question altogether.

It turned out to be easier than she thought. All she did was concentrate on "Maple Seed" on her new menu and feed Mana into it; the sensation and effect were strange, however, because they were like nothing she had ever felt before. When she normally fed Mana into something like a Monster Seed or a defensive trap, it just flowed out of her; this, though, felt like it was being pulled out of her Core and then shoved back into a separate compartment. When she had fed the requisite 5000 Mana into it, the Mana "popped" out of her Core and dropped to the floor in a semi-visible sphere of condensed Core energy like one of her Monster Seeds.

She could barely see it unless she concentrated on it, but she could definitely tell it was there; without thinking about it too much, she created the other necessary Seeds – 3 Average

Natural Elemental Orbs and 2 Average Tin Orbs – and had a Tiny Automaton nearby transport them so that they were all in a pile. That was apparently all it took, because all 6 Orbs (the 5 material and 1 Mana-filled one) suddenly melded together and there was a brief flash of light so bright that it actually blinded Sandra for a moment. When she opened them back up, she saw a small greenish seed on the floor where the Orbs had been. It had two flat "wings" on it that were attached to a central seed pod; she remembered seeing thousands of them over the years as they floated and spun down from Maple trees back in Muriel.

New Origination Material found!

Maple Seed
While the Maple Seed cannot be used directly as a Monster Seed, it can be used in specific applications to create a whole new Monster Seed.

And just like that, Sandra did it. She had used her new skill to essentially "buy" a new Origination Material; it wasn't quite the same as creating it herself through the use of a crafting process – like the Bronze and Steel alloys she had made previously – but it was satisfying, nonetheless. She wasn't even sure some of the things she could unlock even *could* be crafted in any other way, so she thought her new skill was the best possible use of her available resources.

Excited, she used the same process to unlock the other seeds; Cedar Seed needed Natural and Nickel Orbs; Pine Seed needed Natural, Water, and Bronze Orbs; Birch Seed needed

Natural, Earth, and Silver Orbs; Redwood needed Natural, Fire, and Iron Orbs; and Yew Seed needed Natural, Air, and Gold Orbs. The Orbs were easy enough to create and use, but the Mana took much longer to accumulate. The Cedar Seed only needed a little less than her maximum Mana amount – at 10,000 Mana – and it took just over half an hour to gather that much from outside her dungeon. The others, however, took *more* than her maximum – which felt additionally strange to her Core.

Whereas the 5,000 Mana needed for the Maple Seed – as well as the 10,000 for Cedar – re-entered her Core momentarily as it was accumulated before being spat back out, the others that required additional Mana *stayed* there. It almost reminded her of when she was a newly born Dungeon Core and "ate" too much of her cave; the feeling of being full was there, but fortunately she wasn't shut down and unable to do anything while it was happening. Instead, it was like her stomach was full, but it wasn't debilitating – on the contrary, she felt almost energized.

Sandra tried to pull the Mana back out of the spot it was accumulating in her Core, but it was inaccessible. For better or worse, it was tied up in her "purchase" of the next seed like some sort of down payment being held in reserve at a bank. When she thought of it like that, it made much more sense – she had been a merchant in her former life, after all.

When she added more of her Mana to the "bank", it would fill up and pop out of her Core just like before, where she could combine it with the other required materials to unlock the other tree seeds. As soon as she had access to a new seed, she immediately set her Golems in her growing room to work planting a seed and nurturing it to enough maturity to harvest for its wood.

There was one tree seed she couldn't quite create yet – other than the options with the unknown materials: Ash Seed. She needed to have access to Lead metal as a material, which she hadn't found while excavating underground nor was it an alloy she could make herself. Instead, she needed to unlock it using her new skill; the requirements stated she needed to have Earthenware Clay as a material – which she didn't have yet – so she had to unlock that one first. To do that, she needed Earth and Iron Orbs, which were easy to produce, as well as 5,000 Mana.

When that was unlocked, she combined Earth, Fire, and Earthenware Clay to unlock Lead as another metal she could use as a material. Then, when that was available, Sandra was able to combine Natural, Fire, and Lead Orbs (as well as 15,000 Mana) together to unlock the Ash Seed to produce another type of tree – and another type of wood when it was grown in her growing room.

Sandra thought it was interesting how everything was interconnected in some sort of giant web; to gain access to something, she needed to have had unlocked quite a few other things in the process. She had gotten lucky finding or creating so many of her materials earlier, or else the whole unlocking ordeal would've likely taken much longer.

While she was at it and unlocking different materials, she went ahead and gained access to Stoneware Clay with Earth and Iron Orbs; Jute Seed with Natural Orbs and Oak wood; and Cotton Seed with Natural Orbs and Maple wood (once her Maple tree was grown enough to harvest and gain access to its wood type). She held off on planting the Jute and Cotton Seeds, however, until she was prepared to turn them into usable thread/rope; it was a much lengthier process to turn the plants into usable material than just growing and harvesting the trees. The Flax and Linen Thread was more than enough proof of that.

All in all, it had been a productive two days. Sandra had now acquired access to every single material that didn't possess the "unknown" materials needed to unlock them with her new Elemental Transmutation skill – and then unlocked the larger Monster Seed versions of each type of wood, clay, and Lead metal. She figured she could experiment a little with different combinations of her materials to unlock the others, but they would also require quite a bit of an investment of Mana. Therefore, before she did anything like that, she decided that it was probably about time to endure the crushing loneliness and isolation that upgrading her Core Size always seemed to bring.

To hopefully stave off some of that and bring back some of the familiarity that she had been missing in her last upgrade, she spent a little time – as well as Mana and Raw Materials –

creating some constructs to stay near her during that time. It wasn't much, compared to what she had in some of her defensive rooms, but she thought it would be enough.

Two dozen Singing Blademasters were set up in a loose sphere around her Core, far enough away that they weren't a danger to her – but hopefully well within her perception during the upgrade. Sandra instructed them to move slowly in random directions, only making sure not to run into each other in the process and had them spin and "sing" at different times. She was hoping that if they were random enough, it would give her something to focus on and try to anticipate – rather than concentrate on her trapped consciousness. Winxa also volunteered to keep her company again, so with all of those things, she figured she was as prepared as she was going to get.

Before she initiated the upgrade, Sandra put up another super-intense, Fire-fueled trap in front of the large entrance tunnel leading into her Home from where she had multiple Iron-plated Behemoths waiting to defend her. While a potential attack from the Elves wasn't supposed to come for another week and a half – at least – it didn't hurt to be careful. When everything was as ready as it was going to get, she waited for her Mana to fill up again and started the upgrade.

Her perception faded again, shrinking down to just a small area that comprised only about a third of the way to the edges of her large Home room. Fortunately, her Singing Blademasters were well within that area, so her temporary confinement was provided with strangely satisfying entertainment. The constructs were moving slowly in a random direction, while staying in a loose sphere around her a little more than 10 feet away; every once in a while, one of the Blademasters would start spinning and let out its high-pitched whine, which changed in tone when it moved in a different direction. It only lasted between 10 and 15 seconds, but it was enough to distract her.

Winxa made a game of it. "Let's see...I think it'll be that one right there," she would say, pointing at a particular construct. The Dungeon Fairy was trying to guess which one would be next to "sing" and encouraged Sandra to play along. After seeing how much fun her friend was having, she joined in.

Very rarely would either the Dungeon Fairy or Core be correct in their guess, but when they were it was a cause for celebration. Well, at least Winxa spun and danced around in the air when she got one correct; Sandra couldn't do anything or even communicate which ones she chose, so her own celebrations were in her mind. Regardless, the game passed the time and before she knew it, Sandra's Core Size upgrade was complete.

Core Size Upgrade Stage complete!
11/11 Completed

Your Core has grown!
Current Size: 19

Mana Capacity increased!
Raw Material Capacity increased!

New Constructs option!

Core Selection Menu	
Dungeon Classification:	Constructs
Core Size:	19
Available Mana:	16/15646
Ambient Mana Absorption:	10/hour
Available Raw Material (RM):	6500/41608
Convert Raw Material to Mana?	6500 RM -- > 260 Mana
Current Dungeon Monsters:	14576
Constructs Creation Options:	17
Monster Seed Schematics:	133 (3)
Current Traps:	31
Trap Construction Options:	All
Core-specific Skills:	5
Current Visitors:	1

Rather than be disappointed that she didn't receive another Core-specific skill like the last upgrade, she was happy that she got another Construct that she could make and that her maximum Mana had increased. She was waiting to finish off the rest of her rooms with traps when she acquired more Mana, and now she thought that 15,000 Mana would be more than enough to make them effective – and hopefully deadly toward anyone meaning her harm.

"So, what did you end up with? I got seven correct!" Winxa asked, breaking Sandra from her thoughts. The Dungeon Core was confused for a few moments before she figured out what the Fairy was talking about: guessing which Blademaster would "sing" next.

I only ended up with six – nice job! Thanks for keeping me company again; if you don't mind me asking, how long was it this time?

"You're welcome – it was actually kind of fun. And it was just a few hours over two days that you were under; if I remember correctly, the time you'll be out only increases by a little bit by the time you hit Core Size 20, which I'm sure you're very glad to know," Winxa responded.

That *was* good news, though this last upgrade hadn't been as excruciating as the one before it. Sandra figured she would need to do something similar in the future to entertain herself – and Winxa, if she was there – to make the time go by quicker. That seemed to be the key; if she could distract her mind and make her forget about her – albeit, temporary – helplessness and loneliness, then everything would be fine.

She was just about to check out her new Construct Option, but – as seemed usual by then – something else caught her attention.

Chapter 12

What is this I'm feeling along the edges of my Area of Influence, Winxa?

"Uh...could you be more specific? I don't understand," the Dungeon Fairy replied with confusion and maybe even a little alarm in her voice.

When I concentrate on the underground extremities of where I can reach now with my expanded Area of Influence, I can feel a slight resistance in certain areas. I can push through it quite easily, but I've never felt that before.

Winxa seemed as though she might have an idea when she asked, "Where exactly do you feel these 'resistances'?"

Sandra roamed all around her perimeter and tried to isolate where she was feeling them. The closest one was to the south and slightly east; looking at the extensive underground roots of the forest to the east of the Elven village, she could feel it almost as an invisible curved "bubble" that took a slight effort to pass through.

That wasn't the only one, however; she could feel other ones to the west in the forest separating the Elven and Orcish lands, one to the north and a little east at the border forest between the Orcish and Dwarven territories, and a third far to the east in the forest dividing the Dwarven and Gnomish lands. It was unusual enough to also note that reaching that far now meant that her Area of Influence had increased dramatically with her last upgrade. In fact, from what she could tell, it now included the entire wasteland area.

Passing through the "bubbles" didn't really do anything; as soon as she was through them, she could move her vision anywhere underground that her Influence could reach. Which wasn't far even for the closest spot she came across. Sandra explained where they were located as well as she could to Winxa, who seemed at first shocked and then somehow unsurprised shortly thereafter.

"What you're detecting is the Area of Influence of another dungeon. The 'bubble' you're describing is the perimeter of it, just like your own perimeter and how far you can reach. If you're able to go far enough, you're likely to run into the dungeon themselves."

Why did you look shocked? I would think this would be very common.

"Well, yes – encountering the border of another Core's Area of Influence happens all the time; the difference here, though, is your ability to pass *through* the border. Only Cores with the same element can actually pass their viewpoint through another's border, which makes it very rare since the Creator now ensures there aren't any similar-element dungeons near each other when they are placed. Dungeon Monsters can pass through any of them, but only a small portion of the ambient Mana or Mana from the deaths of living beings will be absorbed in any overlap – unless, again, they're the same element, then it is a full 50% split between the two Cores.

"It's also another reason that Dungeon Monsters don't typically fight over territory, as it doesn't matter even if they win – because it wouldn't get them much in the long run. Typically, Dungeon Cores are spaced far enough apart that only when they are quite upgraded in Size will they actually encounter the border of another Core – and by that time, the overlap really doesn't matter because it's difficult for them to fill their entire territory with Dungeon Monsters, anyway."

Wait a minute – if they're so blood-thirsty and willing to kill anything to get stronger, wouldn't they just try to destroy the other Cores near them and take over the full use of the overlapping Area of Influence?

"If they weren't constrained by their contract from attacking the dungeon of any other contracted Dungeon Core, I would say you'd be correct. As it is, though, there's rarely a reason for them to waste their resources on attacking another dungeon; since they don't receive any Mana from killing a foreign Dungeon Monster – nor can the Monster Seeds they leave behind be absorbed – there's very little benefit in it. Unless, just like the absorption of ambient Mana, they are the same element – then they can actually take the Seed back to their dungeon and absorb it for both Mana and Raw Materials, as well as unlocking the use of it as a Monster Seed if it wasn't previously accessible," Winxa answered matter-of-factly, before she cocked her head to the side in thought.

What?

"Oh, nothing – it just occurred to me that your special situation means that essentially any Core's Area of Influence barrier won't really hinder you or the other Core, so that you can both pass freely amongst each other's territory."

I can see that, but why is that significant?

Winxa spoke slowly, as if she was testing her words to see if they would cause her to be seen as giving advice. "Well, do you remember what I said about the contract Dungeon Cores have to abide by regarding attacking another Core?" Sandra indicated that she did. "Ok, so that only applies to attacking another *contracted* Core – which, if you remember, you definitely are not. Therefore, what that means is that it's entirely possible that they could attack *you*."

So, in addition to being concerned about being attacked by the Elves in a couple of weeks, as well as watching out for the Orcs still, I have to worry about the other Cores when they expand their Areas of Influence so that they can reach me?

The Dungeon Fairy hesitated for a moment before she answered. "Yes…and no. What I failed to mention before about same-element dungeons being next to each other is the main reason why you don't find them like that anymore; it hasn't really happened for at least a millennium, so it didn't really occur to me until now. One special aspect of the pairings is that

131

whichever Dungeon Core has the smallest Core Size has access to the *entire* Area of Influence of the other – though they cannot change anything underground, so you don't have to worry about them digging a hole all the way to you. Don't ask me why this ability exists, because it doesn't make much sense; the only reason I can think of is if it was some sort of method the Creator had designed to have Cores 'mentor' their neighbors, thereby making them more effective. My guess is that it was *too* effective and needed to be stopped, which is why it doesn't occur anymore."

Uh...so you're saying that I could be attacked by hordes of Dungeon Monsters at any time?

"Well, not necessarily. If they are a higher Core Size than you, then you don't really have anything to worry about for now."

But didn't you say that I would have access to their entire Area of Influence if I was a lower Core Size? Because I can tell you that isn't the case here.

"Oh, well then yes, you're in a bit of trouble. Then again, the fact that you don't have a contract could make a difference; I'm not entirely sure if it's a 'contracted' ability or not."

Regardless, I need to prepare for even more now.

Sandra wasn't sure how long it would be before the nearby Cores figured out she was there, but she needed to prepare. Since Winxa said they couldn't just dig a hole all the way to her – fortunately – she only really had to worry about them coming in the entrance aboveground. The problem was, she had no idea exactly what was coming her way; she only had her memories of the monsters the Human Heroes would talk about for reference. She remembered the different Classifications she had been able to choose in the beginning of her new existence as a Dungeon Core, but those were only generalizations.

Therefore, she went straight to work designing what she wanted in her fourteenth room, which was set up just after her room filled with lava. She had filled it full of Mechanical Wolves and Jaguars earlier, so she decided to take advantage of their speed and stealth, respectively. To that end, she expanded the room she already had and used quite a bit of Mana to encase the entire room in a very thin steel plating, fusing the metal to the walls, floor, and ceiling of the 100X100X20-foot space.

Then, using even more of her incoming Mana from the sky aboveground, she extended dozens of lattice-like columns of shiny steel up to the ceiling. The biggest difference between a real lattice – which was comprised of crisscrossing bands in a uniform pattern – and her creations, however, was that the cut-out shapes in the tall columns weren't perfectly square. Instead, they were all twisted up in different directions, going every which way in a confusing blend.

Inside the columns, Sandra left holes spaced out almost randomly all along the length of them. When they were all built and complete, she had her shiny Mechanical Jaguars climb the columns and squeeze themselves into the holes, blending in almost perfectly as they clamped down on the "lattice" with their paws and held unnaturally still. Since they didn't breathe or need anything on them to move to survive, they almost looked like part of the columns themselves; Sandra thought that it was only because she knew they were there that she saw them.

For her Wolves, she left a circular area in the middle of the room clear and placed them in specially made holes near the bottom of the columns surrounding it, where they could emerge from a hidden "pocket" underneath the floor and rush towards anyone passing through. They would be able to attack and retreat without having to worry about looking for a place to hide, because there were eight of the hidden refuges where they could find safety.

As for why the entire room was made of steel, it was because of the trap she was going to place there. It required her to wait for her Mana to fill up completely to place, but it was more than worth it in the end – and what would hopefully be the end of anyone (or any*thing*) trying to invade. By combining the Natural and Water elements together – and using one of the hidden Wolves as the catalyst – she was able to create an extremely potent acid that would spray out of the columns at different heights depending upon where they were triggered.

What took the most Mana was her activation triggers, because she was started to think about what types of Monsters might be coming to invade her dungeon. If they were capable of flight – for example – they wouldn't be stopped by many of her previous traps; sure, there were a couple that would be hard to avoid entirely, but not impossible. In this room, however, the horrifically strong acid would spray at any height out of the columns because the activation triggers were flat planes that went from floor to ceiling. Unless they were small enough to avoid the triggers completely and fly/crawl through the lattice-like columns, of course – but if they were that small, then they were either not much of a threat or else something that would have to be killed a different way.

With that set up, she moved on to the next room...and then paused. Something was wrong; she sent her viewpoint back up to the surface and her AMANS, to try to see what was going on. When she looked around and saw what was causing the commotion in the far distance, she zipped back to her Home room and Winxa, who had been listening to Sandra absently describing her latest room design.

*When you said they might have access to my Area of Influence because of our shared element, you meant **all** of it, didn't you? Not just as a pathway to my dungeon?* Sandra asked, panicking a little.

"Yes, why do you ask—never mind, I think I know. It's the Elven village, isn't it?"

Sandra didn't even think of that, as she was distracted by somewhere else; after sending one of her Small Animated

135

Shears zipping towards the Elven village to check it out, she turned her attention back to the Dungeon Fairy. *No, not there, but I'm checking up on it. It's the Gnome village to the southeast; I'm also sending some Shears there to confirm what I can see from a distance, but it looks like it's under attack.*

"I'm sorry, I didn't even think of that. I was more concerned about *your* welfare that it didn't even occur to me that they would attack the villages nearby."

Sandra barely heard her because she was splitting her concentration between two rapidly flying Shears that were approaching either village. The Elven village was first and she frantically searched around, looking for any threats; after a few moments, she didn't see any monsters streaming out of the forests on either side, so it appeared they were safe – at least for the moment. She couldn't help but think that either the Cores her Area of Influence was touching hadn't noticed the difference yet, or – what she hoped was the reason – they were a higher Core Size than her and didn't have access to it. If that were the case, then it was likely that the ability to share their Area of Influence with a smaller same-elemental Dungeon Core was only for "contracted" Cores like Winxa said.

Moments after confirming that the Elves were at least safe, she sent other Shears towards the Orcs and the Dwarves, though from a distance they looked okay. She didn't have a chance to follow up with them, however, because her Gnomish-land-heading pair of Shears arrived seconds later.

And it was a scene out of a nightmare – at least for the small Gnome village there being attacked by monsters.

Sandra now figured out what had caught her attention: the rapid influx of Mana from the deaths of sentient beings. Normally, when something died in her Area of Influence – especially aboveground – she had to physically have one of her constructs there to absorb it; in this case, however, the special circumstances with the same-element Cores sharing an Area of Influence automatically split anything picked up by either Core. It was those large infusions of Mana that alerted her that something was wrong.

And it just kept rolling in as villagers caught outside the semi-fortified village were swarmed and killed by all forms of reptile-based Dungeon Monsters. The Gnomes by themselves were, in general, only about 3 feet tall and weren't necessarily "fighters" by nature; they had no chance against the surprise attack and viciousness of the larger monsters. Based on the bodies left behind on the plowed field outside of the village, at least two dozen of them had been slain and their corpses left without another look. The Dungeon Monsters weren't attacking because they were hungry; they were attacking because all they wanted to do was kill.

As much as Sandra despised and was disgusted by what she was seeing, she could experience first-hand the nearly insane amount of Mana flowing into her; the rapid influx of the precious resource was exciting and almost euphoric-feeling, leaving her wanting more despite knowing where it was coming from. She had experienced it before when the Orcs had attacked, but she had also taken her time absorbing the Mana they left behind so that she could properly utilize it – it hadn't been coming in so quickly and almost incessantly.

Rather than waste it – because there was nothing she could do about what had already happened – she fed all of that Mana into her Core Size Upgrade stages. Even though it was only half of what was collected from the dead Gnomes, it was soon more than enough to completely finish off all but the last of the 12 stages that were needed for the next upgrade. The flood of Mana stopped shortly afterwards, as the monsters were temporarily stymied by the village's defenses.

Large crocodiles, giant turtles, 30-foot snakes, and even smaller-but-quicker lizards surrounded the village, which – unlike the Elven and Orc villages – was protected by a low wall that filled in the spaces in between the squat-looking houses. It was only about 6 feet tall, but it was enough to hold back the majority of the reptiles coming to kill them; in fact, the only monsters that could get past the sturdy-appearing bricked-stone walls were some lizards who could climb vertically using their sticky feet. Fortunately, they were held back by the Gnomes' other defenses.

Large crossbows attached to a tripod were brought to the flat roofs of the houses and hastily set up. The Gnomes were efficient and worked as a well-oiled team to place the weapons; they aimed, fired, and reloaded them with stacks of deadly-looking 4-foot-long bolts with great effectiveness. The penetration power behind the crossbows were impressive, as whenever they hit one of the large crocodiles, it would practically slide all the way through their bodies – and even occasionally pinning them to the ground.

The only downside, however, was that they took a while to reload; they had to wind up a ratcheting system that would pull the taut string back into position, which could take up to 30 seconds per bolt. With a dozen crossbows in place on top of the houses, they were still doing quite a bit of damage, however – but it wasn't enough. There were...hundreds of different reptiles out there, and more seemed to stream out from the distant forest constantly. It almost appeared as though the nearby Core had emptied its entire dungeon in the hopes that a swarm would get the job done.

And it might just work; there were now so many surrounding the walls that they were starting to somehow get organized and climb on top of each other, using their fellow turtles and crocodiles as a stairway to the top of the wall. They hadn't succeeded quite yet in reaching the top, but Sandra could see that it was only a matter of time.

"What are you going to do?" Winxa asked hesitatingly after she heard a brief description of what was happening. Her facial expression was somehow a combination of fear mixed with hope.

I think you know the answer to that.

Chapter 13

Echo crouched comfortably against the side of the small hill and leaned up against the dry, rough rock to support a little of her weight. An oddly shaped outcropping above her thankfully threw some shade on her hiding spot, which helped to keep her a little cool even in her light, light-brown outfit she was wearing that day. The first day had been miserable as she had worn her leathers and was almost cooked alive during the heat of the day; after that, though, she had borrowed some light and airy cotton pants and blouse from one of the growers back in Avensglen. It would do absolutely nothing to protect her if she was attacked, but she'd rather not die from heat exhaustion in the noonday sun.

She was fairly well hidden behind some other rocks as she kept an eye on the entrance of the dungeon she had found just under a week ago, so she didn't keep her camouflage active the entire time. Echo couldn't possibly do that, of course, even if she wanted to; her capacity for Holy elemental energy wasn't enough to sustain it that long. She knew that as she grew older and learned some of the techniques that the Elites employed, she would be able to expand both her capacity and even find new ways to employ her energy, but for the moment she was stuck where she was. The miniscule energy increases she received from hunting the local monster population just didn't do much for her.

She knew that the stronger the beast – or slime, or whatever the dungeon's monsters were – the more you would absorb a portion of their "soul" when you killed them. It wasn't necessarily a "soul", of course, because everyone knew that those monsters didn't have anything even resembling a soul, but it was named that because it was the easiest way to explain what happened. It wasn't visible or tangible, but whenever you slew a monster, you received a small portion of its life force as a kind of reward; it was what made the Elites so powerful compared to those who didn't fight back the dungeon's expansions for a living.

That life force or "soul" was automatically converted into additional capacity for holding energy, though killing easy beasts like she had been for the last decade and more didn't do much for her. There wasn't necessarily a number associated with how much elemental energy someone could hold, it was more of a feeling; even given that, however, she estimated that she had only improved her capacity by...maybe 5%?...since she started hunting in the nearby forest. It wasn't much, but it was an improvement.

Therefore, she tried to conserve her energy as much as she could; it would regenerate from the nearby environment slowly, though it wasn't nearly enough to sustain her active camouflage all the time. It would fill up completely after a few hours of sleep, fortunately, but that wasn't a luxury she could afford to take advantage of while deep into enemy territory.

After watching for almost five days without seeing much of anything happening outside the dungeon, however, she was reevaluating how much of an enemy it was. There weren't any outward signs of aggression, and even the few times she *knew* she had been spotted when she wasn't in her active camouflage – she wasn't attacked. She was ready to flee and use her Holy energy to hide herself, but it wasn't needed. In fact, she thought that the strange undead monsters were entirely aware of her presence but didn't care for some reason.

That fact alone was enough to raise the hair on the back of her neck.

What is going on in there that is more important than attacking? It was extremely strange, and nothing seemed to make any sense; while the monsters themselves were unusual, none of the other characteristics of a dungeon were making themselves known. The strange, metal-looking skeletons weren't roaming around looking for something to kill – they appeared more as some sort of scouts or defenders more than anything; the strange metal objects in the sky floated around in pre-arranged patterns with precise movements that were unnatural and strangely non-threatening; and not once had she seen an additional monster leave from the dungeon's entrance to join those outside.

That last aspect of the strange dungeon...worried her. Echo had seen the entrance to the nearby beast dungeon many times in her journeys through it and almost every single time she saw it there was another monster emerging from it. That was one of the main reasons she was out there in the first place – to keep the constantly renewing population of monsters down to a manageable level, along with accumulating the loot they left behind when they were killed.

If it isn't sending out more monsters...then what is it doing? Echo didn't know the answer to that, which was why it worried her. She wasn't knowledgeable enough about the dungeons themselves to know what it was capable of, so she had passed on her concerns to the Elder back in Avensglen.

"As long as it doesn't seem to be expanding or sending any monsters in our direction, just keep doing what you're doing and keep an eye on it. I haven't received back a reply from my request for aid yet, but I suspect it will be soon," was what she was told in response to her worry.

She understood it, of course; even if she had known what was going on, there wasn't much that they could do about it. It was the same reason they didn't try to destroy the dungeon themselves – because it was much too dangerous. Therefore, she did as she was instructed and just...watched.

Echo was shocked out of her lazy crouch and lean when she saw something finally emerge from the entrance of the dungeon. Her legs slid out beneath her in surprise – depositing

144

her ungracefully on the ground of the barren wasteland – and she hastily scrambled to her feet as she initiated her active camouflage. She slipped her bow off of her back and nocked an arrow – one of the remaining Ironwood ones she possessed – as she got her first glimpse of the monster that emerged.

It was unlike anything she had seen before; essentially, it was a thick pole made of dull metal that had big, beefy arms emerging from its sides ending with closed fists. There was no visible head or feet – it seemed to just float above the ground with no obvious means of locomotion. The monster immediately zoomed off towards the southeast; she briefly thought it was heading straight towards her village, but the angle was all wrong. In effect, unless it turned or stopped at some point, it was aiming directly towards the Gnome homeland.

That wasn't the end, however. More of the strange poles with arms and fists emerged and joined the first in its journey to the southeast, followed by other monsters who were spitting out from the entrance. Large beast-like undead – made from what appeared to be weirdly flexible metal as well – came out next, looking like some sort of large monkeys. They used their powerful-appearing arms as almost another set of legs as they bent over and loped quickly in the wake of the first monsters.

Next came long, thin poles that floated through the air – again without any visible means of movement – which were draped with something hanging off of them. Echo wasn't sure exactly what it was, but she didn't think it was decorative. They moved quickly through the air and easily caught up with the first groups, who were remarkably far away already.

Soon after that, a half-dozen long, shiny, metallic snakes shot out of the entrance and slithered after the others with surprising speed. They undulated back and forth, gliding over the surface of the dried and cracked ground with insane speed, moving so quickly that Echo thought she might have trouble running from them even with an application of her Air elemental energy.

They were swiftly lost to the distance as more of the skeleton-like wolves and cats emerged from the entrance – dozens of them – and joined the race towards something to the southeast. A noise behind her startled her and she spun around in panic. One of the undead cats already outside jumped down from above her head and landed five feet behind her camouflaged form. She braced for an attack and readied to fire as she turned back around to the new threat, but the cat only stared directly at her for a few seconds before it raced to join the others. Looking around, she discovered that the hills were emptying of even more of the cats, and the wolves that had been roaming outside joined them on the run as well.

Her heart was beating rapidly in her chest as realization dawned on her. *Those undead cats were above me the entire time! They obviously knew I was here, because I was out of my camouflage for **hours**. ...But why didn't they attack?*

146

Seeing the different monsters that had emerged from the dungeon, she realized that if they were all made of some sort of metal like she suspected, then she wouldn't have much chance against them. Her Holy energy hadn't seemed to do much against them, and arrows wouldn't necessarily have anything they could impact and penetrate. So, obviously, they didn't really consider her a threat, nor were they concerned with what she was doing there; it was almost as if she didn't exist.

*If they don't care about me being here, then what **do** they care about?* She emerged from her shadowed hiding place and turned towards the southeast; she took a step to follow them when a swarm of metal objects flew out of the dungeon and shot quickly in the same direction of the previous monsters. They were moving so quickly that she barely got a glimpse of them, but from what she *could* see, they appeared to be some sort of scissors or even shears. *What the...?*

Before she could finish that thought, a half-dozen white cylinders floated – *seems to be a common theme with these monsters* – out and started their journey to the southeast as well, though they didn't move nearly as quickly as the others. Echo waited a few heartbeats for anything else to emerge before she followed slowly after the odd-looking white cylinders. Climbing up a short hill for a better vantage point, she could see the farthest of the monsters were definitely not heading towards her own homeland; on the contrary, they were definitely heading towards the Gnomes. With the kind of monster army that had departed for the southeast, she briefly considered trying to investigate the likely-empty dungeon for additional information.

However, not knowing what was left behind stayed her feet from heading in that direction. Echo was curious – not stupid. She almost headed toward her village to warn them that the dungeon was finally making a move – but she wasn't exactly sure what that move was yet. *Are they heading towards the Gnomes to destroy them?* If that was the case, then it was plain that the dungeon had expanded more than enough to reach Avensglen, as well as the other races' villages that were lined up near the perimeter of the Wastelands. Although she had never visited them, she knew they were there because she could vaguely see them sometimes from afar when she climbed a tall enough mini-mountain in the Wastelands.

Why hadn't they attacked before that then? That was just another question she didn't have an answer to. With quick feet aided by her Air elemental energy, Echo chased after the dungeon's monster army, determined to discover the answers to some of those questions.

Chapter 14

Sandra emptied out half of the constructs in her dungeon, leaving only the smaller and slower Dungeon Monsters in her defensive rooms. She also quickly created a half-dozen Repair Drones and sent them along at the tail end of her force, because she thought she might need them later.

The most-recent rooms that she had filled with deadly traps and constructs she left largely alone, though she did steal away some of the Mechanical Wolves and Jaguars from her latest creation – because they were quick enough to get through her dungeon to join those already leaving. Those Wolves and Jaguars already aboveground joined them as well, and she chuckled a little bit when one of her cat constructs startled Echo, who had been watching her entrance since the morning after the meeting in the village Sandra had witnessed.

She had been tempted to make some sort of contact with the Elven woman over the last few days but held off because she didn't want to seem threatening to her. Looking at it from the woman's perspective was easy enough – because she had been Human once; being approached by a dungeon's monster – even if it seemed non-threatening – couldn't help but put her on guard. Given enough time when Sandra didn't show any sort of dangerous tendencies, she thought she might give it a shot and hope for the best; with the departure of what probably seemed like a giant army towards the Gnome lands, however, she worried that she might have just set her cause back without hope of recovery.

*I'll just have to show her that I'm there to help, not harm. Maybe this is just what I need to prove to the Elves that I'm not a threat; in fact, when they see how much I'm helping, it might convince them to work **with** me instead of against me.*

The other Shears that she had sent towards the Dwarven and Orc villages had seen no danger towards either of them, fortunately, so Sandra was able to concentrate on helping the Gnomes. She kept one of her floating constructs in both places – as well as the Elven village – just in case that should change, but she also hoped that if an attack hadn't happened yet, then they were likely going to be okay for the moment. Of course, if Sandra were to increase her Core Size again, that could change at any time; since it was unknown what the other Core's sizes were, she could inadvertently surpass them and end up opening up her Area of Influence for them to plunder at their whim.

So, knowing that her dungeon was still defended with at least *some* of her Dungeon Monsters – not to mention the ultra-deadly traps she had placed – Sandra sped along with them towards the battle raging at the Gnome village. When she concentrated on looking out through her nearby Shears' vision, she found that things weren't going well for those trapped within the village. Already, two of the crossbow emplacements had been overrun, the Gnomes operating them going down fighting; they were all equipped with long Steel knives that were almost like short swords in their hands, which they used to the best of their abilities – which didn't seem to be much. One of the smaller lizards with frightening-looking teeth and sharp claws ended up getting skewered by a Gnome defender, but the others of the reptile army swarmed over the others without much difficulty.

The Mana from their deaths started to fill her up, so Sandra immediately started to make replacements for all of those she sent to the southeast; she was hoping they would all come back, but if for some reason they were destroyed she would at least have some backup in her dungeon. She was saddened at the wholesale slaughter of the Gnomes, who were doing their best to stave off the rest of the reptiles from climbing onto the roofs of their homes; fortunately, even those Dungeon Monsters that had gotten inside couldn't get to them very easily. The rope ladders that had allowed the Gnomes to get on top in the first place were pulled up, giving them little to no access from below.

The front ranks of her land-bound army were approximately five minutes away, but her airborne constructs arrived much faster. Her group of 100 Small Animated Shears, for instance, had passed the others and were rapidly approaching the battle; the Singing Blademasters were going to arrive before the others as well, but were still about two minutes behind her Shears – they couldn't move quite as fast.

Before they could arrive, however, something at the edge of the nearby forest caught her attention. A large shape lumbered out from the trees, much larger than anything she had seen so far from the reptile swarm of Dungeon Monsters; sending her pair of Shears that was observing the battle closer to it, she looked on in awe as what appeared to be a giant construct cut down the crocodiles and lizards running past it towards the town. It was a good thing that her own constructs already had their orders, because Sandra froze in confusion and shock.

Urging her Shears closer, she began to make out exactly what she was looking at. Standing a dozen feet tall, the construct was created from a combination of wood and metal and looked like a wide, round-chested, headless person with stout arms and legs. Noticeable enchantment runes were written over almost every part of the construct, which were unfamiliar to Sandra – but it was obvious that they were what allowed the deadly mobile machine to move.

One arm ended with a large spiked warhammer, while the other was equipped with a permanent double-bladed war axe; both of which were used liberally on the surrounding reptiles as it slowly walked towards the village. The sight of the construct seemed to lift the morale of the besieged Gnomes, as their rate of fire and aim seemed to increase when they saw it coming to the rescue. It was lifted even further when a second and then a third construct started to lumber out of the trees.

Floating down even closer, Sandra was able to see what appeared to be a Gnome suspended by a rope around his waist, located behind a sturdy metal grate inside the middle of the construct's body. More enchantment runes covered everything but his head, and she instantly saw that they were actually covering a strange suit that he – she assumed it was a "he" by the beard – was wearing. It didn't take more than a few seconds of watching to see that the movements he made were instantly copied by the construct he was...operating? It was just plain genius, and Sandra wanted to know how it was done; there was absolutely nothing like it back in the Human land of Muriel.

Tearing her attention away from the spectacular enchanted constructs was difficult, but she eventually turned back to the battle. Her 100-strong group of Shears arrived, and she immediately sent them to help clear off the encroaching lizards – and even a few deadly crocodiles – that were getting too close to the remaining crossbow teams. They dropped down from about 100 feet up in the air, using their speed to impale themselves into the reptiles with great force, killing over twenty of the smaller lizards instantly.

The others did quite a bit of damage as well, maiming limbs and opening gaping wounds in some of the larger crocodiles, crippling them so that they would eventually succumb to their wounds later. A few missed their targets that moved out of the way unexpectedly at the last moment; some drove themselves into a nearby reptile, causing some damage but nothing fatal; a few even managed to hit the shell of a few turtles, which were a lot harder than Sandra had expected. They bounced off the shells while leaving just a small gouge and the relatively soft metal of the Shears were mangled and destroyed by the impact.

When they had all made their initial attack, she attempted to bring them back up into the air so that they could strike again, but only a single one lifted into the air, damaged but still serviceable. The rest, when she looked for them, had already disappeared and left behind a Tiny Copper Orb; the impacts coming even from a perfect strike were enough to destroy them in the process. She saw that many of the reptiles that had been killed left behind various small sizes of Steel Orbs as dungeon loot, which might be why the Gnomes were there in the first place; Steel was a valuable commodity, and she knew that if Human Heroes were around, they'd be doing all they could to cull the surrounding forest every chance they got.

The Gnomes all paused in confusion when her Shears had attacked, which was the opposite of Sandra's intention – because the attacking reptiles didn't care in the slightest. As a result, they took advantage of their victims' inattention to ramp up their attack, sending up replacements for those she had killed. She used her last remaining pair of Shears to impale the head of a crocodile that was just about to bite an inattentive Gnome. It didn't kill it outright like she was hoping, but the action spurred the others into action, who pulled out their long Steel knives and finished off the wounded reptile.

Unfortunately, the delay in continuing their defense was costly. They fought valiantly still, but two of the defensive placements were overrun before they could recover. With fewer targets to concentrate on, the rest of the reptiles piled up quickly towards the remaining Gnomes; things were looking bleak, but then the first of the Gnome constructs arrived and started tearing into the rear of the Core's army. With a tremendous smash of its spiked hammer, it practically shattered the shell of a giant turtle nearby, while its other hand swept back and forth repeatedly just over the ground, slicing off lizard heads and crocodile heads in the process.

Its success was short-lived, however, as the reptile army wasn't taking that without fighting back. The powerful construct was soon swarmed by dozens of snakes that had been slithering around, unable to successfully climb up the smooth walls of the Gnome village either on their own or through the use of the other reptiles as platforms. What they could do, however, was "snake" their way up the legs of the large construct and wrap around its limbs, constricting so tightly that even the rune-enchanted appendages had difficulty moving. Sandra could hear creaking and cracking as the wood and metal components were strained and compressed tightly; finally, there was a shearing noise as the right leg had some critical part snap inside of it, and it fell to a knee.

The Gnome inside the construct wasn't giving up without a fight, however, as he managed to smash its right arm against the ground, crushing the two snakes that had been constricting it. Freed up – at least momentarily – the Gnome construct swept its axe towards its other arm, slicing up the snake there and freeing the warhammer, though she could tell that the left appendage was now damaged. It still worked well enough to flail wildly, at least, and smash apart another turtle in the process.

But the recovery was only temporary. Unbeknownst to the Gnome, another, smaller snake had crawled up its body and managed to squeeze through one of the holes in the metal grate protecting him; when it was close enough, the small red/orange-colored snake struck directly at his face, biting him just under his eye and latching on to his cheek. The Gnome screamed, and instinctively raised both his hands quickly up to his face – which caused the construct to smash itself with both an axe and a warhammer. The impact was so great that it caused the entire enchanted machine to fall on its back, where it squished a few more lizards in the process.

The small red/orange-colored snake – despite its size – must've been highly deadly; the Gnome, after ripping the fanged reptile away from his face – tearing his cheek badly in the process – started to convulse violently after a few seconds and began foaming at the mouth. The movements were copied by the construct, which luckily managed to squish a few more snakes and even a large crocodile in the process, but after about a minute it lay still as the Gnome succumbed to the deadly venom racing through his veins.

The two other constructs waded in without fear, despite seeing what happened to their friend. Unfortunately, after learning what it took to take one of the massive wood-and-metal machines down, they were also quickly swarmed by the hard-to-hit snakes as they started to climb up and wrap around their appendages. Luckily for them, Sandra's Singing Blademasters had arrived.

The whirring sound of two dozen of them spinning at the same time filled the Gnome village valley, as they split up into two distinct groups; one broke off to help the Gnomes on the wall, while the other group split up again to help remove the snakes preventing the larger constructs from moving. They were highly effective as their spinning blades tore into the snakes, chopping them apart with ease; the only problem was that – when an arm or leg was freed – the large construct started to lash out in response, which ended up smashing and destroying a few of her own flying constructs. In the end, though, she was able to remove all of the snakes from the two constructs and helped to eliminate the few more that were trying to climb up, including another one of those deadly red/orange-colored snakes trying to sneak in and bite another Gnome.

The group that fought to keep the walls free had just as hard of a time, though it wasn't through accidental attacks by the Gnomes. While the smaller lizards that climbed up were fairly easy to attack – by essentially running into them, slicing them into bits – the crocodiles that climbed up weren't really afraid of hurting themselves a little in order to destroy her constructs. Massive jaws clamped down quickly on her Blademasters – even when they tried to avoid the front and attack from the rear – which tore the crocodiles' mouths up quite a bit, but also completely destroyed her constructs. One after another they fell to the powerful attacks of the large reptiles, until the only ones left were near the Gnomes' massive enchanted machines.

The respite her Blademasters provided for the beleaguered Gnomes was invaluable, however. Instead of freezing up in confusion again, they took advantage of the surprise attack and fought back even harder, pumping out bolt after bolt in a barrage that whittled down their attackers' numbers. They were actually making fairly good headway towards keeping them off of their roofs – firing into the reptile-made staircases and collapsing a few of them with some lucky shots – when the first defensive position ran out of bolts. When that happened, all of the Gnomes at that position stood on the edge of the wall and did their best to fend off the lizards and crocodiles climbing up.

For the first time (at least that she observed), Sandra could see them use their elemental abilities, infusing their weapons with a quick temporary enchantment. She saw what appeared to be a Fire-based one that super-heated the edge of a Steel knife without melting the metal; another one used an Air-based one that caused the knife to launch from her hand to strike at whatever she was pointing her hand at, before flying back into her hand, its enchantment depleted.

She even saw an ingenious use of a Nether enchantment, which could extend a solidified shield of darkness around the knife, which the Gnome used to block a snapping attack by a crocodile; when the crocodile struck the shield of darkness, it disappeared, but it also blinded the monster temporarily – which the gnome took advantage of and stabbed deep into the back of its head, killing it near-instantly.

All of the enchantments were temporary; she had only rarely seen temporary enchantments before because Humans tended to like permanency – or at least long-lasting effects. Sandra recognized some of the quick and dirty runes thrown on them, but other ones were completely new – and they were more that she desired to learn. It wasn't as though she needed another reason to save the Gnomes, but the prospect of learning even more enchanting runes from the race that seemed to use them for everything was a driving force as she encouraged her constructs on their way to run even faster.

Sending her scouting pair of Shears up high, Sandra did a quick count of how many of the enemy was left; she was encouraged to see that there were probably less than 100 left assaulting 8 positions on the house roofs. Another two of the crossbows had run out of bolts and the others were dangerously low, but the Gnomes fought tenaciously with their temporarily enchanted Steel knives, making the encroaching reptiles fight for every inch they progressed up the walls. Along with the two remaining Gnome machines attacking from behind, she thought that her own constructs would only arrive to help mop up the remainder.

That was, until she saw another wave coming from the forest, accompanied by something...large.

Chapter 15

What...is...that? How? Where did that come from?

"What are you talking about? What do you see?" Winxa asked, as Sandra stared in shock through her Shears at the gigantic lizard-thing that stomped out of the trees, following in the wake of the other reptiles.

It's...a massive lizard at least 20 feet tall and perhaps twice that long. The head on that thing looks bigger than one of my Apes, and those jaws look like they could snap one of my Basher Totems in half. Where did this thing come from?

The lizard had four legs that reminded Sandra of thick tree trunks, and its long neck allowed the head to maneuver quickly in different directions; its tail cracked a tree in half as it passed into the Gnome village valley like it was nothing. The skin covering the entire gigantic lizard was a mottled green-and-grey color, and it looked thick and extremely durable.

"Does it have wings?" the Dungeon Fairy asked, which tore Sandra's attention away from it for a moment.

Uh...no, not that I can see.

"Good. Then that means it's not a dragon."

Wait, why is that good? This thing doesn't seem good – and where in the world did it come from?

Winxa looked at her Core in exasperation. "Because—" she started with measured patience— "if it were a dragon, none of those Gnomes, and likely none of your own constructs would survive. It could go airborne and attack from the safety of the sky; some could even use elemental energy to attack from afar, which could destroy the entire village within moments.

"This sounds like some sort of version of an ancient Saurian. It was likely one of the more expensive Dungeon Monsters the Reptile-Classification Dungeon Core nearby could produce, and it was probably one that it hadn't had the Mana to before now. Since it obviously has access to Steel as a Monster Seed, it's probably using the Large Steel Orbs as its Seed – or the dungeon had somehow obtained another, stronger Seed at some point in the past."

But this seems a little excessive compared to the other lizards, crocodiles, and even giant turtles out here.

"Well, think about your Iron-plated Behemoths over there in that room," Winxa said, pointing off towards her new massive room she had made to contain her large constructs. "Those are probably on par with what this Ancient Saurian sounds like, so don't complain too much."

Sandra wanted to protest, because the size difference was quite profound – her Behemoths were half or perhaps a third of the size. Though, when she considered that it was made of thick *Iron plates* that would protect it from quite a few attacks, couldn't bleed, and was likely capable of destroying quite a bit with its flails, she had to concede the point. It wasn't completely even, but she could see the similarities.

162

She concentrated on the battle again and saw that the nearly 200 smaller lizards and crocodiles were racing across the distance towards the Gnome village, where they would soon join their brethren and quickly overwhelm the defenders. That was especially true, because the Gnomish machines somehow sensed the presence of a bigger threat behind them and turned towards the Ancient Saurian. Sandra wasn't sure what they could do against the massive monster, but she was determined to help.

To that end, her ground forces were finally starting to arrive. Her Steel Pythons actually arrived first, having overtaken the others with their spectacular speed. All six of them immediately latched onto the nearest enemy they saw near the wall, whether it was a lizard, a crocodile, or a giant turtle. Lizards were quickly crushed by the Steel jaws of her Pythons, crocodiles were wrapped up by their ultra-strong bodies and squeezed to death, and the turtles had their legs crippled by the lightning-fast strikes her constructs could deliver.

Steel Pythons were much more powerful and quicker than the flesh-and-blood reptiles assaulting the Gnome village, but that didn't mean that they were invulnerable; the utter force behind a crocodile's snapping jaws crippled the lower half of one of her constructs when it was able to snatch it up as it passed by. One of the giant turtles – which Sandra hadn't really seen as very effective up to that point – surprised her by extending its neck out from its shell almost four feet, and it bit down on the tail end of an unsuspecting Python with its own powerful bite. It was so powerful, in fact, that it sheared through the entire Steel form and left the Python semi-crippled with about two feet missing from its lower half.

For all that, though, Sandra's constructs were doing quite a bit of damage – but it all took time. By the time they were starting to get closer to the wall and the reptilian staircases being made with pure Dungeon Monster bodies, the enemy reinforcements from the forest had arrived. Looking along the walls, she saw that all but one of the crossbows were now out of bolts and the Gnomes were fighting with their Steel knives – and they were slowly being pushed back.

The additional force of reptiles only made it worse; the initial surge of bodies being recklessly flung up to the walls pushed back and overwhelmed half of the remaining defensive positions, leaving only four intact groups of Gnomes barely holding on. The majority of the newcomers had gone to the now-destroyed positions first, but it was only a matter of time before they fell under the onslaught.

Sandra wasn't going to let that happen if she could help it.

The rest of her constructs (less her Repair Drones, which were much slower and were still about 15 minutes or more away) arrived just then and literally tore a swathe through the assembled reptilian army. Her Basher Totems swung their fists over and over, caving in skulls on the smaller lizards and cracking the backs of crocodiles, crippling them and preventing them from moving much. Her Ironclad Apes picked up the giant turtles (which comprised much of the staircases leading up to the walls) and tossed them away like a flying discus, where they landed at least 100 feet away. They were hurt by the throw, but not fatally; a few ended up on their backs and had trouble turning over. The main point was that they were out of the fight, albeit temporarily.

Her Mechanical Wolves and Jaguars went to work on all of the smaller snakes and lizards by snatching them up with their metal jaws and chewing them to pieces, before spitting them back out again. A few of them even raced up the remaining reptile staircases and fought alongside the Gnomes, who – at least at that point – were so relieved for the help that they barely even paused when her constructs appeared.

The help her constructs provided turned the tide of the battle significantly, but – just like every other fight thus far at the Gnome village – it wasn't without casualties on her side. Getting over the initial shock of her forces appearing, the reptile army turned away from the Gnomes to deal with her constructs; though they had proved fairly resilient – in general – against the Orcs that had invaded her dungeon, against the concentrated assault of a Dungeon Core's retaliation attack...they didn't fare so well.

The smaller lizards and snakes weren't much of a threat, though some of the latter managed to entangle a few of her

Mechanical Wolves and Jaguars, leaving them to be finished off by the stronger reptiles. The crocodiles and turtles – once they were totally focused on attacking her surprise force – were deadly. For the large-jawed crocodiles, they were able to whip their heads around quickly and bite down on to one of her constructs' appendages – for instance one of her Basher's arms; that bite, while powerful in its own right, wasn't enough to do more than crush the metal it was made of a little. Once it had latched on, however, it would spin its body in some sort of death roll, which would rip off limbs or tear apart some of the smaller constructs like they were nothing.

The giant turtles grew wise and hid their feet inside their shells, where they were difficult to get to; when her Ironclad Apes tried to approach them from behind, they would quickly smash their heads into the ground at an angle and literally spin themselves toward her construct. Then, with powerful bites of their spiked mouths, they could rip off entire chunks of iron from her Apes and cripple parts of their bodies.

Even with that, Sandra's forces were superior to the reptiles because of their basic nature; poison, wounds to their basic frame or extremities, and trying to squeeze them to death didn't slow them down like it would a flesh-and-blood monster. Her constructs were slowly gaining the upper hand, which was only helped when a brave Gnome – once the attention was off of them – jumped down off of the wall and started chucking the spent bolts back up to the crossbow positions. There were dozens of them just lying on the ground where they had struck and killed some of the reptiles earlier; when the monsters disappeared and left behind their loot, they also left behind the bolts. Some few were bent from the force of the impacts, but many more were still quite usable.

While they were gaining the advantage – despite the losses her forces were sustaining – over the "smaller" reptiles, the Ancient Saurian was still slowly lumbering towards the village from the forest. It was very slow-moving, fortunately, so it gave the Gnome machines time to close the distance. Splitting up, they approached from different directions, their 12-foot-tall constructs facing off against the 20-foot-tall, 40-foot-long reptile with bravery. At least, Sandra thought it was bravery; she didn't think they were foolish, so they must've had a plan in mind.

When they were within range, they quickly – well, as quick as they were able to move – ran to either side of the massive lizard and started to pound and slash at its belly. Sandra could see a few indents in the Saurian's flesh where their spiked warhammers impacted it, but she didn't think they broke any bones; their double-bladed axes, however, were able to slice big gashes in its side and blood started to run freely from the wounds.

A massive head whipped around from the front of the giant lizard faster than Sandra thought it was capable and bit down on the Gnome machine on its right side, its mouth wide enough to slip over the entire top half. She could hear cracks and creaks as the jaws compressed together, but the construct held its basic form quite well; after a few moments, the Saurian couldn't bite down any harder to do any more damage. Instead of continuing to try to crush it, the massive lizard brought its head down over and over, smashing the Gnomish machine into the ground, battering it and essentially destroying its lower limbs in the process.

The other Gnome construct wasn't forgotten, however; it had widened a huge vertical gash in the skin of the Saurian and Sandra could practically see its insides. The pain was likely enough for the giant lizard to want to do something about it – and it did.

Taking one large step to the right with its front leg, the lizard planted its foot and *pulled* the rest of its body around – including its long and powerful tail. The momentum from its half-spin was enough to catch the Gnome machine with a force capable of crunching wood and metal, and the impact was so tremendous that the heavy, rune-enchanted construct went flying. It was hit so hard, in fact, that it was launched the remaining 300 feet between the Saurian and the Gnome village.

It bounced once with bone-crunching force off of the reptiles who were starting to bunch up for a counterattack versus Sandra's forces – crushing a dozen crocodiles and three giant turtles – before taking to the air again. Fortunately, it completely missed hitting any of her dwindling construct army; unfortunately, once it bounced off the reptilian forces, it smashed right through two of the four remaining crossbow positions.

The Gnomes there were caught completely unprepared; they didn't even get a chance to scream as the large construct smashed into them, wiping them off their roofs and tossing them aside. Sandra couldn't see if they had all been killed outright, but it didn't look good; a few rapid influxes of Mana proved that at least some of them had landed near either her own Dungeon Monsters or some of the other Core's, but it was hard to tell with everything going on. She did see where the Gnomish machine landed, however, and it was a broken mess of wood, metal, and destroyed runes; the Gnome controlling it was miraculously alive – injured, but alive – inside of it, but without some major repairs, the construct was essentially a pile of parts.

The wiping out of a portion of the smaller reptiles was enough to give her constructs an even greater advantage, despite the loss of two of the Gnomish crossbow positions. They attacked with renewed determination, whittling down the enemy army from just under 200 to less than 50 in a matter of minutes. The last two Gnome crossbows ran out of ammunition again, but by that time it was only a matter of cleaning up the rest with the now-more-equal amount of Dungeon Monsters on the field. Without the advantage of numbers, the reptiles finally fell under the fists of her three remaining Basher Totems, four Ironclad Apes, four Steel Pythons, two Singing Blademasters (who had broken off from the Gnome machines when they went after the Saurian), fourteen Mechanical Wolves, and thirteen Mechanical Jaguars.

By that time, the massive lizard had finished smashing the lower half of the Gnome construct apart; with a release of its jaws, the crushed-but-still-largely-intact upper half fell on the ground, the Gnome inside looking dazed, slightly injured – but alive as well. The machine's arms had been trapped inside the jaws while it was held, but now they were free. With a visible effort of will, the Gnome inside used its arms to sit the entire construct up; without legs or feet, though, it couldn't really move. It started to swing its arms though, trying to attack the nearby Saurian...but was stilled when a tree-trunk-like leg came crashing down and smashed right into the construct.

The frame cracked but held for the moment. A feeble arm movement was the only sign of life inside the machine, but even that faded after the Saurian's foot stomped down three, then four more times. On the fifth stomp, the construct finally cracked completely, destroying the Gnome and half of the wood and metal comprising the machine at the same time.

That happened just as Sandra's own constructs finished off the rest of the smaller reptiles, and she turned them toward the greater threat.

Chapter 16

During the battle, Sandra had been using all of the Mana that she had been – unfortunately – receiving from the slain Gnomes to replenish those constructs that she had sent to help. At the first sight of the massive lizard, however, she had started to send most of those she had created out to help as well, but they weren't going to arrive in time. The Ancient Saurian was going to reach the Gnome village before the dozen Apes, two dozen Bashers, and even the four Steel Pythons could make it.

She briefly thought about utilizing a portion of her AMANS for some sort of concentrated Shears attack, but she didn't think they'd be able to penetrate the Saurian's skin effectively enough to make it worthwhile. It was more likely that they'd just bounce off like they had against the shells of the turtles they had inadvertently hit earlier.

That meant she only really had the constructs she currently had there to fight the 20-foot-tall Ancient Saurian. While it was heavily wounded along its side, it didn't look like it was a fatal wound; in fact, the blood was already starting to slow down in its effort to leave the massive lizard's body as it began to clot. Therefore, she couldn't expect it to be too weakened from blood loss to make it an easier fight – she was going to have to use some strategy to defeat it.

It was too bad that her superior knowledge crafting didn't really lend itself to the art of fighting and warfare strategies.

Most of the fights so far had been essentially slugfests, where she just sent her constructs in and hoped they knew what they were doing. There were a few times when she directed particular ones in *where* to fight, but she largely left the *how* to them. She had a feeling that if she sent them in as they were against the massive lizard, they would end up just like the Gnome machines – broken and destroyed. But...she didn't have a clue what else to do.

Fortunately, she wasn't alone in the fight.

The Gnome that had been controlling the construct that had inadvertently wiped out two of the crossbow positions had managed to free himself from the wreckage, drag his battered and bruised body to the closest house where there were still other Gnomes present, and climb up the rope ladder they tossed down to him. Despite his age, which Sandra had no frame of reference to – she was only going by the white hair, wrinkles, and scars all over his face – he was sitting down on the roof and barking orders. It looked silly for him to just sit there, until she realized that the lower portion of his left leg was jutting off at an angle it probably shouldn't have been. Her respect for the grizzled Gnome rose a few notches as she realized he had *literally* dragged himself there through sheer force of will.

"Aim for the wound I made on its side! The only way to take it down is to pierce its heart – any other way will take too long!" he belted out, easily heard by the adjacent crossbow position. One of the four Gnomes at each position dropped down to the ground outside of the village and started tossing up more bolts, all the while keeping a wary eye on Sandra's constructs.

"Felbar, have you ever seen these things before? Are they something new from the Warmaster's College sent here to help?" a female gnome with long brown hair and blue/purple-colored eyes asked softly. She was standing near the old Gnome who appeared to be keeping himself upright through pure determination alone.

"What? Of course not, Violet. Do you see any runes on them? No – they're not from the College or from one of the few Master Enchanters we have left. If you've been paying attention like I've been trying to teach you, you'd see that when these new ones die, they disappear just like those blasted lizards." He looked at the female Gnome for a second as if waiting for a response; when nothing was forthcoming, he sighed heavily and said, "They're a dungeon's monsters, Violet."

"What? That doesn't make any sense – why are they helping us then?"

"I have no idea. But unless one of you slackers can manage to strike the heart through the wound in its side, they're our only hope," the one Sandra guessed was called Felbar

173

responded, raising his voice so that everyone could hear him. Including herself; she now had an objective, she just needed to figure out how to do that.

The Ancient Saurian was already headed towards the village by that time, after making sure that the other Gnome construct was completely destroyed. Its slow, lumbering steps made it look like it was moving in slow motion, but its stride length was still impressive. In less than a minute, the massive lizard was within 100 feet of the village's walls, and the crossbows let their payloads fly.

Since it was facing directly at them, it was difficult if not impossible to hit the wounded side of the Ancient Saurian. Instead, they had aimed at its face in the off chance that they scored a critical hit in its eye, its large nostrils, or even its slightly open mouth. Unfortunately, the same quick movements that it had displayed before with its neck allowed the massive lizard to twitch its face out of the way in more than enough time, and one of the bolts missed completely, shooting off into the distance when it didn't hit anything.

The other bolt hit its neck and stuck in its thick skin, having penetrated a couple of inches but was unable to go any farther. It hung off the throat of the Saurian like a large needle, just deep enough to get stuck but with not enough penetrating power to even draw any blood. Seeing that, she was doubly glad she didn't bring her AMANS in for an attack, because they likely would've bounced off without being able to do any damage.

What they needed was for the massive lizard to turn to the side, so that they would have a chance to penetrate to its heart; while its skin was really tough, its insides were just as squishy as any other living being's internal organs. That was where Sandra's constructs came in.

Knowing that it was a suicide run for most of them, she spread out her constructs and sent them to the Saurian's left side where the wound was located; instructing them to stay back and make only quick attacks before retreating, they got into position out of range of the head – were it to swing towards them. Then, starting with her Mechanical Wolves and Jaguars, she sent them to start biting its left hind leg, far enough away from the front where the neck couldn't stretch around and let its massive mouth snatch them up.

After the tenth attack, her plan had the desired effect; just as had happened when the Gnome machine had been attacking it – it was the grizzled old Felbar once she thought about it – the Saurian's right front leg stepped to the side and dragged the massive lizard to the side. A humongous tail whipped around and smacked right into the Wolf attacking it, launching it straight ahead, where it impacted the village's stone wall and shattered a portion of it. Her construct didn't fare that well, either, as it was mangled and destroyed upon hitting the barrier.

Two large crossbow bolts came flying out from the village, aimed *almost* perfectly; both hit the wounded side with precision, but one of them impacted a bone underneath the fleshy meat and was stopped cold, while the other went in at a strange angle and didn't hit anything vital. The lizard hissed in pain, however, so maybe it *had* hit something vital.

Either way, even if they had been able to reload and fire again almost instantly, the Saurian turned away before they could've gotten a shot off. It continued to drive itself forward towards the short village walls, undeterred, and Sandra tried to get it to attack the same way again by attacking its flanks a second time. Ten, then twenty, then thirty attacks went by without any result and — while her attacks were beginning to wear away some of the skin and caused the massive lizard to bleed a little, it completely ignored her efforts.

They had less than a minute before it was in range of the village, so Sandra threw everything she had at the Saurian to get it to turn. When nothing seemed to work, she grew frustrated and worried for the still-living Gnomes.

"You have to remember that it's likely being controlled by the other Core right now; while they might be insane, murderous psychopaths — they're not stupid. It knows by now that your constructs are worth nothing to it, so the only objective it has is to kill the other sentients nearby — even if it has to sacrifice its own monsters to do that," Winxa remarked after listening to Sandra get frustrated.

That's...a very good point. It seemed as though the Core was now so focused on the Gnomes just sitting there, ripe for the killing, that it was ignoring everything else. And if that was the case, then maybe she could get it to pay attention to her...

Instead of her constructs trying to get it to turn, Sandra instead had them all attack its front: legs, chest, face, and neck. Her Wolves and Jaguars latched onto its legs, ripping out chunks of skin little by little; her Basher Totems started pounding on its chest, doing their best to break something internal; her two remaining Blademasters went right up into its face and started attacking its vulnerable eyes and likely-sensitive nose; finally, her Apes jumped up and caught hold of its neck, where they secured themselves and started pounding away, using their Iron-fueled strength to try to rearrange the bones underneath them.

It worked – for better or worse, she wasn't quite sure yet. Sandra thought it was the spinning Blademasters aiming for its eyes that snapped the Core out of its single-minded pursuit of the Gnomes; the Saurian immediately snatched both constructs out of the air and bit down on them. They were destroyed instantly, and though they probably ended up cutting the inside of its mouth in the process, the damage done to the massive lizard was superficial.

It then did something she hadn't seen it do before. The Saurian bent down its front legs momentarily, shaking a few Wolves off in the process, before extending them quickly, causing its entire front end to launch off of the ground and raise almost 30 feet into the air. Most of her constructs were still hanging on through the use of their teeth or arms – in the case of her Apes – but her Basher Totems were still on the ground waiting for the large lizard to come back down.

And it did, though it extended itself slightly forward and sped up its descent with a bunching of its muscles; the impact when it hit the ground – and flattened her Totems – caused some of the village's walls that were damaged previously to crumble apart. Most of the Gnomes lost their footing as well, but her constructs had taken the worst of it.

All but one of the Apes were shaken off the Saurian from the impact, and her Mechanical Wolves and Jaguars were thrown to the ground and most of them were slightly damaged – but still able to attack. Her Totems were completely destroyed and one of the Apes that fell off had one of its arms sheared away, exposing its vulnerable glowing light at the center of its chest.

Before they could climb back on, the massive lizard surged forward, displaying more speed than it had previously; Sandra suspected that the lizard was utilizing elemental energy for some sort of special ability. It managed to move the remaining 40 feet to the village walls – and the Gnomes that suddenly stepped back in fright – within a couple of seconds, far faster than her constructs could plan for. And, despite her remaining Ape pounding away at its neck – to only mild effect – it reared its head back to strike at the closest group of Gnomes...

...and it suddenly froze at the apex of its strike. The Saurian's eyes glazed over, and its neck fell forward, narrowly missing the house where the Gnomes were standing with their Steel knives out. It hit the stone wall nearby, causing it to crumple under the weight of its neck, while the rest of the Saurian collapsed to the ground in death.

Within a few moments, the massive lizard had dissipated, leaving behind a remarkably small blue Monster Seed in its place – as well as a single damaged Steel Python where its belly used to be. Unbeknownst to the Ancient Saurian, her three remaining Pythons had crawled inside its side wound while it was distracted by her other constructs. They were searching for its heart – which turned out to be a bit farther back in its body than she was expecting – though when the massive lizard reared up, the pressure and bones inside the Saurian rearranged themselves a little, which ended up crushing two of them and damaging the third. Fortunately, it was able to continue its search and struck at its heart just in time to save everyone.

Well, save everyone who was still alive...all nine of them.

Nine out of just over eighty Gnome villagers (if she counted the bodies right) were still alive; not necessarily a good result, but at least *some* of them survived. What made it worse for Sandra, however, was that she knew that her presence was what was ultimately led to that outcome, regardless of what she did to save them. It was her connection with the other Core that allowed the reptiles to attack in the first place; she only wished she had known about the danger sooner, so that none of them would've died.

179

With the massive Ancient Saurian dead, the remaining Gnomes and her constructs stood staring at each other. She hadn't thought that far in advance, so she wasn't sure what to do; she still couldn't technically communicate with them, though she was hoping that her demonstration of their defense would do the talking for her.

Fortunately (or unfortunately, depending on how you looked at it), being unable to communicate didn't matter in the end. The one she thought was called Violet stepped forward to speak, but her eyes caught on something in the distance and opened wide. Sandra turned her Shears' attention to where the little female Gnome was looking, and her figurative heart dropped.

Standing on the edge of the forest were two more of the Ancient Saurians, as well as a hundred or more smaller crocodiles and turtles.

Well, that's not good.

Chapter 17

"Look, I don't know who you are or where you came from, but I'm willing to bet that you aren't here to try to kill us. I do know that staying here is out of the question, unless you have another army of 'friendly' monsters nearby," Felbar asked loudly, the pain in his broken leg he had been trying to ignore up till then now plain in his voice. Violet couldn't help but wince whenever she looked at his bent-out-of-shape lower appendage – she knew that she would've likely passed out from the pain long ago.

"I'll take that as a 'no'," Felbar continued, when the strange...things made no indication otherwise. She still couldn't believe that they were monsters from a dungeon, despite their fantastical appearance; however, she couldn't deny that she had seen them fade away just as quickly as those darn lizards and crocodiles, leaving behind some dungeon loot in the process. Most of them that had been destroyed had been leaving steel behind, which was the village's main purpose for being on the edge of the wasteland in the first place. "Then, what do you suggest we do?"

Violet looked at the old Gnome in surprise; that was the first time she had heard Felbar ask someone – or some*thing* – else for advice. He was the one in charge of their operation there in the village, and he always seemed to know or have an answer for everything. She was glad that he had survived the attack, even if he was wounded. Although, she knew he would probably blame himself for the deaths of everyone else, even if it wasn't his fault and he did everything he could to save them – that was just the kind of leader he was.

The strange monsters obviously couldn't speak, being made of metal and all that, so Violet wasn't expecting any type of verbal response. Before they could do anything else, however, something else arrived before they could react. Six weird white cylinders floated in from beyond the village and parked themselves next to the metallic monsters. Suddenly, as if from nowhere, two thin arms emerged from the cylinders with squarish metal pads on the ends.

Violet tensed up for a moment, before she saw them approach some of the strange metallic skeleton wolves, where they placed their pads upon the places most damaged. Before her very eyes, a veritable rainbow of colors was transferred between the two, and the wolves' bones repaired themselves quickly – almost like a miracle. With a mental click in her head, she realized the cylinders were healing the others; the only elemental energy she knew of that could heal like that was Holy energy, so she reasoned that the monsters couldn't be *all* bad.

And if they can heal their own like that, maybe they can heal Felbar.

Looking at him again when he didn't speak anymore, she realized there was a small pool of blood underneath his broken leg. It wasn't a life-threatening amount yet, but unless he got some care soon, he was going to die. She knew of a few runes that could be used to heal him, but she didn't have any of the materials needed to place the enchantment on; there were a few in the village, but they didn't have time to find what she needed *and* save his life before the new lizard monsters could arrive.

Stepping up and making the decision for him – mainly because he had gone super pale and appeared to be struggling to stay upright – she called out in just loud enough of a voice to carry to the strange monsters waiting below, "If you can bring us somewhere safe, we would be forever grateful. And if you have some way of healing Felbar here, we would be even *more* grateful."

"Girl, don't worry about me – take everyone else and run. Leave me here...I've not got long, but I'll do everything I can to delay them," the old Warmaster weakly told her, before collapsing back as his strength finally left him.

Violet ran to his side and checked him over quickly; she sighed in relief as it seemed that he had just passed *out* and hadn't passed *on*. Still, though, if he didn't get help, she didn't think he would last more than a couple of hours. She didn't know what kind of internal injuries he had sustained from the horrific crash his War Machine had undergone, so it could be even less.

Out of the corner of her eye, Violet saw a line of the metallic skeleton wolves who had been miraculously healed by the white cylinders bend down so that they were lying flat against the ground. She counted them and saw that there were eight of them – exactly the same number of Gnomes that were still standing.

"But what about—?" she started to protest, before one of the metal monkeys – she thought it looked like it was made completely out of iron – patted its chest. It ran over to the wall in front of her and jumped up, catching the edge of the roof and easily pulling itself up.

Everyone else but her pulled their knives again and held it towards the metal monster, but it ignored them and gently picked Felbar up in its arms, cradling him like a baby. *If he ever finds out this happened, I shudder to think how he'll react*, Violet couldn't help but think. *Of course, he's got to survive first.*

The monkey jumped off the roof with Felbar still cradled in its arms and moved to the front of the column of skeleton wolves. Knowing there wasn't much choice, she jumped off the roof as well, tumbling forward as she hit the ground; she used to practice that move as a child when she was growing up in the ELA – or better known as the Enchanters Learning Academy – but it stopped when her tutors found out she was jumping off of houses for fun.

Approaching with what she hoped was visible confidence, Violet walked up to the first skeleton wolf and placed her hands on its back. Rather than feeling like old bleached bones like she briefly thought they would, it instead felt warm to the touch, though only on the side facing the warm sun; it was a hard-but-smooth metal that was unfamiliar to her, but she definitely knew it wasn't steel. She – as well as everyone else in the village of Glimmerton – knew their steel, and this certainly wasn't the same metal.

Without thinking about it too much, she lifted herself onto the top of the skeletal wolf – though, now that she was closer, the "bones" were looking more and more like metal bars with gears connecting the joints – and settled onto its back, gripping on tightly to its ribcage for support. She looked back over at the others still on the roofs looking at her with horrified expressions on their faces.

"C'mon, what are you waiting for? If they wanted to kill us, they could've done it at any time. Besides, I don't know about all of you, but I don't want to get eaten by those giant lizards over there," she told them with a little admonition in her tone. They were being ridiculous; they had been saved and were being given a way out, and *still* they hesitated.

Her words must have convinced them, however, because first one and then all of them quickly jumped down and ran towards the…mechanical? wolves. Only a few of them hesitated more than a moment, but they were soon all on and as ready as they were going to be. It was just in time, too, because the other monster army was almost upon them.

*I wonder if **that** had anything to do with their decision to come.* She thought it was her words, but it could've easily been the sight of monsters out for their blood that spurred them on. *Regardless, they're coming – that's all that matters.*

Without any type of signal that they were starting, the iron-looking monkey started to run, still holding the unconscious form of Felbar in its left arm – the right one was used to help the metal beast move and support itself, because it couldn't run very well on just two legs. The wolves followed immediately after it, and she was almost knocked off of the back of her strange ride when it stood up and sprinted forward at full acceleration. Luckily, she had grabbed on tightly beforehand and was able to hold on – though just barely.

Settling herself into its surprisingly gentle stride, she looked back to see the others following behind, expressions of fear and wonder warring with each other on their faces. She thought that the same was probably on her face as well, though she had to admit that wonder and even a little enjoyment was at the forefront of her experience. She'd never moved that fast before – at least when she wasn't sealed up in a safe Mover box back in the capital; the unique and handy people-transportation system utilizing the Movers – that the Master Enchanters had created centuries ago – were great, but they barely even felt like she was moving. Here, though, the air from their passage whipped her long brown hair back and every which way, and the steady movement of the metal wolf beneath her was almost hypnotic.

Looking farther back, she saw the other strange metal monsters following after them, though they held back as if they were presenting a screen of safety against the lizards and crocodiles that had turned to follow after them. Fortunately, those dangerous reptiles were quite slow when compared to their rides, as well as the steel snakes and metal monkeys joining them. The white healing cylinders weren't left behind, either, as they were either picked up by one of the monkeys or placed on the back of one of the metal cats, where they appeared ready to topple off at any moment. Fortunately, none of them actually did, which was encouraging for their survival.

Even farther back, she saw the metal monkey that had gotten its arm ripped off and another white cylinder with its tiny arms pressed against it. If she wasn't mistaken, the arm was actually *growing back*, which was just...crazy awesome. However, she realized that unless they moved in the next few minutes, they would soon be overwhelmed by the following horde of reptilian flesh.

There was nothing that she could do about it, and she wondered why she even cared. They were dungeon monsters, after all...right? Despite that reasoning, though, she couldn't help but hope that they escaped before they were swarmed over and destroyed. It might have been gratitude from being saved by them, or even that one of them seemed like primarily a healer and not a fighter; regardless of the cause, though, she didn't want them hurt.

They were moving very quickly over the wasteland and none of the strange metal monsters seemed to have any difficulty navigating their way around the hills and valleys and devastated land. In fact, they were so efficient that Violet didn't even realize where they were going until they started to slow down; she had expected them to keep going, perhaps even into the Orcish-controlled lands of Orcrim, which was where it appeared they were going.

She was okay with that, if that was where they were going; the Orcs wouldn't kill them outright for passing into their lands, though it would be difficult to stay safe there. She had heard that the dungeons had expanded even farther there than they had in her own land of Gnomeria, though with the sudden expansion of the reptile dungeon back near her village she wasn't so sure anywhere was safe anymore. It had caught them completely unaware and unprepared; even if they had left the dungeon alone and stopped culling its monsters for years, it still wouldn't have reached their village. Felbar and the two other War Machine pilots had been culling in the forest when the attack started, in fact, and she was sure they were just as surprised as everyone else.

Thoughts of those that had died filled her with sorrow, but she tried to push it away as she took in where they were. The time for mourning was for later, once they were all safe;

being one of the few Apprentice Enchanters that had survived the destruction of the ELA meant that she was technically in charge of the well-being of the village, especially since Felbar was down. She would've given anything for him to be there to help make the kind of decision she had to ensure their safety – he was a salty old War Master, but he always had their best interests at heart.

As the metal wolves slowed down to a walk, Violet realized they had arrived at their destination already. And, if she wasn't mistaken, she was staring at the entrance of a dungeon.

Chapter 18

As soon as the group had left the Gnome village, Sandra had pulled back the new constructs that had been heading there to reinforce them; they weren't really needed anymore, especially when she saw the relatively slow speed of those chasing after them. While some of the snakes and smaller lizards could move fairly quickly, the large crocodiles and giant turtles couldn't. And as for the two new Ancient Saurians, they traveled the slowest of all with their lumbering movements.

She was both pleased and saddened by how the Gnomes had been practically forced into coming with her constructs. Sandra was glad that she had been able to convince them that she meant no harm, though when they learned the truth of the entire situation and that it was ultimately her fault that they had been attacked in the first place, she didn't know how they would react. Since the deaths of the Gnomes had likely fueled the creation of the first Ancient Saurian – as well as the additional two – Sandra didn't think they'd take the news well.

Her remaining forces were easily able to keep far ahead of the reptilian army, which was now separated into two major groups, which she kept track of via her Shears above. The first was comprised of the smaller reptiles like snakes and crocodiles and they stuck together instead of traveling at different speeds. That alone showed that they were being controlled by another intelligence, because otherwise they would've been spread out and it was possible that some of the smaller-yet-faster lizards could've caught up; the fact that they were held back from doing that proved that the Core controlling them knew that attacking as a group was preferable to attacking alone. While Sandra didn't have much experience in the ways of battle and fighting, she knew that much at least.

One of her Repair Drones had stayed behind to continue repairing the one-armed Ironclad Ape still near the Gnome village. She *could've* stopped it if she really wanted to and had it escape with the others even if the repair was only half-done, but she reasoned that it might be prudent to employ a small delaying force. Granted, it would be a very small force comprised of a single Ape and a defenseless Drone, but every little bit would likely help.

The repair and "regrowth" of the Ape's arm was complete only seconds before the Core's reptilian army arrived. As soon as it was done, though, she had her larger construct go wild, tearing into the enemy with flying fists and leaping from place to place, in an effort to do as much damage and cause as much disruption as possible. Sandra knew that it wouldn't be able to do much to stop them, but that wasn't the point – they just needed to be delayed.

It worked...up to a point. For more than a minute, her Ape jumped around and did its best to avoid attacks by the reptiles; it ended up killing a crocodile and a half-dozen smaller lizards while it was on its rampage, but it was eventually pulled down by another crocodile that was able to clamp down on her construct's leg with its jaws. Without the ability to jump away, her Ape attempted to free itself, but was quickly overrun and literally torn apart. Even though they were weaker flesh-and-blood monsters in comparison to her constructs, they were powerful in their own right.

Her Repair Drone didn't even try to fight or run, as it was incapable of defending itself and couldn't move faster than the reptile army. It was surrounded after Sandra's Ape went down and with a quick clamp of a crocodile's jaws, the white cylinder was crushed and destroyed. Shockingly, however, the puncturing of its form caused something unexpected to happen – it blew up. An explosion of multi-colored light erupted in all directions, which caused the jaw of the crocodile crushing her Drone to be completely blown apart. With half of its head missing, the deadly reptile faded from view as it dissipated in death.

The surrounding reptiles were blown away as well, though none of them looked seriously hurt from the explosion. Only the one that had destroyed her Drone had been killed, though even that was a surprise – she had no idea that her construct would do that, and she had to keep that fact in mind for the future.

Without anything else impeding them, the smaller-yet-more-numerous reptile force investigated the village for any survivors and then took off after Sandra's constructs – and the Gnomes tagging along. As she had stated before, they kept together in one large bunch, even though they moved at the speed of their slowest monster – the giant turtle. Even given that it couldn't move faster than Sandra could quickly walk in her old Human body, it was still much faster than the Ancient Saurians in the second group.

When the village was cleared by the other group, the massive lizards immediately turned to follow after Sandra's constructs as well. They moved so slowly, however, that unless they used that special ability that she had seen from the first one just before it died, it could take them a full day or more to reach Sandra's dungeon. That didn't seem to perturb them, though, because they just plodded along, intent on getting to the Gnomes she had stolen away.

Before she had her pair of Shears leave the village and follow after the reptilian army, she noticed a veritable swarm of much smaller lizards emerge from the forest where she assumed the other Dungeon Core was located. They were at most a foot long and only half that tall, so Sandra was confused at what purpose they could serve; they reminded her of her smaller constructs that were useful when she had been growing and expanding her dungeon, but they weren't as useful for defense now as her other bigger and deadlier Dungeon Monsters.

Her answer was quickly delivered as the surprisingly quick lizards roamed over the field in front of the village and started to pick up in their jaws the Monster Seeds left behind not only from its previous own killed monsters, but from Sandra's as well. She saw them run back to the forest, where she assumed they would deposit them inside the dungeon where the Core there could either reuse them or absorb them for Mana and Raw Materials.

When the field was clear, dozens of them roamed through the village and literally plundered it, stealing whatever was small enough to carry off. Sandra couldn't help but think how many materials she could've found inside there too, which she had a feeling would be completely wasted when it came to the other Core. They would likely all be only used as Monster Seeds instead of actual materials, which was a shame.

The one thing they didn't carry back, however, was a shiny blue stone clutched in the jaws of Sandra's Steel Python; she didn't have a lot of time before they had to leave the Gnome village, but she made sure she grabbed the Seed dropped by the Ancient Saurian before they escaped. While she didn't get a chance to get a good look at it before her construct snatched it up, she had a suspicion of what it was – but she'd have to wait until it was back in her dungeon to be able to tell for sure.

Which was only a relatively short time later as her constructs carrying and protecting the Gnomes arrived at the entrance of her dungeon within a half hour. Sandra's Mechanical Wolves could've run even faster, but they had to match the speed of the Ironclad Ape holding the broken and unconscious body of the old Gnome. *Felbar,* if she remembered correctly what the young woman had called him earlier. He was definitely still alive, but there was a sporadic blood trail being left behind them as they ran, which meant that he needed some healing before he lost too much of his precious life-sustaining fluid.

Fortunately, she had prepared as much as she could while they had been traveling. She knew it was a bit of a risk letting them all into her dungeon's safe rooms, but she knew she had to start somewhere.

"Just make sure you're protected; you don't know these Gnomes like you knew Kelerim, and it's always possible they could betray you. Especially if they end up learning what actually happened...unless you choose to keep that a secret," Winxa noted, as Sandra's Wolves slowly brought the refugees inside her entrance. As soon as they passed the threshold, she felt her ability to manipulate many of the things of her dungeon dampened like they did when there was an "invader" present.

I'm not going to keep that from them, as I want to be as honest as possible. Of course, that is probably the biggest risk, but I'm hoping that once they get to know me a little, they'll understand that it wasn't intentional. Besides, even if they **do** *decide to attack me out of revenge, I have plenty of traps and defenders in my Home to protect me.* As soon as she had decided on her course of action, she brought quite a few of her new constructs into her Home for protection, before sealing off both entrances with her deadly Fire trap. She had already moved everything out that she'd thought she'd need over the next couple of hours, so keeping herself essentially sealed up wasn't going to cause her any hardships.

Sandra watched as the Gnomes entered her dungeon and she thought again about carving some sort of mural or something like that on the entrance tunnel to portray her non-threatening nature. *Or, if I can learn how to carve the stone along the outside, I can control one of my Apes and have them do the work for me.* That would require quite a bit more effort than just visually eliminating the stone through her normal Core absorption process, but she thought it could be done.

Despite the danger coming toward her dungeon, she had eliminated the Nether trap in the first room and the Holy trap in the second, so that it wouldn't freak the Gnomes out and cause them to want to attack blindly – literally. If Sandra didn't have the newer rooms completed farther down, then she would've hesitated to remove them; as it was, however, she was fairly sure that they wouldn't be as effective against the reptiles as she would hope, as she knew that most of them relied on senses other than eyesight to move about the world. Of course, if she was able to re-establish them before they arrived, she was planning on boosting their effectiveness a bit – she had access to much more Mana since she had initially set them up.

So, while the traps weren't present in those two rooms, her constructs certainly were. In the first room, a dozen Basher

Totems were lined up against the walls, along with four Ironclad Apes; they were completely motionless and almost appeared to be statues, except that they followed the incoming Gnomes with subtle turns of their heads – or in the case of her Totems, their entire bodies. In the second room, two dozen Singing Blademasters were floating in the air at different points, their blades lying limply along their long pole bodies since they weren't spinning at the moment.

All but the female Gnome in front – *Violet* – seemed nervous seeing all of the constructs around, though Sandra thought it could also be the fact that they were inside of a dungeon at all that caused them to use one of their hands to grip one of their Steel knives at their sides. Violet, on the other hand, looked wary but not necessarily afraid or worried; Sandra was starting to like the small woman – her fortitude during the attack and her determination to save her fellow villagers were excellent qualities in a leader. And a leader she suspected the young Gnome was in actuality, though obviously a reluctant one at that.

In the tunnel leading to the third room, they were turned aside by the stone door that was opened in the side wall, and the Ape holding the old Gnome and the Wolves following them immediately stepped through the doorway. As soon as they were all inside – including a Repair Drone (the rest had stayed behind or were outside the dungeon again), the pair of Shears that was essentially the gatekeeper swung the door closed

197

silently; it was only when it was locked a noise was made, and it was the first indication to the Gnomes of what was happening. A few of them looked back nervously at the now-closed entrance as they realized they were trapped inside of a dungeon with no visible way out. It couldn't have been the most comfortable of feelings, but she couldn't explain that it was for their own safety.

A short hallway led to the top of her VATS, with the two holes in the floor: one hole was where you could drop down and the other for when you came up. Just like Kelerim, these Gnomes were highly confused, though Sandra wasn't expecting them to move from there yet. Without instruction and the promise that they wouldn't die if they jumped down, it was unlikely that they would attempt it anyways.

Instead, they were greeted by an Articulated Clockwork Golem...and a good-sized pile of Large Elemental Orbs Sandra had moved up from her "treasury". *It's time to get to work.*

Chapter 19

This was much easier with an unconscious Kelerim, Sandra couldn't help but think.

She needed to accomplish two things; one, establish a mode of communication; and two, heal the grizzled old Gnome, Felbar. To do both of those things, however, she needed to use her Dungeon Visitor Bond skill on at least one of the Gnomes to get things started, but it was proving harder to do that than she thought it would be.

With Kelerim, she had needed to try out every Elemental Orb and then combinations of the elements to eventually figure out that he had access to Fire and Earth; of course, that was made so much easier because he couldn't stop her or question her methods. Trying to communicate what she wanted to do to the confused and nervous Gnomes was outrageously harder. Any amount of her Golem's or her Ape's pointing and hand-waving wasn't getting them anywhere after about five minutes where the entire Gnome party started to get more and more agitated.

"I don't understand what you are trying to say. What are those small orbs you're pointing at there? I've never seen anything like them before, but for some reason a few of them...*feel*...familiar," the one called Violet said after none of them seemed to understand what Sandra was trying to convey.

Ah…that might be the solution, then. She had been trying to point towards the pile of Elemental Orbs and then to the chests of the Gnomes, but that was doing absolutely no good. She had no clue how to improve on her message before, but with Violet's last statement, she thought she might have an idea. It was the fact that a few of them *felt* familiar that led her to try another tact.

From the battle back at the village, Sandra remembered seeing the woman using the Natural element as part of her temporary enchantment on her Steel knife; the quick rune she had etched on it had created three long spiked thorns that erupted from the blade when she struck at one of the lizards attacking her. It only lasted the one strike, but it was damaging and effective enough that it left an impression on Sandra.

She took control of her Golem and used its clamp hand to pick up one of the Large Natural Elemental Orbs she had in the pile; bringing it over to Violet, she held it out to the Gnome. After another small bout of confusion, the small woman held out her hand and Sandra let it go, letting it land in Violet's outstretched hand. As soon as the orb touched her skin, the Gnome gasped in shock and what appeared to be wonder as she gazed down at the glowing green orb in her hand.

"Th—This is full of Natural elemental energy!" Violet exclaimed, before looking at the elemental orb closer. "At least, that's what it feels like, but it's subtly different," she slowly said after a moment. "I feel a connection to it, though; it's almost as if it resonates with the Natural elemental energy I can access..."

Suddenly looking up and at the pile, she walked over and reached down, pulling out a yellowish orb. "And this feels like my Spirit energy!" she exclaimed, looking at the two orbs in her hands with wonder.

That was apparently all it took, as the others scrambled over and picked out whatever orbs called to them; there were plenty for everyone, fortunately, because Sandra had made sure that there were nine of each Elemental Orb, just in case there were repeats. It was interesting to note that only Violet had access to two elements, while the others only had one.

With that step at least partially communicated to the Gnomes, Sandra needed their help to save the old Gnome, Felbar. Again, using her Golem – she found it was easier and likely to be less intimidating to them with the smaller construct, since her Ape towered over them – she pointed to the pile and then to the rapidly dying Felbar, trying to convey what she needed. While she could theoretically just keep trying different combinations, it might end up taking too long and they didn't have any time to lose.

Violet, just like all the other times, caught on before everyone else. "You want to know what elemental energies Felbar has access to?" she asked. Her Golem didn't really have a neck with which to nod yes, so she instead just shook her arm up and down. That was all that was needed, fortunately, and Violet immediately picked out two orbs out from the only slightly diminished pile and placed them in front of Sandra's construct.

"I'm assuming this is Fire and I know this one is Spirit," Violet stated, pointing to a red one and a similar yellow one like the one still in her hand. Sandra immediately picked them up and hurriedly placed them on Felbar's chest. After stepping back, Sandra concentrated on establishing a Dungeon Visitor Bond with the dying Gnome – and she felt the tugging at her Core that signified that it was starting to work.

While establishing the bond with Kelerim had taken 1,000 Mana and 5,000 Raw Materials to complete, only half that amount was consumed in the creation of the bond with the old Gnome. She wasn't sure if it was the smaller size of her target or if that had only been a one-time thing; either way, it meant that the resources she currently had at the moment filling up her core would be plenty to establish a bond with all of them.

The same bright golden glow erupted from Felbar's chest as it had when she bonded the half-Dwarf/half-Orc, and the others screamed out in pain, closed their eyes, and looked away. The light fortunately only lasted a few moments before it faded to a lower level, leaving the sight of the old Gnome with the front portion of his strange faded-rune-covered suit burnt away and a bronze-colored gear covering his chest like a tattoo. And, just like Kelerim's had been, if Sandra looked at it in a certain direction, she could see little flecks of red and yellow inside, signifying his elemental affinities.

When they could see again, the Gnomes looked at Felbar and shouted out in surprise, Violet included. "What did you do!?" she yelled out, kneeling down by his side and hesitatingly reaching out to touch the tattoo covering his battle-wound-scarred chest. Before anyone else could freak out, they all stopped their yelling when the Repair Drone hovered over and brought out its two thin arms; placing the metal pads on the old Gnome's broken leg, Sandra saw red and yellow energy flow out from her Drone and into Felbar.

The healing of a flesh-and-blood entity was surprisingly much faster than fixing up her constructs; Sandra thought it probably had something to do with needing to use all of the elements to heal her Dungeon Monsters as opposed to just two for the Gnome. Or even that the materials were so different that it was possible that metal took longer to create than blood, flesh, muscle, and bone. Regardless of the reason, the Gnomes all watched in awe as the leg visibly straightened and repaired itself, the pallor of his skin faded and returned to normal, and his body "re-inflated" a little as internal injuries were repaired and blood was returned to a healthy level. All of that took less than a minute, which made it all that much more miraculous.

Unfortunately, Felbar didn't wake up; it was possible that bonding and healing an unconscious individual caused them to *stay* unconscious for a while, but Sandra didn't really have a good frame of reference. For all she knew, it was possible that the same would happen if they were conscious and healthy —

the only one that she had done it on had been in the same state as the old Gnome had been.

"How—?" Violet began to ask incredulously, before cutting herself off. "Never mind that – why isn't he awake?" she asked instead.

Sandra had no way of answering; she was hoping that Felbar would wake up and allow her to explain everything to him. Instead, she just pointed toward Violet and the Elemental Orbs in her hand.

"What does that mean? What do these have to do with why he isn't awake?" Violet asked. "Don't get me wrong, I'm very grateful for the healing you did on Felbar, but what is that on his chest? Is it some sort of slave mark?"

What is it about slave marks here? Is that common in this part of the world? Sandra asked Winxa quickly, while she tried to figure out what to do.

"It used to be – especially in the Orc lands – when their population was much greater. Now, though, everyone is working together to defend against the dungeons that they can't afford the luxury of having slaves that may or may not help fight," the Dungeon Fairy answered.

Filing that information away, Sandra used the Golem to touch the gear tattoo on Felbar's chest, followed by his mouth, and then to his temple. She was trying to convey that the bond would allow her to talk to his mind, but she wasn't sure how successful she was at it.

"This...will allow you to talk to us?" Violet said, pointing towards the bronze gear.

I guess I was more successful than I thought. Sandra again waved her Golem's arms up and down in affirmation.

"Ok...then do it," the small woman said.

"What?! No, don't do it, Violet – you don't know what it will do to you!" said one of the other Gnomes, who tried to move her away from Felbar as if the gear on his chest was some sort of disease that could be spread. Violet shook him off and repeated her request for Sandra to do it.

Before the Gnome woman could change her mind, Sandra initiated the Bond again and felt Mana and Raw Materials stream out of her. To her surprise, only 100 of the former and 500 of the latter was needed to complete the Visitor Bond; neither she nor Winxa had any explanation for the difference, though the Fairy mentioned that it might have something to do with the Gnome's willingness and her lack of unconsciousness.

The same light blinded everyone again and Sandra heard Violet scream out in pain; fortunately, it was over just as fast as it began, and she saw the Gnome woman blinking her eyes and trying to stare at her hands. The Natural and Spirit Elemental Orbs were gone – as Sandra had expected – but in their place were two bronze-colored gears on either palm. They were similar in appearance to the larger one on Felbar, but of course a bit smaller; on one, Sandra could see flecks of green; on the other, she saw flecks of yellow.

The Repair Drone moved over to Violet and did its whole healing thing again, though this time with green and yellow energy streams pumping into her. The Gnome seemed to be frozen during the process, but it was only temporary; within seconds, the Drone was done, and it moved off after putting its arms away.

"Thank you – I can see again," Violet said absently, now able to see her palms and was staring at them in shock. "Wh— what was that? What are these things?"

* Sorry about the pain – I haven't created a bond with someone conscious before and didn't know. *

Violet looked around wildly at Sandra's voice, though she recovered much faster from the shock of hearing a voice inside her head than Kelerim had. "Who are you? What did you do to me?"

Sandra started by explaining that she was the dungeon and that she was there to help and not harm them all. She followed that up with what she thought was the reason Felbar was still unconscious, but that he would wake up eventually (she hoped). Then, with another few quick thoughts toward the woman, she described the bond that allowed her to speak to the Gnome and also explained that they were not "slave marks" or anything of the kind – and that they were free to leave at any time they wanted. However, she stressed the need to hurry and convince the others to agree to the bond as well.

*I need you to convince the others of the need to perform the Visitor Bond as well, otherwise my hands are tied when it comes to changing the dungeon around while there is an 'intruder' inside. I was forced to do it for Felbar there without his permission to save his life, but I won't do it for anyone unwilling. However, if they don't agree, they'll have to leave – at least temporarily; the other Dungeon Core's reptile army is about an hour away, so there is time to escape if they want to. Escape to where, I honestly don't know – it'll be highly dangerous anywhere they go. *

Sandra heard Violet start to explain what was going on to the other Gnomes, who had been staring at her essentially talking to herself; fortunately, instead of thinking she had lost her mind, they listened raptly to her words. Apparently, the Gnome woman held a greater position in their village than she had thought, as the others all agreed to the bond. Most of them still seemed reluctant, but they still gave their permission.

Rather than doing them one at a time, Sandra did a mass bonding on the other seven, concentrating on each of them and holding the Dungeon Visitor Bond at the forefront of her mind. Just as Violet's bonding had been, the Mana and Raw Materials were much less than Felbar's and it only confirmed that being willing and conscious probably had a lot to do with the amount she needed to spend to form the Bond.

And, just like Violet, they were all slightly blinded from the light, which was quickly fixed by Sandra's Repair Drone going from one to another. Unlike Violet, however, they only had one bronze-colored gear on a single palm – depending on where they were holding the Elemental Orb that matched their affinity. Sandra spoke to each of them individually and then as a group, and by the time they had gotten over the strangeness of her voice in their heads, the inevitable question came up.

"Why are you doing this? Better yet, what are you going to do with us?"

*That's a bit of a long explanation that we don't have time for right now; I need to prepare for the small army of lizards, crocodiles, and giant turtles about to descend on my dungeon. Rest assured that I mean you no harm and in fact want to help – but I'll have to explain it a little later. Right now, I need to get you all somewhere safe where you can rest and even get a little something to eat if you want. You **do** eat meat, don't you?"*

"Well, yes – though it isn't often that we have access to it—" Violet started, before Sandra cut her off.

Then let's get you below and settled in and I'll keep you all apprised of what's going on with the reptile army heading here.

"But what about those massive lizards? Do you have something that can kill them too?" The Gnome woman pushed her questions out and practically forced Sandra to respond. The problem was, Sandra had no idea what she was going to do about them, but she still had at least a day before they arrived.

Honestly...I have no idea what to do against them. Let me worry about this initial wave first, and if we all survive, we'll see what we can do. *

"What do you mean, 'if we all survive'?" Violet asked.

Wow...I wonder if I was this annoying when I was pestering the crafters to teach me what they knew back when I was Human? I bet that's why they taught me in the end, just so that I would stop asking questions. Sandra tried to answer the rest of her questions as best she could, all the while itching to get back to preparation; she had trouble carrying on a conversation that required she listen and respond while doing something else at the same time. When she would recite what she was seeing and what was happening to Winxa back near her Core, it was usually just a one-way conversation – this was much more complicated.

Fortunately, as soon as Sandra showed the Gnomes her VATS, they turned their attention to that instead. Freed up from having to answer difficult questions and only needing to lead them to where they needed to go, she could finally concentrate on more important matters.

At least, she *thought* survival was pretty important.

Chapter 20

First, Sandra checked her Non-threat Visitors List to make sure that everyone was on there from the Bonding process, though she was sure it worked because she could feel her ability to manipulate things inside her dungeon as soon as it had completed.

Non-threat Visitors List (Currently Present)		
Name	**Race**	**Elemental Access**
Winxa Flamerider	Dungeon Fairy	Spirit
Felbar Warmaster	Gnome	Fire, Spirit
Violet Apprentice	Gnome	Natural, Spirit
Jortor	Gnome	Nether
Saryn	Gnome	Earth
Lankas	Gnome	Air
Kasdon	Gnome	Water
Wilser	Gnome	Air
Pomend	Gnome	Fire
Junipar	Gnome	Holy

Just as she thought, an additional nine names had been added to the list, though it was interesting to note that no one other than Felbar and Violet had surnames. Warmaster and Apprentice didn't seem like the typical surnames passed on to other generations; instead, they almost sounded like *earned* titles instead of ones just given to them at birth. It was also fascinating to see that their elemental access ran the entire spectrum – only Fire and Air were repeated. She wasn't sure if that meant something, but she was hopeful for potential applications in the future — if the Gnomes were willing to help her with her crafting, that was.

Unfortunately, she didn't have time right now to continue those crafting pursuits; with another Dungeon Core's army of reptiles on the way, she had to concentrate on defense instead. To that end, she also checked on her current resources to see what she was working with; if she was guessing accurately, the reptiles still had another 45 minutes before they would arrive, which would give her another 13,000 or so Mana, minus what she was going to spend on the Gnomes to feed them — which fortunately wasn't much.

Core Selection Menu	
Dungeon Classification:	Constructs
Core Size:	19
Available Mana:	8215/15646
Ambient Mana Absorption:	10/hour
Available Raw Material (RM):	26250/41608
Convert Raw Material to Mana?	26250 RM -- > 1050 Mana
Current Dungeon Monsters:	14121
Constructs Creation Options:	17
Monster Seed Schematics:	133 (3)
Current Traps:	31
Trap Construction Options:	All
Core-specific Skills:	5
Current Visitors:	10

Looking at the list, she realized that she had neglected to check out a few things with everything that had been going on with the preparations she was making in her dungeon right after her Core Size Upgrade, the attack on the Gnome village, and then bonding the survivors so that she could operate her dungeon properly. Speaking of them, they were all sitting down on the kitchen floor after enjoying their trip down the VATS – completely the opposite of a certain half-Dwarf/half-Orc – and eating some Bearling steaks her Golem had cooked for them. Felbar joined them, still unconscious, when her Ape brought him down and deposited him there, and the others kept him as comfortable as possible; remembering what had happened with Kelerim, she made sure a Repair Drone was nearby to help sustain him through his unconscious period.

Sandra had told them that they could visit the forge in the next room (Kelerim's old one), but to avoid going anywhere else for the moment. There weren't too many dangerous spots in her workshops, but she didn't want them accidentally trying to walk into her Home room while she was distracted; being burnt to a crisp from her Fire trap she had set up after just being saved didn't sound like a good ending for one or more of them.

Therefore, unless they started making trouble – she thought Violet was level-headed enough to keep them all in line – she ignored them for the most part. Sending her attention skyward, she instructed a thousand of her AMANS to spread out in the direction the reptiles were coming, just for extra coverage in case some of them split up and went somewhere else – or even to try to sneak in while she was distracted. She also checked on the Shears hovering far overhead of the other villages near the wastelands and was relieved to see that everything looked as normal as it was before.

Sandra briefly wondered what had happened with Echo, the Elven woman watching her dungeon. She had lost track of her after she saw the woman running after her Repair Drones on their way to the Gnome lands; she had been visible for more than half of the way there, but then she disappeared with her special elemental ability. Since that last glimpse of her still following the Drones, Sandra hadn't seen even an "echo" of her presence anywhere. She hoped that she hadn't been caught up with the reptile army and had gotten out of their way.

Putting that out of her mind, Sandra worked on finishing the things she had been putting off. First, something she thought would be easy enough to take care of, she had her Steel Python spit out the blue-colored rock it had picked up in the Gnome village. She thought that it was about time to see what the Ancient Saurian had left behind after it had died – so she ate it with her Dungeon Core powers immediately.

New Monster Seed and Origination Material found!

Sapphire
While Sapphire can be directly used as a Monster Seed, it can also be used as a material for use in the dungeon or other purposes.

You now have access to:
Tiny Faceted Sapphire Sphere
Origination Raw Material Cost: 12000
Origination Mana Cost: 3500
Monster Min. Mana: 3500
Monster Max. Mana: 8500

A Sapphire with those Mana and Raw Material costs was much better than she had expected; if she were to unlock the larger sizes, then in some ways it would be more affordable than her Large Steel Orb in terms of Raw Materials, and the Small size would actually give her an alternative to the Small Dragon Glass Sliver when it came to the maximum Mana she could use for a Monster Seed. She didn't have the time or resources to spare to unlock it then and there, however, so it would have to be later.

The second thing she had completely ignored until now – and which she was hoping would help with the defense of her dungeon – was the new construct option she had received as a result of upgrading her Core Size up to 19. She couldn't even imagine what it could be, since her Iron-plated Behemoth had cost 10,000 Mana to create; *if it costs even more and is even bigger, can I even contain it inside my dungeon?*

With strange trepidation and eagerness all rolled up into one, she brought up her Constructs Creation Options menu.

Constructs Creation Options	
Name:	Mana Cost:
---------	----
Ironclad Ape	6000
Steel Python	8000
Iron-plated Behemoth	10000
Gravitational Destruction Sphere*	15000

Uh…huh? Not only did "Gravitational Destruction Sphere" make absolutely no sense to her, but it also had a strange symbol next to it that she didn't recognize. It almost looked like a star, but unlike anything she had ever seen before. The only one she could ask about it had no idea, either.

"I've never heard of that before. There must be a reason for it to have that symbol; maybe you need to concentrate on it to see if it gives you any more information," Winxa added with a shrug. It was an overly simple solution to her problem, so of course it worked.

Gravitational Destruction Sphere*

* This unique construct is limited to being created only **1** time every **60** days. Each Sphere will maintain its existence for **24** hours before dissipating while also consuming whatever Monster Seed it was created from, no matter if it was used or not. Range limit: **300** feet from dungeon entrance. *Warning: Use of this construct is not advised inside of a dungeon.*

That was a lot of limitations for something so expensive in terms of resources, which at the moment was almost her entire maximum Mana; in addition, whatever Monster Seed she used for its creation was set to be consumed at the same time, even if she didn't "use" it within 24 hours. *Speaking of that, if it isn't advised to be "used" within a dungeon for defense, what good is it?*

Winxa answered even if Sandra wasn't actually asking her. "That sounds extremely dangerous. I can't give you any specific advice, but I'm sure you can guess what I would say."

Yes, and I agree; I won't use this new construct unless it's absolutely necessary. Sandra was wary of using anything that had an actual *warning* attached to it; everything else that she could make – including her deadly traps – were fine, apparently, but she was planning on staying away from something that could potentially harm her as well.

With the new construct essentially a bust, Sandra turned her attention back to what she could do to increase her defenses. With what appeared to be at least 200 various reptiles (not counting the two Ancient Saurians farther behind them) heading her way, there were a number of ways she could defend herself; first, she could intercept the army with a force of her own before it even got close; second, she could use her AMANS to attack from above, killing many – if not all – of them, but it would end up destroying hundreds or even thousands of her Shears in the process; or third, she could let them come to her dungeon and let the constructs and traps inside do the work for her.

As for the first choice, it had the benefit of not revealing where her dungeon was located, though she was sure if they looked hard enough they could eventually find it. As it was, Sandra could see that they were following the sporadic blood trail left behind by the bleeding and unconscious form of Felbar, as well as her constructs' tracks through the wastelands. Therefore, while her own Dungeon Monsters would prevent them from initially finding her entrance, doing it like that would likely end up with many casualties – which couldn't be as readily replaced to face the Ancient Saurians once they arrived.

The second option was also tempting, because it also helped protect her location while killing the reptiles from above. The only issue was whether or not she could kill them all; the giant turtles, for example, were essentially impenetrable in their shells, and she had already seen that they could bring their heads inside to protect them from harm. It was entirely *possible* that she could get lucky and manage to score a direct hit from her Shears bombardment, but it wasn't *probable*. Hitting their legs might work, but if they had advanced warning of her attack from above, they could bring those inside their shells as well.

A combination of the two options would work even better and would be sure to devastate the reptilian force, but there would still potentially be quite a bit of destroyed constructs on her side. While that was potentially fine, with the threat of the two Saurians on the horizon, she wanted to ensure that she had enough constructs left to defend her dungeon and, ultimately, her Dungeon Core from their threat.

Not only that, but when she thought about it a little more, Sandra *needed* the Reptiles to find her entrance; the last thing she wanted was to give them a reason to start searching around and potentially find another village of Elves, Dwarves, or Orcs. None of them appeared to be prepared to fend off an assault like the one that befell the Gnomes; in fact, it was a miracle that *any* of them had survived – though it looked like that was probably due to their walls and preparations they had made as a normal part of their defenses. None of the other villages had anything approaching that level of preparedness.

Which only made sense; it was only an unfortunate fluke of Dungeon Core rules and abilities that had granted the Reptile Core access to the Gnomes when it shouldn't have been possible. They had unknowingly paid the price of Sandra's mere presence, and she'd be darned if she would let any of the others suffer the same fate.

Decision made, she abandoned any plans to fight outside of her dungeon. Instead, she did what she could to enhance her defenses inside; there wasn't much she could do that hadn't already been done, especially when she didn't have the time (or Mana) to finish trapping the last couple of rooms near her Core. Well, technically, if she wanted to convert some of her treasury into Mana and Raw Materials she'd have enough resources, but she still didn't have the time – and it wasn't something she wanted to rush if it wasn't necessary. Besides, she wasn't too worried about the reptiles even getting anywhere near her Core; it was their much bigger cousins that were going to be a bit more of a problem.

Therefore, Sandra used most of her Mana she currently possessed and what she accumulated in the time before their arrival to reset the first two rooms' traps, though with a lot more Mana than had previously been invested. She ditched the blinding darkness of the Nether-based trap – knowing that it probably wouldn't affect the other Dungeon Monsters as much as it would a sentient – and instead used the Nether element to create a trap that would be much more useful.

A dozen flickering bands of pure darkness would extend down from the ceiling like writhing vines, wrapping around any enemy they came in contact with. The Nether energy would solidify and keep them trapped in place, while Sandra's Basher Totems and Ironclad Apes would take advantage of their immobility; it would honestly probably be a slaughter, and it was entirely possible that none of the reptiles would even get past the first room.

If some did manage to make it through, they would face the second room which had its trap revamped; not only was the Holy light suffusing the room even brighter and more blinding, but – with a little quick experimentation – she had discovered how to create small little spheres of intense Holy elemental energy. These spheres wouldn't necessarily do any damage, but anything that touched them would be repelled with great force, flinging them all over the room – and into the spinning blades of the two dozen Singing Blademasters floating around the room. Since the reptiles were all land-bound, she placed 10 spheres near the floor and out of the way of her constructs, so that they would be free to do what they needed to stop the invasion.

The only downside to the more powerful traps in both rooms, however, was that they only had a limited time that they were active; the boost in Mana pumped into them helped extend the previous time limit from approximately a minute or a minute and a half to about three minutes, but it was well worth it for the extra benefits of them.

Sandra wanted to enhance her other initial traps, but there wasn't time nor Mana to do it. With a lack of either resource, all she could do was wait for the lizards, snakes, crocodiles, and giant turtles to arrive.

Chapter 21

Echo collapsed behind a rocky outcropping, her legs giving out beneath her from exhaustion. She let the last vestiges of her active camouflage fade as her energy reserves were practically drained; she had held it for as long as she could, but without a bit of rest she wouldn't be able to sustain it much longer. She dragged herself deeper into the small shadow the rocks afforded her as she attempted to keep herself out of sight of the rapidly approaching army of vicious-looking reptile monsters.

While Echo had no trouble fighting and killing beasts or even the slime monsters located near the other forest dungeon, she had an unnatural fear of snakes; the larger lizards, crocodiles, and turtles didn't affect her the same way, nor did the metallic-looking snakes she had seen slither quickly out of the dungeon she had been watching earlier. It was just something about the size and shape of a real snake that made her freeze up; some combination of its scaly skin, forked tongue, and even lack of legs that both creeped her out and made her a bit fearful. *Ok, maybe a little more than a "bit".*

After following (but staying far back from) the strange white cylinders that trailed the other undead monsters – she had to revise her thought that they were undead, however, after seeing the metallic monkeys and other assorted objects that emerged from the dungeon – she had finally arrived at the Gnome village on the border of the wastelands, just as she had earlier thought they were heading towards. She had already activated her active camouflage a bit earlier as she approached what she was sure was their destination, so she spent some time moving forward cautiously, not wanting to get caught up with whatever was happening.

She feared the worst for the Gnomes ahead but knew there was nothing she could do to help; even if she had gone to her own village first, gathering up enough to help them out would've taken a while because many were out hunting. Even if she had been able to assemble some sort of assistance force – which wasn't likely, as they had been forbidden contact with the other races because of some longstanding issues -- they would probably arrive too late to help.

From a distance she had heard what sounded like the sounds of an odd battle, with the gongs of hollow metal being banged around and the heavy footsteps of something walking, but because of the lay of the land she was unable to see what was happening. When she had finally gotten close enough to get a good view, she had seen the devastation of its walls, the small forms of dead Gnomes littering the fields and roofs of their squat houses, and the metal monsters surrounding the village, ready to finish off the remaining survivors.

At least, that's what it looked like; in reality, things were confusedly different.

She remembered seeing one of the metal monkeys jumping up on top of one of the roofs and she thought that was it for the Gnomes; she had nocked an arrow, despite it being at the extreme range of her bow and what would likely be a futile attack. However, she couldn't have just done nothing and watch them be slaughtered without at least helping a little, even if it was just a token resistance. Instead of killing them all, though, the metal monster gently picked up what appeared to be a wounded Gnome and jumped down with them cradled in its arms.

She had watched with shock as the other Gnomes jumped down as well and climbed on top of the metal skeleton wolves – and then *rode them away!* Initially, Echo had thought they were being taken prisoner somehow, though it didn't make any sense; then she saw all of the Gnomes looking off to the western edge of the forest between her own lands and theirs. From her vantage point, she could see something emerging from the trees but couldn't quite make it out.

Rather than follow the metal monsters right away, she stayed to see if she could see what they were looking at. Along with her, Echo saw that one of the metal monkeys and a white cylinder were still there as well, though the larger monkey was missing an arm – at least temporarily. It was too far away to tell for sure, but it almost appeared as though its arm was growing back, albeit slowly; she wasn't sure if the white cylinder pressed up against it had anything to do with it, but in the end it didn't matter.

Echo stayed crouched down on top of a short hill still in the wastelands as a mass of lizards, crocodiles, turtles, and of course *snakes* swarmed over the two metal monsters left behind. She watched as they began to fight against each other – which was something that she'd never seen before. The white cylinder ended up exploding in a spectacular array of colors, which she could tell surprised the reptiles as well.

She had no idea what was going on; it almost appeared as though the dungeons nearby were warring against each other, even though she had never heard of that ever happening before – despite her people's long history and recorded knowledge. What it portended and whether the Gnomes that had been snatched away were to be pawns in some sort of unseen war was yet to be seen. She pondered those questions as she watched the lizards and other monsters swarm over the now-abandoned village, looking for any survivors.

Her thoughts were elsewhere as she crouched there in her camouflage watching them work – which was why she only realized at the last moment that the reptilian swarm had finished and were on the move.

Straight towards her hiding place.

Though, technically, they weren't heading straight for her, but they had spread out and advanced quickly through the wasteland in a wide line in a sweeping formation. It was another thing that Echo had never seen before, a mass of dungeon monsters traveling together in a silent but determined group towards an objective. She had seen small groups working together in the forest before, but nothing at all like what she was witnessing.

She took off as quickly as she could while trying to avoid the echoes that were her namesake; they usually only happened when she moved too quickly, so she had to maintain a quick but not too fast of a pace. She knew she could probably outrun them if she wanted to, but since they were all keeping together and regulating their pace to their slowest members, she didn't want to take the chance that a few of them were much faster. She had seen those metal snakes that came from the strange dungeon move nearly as fast as she could even when she used her Air elemental energy to boost her speed, and she didn't want to risk a flesh-and-blood one having the same ability.

So, Echo maintained her constant speed ahead of the army and even managed to put a little distance between them before she arrived near the dungeon in the middle of the wastelands. She had briefly considered running straight back to her village to warn them of all that she had seen but held off for fear that the reptiles following her would somehow be able to track her to her village. The last thing she wanted was to lead them there; it was much better if they attacked the strange dungeon and destroyed it, making the incoming Elites' job unnecessary. Of course, it would probably result in all the

Gnomes that had been taken being killed as well, but it was probably a better fate than whatever plans the dungeon had for them.

As she watched the lizards and the other reptiles get within 500 feet of the entrance, she watched them break formation and the fastest of them surged forward. The smaller lizards reached there first, with the crocodiles and then the turtles entering next; the snakes were left behind, as they had difficulty slithering up and down the broken hills and valleys of the wastelands.

From where she was positioned, Echo couldn't see anything inside the entrance, but she definitely heard the sounds of metal pounding against rock, frantic hisses from struggling reptiles, and the snap of crocodile jaws opening and closing. She even thought she heard the cracking of what she presumed were the shells of the giant turtles, as there were multiple wet-sounding *cracks* echoing out from the tunnel leading in. In a remarkably short time, the sounds stopped just as the snakes reached the dungeon, where they disappeared inside without a sound.

Silence descended upon the broken valley where she found herself at a loss of what to do. On the one hand, she was exhausted and needed to rest; the best idea for her was to go back to her village and tell everyone what she had seen that day and let them decide what to do with the information. On the other hand, she was curious whether or not the reptile monsters had managed to destroy the heart of the dungeon. Either prospect involved moving, which was not something that she wanted to do at the moment.

Therefore, she decided to wait for a little bit to see if anything emerged from the entrance. If some of the foreign reptile monsters ended up succeeding and destroying the heart deep down inside, then they would likely try to leave before the dungeon collapsed – or at least that's what she heard happened when the dungeon heart was destroyed. It usually took a few hours for it to fully collapse – from the stories that she had heard – which was why there were survivors in the first place to pass on the tales.

After about 30 minutes, nothing seemed to be happening; the reptile monsters' success was in doubt, as nothing had stirred since the last snakes went inside the entrance. Picking herself up with a weary sigh, Echo got ready to make the trek back to Avensglen; her Holy elemental energy was almost nil, but her Air energy was still relatively full – so she should be able to outrun anything that saw her without her active camouflage. Though, she had to admit that the recent events had been extremely odd, and the verdict was still out – in her mind, at least – on whether or not the dungeon there actually posed a threat or not.

Elder Herrlot will know what to make of all this. She's older than dirt and she's seen just about everything—

As Echo was thinking that she took a step out of the shadow she was hiding in and felt a piercing pain in her left calf. Looking back, she saw a red/orange-colored snake latched onto her leg, the light and thin clothing she had borrowed providing very little protection against its fangs as they sank deep into her calf.

She involuntarily screamed louder than she had ever screamed before; whether it was from pain or from the sight of a snake so close to her, she couldn't tell. She grabbed the knife off her belt while still screaming and started to bend down to try to cut it off – but her vision started to swim, and she almost lost her balance. Two quick whistling sounds followed by a *thunk* *thunk* sharpened her awareness as she looked for the source of the sound while trying not to fall down.

Two of the metal scissors that she had seen up in the sky had impaled the snake, cutting it in half down below before slicing through the bottom of its neck. All three dissipated after a moment, leaving dungeon loot behind – but by that point, she was nearly incoherent with pain and didn't even see what they were. Echo finally lost her balance and collapsed onto her side, her prized bow tumbling away from her as she fell; she tried to rise, but she was having trouble even moving. In fact, she was having trouble even breathing, as each breath was getting harder and harder to bring into her lungs.

The last thing her eyes saw before they closed – for what she feared was the last time – was a large shape emerging from the dungeon entrance.

Chapter 22

If Sandra was honest with herself, the "invasion" of the reptile army was less of an invasion and more of a slaughter. She had watched them break from their cohesive formation and race inside, which was their first mistake. Or, she should say, *the Core's* first mistake by being too eager to get inside and to the Gnomes that were within. Obviously, it hadn't really considered that she would be prepared with traps and defenders; then again, she wasn't sure how long the other Core had existed, and it was doubtful it had ever been up against another. It had probably grown complacent over the years and didn't consider much – if anything at all – a significant enough threat to employ any great strategy.

The lizards that came in first were practically useless against her Bashers and her Apes; they had deadly claws and teeth, but no real force behind them. Sandra was sure they were deadly against other beasts and even an unwary Hero – or whatever the Gnomes called those who culled the dungeon monsters – but they couldn't do more than scratch her constructs superficially. What they did have going for them was speed, and dozens were able to escape the clutches of her Nether "vines" and make it to the second room – where they were instantly blinded and tossed about the room by the special Holy-based spheres she had made. Most of them were sliced by the Singing Blademasters that guarded the room, but six somehow made it through even that gauntlet.

The lizards were so fast that they – despite being blinded – flew over the shallow water in the third room and two of them luckily were missed being impaled and killed by the ice spikes that shot up out of the water as they passed by. The relatively slow Small Armored Sentinels holding their steel swords didn't even get a chance to swing before they escaped to the tunnel leading to the next room. Of course, those "lucky" lizards that made it to the fourth room were burnt by the massive flame jets that shot out of the floor, ending their attempt to reach the end of her dungeon.

The crocodiles were next, and they proved to be more of a challenge – but not much of one, for all that they were bigger and deadlier than the lizards. The Nether vines wrapped them up one by one as they came in and secured them in place, but failed to secure their heads – and jaws, especially. Two of her Bashers had their arms ripped completely off before they were able to pulverize their crocodile victims, and an Ape had its left foot snapped off from the pure force behind the reptile's snapping jaws. There were a few other minor damages to her constructs in the first room, but overall the casualties were almost completely one-sided.

The giant turtles also proved to be tougher, but in a different way. They moved much slower than the others, and by the time they arrived all but two of the crocodiles had been dispatched – and none of those deadly reptiles had even made it to the second room, technically doing worse than the initial lizards. The turtles were more difficult because they were almost impossible to grab – let alone hold onto them – with Sandra's Nether vines; either their size prevented them from wrapping completely around the turtles, or there was something about its shell that was...*slippery*, was probably the best word for it.

Regardless, Sandra's Bashers and Apes did their best to slow them down, but the turtles moved forward without even caring about defense or fighting back; the few times that one of her constructs got in front of one of them, the shelled reptiles struck out with their snappy-beaked mouths and took chunks out of them – but kept moving seemingly without a care. Dozens of the turtles fell in the first room through the sheer fact that – with enough hits in the same place – even their hard shells couldn't withstand heavy sledgehammers of force smashing into them. After around ten or so bashes from a Basher or Ape, the shell would crack like a walnut and it was easy to finish them off after that.

However, as a result of the shelled monsters not sticking around to fight back, 20 of them made it to the next room, where they were bounced around and blinded, but ultimately couldn't be hurt that much because her Blademasters had trouble targeting anything but hard shell. One was bounced so hard against a wall, though, that its shell cracked and fell apart –

which her constructs took advantage of and finished it off; other than that, 19 turtles moved on to the third room.

Ice spikes didn't really do much to the hard shells of the turtles other than launching them through the air, and the Sentinels were relatively ineffective with their short Steel swords, though a few managed to slice up a few legs pretty good. Two of the shelled reptiles ended up on their backs after being flipped by ice spikes, however, and were stabbed repeatedly by her constructs through their leg holes; the one time a Sentinel tried to attack a turtle head, it was snapped at and destroyed with one hit by the sharp-beaked reptile.

Seventeen of the enemy walked into the fourth room and sixteen walked out, though they were all singed in places; the flame jets only managed to catch a single turtle full-on and baked it alive in its shell.

The poison clouds in the fifth room seemed to do just about nothing, but the Segmented Centipedes that fell from the ceiling had been surprisingly the most effective construct (in terms of cost and size) at defeating the turtles. The Centipedes were small enough to land on top of their shells – which they couldn't break through – but they *were* able to crawl towards the turtles' leg openings and chew their way inside the exposed soft flesh. Just like the Centipede that had chewed up one of the Orcs from the inside, they were able to burrow inside and slice up the shelled monsters' vulnerable internal organs.

Only half of the sixteen that had entered the fifth room survived to tackle the sixth room, which was also not really a problem when all of the air was removed from the room – if Sandra remembered correctly, they could survive a while without breathing because they had a very slow breathing rate. The Articulated Clockwork Golems with double-bladed axes managed to gang up and chop off the legs of one of them, but that still meant that seven turtles were able to make it to the seventh room.

Web illusions through the use of the Spirit trap and Clockwork Spiders did absolutely nothing to faze the turtles; the Spiders couldn't even penetrate the softer leg tissue when they managed to get close enough.

Therefore, seven of the enemy entered the last of Sandra's original dungeon rooms, where they were greeted with stone spikes jutting out of the wall and a rotating funnel of Small Animated Shears. Of course, whoever was controlling the turtles didn't care to try to go around the funnel and instead drove the turtles straight through them, where only one managed to get three of the Shears – which were destroyed as a result – through its neck; it continued on for a little while, but the Shears dissipated and it bled out from the wounds shortly thereafter. Learning from that, the rest of the shelled monsters kept their heads inside their shells and made it through with only a couple of superficial wounds to their legs.

Which brought them to Sandra's brand-new room that hadn't been tested...and it was over in less than a minute. The extreme heat in the room literally cooked the turtles alive as they attempted to navigate the Steel-walled maze. Their feet sizzled against the floor and the softer, more-vulnerable flesh in their leg and neck holes were cooked like tender meat in an oven.

She was strangely disappointed that they hadn't gotten any further, because she wanted to see how her other rooms would fare against them – but she supposed that a positive test of one of the newest rooms was a good result.

While the turtles were still navigating through the rooms to their demise, the snakes that had come with the group had finally entered...and were squashed or pounded flat by her constructs in the first room. The Nether vines didn't even really have to restrain them, because they actually went for her Dungeon Monsters for some reason, though their venom and sharp fangs were no match for metallic bodies. In fact, the snakes that came in were actually defeated before the turtles met their end, so as soon as that happened there weren't any more of the reptilian army to worry about.

Other than the two Ancient Saurians on their way, but that was something that she wouldn't have to worry about for a while.

She waited to see if any more were hiding nearby and waiting to enter her dungeon, but after a couple of minutes she didn't see anything moving out there. Echo had finally showed up at some point, however; she was covered in sweat and looked exhausted as she attempted to hide in the shade behind some rocks, but since she didn't have her invisibility thing going on, she was more than visible to her AMANS up above.

Overall, there were some repairs to many of her constructs that needed to be completed, which her Repair Drones that she had stashed just inside the topmost VATS room immediately went to work on as soon as it was all clear. Only one of her Small Armored Sentinels had actually been destroyed, in fact, which she immediately replaced – though she waited to send it back up until she was sure enough of the Gnomes that were brought in earlier were safe enough to trust. She'd have to take down her flame traps in her Home in order to do that, and a single Sentinel wasn't enough of a reason to do that quite yet.

While she was thinking of that, she checked back in with them and saw that they had already finished eating and were sitting around talking.

"…not sure what we should do. The voice in my head said that we were free to go anytime, but can you really trust a dungeon? Sure, there are some very strange things here, but I can't help but think we're being held captive here like the other races hold livestock – so that it can eat us later when it's hungry," one of the Gnomes was saying to the others. She wasn't sure of the male Gnome's name yet because she hadn't yet had a chance to learn them; while she had a listing of their names through her Non-threat Visitor's List, she hadn't been able to put a face to each of those names.

"Let's just wait a little bit longer before we start throwing out wild theories; I have an odd feeling that this dungeon is quite a bit different from every other one," Violet responded. "For one, the fact that it spoke to us shows an intelligence there that is utterly unlike the others. And two, look at this place! This looks more like a home than a dungeon; granted, it's made completely of stone, has monsters made of metal, and it's a bit dreary and drab, but I've never heard of anything like this anywhere else. It's unique, and that might make all the difference."

The others still didn't look completely convinced. Sandra eavesdropped on their conversation while she waited for her Mana to refill; when she was Human, she would've felt a little bad about it – especially since they were mainly talking about her – but now she was more interested in what they thought of her dungeon. And, to be frankly honest, she was a little worried about the two Ancient Saurians that were still heading towards her dungeon. Well, she *was* worried...until she checked on their progress and saw that they turned around and were heading back towards where they came from.

Winxa, why would those Saurians be turning around? I would've thought that the temptation of the Gnomes here would keep them coming, Sandra made sure to send her thoughts towards the Dungeon Fairy alone.

"I tried to tell you before, the other Cores are insane and homicidal, but they aren't stupid. You completely annihilated his force back at the Gnome village and then destroyed their reptile army here without suffering many casualties yourself; after getting a look at your dungeon and your traps, they probably decided it was a lost cause. I'm sure they ended up gaining more Mana today than they had in the last decade, so it makes sense if they want to pull them back," Winxa said matter-of-factly. "Especially if they are ready to upgrade their Core Size; you probably eliminated many of their actual 'dungeon monsters' defending their dungeon but having two massive Ancient Saurians standing guard outside will go a long way to defending themselves."

She hadn't thought about that before; it was still strange to think of the other Cores as thinking beings instead of mindless homicidal floating stones, especially given what she knew about them and their history. And not "throwing good money after bad" was a common expression while she was a merchant; the other Core had already wasted a significant amount of Mana with the failed invasion of her dungeon. All of the Monster Seeds left over from the reptiles dying had already been collected and deposited in her upper VATS room, where she was planning on bringing them down later. Unlike in the Gnome village, the reptile Dungeon Core wasn't able to collect them for reuse.

So, with that threat at least temporarily off the table –
for now – she turned back to her immediate problem: Gnomes.
Sandra had some ideas of what she'd like to do with them if they
were willing, but she knew that she would have to explain a few
things to them first. She wasn't looking forward to that
conversation.

Before she could interrupt them and broach the subject,
however, a woman's scream from somewhere captured her
entire focus and attention. She discovered it immediately
aboveground near her entrance, through one of her Mechanical
Wolves standing sentry nearby. Sandra immediately instructed
two of her nearest AMANS to propel themselves downwards,
where they sliced cleanly through the snake latched onto Echo's
calf muscle, destroying all three in the process.

The Elven woman fell to the ground and convulsed a few
times; Sandra could see her struggling to rise but failing to find
the strength. Judging by the coloring of the snake, she guessed
that Echo only had minutes to live; the Gnome that was bitten
by it back at the village had been struck in the face, so the
venom inside the snake's fangs had gone straight to his more
vital areas. The Elf wasn't foaming at the mouth quite yet, so
Sandra thought she might have a little bit longer before it was
too late.

One of her Ironclad Apes quickly ran out of the
dungeon's first room and threw her over its back in a hurry;
Sandra didn't have time to be gentle. It ran back inside and

went immediately to the VATS room Sandra had opened up and deposited her a little more gently on the floor.

Is there something about my dungeon that draws unconscious people, or am I just lucky?

Chapter 23

Sandra knew she didn't have a lot of time; as soon as her Ape put her down, Echo started to foam at the mouth. Thinking quickly, she had the Golem still there walk to the Elemental Orb pile; Sandra had to guess correctly because she didn't think she'd have more than one or two tries to get it right. Thinking about the Elven woman's abilities and what type of elemental energy she used, Sandra remembered seeing the white of Holy energy dissipating after she had dropped her invisibility; her superior speed had to be either an infusion of Earth to her body to increase her muscle strength or an outward application of Air to reduce the resistance as she ran.

Remembering what Winxa had said about Elves being the masters of manipulating the elements – but not necessarily inside their bodies like the Orcs did – Sandra reasoned that Air was the likely one. Grabbing an Air and a Holy Large Elemental Orb, she brought them over and placed them on Echo's chest – which she immediately bucked off as she convulsed violently again. Picking them up via her Golem, Sandra looked for a solution; the woman was in her death throes and she didn't think she could get them to stay anywhere on her body...well, *almost* anywhere.

Knowing that she probably couldn't breathe anyway, Sandra shoved them in her mouth and pushed them to either side of Echo's inside cheeks. Then, before they could escape or be involuntarily spit out, she activated the Dungeon Visitor Bond for the third time on someone unconscious in her dungeon, hoping for the woman's sake that she had guessed correctly.

Just like the bond with Kelerim, 1,000 Mana and 5,000 Raw Materials flowed out of her Core and into Echo's still-convulsing body. The now-familiar bright light erupted from around her face and even Sandra had to look away; when it was done, the Elven woman was completely still – and with a bronze-colored gear tattoo visible on each cheek. She didn't bother to check, but she wouldn't be surprised to see white Holy flakes in one and grey Air flakes in the other.

Immediately, a Repair Drone had its arms out and pads pressed against Echo's inert body; bright white and grey light flowed in between the pads and the Elven woman, though it started to fade after a little bit. Sandra hoped that she wasn't too late; she had placed two other Drones in the room previously, as they had just finished repairing the constructs that had been damaged by the reptiles. With a quick order in their direction, she ordered them to help, which they immediately floated over to do.

As soon as they joined in, Sandra could finally see a change come over Echo's body. The pant leg covering the puncture wound had been dragged up as a result of moving her unconscious form, and she could plainly see a thick liquid being rapidly expelled from the holes the snake had left in the flesh. It was actually quite a bit more than Sandra had expected, as it created a sizable puddle on the stone floor by the time it was all removed from the Elven woman's bloodstream. As soon as it was all out, the wounds closed over in an eyeblink, and the color started to come back to Echo's skin – and her breathing resumed normally. Sandra breathed a figurative sigh of relief that she had been able to save the woman.

Of course, she was still thoroughly unconscious.

Regardless, Echo hadn't died and would be ok; better yet, Sandra would be able to speak with her and be able to explain who she was and that she wasn't a threat to the Elves – or any of the sentient races. Granted, the Gnomes – and Orcs, for that matter – could partially refute that statement based on how many had died since she arrived as a Dungeon Core, but nothing that had happened was intentional.

Just to ensure that everything was indeed okay and that the woman was indeed alive – despite the physical evidence that she was fine, Sandra couldn't help but realize that Echo had been extremely close to death, if not *actually* dead for a short period – she checked the list for her name.

Non-threat Visitors List (Currently Present)		
Name	Race	Elemental Access
-----------	-----	-----
Emmalyra Arlen	Elf	Holy, Air

And there she was, right at the bottom of the list; however, instead of it saying Echo, it said Emmalyra. Sandra figured that Echo was actually a nickname the Elf had earned based on her special invisibility that left echoes of her form if she moved quickly enough. She was glad that she had guessed her elements correctly and that there were only two; thank the Creator that there weren't three or more – Echo probably wouldn't have survived long enough to bond and be healed.

Now that Echo was as healed as she could get her, Sandra had the Ironclad Ape pick up the unconscious Elf's body and used the VATS to bring her down to the kitchen. While she had been working to save her life, the Gnomes had chosen to finally get up and explore a little; they were currently looking at her oven/stove she had made, as well as her faucet.

"...don't even see any enchantment runes anywhere— what is an Elf doing here?" Violet looked up in surprise as Sandra's Ape walked through with the limp form of Echo in its arms.

*She was bitten by a venomous snake and I had to bring her inside to heal her – I'll explain everything in a few minutes. The threat from the other Dungeon Core has passed for the moment and the reptilian force has been completely destroyed. *

"Dungeon Core? What is that? And you said the entire force was destroyed? Even those giant lizards?" Violet asked in

245

surprise as Sandra's Ape placed Echo's body next to Felbar. The two healthy-but-unconscious people looked peaceful lying there together, though Sandra knew as soon as they woke up they would be anything but peaceful. From what she saw of him back in the village, Felbar didn't seem like one to take the bonding against his will very well and Echo was already suspicious of her dungeon in the first place.

When that was done, the Gnomes crowded around her Ape as they looked for answers, despite that not actually being *her*; she supposed it was easier to talk to something physical rather than talking to a voice in their heads. So, now that she had the opportunity, Sandra began to explain everything to them – or at least everything she thought it was safe for them to know.

*　　*　　*

Violet's head was reeling as she listened to the dungeon – who she now understood was something called a Dungeon Core – explain her existence there in the wastelands. Sandra – an interesting name for the intelligence behind the dungeon – was apparently Human at one point, and she also indicated that all of the other "Cores" were once a sentient race at one point in the past, but that they had gone a bit insane (hence their homicidal tendencies). Contracts and whatnot were also spoken of, but that didn't really interest her.

The fact that the mere presence of Sandra's dungeon being there was the cause of the attack on her village, however, *did*.

*...entirely unintentional, and I had no idea they would attack your village. As soon as I learned of them there, I sent my constructs to help defend you – and you know the rest of what happened from there. The smaller reptilian army that was following us here entered my dungeon and was annihilated fairly quickly from my defending constructs and traps, but the two massive Ancient Saurians turned back soon after that happened. They're not quite back to their old territory yet, but they'll be there soon. *

Violet didn't know how to respond. She was just slightly relieved to learn the reason they were attacked in the first place when it should've been impossible; knowing that every dungeon around her homeland wouldn't be doing the same and attacking everyone at once took a little weight off her shoulders. That didn't excuse what had happened, though, and she wasn't sure how she felt about it.

If the dungeon intelligence could be believed – she was still accepting the fact that it *was* intelligent and could communicate with them – then what had happened was unintentional, and that Sandra had done what she could to rectify the situation. That in no way excused the deaths of 71 of her fellow villagers.

I understand completely after learning about all of this if you wish to leave and I will in no way stop you. In fact, if you do want to leave, I'll even send you back out with transportation from my Mechanical Wolves again, as well as some supplies.

That was also a relief to know that they weren't prisoners in the dungeon; despite the assurances when she had first communicated with Sandra, Violet wasn't wholly convinced that this all wasn't some sort of ploy meant to lull them into compliance. Compliance into what, she didn't know, but her knowledge and experience regarding dungeons in general was quite limited.

"Where would we go? Glimmerton is destroyed and there are only a few of us left. If this dungeon is to be believed, then those lizards could be back to attack at any time and we don't have any more War Machines left that are operational. I'm sure we could repair the basic shell of one of them, but without a Master Enchanter—" Kasdon looked apologetically at Violet— "we can't completely repair the runes to get it to work."

That was a sore spot for her; Violet had been one of the "lucky" ones that had been away from the ELA when it was overrun by the nearby dungeon. She had just started her training in the art of War Machine rune-making, but the Academy had been destroyed before she could learn more than

248

the most basic enchantments. When many of the Apprentices, Adepts, and Master Enchanters were killed, much of the knowledge was lost with them. That wasn't the only thing that was lost; her parents – Master Enchanters themselves and essentially all of the family she had left – had also fallen as part of the attack.

There were still a few retired Master Enchanters living elsewhere that were attempting to pass on their knowledge, but everyone was worried that they would die of old age before they could teach everything they knew. It took nearly a decade of study and constant practice before one could become a Master Enchanter, and there were very few Gnomes left anywhere that had the necessary elemental affinities to learn how to maintain, repair, and craft new War Machines – their ultimate defense against the dungeon monsters encroaching on their lands. The loss of three Machines was a significant tragedy; production had essentially stopped after the ELA fell, so what they had now was – potentially – all they had for the future.

Since Violet herself could maintain them and repair the most common rune problems on the War Machines, she had been sent to Glimmerton to ensure they were in top working order. The supply of steel and other metals – which were dropped by the lizards, crocodiles, and turtles when they were culled – was important to maintain those same War Machines, as well as providing material to craft other weapons like the defensive crossbows they had used to defend the village. With new War Machine production stalled, other weapons – using those same materials – were being designed and created to help them against the monsters getting closer to their settlements every day. Of course, they weren't nearly as effective as the powerful Machines, but they were doing what they could.

"Even if we were to repair one of them, if those massive lizards are still there, it would just be smashed apart again. With the threat of them there in the forest, there's no chance of culling the monsters for loot anymore; which in turn means that the entire point of the village being there is lost," Jortor contributed, gloominess in his voice as he commented. "I suppose we could go back to the capital, but then what? We were supposed to be in Glimmerton for years, supplying much-needed material, and I don't know of any other dungeons nearby that would be able to provide what we've just lost." He looked extremely downcast, and Violet couldn't blame him – she felt the same way.

There didn't sound like there was a good solution anywhere; even ignoring the fault of Sandra in the role she played in killing so many of her friends and the destruction of the village, that didn't change the fact that it happened. They couldn't change the past and she needed to look towards the future; not only *their* future – herself and the others with her in the dungeon – but the future of the entire Gnome race. The loss of Glimmerton and the materials it gathered and supplied was significant and would put a major dent in their weapon production; she couldn't see any way to recover from that without years of work and establishing another outpost elsewhere – if a suitable dungeon supplying what they needed could even be found.

If you do decide to stay, at least for a while, I can help you. *

Help? What could a dungeon do to help? And why would we want help from someone who has done so much harm to us already? Angry and sorrowful thoughts flowed through her head as she remembered dozens of her friends being cut down outside of Glimmerton's walls earlier that day in the fields, after being overrun by the surprise attack by the dungeon's monsters. However, reason and curiosity cut through those thoughts as she thought about what Sandra had said. "Help how? Keep in mind that I don't entirely trust you, or forgive you for what you did, and this better not be some sort of trick."

It's perfectly understandable for you to feel that way, and I assure you that this is no trick. I'm not like all of the other dungeons in the world; I already told you that I'm not looking to attack or harm anyone. Honestly, I just wanted to be left alone.

You see, crafting is my passion and is really all I wanted to do. Of course, that was before I learned about the nearby races here: Orcs, Elves, Dwarves, and then you Gnomes. All of you are facing a crisis, even if you can only see a glimmer of it right now. Eventually, given enough time, the dungeons around your lands will become too powerful for you to fight back against and you'll be wiped off the face of the world. If you don't believe me, just look at what happened to your Enchanter's Academy or even your village once a dungeon started killing innocent people.

* If that scares you, it should. You need to fight back now before it's too late, and I think I was brought here to help you do that. *

How does she know about the ELA? Did she have something to do with that, too? She desperately hoped not, because then that meant that the dungeon was even more powerful than she previously thought. After a moment's reflection, though, she realized that it was highly unlikely that Sandra had anything to do with that attack given that it was almost a month's travel away from her dungeon.

And, as much as she wanted to deny it, what the dungeon had said about their eventual fate *might* be true. Recovering from the destruction of the ELA was nearly impossible, and try as they might, Violet didn't think that they'd ever be at the same point they were just a few years ago. From the information she had been able to gather, the expansion of the dungeons had been held in check for centuries through the use of their Master Enchanters and Warmasters, but given the recent reduction in culling, it wasn't likely they'd be able to keep that same equilibrium they had enjoyed before.

"Okay...say I believe you. What can you do to help?" Violet finally asked as the others all seemed lost in their own depressed thoughts while thinking about their homes and families.

Well, for starters, I can supply as much—where did that come from?

Violet looked around to see what had made the dungeon pause in its explanation. The only thing she saw was Jortor eating an orange; the others also looked at him in confusion and not a little bit of consternation. When they were all eating meat earlier – which wasn't her favorite, but she could eat it – none of the other Gnomes had spoken up about having any other food on them.

"What? Why are you all looking at me like that? You know that I always eat when I'm depressed...or nervous...or happy. So, I like to eat – is that a problem?" Jortor answered defensively, attempting to hide the orange in his hands.

That's not a problem, but if you don't mind, can you drop one of the orange seeds on the floor?"

Without responding except with a shrug, Jortor plucked out a seed from his orange and dropped it on the stone floor. It disappeared so fast it barely had a chance to bounce.

*This should work for a demonstration, actually. If you would follow my construct here, I'll show you what I can do to help. *

The large metal monkey moved off towards a tunnel leading slightly downwards and Violet and the others hesitated. She looked over to Felbar in worry, as she didn't want to leave him there alone.

*Don't worry about him, he'll be fine. My Repair Drone is right there in case he needs any healing. *

With an expression that mirrored Jortor's from earlier, she shrugged and followed the dungeon's "construct" through the tunnel, leading to some unknown destination.

Chapter 24

Sandra watched the faces of the Gnomes as they followed her Ape through various workshops in between the kitchen and her growing room. They passed her Gem-cutting station in one room, her Gold/Silversmithing/Jewelry worktable in another, her Leatherworking Workshop next, and then at her room with the boiling vats before they arrived at the Textile shop, which was where her growing room was located, just off of it. It took longer than she was expecting for them to arrive, mainly because the Gnomes couldn't help but ask questions about everything they saw. She answered them as well as she could while trying to usher them through, until finally they arrived where she was planning on showing them something interesting.

There was a lot inside her dungeon that she could show them about her crafting initially — which, if they agreed to stay for a little bit, she was still planning on showing them — but she wanted to show them that she wasn't all about war and fighting. Kelerim had been suitably impressed by the weapons and armor she could craft using her forge because he came from a society that prized warriors and fighting prowess — or at least half of him did. The Gnomes, on the other hand, knew how to create great and interesting machines through the use of their Enchanting; they would be less impressed by a longsword she could masterfully craft in her forge. Even the Steel knives at their sides were actually quite well made — not mastercraft quality, certainly, but they were worlds better than anything she had seen come from the Orcs.

Nor could she craft something as impressive as their War Machines, though she had thoughts about how to do that; she would be missing the enchantment runes, of course, but if she had some sort of schematic she thought she could build one if she had enough time and a brand-new room entirely just for that...

Anyway, since neither of those would impress upon them her willingness to help, Sandra knew she had to do something else. When she had seen the orange, another idea had popped into her mind. While she didn't think it was as impressive as, say, forging weapons or building War Machines, she thought its impact would better convey the message she was trying to get across.

As soon as they were assembled in the room and lined up along one walkway, she used her Mana to produce a large pile of Orange Tree Seeds like the one she had absorbed in the Kitchen area.

New Origination Material found!

Orange Tree Seed
While the Orange Tree Seed cannot be used directly as a Monster Seed, it can be used in specific applications to create a whole new Monster Seed.

If the sudden appearance of the pile of Orange Tree Seeds startled them, then the sudden movement of dozens of Articulated Clockwork Golems all around them freaked them out. They all pulled their knives out and held them in front of themselves defensively, but none of the Golems even came close to them. Instead, they picked up seeds and started to dig and plant them in one of the dirt plots, seeding one entire 100-foot plot. As soon as they were done they stepped away from the plot and her Singing Blademasters went to work; she had enough inside the room to completely cover an entire plot with water as soon as it started to pour down.

She had the Rolling Force above start the water trap and water started to pour down on her spinning constructs, and soon enough the sprouts from the Orange Trees were popping out of the dirt, reaching up to the bright light that was also emerging from the ceiling. Fruit-producing trees apparently took much less time to grow, because within minutes they were already two feet high and growing at a rapid pace from there.

The Gnomes all looked shocked at what they were seeing and were completely silent as they watched the trees grow; Sandra had seen the Elves using their elemental energy to increase the speed at which plants grew, but the Gnomes didn't really utilize their energy in the same way. She could also say without any type of false modesty, that *her* plants and trees grew much, much faster than anything she'd seen the Elves accomplish.

Within a half hour, the Orange Trees were already tall and mature enough to start bearing fruit. Large, juicy oranges were already hanging low on the branches nearest the Gnomes, and it wasn't too much hardship for them to reach up and pluck one off for themselves. After peeling the skin back, they tasted them and exclaimed in surprise.

"These are so much more delicious than anything we get from the capital! I guess that having it fresh instead of shipped out to us on the border makes all the difference," Jortor added after he had eaten the entire orange and was licking his fingers.

"Okay...so you can feed us. I'm actually very impressed – I've never seen anything like that before, and it amazes me how you can grow *anything* down here, let alone fruit trees. However, we're not exactly starving for food right now, but it's nice to know that you can help provide some if we need it. What I'm more fascinated by, though, is how you made those seeds appear out of nowhere."

* That was actually what I was trying to demonstrate to you. I can reproduce almost any material that I have initially absorbed, but it needs to be crafted or grown as you've seen here. So, while I can supply you with all the Steel you might need— *

Sandra used her Mana to create a big brick of pure Steel and made it appear where the Orange Tree Seeds had been, to the shock of everyone there.

* —I have to manually craft everything that is a finished product. Hence, the workshops you've seen on the way down here, as well as the other workshops down below. *

She saw Violet look at the large brick of Steel and to the Orange Trees – which had stopped growing when Sandra turned off the trap – but it still had plenty of fruit growing on it. "I see. We could definitely use the material now that our village has been destroyed—" the Gnome said, anger in her face and voice— "but why would you help us? And what do you want in return for all of these 'gifts' you want to bestow on us?"

They were fair questions, though it was hard for Sandra to answer. She knew exactly why she wanted to help them, but as far as what she wanted in return, it was something that they might not want to provide.

* I don't want to help just you – I want to help all the races around here. And the only way to do that for you is to help you in any way I can, to gain back what was lost when your Academy fell to the dungeons. Not only that, but I think there might be a way for everyone to survive the coming dungeon monster invasion that is sure to come if something isn't done about it. *

"How can we gain back what we lost? There are very few Master Enchanters left to teach us all, and even if they could teach what they know in time, there is a serious lack of Apprentices that could even learn how to do it."

That's where you all come in. Currently, I don't have the ability to do any enchanting, but I'm hoping that will change soon. I used to be what you would consider a Master Enchanter when I was still Human, despite having never enchanted anything at all.

"What? That doesn't make any sense—"

However, I've never seen anything like the runes placed on the War Machines Felbar and the other two Gnomes were controlling. If you teach me how to make those, I can in turn teach others, as well as start making some of those War Machines myself.

"But I only know a few of the runes, as I hadn't finished— wait a minute," Violet said, before stopping herself. "Are you seriously asking *me* – a Gnome – to teach *you* – a dungeon – how to craft and make a War Machine, the only thing that has kept our people alive all these years from the monsters coming from *dungeons* roaming around our borders?"

When she put it that way, it sounded ludicrous. Sandra didn't know what she could say to convince Violet of her sincerity, so she said nothing. They were both silent as the

Gnome seemed to have some sort of internal struggle in her mind.

"What guarantees can you give that you won't use the information against us?" Violet finally asked.

The others immediately protested. "You can't seriously be considering that, can you?" "Are you crazy? This is a *dungeon* we're talking about!" "That's a very bad idea, Violet; Felbar will kill you when he finds out!"

Violet held her hand up to shush them, which they did almost immediately, as she waited for Sandra's response.

There isn't any guarantee that I can give to you that you would believe, especially coming from a dungeon. However, I hope that my actions of late and the sight of my workshops here have shown you that I'm a different kind of dungeon than you're used to.

The Gnome seemed to think that over for a bit, before nodding her head once. "That'll have to do, I suppose; if you had actually tried to give me guarantees, I probably wouldn't have believed you. I agree with your proposition, for the survival of my people, if nothing else. But, like I was saying, I only know a few of the runes; I had only begun to learn how to create the other one when my parents—I mean, the Enchanters Learning Academy was destroyed," Violet choked out, sounding a little emotional.

There was some sort of personal story there, but Sandra didn't pry – because it also sounded like it was private and still a bit raw. She assured the Gnome woman that with enough experimentation, she could probably figure it out if she had a starting point; she had enough instruction in Enchanting over her decades-long pursuit of crafting knowledge that she thought she could work out a solution.

Also, I would love to learn more about your temporary enchantment runes I saw you use on your Steel knives; Humans tend to do enchantments with permanency, so I've never actually seen more than a few temporary enchantments before.

Violet looked skeptical. "Are you sure you were a 'Master Enchanter'? Even our children can use simple runes like that." Sandra didn't bother to answer her, as she didn't want to explain everything about her own history. "But I'll see what I can do to have the others teach you what they know."

Thank you. If you all want to head up to the Kitchen again and through there to the forge in the next room, I'll see about converting an old room into a place where you can all sleep for the night. The sun is starting to set, and I know that today has been a bit exhausting."

Sandra saw them file out, the exhaustion that they had been ignoring with everything that had been going on visibly hitting them as they headed up. Before Violet left the growing room, she stopped and turned to face one of the Articulated Clockwork Golems nearby. "By the way, what's the deal with the Elf?"

* Oh, that's right, I forgot to mention that. In a little over a week, a special party of Elven Elites are supposed to be coming here to destroy me unless I can find a way to stop them. They think I'm some sort of danger or something. *

Violet just shook her head and departed, mumbling under her breath. "What did I just get myself into..."

Chapter 25

It was easy enough for Sandra to send an Ape into Kelerim's old room and disassemble the bed there; as soon as the leather mats were gone, she was able to manipulate the stone bed frame, add to it, and create 8 separate, smaller beds. A quick use of her dungeon ability to eat away at a portion of the crude – nearly rancid, actually (she was going to have to make some more soon) – leather mats to divide them up to fit on each bed like a hard mattress. It was a little cramped in the room now, but it was better than nothing.

The Gnomes didn't care, however; as soon as they saw somewhere to sleep, they each picked a bed and collapsed, falling asleep within minutes of arriving. Sandra figured they would be out for quite a while, which was alright for her, since she needed to get caught up on a few things. Not only was there more crafting that she wanted to accomplish, but she needed to get some things ready for when her new Visitors all woke up. First, though, she needed some information.

Winxa, I have a couple of questions. First, the Core that had all of the reptiles; does its Core Size Upgrade take the same time as mine will? And second, will the Gnomes here be able to help me stop the Elves from attacking by speaking to them?

The Dungeon Fairy had been listening to everything Sandra had been telling her for the last couple of hours with great interest. Once the Gnomes had gone to sleep, she had even checked out Sandra's growing room with the Orange Trees there, as well as looking over the sleeping/unconscious forms of all of Sandra's Visitors.

"That first question is the easiest, so we'll get that one out of the way. In general, the Core Size Upgrades take approximately the same time for each Core, though they can differ slightly depending on the kind of Core it is. The difference is barely noticeable, however; a few minutes longer or shorter when it already takes 48 hours – or more – isn't that big of a deal. I'm assuming that you're asking because you want to know how long you'll have until you need to worry about them attacking you again. On the low side, I'd put them at least a day and a half out before they likely finish their Upgrade, but keep in mind they will likely be fairly depleted just like you usually are after your own upgrades.

"As for your second question...I'm not sure. Remember, just because you can understand them all and 'speak' to them, that doesn't mean that the Gnomes will be able to speak Elvish. It's more likely that at least some of the older Elves will speak at least some Gnomish, but I can't guarantee that. And before you ask, the same goes with the written language – they won't be able to write anything that will be understood by the others, unless the Elves can read Gnomish, as well."

What about you? Do you think you can teach them enough to communicate with the Elves?

"The same ability you possess lets me understand and talk to any race, which is how I can speak with any Dungeon Core I am supposed to be guiding; only a fraction of the Cores I've met personally were Human, you know. Just as you can, I can read any language – but I can't write anything. Besides, Dungeon Fairies interacting with or helping any of the races is kind of frowned upon, though not necessarily forbidden – and I don't want to push my luck with that right now."

Essentially what you're saying is that unless one of the Elves speaks Gnomish, I'm likely out of luck. I may just have to see if one of them would be willing to try, however; it can't hurt, right?

Winxa told the Dungeon Core that it was up to her, though the Fairy didn't hold out hope. Sandra was more positive and thought it might have a chance of working; if it did, then she wouldn't have to worry about the arrival of an Elite team of Elves bent on her Core's destruction. If it didn't...well, she would worry a bit more about it after that.

That was for later, though, because right now she got started on a few crafting projects that she had been neglecting. First, she wanted to finish her plant growing and Thread-making crafts with Cotton and Jute. It felt unfinished and she didn't like things to go unfinished once she started down a path.

In her growing room, she ate and absorbed one of the Orange Trees; just as she had hoped, it had given her access to a new type of wood.

266

New Monster Seed and Origination Material found!

Orangewood
While Orangewood can be directly used as a Monster Seed, it can also be used as a material for use in the dungeon or other purposes.

You now have access to:
Tiny Orangewood Chip
Origination Raw Material Cost: 500
Origination Mana Cost: 100
Monster Min. Mana: 100
Monster Max. Mana: 200

Sandra left all of the other trees alone for the moment, as she wanted to keep the fruit for the Gnomes to eat if they wanted it. She had plenty of other space in the room for growing more plants, after all – which was precisely what she did. Using her helpful little Golems, she created Jute and Cotton Seeds and planted them in two different plots. She alternated the trap triggers so that they were active for approximately five minutes for the Cotton and twice as long for the Jute, as she knew it would take longer to grow.

Rather than watch that for the hour or so that it would take for both of them to mature enough to be harvested, she spent that time seeing to some more unfinished business. As soon as her Mana had filled up to nearly full again – which only took about 50 minutes or so – she began placing traps in the rest of the rooms she had created for defense earlier; just because the threat from the reptile-based Dungeon Core was on hold and the Elven hit-squad wasn't supposed to be there for another week or more, that didn't mean she wanted to leave her dungeon unprotected any longer than necessary. Therefore, she finished what she had been doing before the Gnomes had been attacked.

The fifteenth room down from the surface was filled with exactly 1,000 Segmented Centipedes; she wasn't exactly sure what she was thinking at the time when she had originally placed them all there, but she thought she had an idea on how to use them now. While the Centipedes were not too dangerous by themselves, Sandra had seen first-hand in the Gnome village attack how deadly a swarm of smaller monsters could be. By utilizing a trap that combined Nether and Spirit, she was planning on taking advantage of their greater numbers.

Unlike her tenth room that combined Holy and Spirit elements together to make victims feel euphoric while they were killed, this one would instill quite the opposite emotion: fear. Shadowy "apparitions" would float around the room that were about the size and shape of a 5-year-old Human child; when they touched someone or some creature/monster, an illusion would pop up of whatever their victim feared the most, sending them into a panic. That panic would spell their doom – or so she hoped.

The room was fairly small – only about 30 feet wide and long, and 10 feet tall – and there was a 4-foot-wide walkway running down the length of it in a straight shot to the exit tunnel. On either side of the walkway, however, Sandra created two shallow pits – only about 5 feet deep – that each contained

500 Segmented Centipedes constantly moving around in a writhing mass of potential death. If something were to fall inside while still in the throes of whatever illusionary fear they were suffering from, they would be instantly swarmed over and covered head to toe in Centipedes. It wasn't a pleasant way to go, but Sandra wasn't planning on it being an enjoyable experience – she was only doing it to protect herself. And better yet, she was able to tie the double-element trap to a single one of the Segmented constructs in the pits, meaning that it would probably take the destruction of almost all of them to deactivate the trap.

In the sixteenth room, Sandra went from illusionary fear to one of the real fears she held herself when she was still Human: drowning. She had never learned how to swim, and her deformed hands made that difficult in the first place, so she had tended to stay away from any bodies of water larger than a shallow bathtub. By utilizing Air and Water in a trap, she was able to make a nightmarish – at least for herself, and hopefully others – underwater maze that forced whoever entered to hold their breath for a minimum of 10 minutes on their way to the exit.

At the entrance, anyone entering would take two steps inside and activate the trigger. Thin walls of clear hardened Air would snap into place in the 50X50X20-foot room, creating narrow hallways that would meander throughout the room in different directions – including straight upwards and downwards. There were three initial entrance choices for whatever dared to attempt her labyrinth, though it was hard to tell because the "walls" of Air were invisible. All three entrances actually led towards the end, though only one of them was shorter; even if they chose the shorter one, as soon as they crossed into any of the entrances, the hallways made from invisible air would start to rapidly fill with clear water.

Whatever tried to navigate through the filled hallways would have trouble finding the walls and the way through as everything was clear; occasionally, they would need to wait for the portion of the maze they were on to fill with water to float them upwards, though of course they wouldn't necessarily know that there was a gap they could go through. It was likely that they would think it was a dead end and turn around, not knowing that they would have to go upwards.

Within a minute, the entire labyrinth of solid Air walls would fill with water, and then it would be a race to the end – if they could find it. And even if they could navigate their way through and hold their breath, Sandra didn't make it easy on them; a dozen Ironclad Apes were scattered throughout the maze-like labyrinth. They were easy to see through the clear Air and Water, but it was almost impossible to determine when they would actually be encountered. Since they didn't breathe, Sandra didn't have to worry about them running out of air as the labyrinth filled up with water. If anything survived 30 minutes within the air and water-filled maze, the trap would run out of

Mana and collapse, leaving them free to get to the exit – and contend with whatever Apes were still left.

And that finally brought her to the final, massive room she had constructed to house her Iron-plated Behemoths. Nine of them were currently inside the 200X200X25-foot room, and Sandra needed something to make up for their relatively slow movement speed. While they could spin around quickly and smash apart their opponents with their flails, they couldn't walk very fast; it was entirely possible that someone or something could literally run right by them without even engaging them. Sandra thought about Echo and the way she could increase her speed by using Air elemental energy – *she'd probably run circles around my Behemoths.*

To counter that, she created walls of thick stone inside the room, separating it into three distinct areas; the first was a fairly small circular space and contained a single Behemoth that was stationed in the middle. When it spun around, its flail-tails would be able to reach every edge, closing off any avenue of escape if someone just tried to avoid her construct in the first place.

Given that whoever made it that far had to have some expert survival skills, even Sandra didn't think that was quite enough to stop them, however. Therefore, she abandoned the dual-trap theme for the last room and used pure Air – and a whole lot of it. The trap she created would thicken the air until it was so dense that it was almost – but not quite – solid. Her

Behemoth even had a little trouble getting its rotation up to speed, but once it had momentum, it would cut through the air like a knife through thick porridge. Even if someone like Echo used her Air elemental energy to thin the air out enough to move at more than a walk, they would have to expend a lot of energy to make it happen.

And then they would have to go to the next space, which was essentially three long hallways that were just wide enough to hold an Iron-plated Behemoth. The same trap would thicken the air there as well, which was why her constructs were located at the end of each of the hallways; they would be able to start moving and pick up some momentum with their massive heavy bodies, until they got up to "ramming speed" – which was essentially the speed of a quick walk. Instead of trying to hit the enemy invader with a flail-tail, these three Behemoths would just run them over and smash them flat.

In the final space she made, five Behemoths were stationed in a large circular arena, where they were free to move about and attack whatever made it that far together. It was simple yet she was hoping effective, as they were her strongest Dungeon Monsters; if someone was able to get through them, then there wasn't much more she could do to prevent her demise. Even her super-hot flame wall trap blocking the inside entrance to her Home probably wouldn't stop someone so determined to reach her Core.

All in all, she was pretty happy with what she had created for her defense. There were 17 fully trapped and defended rooms, each one deadlier than the last. She was pretty sure that it could stop anyone or anything – but she was also hoping that she didn't have to test that. It was one thing killing the reptiles that had tried to invade her dungeon; it was quite another to kill any sentients like the Orcs that had invaded, or the Elves that were planning on attacking her as well.

There was nothing she could do about that quite yet, though, other than prepare for the worst. Which, looking at her entire dungeon, she was pretty sure she had done. She would still strive to prevent that "worst" from ever happening in the first place, but she was prepared if it should come knocking on her door.

Chapter 26

Compared to the growth of the Orange or any of the other trees Sandra had grown in her growing room, Cotton and Jute were relatively quick to grow. She worked on harvesting them when she was in between finishing the traps in the rest of the rooms, and she was as done with them by the time she was finished with the defenses as she could be.

The Jute was the easiest of the two to handle, as it was a very similar process to the Flax plant when Sandra had been making Linen. After the large stalks were grown enough that they began to flower, she had her Golems rip them out of the ground and use their clamp-hands to cut off the roots. Then bundles of the Jute Stalks were brought into the boiling vat room to soak inside the constantly churning warm water there to start the retting process. Easy as that – the rest would come later.

Cotton, on the other hand, was something she could see through to the end right away – though it took a bit of work. Normally she would just have her Golems pick the cotton buds that bloomed on the plant, but they were a little more difficult to get to with her construct. Fortunately, she didn't need to keep the plants around afterward; instead, the Golems just ripped the plants all out and picked the buds off when they were more accessible.

From there, Sandra used them – as well as some Segmented Centipedes she had used previously on the Flax plants – to pick out the seeds and any other foreign elements. Then – making sure she had plenty of Mana to throw it up again if she needed to – she took down her Home Fire wall trap and created 200 Clockwork Spiders, who went to help with the rest of the process. When they arrived, they used their legs to start breaking up the cotton bolls, pulling them apart and making the densely packed buds light and fluffy.

From there, it was a simple process of combining the fibers into a single strand that used the same process as the Linen thread, where they would start as large strands and be trimmed down using a spinning wheel and into a fine thread. When that was done, she finally had access to Cotton Thread to make into clothing at a later date.

New Monster Seed and Origination Material found!

Cotton Thread
While Cotton Thread can be directly used as a Monster Seed, it can also be used as a material for use in the dungeon or other purposes.

You now have access to:
Tiny Cotton Thread Bobbin
Origination Raw Material Cost: 15
Origination Mana Cost: 10
Monster Min. Mana: 10
Monster Max. Mana: 20

The Jute would be done at a later time, when the retting process was complete, but she had made good progress with her crafting and advancing what she had for material. Cloth (soon to be made with the thread), leather, wood, and metal – four very important components to many of the crafting recipes she could make now. There were other materials which would help, of course, but having those four staples meant that she could make quite a bit now.

Before she used her Mana to start anything else or unlock some of the larger sizes of her new Monster Seeds (Sapphire, Orangewood, and Cotton Thread), she checked out what other new options she had in her Transmutation Menu.

Organic/Inorganic Material Elemental Transmutation Menu				
Transmutation Options	Elemental Orb Required (Size/Qty)	Mana Required	Additional Seed Material (Size/Qty)	Unlocked (Y/N)
Precious Gemstones				
Citrine	Air (Large/6)	0/80000	Gold (Large/5)	N
Hematite	Spirit (Large/6)	0/100000	Silver (Large/5)	N
Onyx	Nether (Large/6)	0/200000	Iron (Large/5)	N
Sapphire	N/A	N/A	N/A	Y
Topaz	Earth (Large/6)	0/400000	Tin (Large/5)	N
Ruby	Fire (Large/6)	0/500000	Copper (Large/5)	N
Emerald	Natural (Large/6)	0/1000000	Bronze (Large/5)	N
Diamond	Holy (Large/6)	0/10000000	Steel (Large/5)	N
Moonstone	?????	0/20000000	?????	N
Dragon's Eye	?????	0/50000000	?????	N
Magistone	?????	0/100000000	?????	N
Fruit-producing Tree Seeds				
Apple	Fire (Average/3)	0/10000	Oak (Large/4)	N
Pear	Natural (Large/2)	0/15000	Maple (Large/4)	N
Peach	Fire (Average/3), Holy (Small/2)	0/20000	Cedar (Large/4)	N
Plum	Nether (Large/3)	0/25000	Ash (Large/4)	N
Apricot	Fire (Large/2), Air (Small/2)	0/30000	Pine (Large/4)	N
Orange	N/A	N/A	N/A	Y
Lemon	Air (Large/5)	0/50000	Redwood (Large/4)	N
Lime	Natural (Large/5)	0/60000	Yew (Large/4)	N
Coconut	?????	0/100000	?????	N
Elderfruit	?????	0/1000000	?????	N
Ambrosia	?????	0/25000000	?????	N

Theoretically, she could unlock quite a bit of different materials using her skill, but that would require a bit of an investment of Mana. There were some gemstones and fruit that she had never heard of or only whispered as something that might exist – somewhere – but she had never actually seen them before. Dragon's Eye and Magistone were unheard-of-before gems that seemed extremely intriguing and might have some interesting properties, while Elderfruit and Ambrosia were only rumored to exist while she had been Human. She had no idea what any of them did, but with Mana requirements to unlock them from 1 to 100 million, they had to be beneficial for some reason.

"Sandra," Winxa suddenly said as the Dungeon Core was about to move onto something else, feeling almost scatter-brained with the options now open to her. "I was wondering – what are your plans? I'm in no way going to give you advice – for obvious reasons – but I figure it couldn't hurt if you want to share what you have in mind. It might help to sharpen your focus so that you can accomplish what you want to do without getting side-tracked."

It was actually quite amazing how the Dungeon Fairy could guess that; Sandra had to admit that she was starting to get a little overwhelmed with everything going on. From the eight sleeping Gnomes and the unconscious one, the Elf that was supposed to be their watcher almost dying and then bonding with her Core, to the upcoming threat of a dangerous Elite party of Elves coming to destroy her, and of course the reptile-based Dungeon Core that could wake up from its Upgrade at any time and send another army to assault her dungeon – or worse, find another of the nearby races' villages and slaughter them. She counted herself lucky that the other Core hadn't already discovered them, but it was probably because it had to physically send one of its Dungeon Monsters there; for all she knew, the other Core may assume that there weren't any other races around it if it had only seen Gnomes for countless years.

Then again, one of its snakes had almost killed Echo the *Elf*, so they might not be a secret anymore.

Ultimately, I want to save everyone from the dungeons everywhere, but I know that probably isn't possible without some loss of life; the battle at the Gnome village was proof of that fact. I was also slightly underwhelmed by my constructs during the fight; I had thought that they were superior to every other type of Dungeon Monster with their all-metal bodies, but they're just...different. Superior in some ways; weaker in others. If the other Core had been smarter and maybe not as "insane" with trying to kill the Gnomes, I'm not sure if it would've been the same successful outcome.

*So, what I think needs to happen is to establish my presence with the sentient races one at a time as a **good** thing, and not something to be feared. While we're not off to the best start with the Gnomes, they are probably the only ones I can* *actually work with right now. The Orcs – barring if Kelerim suddenly changed all of their minds about me – are out at the moment, I haven't even met a full-blooded Dwarf yet, and the Elves already want to destroy me. But now I have a chance to prove myself to the Gnomes and help them out with what they need to fight back in the future.*

I'm hoping that we'll be able to stave off an attack by the Elves with the aid of one of the Gnomes communicating with them, but if not, I'm hoping that Echo will wake up in time to stop them. Regardless of that, I'm as defended as I'm going to be, and I need to take the opportunity that has been presented with Violet and the others being here. To do that, however, I need to...hmm...

Sandra really didn't know what she needed to do, which was why it was good to explain her plans and really think it over. She knew what *she* wanted – to craft and to learn more enchantments – but she had no way of learning enchantments with the present state of her constructs...or did she? There was a way of preserving even temporary enchantments, though they would have to be used on the same medium as they normally were – Sandra just hoped that Violet had learned the enchantment in her limited time as an Apprentice Enchanter. It required the use of Spirit and Natural elemental energies, so there was a good chance that she had.

Whether or not the Apprentice Gnome knew it, Sandra knew that she needed to make a room where the enchantments could be performed and even stored, until she had some way to practice them. In the future, she even thought it would be possible to preserve enchantments in stasis, so that they could be used as a sort of visual repository for teaching others. The answer was so simple to her that she didn't know why it hadn't been done before; then she remembered the secrecy and unwillingness to share attitudes of most of the Enchanters she had learned from when she was Human. She didn't have to wonder too much after that.

With her plans set – at least for the moment – she told Winxa what she was planning on doing. The Dungeon Fairy seemed surprised, but also approving. "That's a great idea, Sandra – but what are you going to do after that?" she pushed.

After that, I'm going to have to wait for all the Gnomes to wake up, because I'm going to need some questions answered.

"Fair enough," Winxa responded, leaving Sandra to do what she was thinking about.

Using her Dungeon Core abilities, she ate away a large 200X200X10-foot room branching off from her Display and Storage Room, which was the third room up from her Home. It had been previously used as a place to display all of the weapons and armor pieces that she had practiced making over the last month or so, storing it until it was needed. She was still hoping Kelerim would come back and ask for help moving some of them out for Orcrim; if he didn't, they'd still be there in case someone else wanted them.

The new room, however, was empty of any decoration initially. To change that, Sandra used her Mana to create large, solid cylinders – with "arms" of varying lengths and thicknesses sticking out of them like some sort of mutated porcupine, as well as one fully flat side – of different metals, woods, and clays, approximately a foot in diameter and four feet tall. She also made a smaller cylinder about 10% of the size made completely out of Sapphire and Dragon Glass; she wanted them to be the same size, but it was expensive Mana-wise to create even that much of the material. She then had some of her spare constructs she had roaming around her workshops move them into separate areas in the room, so that the types were kept together.

Some enchantment runes were best used – or could only be safely used – on certain types of metal, wood, clay, or gemstones, depending on what they were. These different areas would allow her to keep a record of what worked best on which material, as well as the shape of the rune; if the preservation/static enchantment circle rune – which Sandra prayed that Violet knew – worked the way she hoped, it would also preserve the precise way that the rune was created. That was almost as important as what it looked like, because if you were to place a line out of order, it could change or even destroy the entire enchantment.

Runes came in many different shapes and sizes, but they also didn't always align in two dimensions. While there was a flat side on each cylinder that could take runes that were straight-up flat-formed, the arms sticking out of the Rune Repository Pillars, or RRPs (a name she decided on after looking at them for a while), were there for the three-dimensional type runes. They were common on long swords, staves, and other long objects, where the rune would "wrap" around the material being enchanted. The curved cylinder part of the RRPs would accommodate runes that were used on curved surfaces, usually found on armor and round objects like spheres.

While all of those were being adjusted, Sandra also started the process of stripping some more Raw Bearling Hides to use as leather, because she wanted to include some leather – as well as cloth – RRPs into the Enchantment Repository, because even more enchantments worked best on those materials. She had made the room large enough to hold all of the materials she already had access to – which made her realize she hadn't made a stone one and quickly did that – and she had room to expand it when she acquired even more varieties.

Next was weaving some Cotton and Linen cloth from the Thread she had acquired earlier. She had made an extremely simple-yet-effective warp-weighted loom for the job, where the warp threads were suspended from a top bar and weighted with small Lead weights holding them taut over two heddle frames. She hadn't figured out how to automate the process quite yet using a trap, but once she had a chance to play around with one she thought she might be able to figure it out. Currently, she was going to have to have her Ironclad Ape physically move the pick holding the weft thread back and forth to create the weave; fortunately, her construct didn't get tired and could do the repetitive action standing up without complaint for years if she needed it.

However, before she could really get started, the sun came up and there was movement just outside her dungeon. The figure of an Elf carefully picked his way over the rocky barren wasteland, keeping to the shadows thrown over everything by the sunrise to keep as hidden as possible. Sandra vaguely recognized him from the village, though she didn't know his name – but Echo had greeted him when she had originally returned after visiting her dungeon.

He was obviously looking for something, though he was moving very slow and was extremely careful with his movements. In fact, if it weren't for the fact that she was watching it all from above, she wouldn't have even known he was there – her Mechanical Wolves and Jaguars she had roaming around hadn't made him out. She was a bit paranoid about another attack, though, which was why she had been fairly diligent in watching for any threats outside her entrance.

He crawled close to the ground and almost seemed to be sniffing like some sort of animal, which was unusual to her; whatever ability he had with the use of his elemental energies, however, seemed to be working. He honed on the spot where Echo had been attacked by the venomous snake and collapsed, and where her Ape had picked her up. *He might find a little blood there, but that doesn't mean it's hers—*

And then she saw it as soon as the male Elf did: Echo's bow.

It had fallen away from the dying Elf woman the night before and Sandra had forgotten about it in her hurry to save Echo's life. The Elf quickly scuttled closer while looking around for danger, and he picked up the bow and frowned as he recognized it. Sandra could see him analyzing some tracks left by her Ape when it had come out of her entrance to pick the woman up, the miniscule drops of dried blood spots on the ground from Echo's puncture wounds, as well as the slightly deeper prints leading back to the dungeon. It didn't take him long to come to a conclusion (however wrong it might actually be) and take off again toward his village, holding Echo's bow tight to his body.

Well...that's...not good.

Chapter 27

Violet woke up with the smell of rotting carcasses in her nose; or at least, the rancid remains of an ill-prepared leather hide that wasn't cured properly to maintain its "freshness". She wasn't an expert on tanning and leathermaking, but when she looked at what she was lying on as she sat up, she saw that it appeared well done, but it was lacking the finishing touches that preserved it for longer. What those were, exactly, she didn't know, but she knew that some sort of substance was supposed to help with the process.

Regardless of the smell, the bed was actually quite comfortable; she didn't remember waking up at all after she lay down...*last night?* It was impossible to tell, unfortunately, because the light in the rooms was the steady source-less illumination she was told that all dungeons had in each room. From what she could tell, it might've been only hours since she fell asleep, or it could've been days – it was impossible to tell; judging by how refreshed she was, she figured she had slept 8-9 hours straight.

Violet peered around the room at the others still sleeping, passed out from the night before and looking like they had fallen into bed and not moved since then – almost like they had passed on and joined the Creator. She suddenly remembered all of those that had perished because of a sudden dungeon raid just the day before, and that everyone she saw there were the only ones left. Well, not everybody; Felbar wasn't in the room, but she supposed he was still lying unconscious in the other room. Next to an Elf, to boot – *he's going to rant and rave as soon as he finds out he was sleeping with an Elf!*

* Good morning, Violet. Did you sleep well? *

The voice in her head startled her, as she had momentarily forgotten the voice of the dungeon, Sandra. Everything else about yesterday came flooding back, and she straightened up on her bed as she tried to comprehend where she was and what it meant that they were still alive in the dungeon. She half-expected – even after all the Dungeon Core had demonstrated to them – that she wouldn't wake up in the morning...or whenever it was.

"Yes, I did actually. I'm hungry again, though," Violet whispered, not wanting to wake the others up if they weren't ready to get up yet. *Let them sleep – yesterday was a day none of us want to remember.* Of course, her attempt at being quiet didn't work too well, as it was completely silent in the room and it woke one of them up.

She couldn't blame Saryn, honestly, for waking up screaming; the horrors of the previous day were enough to want to do the same thing. She just wished he wasn't so loud that everyone else woke up screaming and looking around in fright. At that moment, of course, one of the metal monkeys walked into their room carrying a tray full of food.

Jortor immediately stopped screaming when he smelled the cooked meat and halved oranges on the large tray. "Ooh, don't mind if I do."

Jortor and his food, Violet couldn't help but inwardly chuckle at his overwhelming love of eating. Though, you couldn't tell by looking at him; for as much as he ate, he sometimes looked like he was half-starving.

* Sorry about that, everyone – I didn't mean to startle you. Here, eat up. We have a long day ahead of us. *

Everyone had stopped screaming by that point, and she dug into the meal just as quickly as the others; she didn't think she'd be that starved after just eating the night before, but she was practically ravenous. Or it could be because everything smelled so fresh and delicious, whereas they usually had to get food like what they were eating delivered to them from the capital.

"What do you mean about a long day? What are you going to do with us?" Violet asked, concerned.

** Don't worry, it's nothing **too** strenuous, at least I don't hope so. I have need of your enchanting abilities. When you're finished,*

*we'll talk about what you're going to do today as you follow my Ironclad Ape, and what I can do to help you. ***

That was something she could do at least. Violet finished stuffing her face around the same time as the others and followed the Ape out of the room. The air felt fresher as soon as she stepped out and she was thankful that the rotting smell of leather was confined to the other room; with a sniff at her clothes, however, she realized that some was going to linger on her for a little while. They passed through the blacksmith's forge and to the kitchen-type room where she saw Felbar and the Elf unconscious side-by-side, a *Repair Drone* – if she got the name right – hovering nearby both of them.

"How long did you say he's going to be out?" she asked, worried that his condition hadn't changed even a little bit.

* The last time something like this happened, Kelerim was unconscious for approximately two weeks. His injury was to his head, however, so I don't know if that played a factor in the length of time or not. *

Sandra had mentioned Kelerim at some point the night before, but Violet was still too scatter-brained at the moment to recall it properly. She guessed that it didn't really matter in the long run, though, so she put it out of her mind. *I hope he isn't out that long. I could really use his guidance – the sooner, the better.*

They passed through some semi-familiar rooms on the way to the growing room where they had seen orange trees grow in a matter of hours instead of years – and then went past it to someplace new. The next room looked to be some sort of pottery-making space with a kiln and everything set up, though it didn't look like it had really been used yet. After that was a woodworking workshop, filled with strange cutting implements and the smell of sawdust in the air.

All the while they were heading downwards, Violet and the others were having a conversation with the voice in their heads.

* First, we're going to a new room that I just created; once we get there, I'll explain what's going on with it and what I need all of your help with. Until then, I have a few questions for you. The most important one, for me at least, is: do any of you know how to speak or write in Elven? *

That's an odd question. Violet looked at the others with a question in her gaze, though she thought she already knew the answer. They all shook their heads in response – it was just as she thought. "No, none of us do. It's possible that Felbar might, as he's been around longer than any of us, and it always seems

289

there's no end to his knowledge. Why do you want someone to speak Elven?"

Violet actually thought she heard the Dungeon Core sigh in her head before she heard a response.

*Well, I'm pretty sure the Elven village nearby thinks I've either killed Echo – the unconscious Elf lying near Felbar – or have her captive here. I have no way of communicating what had actually happened, and this just makes the likelihood of them attacking when the Elites arrive more of a certainty. *

"Why don't you just have one of your...constructs?...bring her back?" That seemed like the most logical solution to Violet.

*I'm worried what will happen to her outside my dungeon after she leaves; the Visitor Bond I was forced to create with her might not be fully complete yet, which is why I think she – and Felbar – are still unconscious. My Repair Drone is also keeping them both alive, as well, because they can't eat or drink anything right now. If I return her, there's a good possibility that she could die if they can't sustain her body during this process. *

Violet thought that made sense; it wouldn't be good to return the Elf with strange markings on her face – very similar to the ones Violet had on her hands – only to have her waste away and die within a week or two. "Okay. So, what's your plan, then?"

*Well, I was wondering if any of you would volunteer to go to the Elven village and speak to them for me. To tell them that Echo is alright and that she is recovering, as well as that I'm not a threat to them and that they don't need to attack me. My hope is that someone there speaks Gnome, as they are quite long-lived and are likely to know other languages. *

Of course, none of them volunteered. Even the prospect of leaving the dungeon wasn't enough for them to risk going into another peoples' territory; everyone knew that the Elves killed any intruders to their lands. "We'll see. I don't know if it will be safe to go, and it'll probably take half a day just to walk there," Violet said uncertainly.

*Don't worry about that; whoever goes can ride one of my Mechanical Wolves to get there much faster. That's all for a little later, anyway, so we can see if we have any volunteers then. Before we get to the new Enchantment Repository, I want to tell you what I can do to help you all out. I want to provide you with whatever supplies your people need to continue to fight against the other Dungeon Monsters throughout your land. You've already seen that I can provide pure Steel, but I can provide various woods, Linen and Cotton thread, and various other materials. The only problem would be transportation. *

"That sounds wonderful; those supplies will really help out, especially since Glimmerton...no longer exists," Violet choked out, the memory of dozens of her friends dying in the field flashing through her mind. "But what do you mean about transportation? You can just have one of your monsters pull a simple wagon and—"

* Unfortunately, my constructs can only travel a little bit past your village, as my Area of Influence only extends that far. *

That certainly wouldn't work, then. Violet felt like they had just discovered a massive cache of valuable materials...but couldn't bring it back home because it was too much and too heavy to carry. What they could carry on their backs would barely be what the village could harvest in a week and transporting it by foot would take forever — even if they were able to obtain a ride to the village. If only they had some Haulers...

"Wait — I think I have an idea. It's going to take a bit of work, but if you really can help with the crafting part of it, I think I may have a solution. We use special Haulers to move large shipments of materials; if you can help make one of them, I think I can figure out how to enchant it. It uses a basic input

feedback system, which I was just starting to learn when..."
Violet trailed off as she remembered the devastation she had
come back to after the complete destruction of the ELA. *So
much tragedy has happened to me over the last few years that
I'm not sure if I can handle any more.*

** That would help immensely; all I would need is some idea of
what it needs to look like, and I can help with that part. Which
brings up another question – how many different enchanted
machines do your people use? **

"Oh, we use quite a few, though only a few of them are
big enough to transport people/goods or to fight for us against
the monster scourge. The War Machines you saw before are
used primarily for culling and harvesting materials outside of a
dungeon; they aren't the largest, either – but they
are...*were*...suitable for what we needed near here. We also use
a much smaller version called a Deep Delver for...uh...destroying
dungeons, as the larger War Machines wouldn't be able to fit
inside the rooms and tunnels. We have very few of them left,
unfortunately, as many of them were destroyed unpiloted at the
ELA when it fell, as they were undergoing routine maintenance
at the time. There are a few others, but along with the Haulers,
that is the majority of the ones we use," Lankas spoke up for the
first time.

Violet looked at him in thanks, as she didn't want to mention the destruction of the ELA again. Each of the others that had survived the fall of Glimmerton had a little something to do with the normal maintenance of the War Machines and had to deal with Haulers frequently as they helped to receive supplies and ship out the village's harvested materials. While they didn't necessarily *build* the machines, they knew their forms fairly well; their enchantments, however, fell under Violet's purview.

* One last question before you arrive at the Enchantment Repository: Violet, do you know how to create a Preservation Barrier? *

"A Preservation Barrier? Is that like a Stasis Field? As in, a field that will keep most objects inside it from experiencing the passage of time?" Violet asked, confused by the terminology. The Stasis Field was a common enchantment, used commonly even in transporting foodstuffs, as it prevented the food from rotting and was kept as fresh as it was when it was put inside the Field. It only worked on non-living objects, though, so plants, animals, and Gnomes wouldn't be affected by the Field.

After Sandra confirmed that they were one and the same, Violet said, "Well, yes – I can make one of them. But what do you want to use it on? Based on what I saw yesterday, I doubt you want to preserve food for any length of time, as you can just make more of it with...whatever you're using to do that."

Following the metal monkey, they passed into another room that had racks and piles of weapons of every discernable shape and size, collections of full-metal armor pieces, and other things she didn't even recognize. There was enough weaponry there to practically outfit an armory, and most of it looked to be extremely well-made – if not masterwork quality.

*This is my display and storage room – I think I told you that I like to craft, and this is a result of a couple of weeks of crafting. Anyway, we're almost to our destination; you'll see what the...Stasis Field...will be used for in just a moment. *

She could barely tear her eyes away from the insane number of weapons in the dungeon's armory, but when she did, they were already walking through another tunnel. When they finally emerged into another, larger room, she looked at the multi-armed cylinders made from different materials scattered around the space.

*Alright, here we are. Let me explain how this is going to work... *

Chapter 28

Sandra was relieved that Violet was able to create the Protection Barrier – or Stasis Field – enchantment, otherwise none of what she had planned in the Enchantment Repository would work. *Yet*, at least; Sandra still planned on eventually acquiring a monster from another Classification that would allow her to craft enchantments herself. Still, the fact that Violet could do it would make the whole process much easier.

She explained what the purpose of the room was, how it was to work, and how she desired for it to be a sort of "library" of enchantment knowledge that could be used to teach others. While the Gnomes were able to create enchantments as easy as breathing, they didn't always have the learning and experience needed to make *everything*; from what was explained to her through a combination of speaking to Winxa and conversing with Violet, most Gnomes knew maybe five to ten enchantments using their specific elemental energy, with half of those being only temporary. The rest that they knew were permanent utility enchantments ranging from a simple rune that would repel dust off of a surface to a slightly more complex rune that would keep pests away from a building.

"That's...quite genius, actually. I can see how that would work to preserve even the temporary enchantments, while also not letting them activate in the first place because of the Stasis

Field. However, I'm worried that a Field the size you need will consume quite a bit of energy; I can set four or five up quite easily, but I don't have enough Spirit energy to finish the rest. That, and the Stasis enchantments will only last I'd say...hmm...about a week, give or take a day."

That was going to be a problem, especially since she wanted to keep the RRPs around for a long time to preserve that knowledge. The only Preservation Barriers she had personal experience with were much smaller, though, which was probably why she had thought they would last for years or decades; apparently, the bigger they were, the more energy they consumed to maintain the Barrier – or Field. *I guess it makes sense why something like this wasn't ever done back when I was Human; from what I remember, the Barriers can't be recharged once they are formed, though an additional one can be formed over the previous enchantment.* While that was an option, forming another Stasis Field would disrupt the first one and it would take a few seconds for the new Field to establish itself. It didn't matter too much for things like food to be out of the field for a few seconds, but she wasn't sure what it would do for the enchantments – especially the temporary ones. That, and the Field would suspend the rune and prevent it from activating; any disruption would possibly cause dozens of enchantments – or more – to activate at the same time, which could be harmless...or catastrophic.

*We'll cross that bridge when we come to it. For now, if you could craft a Stasis Field on the Steel cylinder right there, I would love to see if it will work. *

Violet shrugged her shoulders and walked over to Sandra's multi-armed Steel RRP and started the process of creating a Stasis Field. It was a Spirit-based enchantment, so Sandra had figured that the Gnome had knowledge of it – and she was glad she was right. She watched, fascinated, as Violet worked quickly and efficiently. Sandra always enjoyed watching crafters at work, and enchanting was no exception.

A line of light-grey glowing Spirit energy seemed to spill out of Violet's right finger as she traced a large circle on the floor that encompassed the entire RRP, including the arms extending outward. It was slightly larger than necessary, probably, but it appeared that the Gnome was ensuring that if the cylinder was shifted even an inch that it would still contain everything that was currently inside the Field.

Once the circle was drawn on the ground, she extended her hands above her head and drew another circle in the middle of the air, tracing the same path the circle on the floor followed. When she was done with that, she started to create simple runes that floated in the air at about chest height on her, again following the same circular path as the circles before. The runes were two-dimensional, though they weren't necessarily flat;

they curved slightly, as if they were drawn on the side of a large cylinder similar to the Steel one inside the field.

That was, in fact, essentially what was being created – a large cylinder made of Spirit elemental energy that would preserve anything inside. The runes were all connected to one another as there was no break in between them – and Violet expertly continued to create them around the entire outside of the Field, before eventually connecting it to where she began. By the time she was done – about 15 minutes later – the entire column of Spirit energy was filled with three simple repeated runes that were flawlessly executed. *Gnomes really **are** naturals at enchantments; if she was just an Apprentice, I can't even imagine what a Master could do.* While Sandra knew many, many enchantments, she'd never actually made one before and she didn't think she'd have that same sort of expertise as Violet showed.

The cylinder of glowing elemental energy flashed brightly once when the Gnome was complete, before collapsing down to the floor in activation of the Stasis Field. Now, around the entire RRP, the circle that was drawn earlier was filled in with the same runes that Violet had just crafted around the outside, as if it had been squashed flat and was now covering the stone floor inside the circle. It glowed the steady grey color of a Spirit enchantment, and Sandra had no doubt that it would work perfectly.

Violet sagged a little bit when the enchantment activated and blew out a big breath. "That took a little more out of me than I thought; I've never created one that large before – they are usually made to encompass something the size of a small crate, which uses much less energy to create. I might be able to do another two, but that'll probably be it for today."

*Nice job and perfect execution! Rest a little bit and don't worry about doing any more for now, I want to make sure it's working. Ok, the rest of you, I want you to craft whatever enchantments – permanent or temporary – that you know works best with Steel and place them somewhere on the Rune Repository Pillar. *

Sandra further explained the nature of the arms and the flat sections, and Jortor immediately stepped up to the RRP. He extended his finger against one of the thinner arms sticking out and started quickly tracing Nether elemental energy around it in a fairly simple rune. The rune almost appeared to be shaped like a shield with a tapered oval on the face of the shield; it wasn't overly complex, but Sandra thought it would take her at least 15 seconds to craft it accurately. Jortor, however, was able to make it in just over a second, showing how natural the entire enchanting process was to not just him but Gnomes in general.

The rune looked vaguely familiar to Sandra, and after a moment she realized that Jortor was the one she had seen use his Nether energy to create a shield of darkness that blinded a crocodile when it was struck. Most runes weren't exactly that literal when it came to their form, but this one appeared to be a fairly accurate representation of what it did.

Jortor stepped back and looked at his enchantment, and the others stepped up to see what was happening as well. It was slightly difficult to see it within the black-colored Nether energy that characterized the element, but there was a slight directional flow in the glowing rune pattern, which followed the same path the Gnome had taken to create the enchantment. Looking at it for a few moments, Sandra was easily able to see where his finger started, where it went next, and all the way up to where it was finished.

"How does it do that? Better yet, how did you know it would do that? I've never seen anything like it before," Violet asked in wonder as she too stared at the glowing rune.

*It was kind of a lucky guess, actually. I hypothesized that the Stasis Field would capture the exact form of the enchantment before it sunk down into the material, activating it at the same time; however, I guessed – and hoped – that it would capture the directional energy flow as it was created. It turns out that I was right, thankfully. *

Sandra knew that it wasn't just the way an enchantment rune looked like that mattered if it would work or not; it was *how* it was created that mattered almost as much. That was the main reason there were very few simple runes that were recorded in books with detailed instructions; anything more complex had to be seen being constructed to know the proper way to craft it.

Temporary enchantments didn't last very long, sometimes as much as a couple of minutes, so everyone was excited to see that the enchantment Jortor had made was still as strong and intact even ten minutes later. As soon as they saw that, everyone except Violet crafted their own temporary enchantments on the Steel RRP, only stepping back when they were done.

Colors from every element except for the grey of Spirit encompassed the runes covering about a third of the RRP; black, yellow, green, red, blue, white, and brown represented Nether, Air, Natural, Fire, Water, Holy, and Earth, respectively. All in all, it appeared as though each of the Gnomes had been able to add two temporary enchantments that were best used on Steel; it wasn't as though they couldn't use other runes on the material, but they wouldn't be as effective. For her repository to make sense, Sandra thought it was best to separate the enchantments based on material, instead of by use or even by element. She figured if she had the opportunity in the future, she would be able to make some sort of chart to cross-reference them all, but there wasn't nearly enough in the room to need something like that...yet.

After conferring together, they all decided that Oak wood and – strangely enough – Copper were the two materials they had enchantments best for, so Violet created another two Stasis Fields on those two RRPs. When she was all done, she sat down on the floor looking exhausted, while the others went to work placing enchantments – some permanent, even – onto the cylinders wherever they could.

During that whole process inside the Enchantment Repository, Sandra had her mind split up and work on another project. It was simple at first, as she was only clearing away rock and dirt; which, when she really looked at how fast she could clear it away now compared to when she first became a Dungeon Core, she realized that it was nearly 20 times as fast...

"Yes, your Core Size does affect how fast you can clear out and create a new room; I had thought you would've realized that by now," Winxa told her with a smile, taking any sting away from her words as she listened in on Sandra's internal conversation.

That's beneficial, at least. By the time the Gnomes had finished enchanting all that they could – crafting just under 50 enchanting runes that were suspended in stasis, Sandra was done clearing her new room. She looked over the RRPs and saw that most of the permanent enchantments she already knew; on the flipside, however, almost all of the temporary enchantment runes were new to her. Overall, it was a great start to her Enchantment Repository.

Now it was time to repay the help they provided with something only Sandra could provide: a way home.

Chapter 29

A trip back to the Gnome homeland wasn't an easy affair, however. While Sandra could easily create supplies for them to take back, transportation – as she had told Violet earlier – was an entirely different affair. Making wagons were easy enough; with her Mundane Object Creation skill, she could easily produce the components necessary to put them together. The skill didn't lend itself to just creating an entire wagon out of nothing as it technically had "moving parts", but the simple components were easy enough to create out of wood using Mana. All they had to do was put it together.

She created a 4-inch-thick, 5-foot-wide, and 8-foot-long wooden sheet of stout Oak wood to be used as the baseboard for the wagon, and then created 2-foot-wide planks that would attach to the side of it so that it would look like a large open-topped box. Four inch-thick solid Steel wheels and two Steel axles rounded out the major components, of what was needed; they were a bit on the heavy side, but it was balanced out for the need to have something that could travel over the extremely rough terrain of the wastelands before even getting to the Gnome village and beyond.

There were other, smaller components that were needed, of course; long and short Steel braces for underneath the carriage, Steel pins to keep the wheels on the axles, Steel bolsters and clips, and other minor – yet important – parts. She had spent an entire day watching a wheelwright and a carpenter making a wagon one day, though she planned on cheating quite a bit in the process compared to what they had to go through. First off, she didn't plan on attempting to weld anything, nor was she planning on having her constructs hammering hundreds of nails into it.

She didn't have time for that.

Sandra had built her new room directly across from the hidden VATS access door in the tunnel after the second room. All she did was cut out another tunnel going *outwards* from her normal defensive rooms and then created a large 200X200X30-foot room that contained a small forge – just in case – and a large area where she could start accumulating supplies to place in the wagons once they were done. The first of which was just beginning to get assembled when the Gnomes had taken a ride up the VATS from down below and walked into Sandra's new Assembly and Staging room.

She had created it so near the surface for one reason, and one reason alone: she couldn't fit a wagon through her normal dungeon tunnels. Winxa mentioned that most of the other Cores, when they got access to Dungeon Monsters such as the Ancient Saurians, they built another, larger tunnel leading from their Core Room to their first room near the surface, and then they just made their entrance tunnel larger. They would then seal it off with a stone wall when they didn't need it by

306

using a bit of Mana, so that they wouldn't leave direct access to their Core. It apparently worked and didn't violate any rules, because there was still a route to get to their Core through the regular defensive dungeon rooms.

That wasn't something that Sandra wanted to even contemplate, however. If, for some reason, an invader somehow got inside when that large tunnel was open, there would be very little stopping anyone from reaching her Dungeon Core. And – unless you filled up the entire tunnel with stone – an invader powerful enough could potentially break down the stone wall and gain access that way. Neither of those seemed like a great idea, so she chose to abandon any hope of moving her Behemoths out from far down below and instead opted to make it easier to reach the surface from the new room. Instead of going through the main entrance, however, she created an exit that actually emerged inside the Bearlings' old lair, though it was mostly hidden behind a hard-to-see turn in the stone wall surface.

Even if someone found it, all they would bypass in her dungeon were the first two rooms. If that happened, though, she would move all of her constructs from those two rooms and fill up the third, making it much harder for anyone to advance down from there. It wasn't perfect, but it was the best solution she could think of.

When the Gnomes walked in after doing their best to fill up Sandra's RRPs with enchantments, they found four Ironclad

Apes holding different components together while she applied some of her Core abilities to fuse them together with an application of Mana and Raw Materials. No hammers, no nails, and no welds were needed; in essence, it was cheating the crafting a little bit, but she was now on a time constraint.

Because she wanted to be done before the other Core finished its upgrade. It was more than possible that as soon as it finished upgrading its Core Size it would send all of its Dungeon Monsters out again, making travel next to impossible. It might take all night, but Sandra was hoping to have everything built and ready to go by morning. The Enchanting might take a little longer, but hopefully not too long.

"What are they doing? And *how* are they doing that?" Violet asked, as soon as she saw the pieces joining together without any obvious methods.

*They're building a very nice, sturdy wagon to transport you and many of the supplies I told you I'd create for you. You can see what I mean over there in the corner. *

Indeed, the rapid influx of Mana from her AMANS made it possible for Sandra to turn most of the Raw Materials she had absorbed from the creation of the newest room into supplies for the Gnomes to take back with them. There were bars of Copper, Iron, Steel, Silver, and Gold — all useful for different applications — stacked up in neat piles up against the wall, with Steel being the most numerous of the groupings. Planks of pristine Redwood and Yew wood were stacked up in large piles, a few thin plates of Dragon Glass, and even some Skeins of Cotton Thread that she had just decided to spend some of those incoming resources to unlock were there. When she looked it up, she found that it didn't cost that much to unlock them all.

Monster Seed Origination				
Name:	Raw Material Cost:	Mana Cost:	Min. Mana:	Max. Mana:
Tiny Cotton Thread Bobbin	15	10	10	20
Locked Seeds:	Unlock Requirements:	Mana Cost to Unlock:	Min. Mana:	Max. Mana:
Small Cotton Thread Spindle	2 Tiny Cotton Thread Bobbins	20	10	40
Average Cotton Thread Spool	4 Small Cotton Thread Spindles	80	10	160
Large Cotton Thread Skein	2 Average Cotton Thread Spools	160	10	320

The Linen Thread she could create was even less expensive in terms of resources, so she unlocked those as well and included those with the growing pile of supplies being held inside the room. She first tried to use her ability to create the material, but it ended up in a large pile instead of an organized Bobbin, Spindle, Spool, or Skein like the Monster Seeds, so she ended up making the Seeds and using a few nearby constructs to transport them above. They were relatively inexpensive even for the largest size, so it was no hardship on her resource wallet.

*As for how they're putting them together, I'm using one of my abilities to sort of weld together the pieces, so that we don't have to waste time with the construction. Don't worry about them, though; I need to know what I have to provide so that we can make one of these "Haulers" you told me about. This wagon isn't going to pull itself, after all. *

"Right, yes, we can do that," Violet said, after watching with fascination how easily Sandra's Apes were moving the thick wooden bed of the wagon around, as well as the thick steel braces and wheels. Sandra didn't really have the best grease for allowing the wheels to turn without too much friction, but she figured that the thick oily grease from all the Bearling meat she had cooked earlier would have to do for now.

Now that she had access to wood, Sandra hoped that she could make paper for the Gnomes to help create a blueprint of sorts to draw what was needed. Alas, it was apparently an object that needed to be created first, as it didn't appear when she thought about making it via her Mundane Object Creation; she figured it was the same as not being able to make cloth now that she had Thread – both were essentially next-stage products and needed to be created first. Therefore, instead of paper, she provided them with various sizes of pure Maple wood boards, which had a very even blondish color to it, making it easy to see marks left by the small coal pencils she also provided to the Gnomes.

None of them were artists – or even particularly good at drawing – but when there were eight of them trying to draw the same things, Sandra got a fairly good idea of what it was going to look like. In the end, it was fairly simple in design, but she thought it was going to be difficult to execute.

In its simplest form, a Hauler was a box attached to two rotating spiked metal bands on either side of it. The somehow-flexible bands – which also had holes in them periodically -- were affixed to smaller gears that stuck into the holes and propelled the machine forward. There was a platform for a Gnome to stand on cut into the backside of the box, with two vertical rotating "steering wheels" – or at least that's what the Gnomes called them. When the operator on top of the box wanted to move the Hauler forward, they would rotate both wheels forward at the same time; if they wanted to turn left or right, they had to rotate just a single wheel; if they wanted to back up, they rotated both wheels backwards.

The way the enchantment worked was through what Violet called an "input feedback system", which was completely new to Sandra – and she was eager to learn what it was all about. If she understood the theory behind it, two Spirit-based enchantments would be paired together in a uni-directional matter, where what you did to one object happened to the other – but not the other way around. Therefore, as you turned one steering wheel, it would rotate the paired gear connected to the band, which would then rotate the band forward – and thus the machine. It only worked one way, however, so that anything happening to the gear below wouldn't transfer back to the steering wheel.

Frankly, Sandra thought it was genius.

"In its very basic form, the input feedback system is what allows our other combat-oriented creations – like the War Machines you saw before – to work, though those are done on a massively complex scale. It would be like trying to compare a shoddy iron dagger that a novice blacksmith attempted to make, to a masterwork mithril short sword that a master at their craft could present. While I'm not exactly a 'novice', I'm nowhere near being able to create that kind of complexity yet. At best, I can help maintain and repair what's already there, but designing and putting together something like that boggles my mind," Violet explained.

*But you think you can put the enchantments on a Hauler together? *

The little Gnome hesitated only for a moment before replying. "Yes, I believe so. I know the basic principles behind it, and I was able to put together a simple feedback system on a model back at the ELA."

With that being just about all the reassurances she was going to get, Sandra got started creating parts for the new Hauler. While she was at it, she spat out parts to make two more wagons; she figured if the Hauler worked the way it was supposed to, then she could link all three wagons together so that they could take as many supplies as they could.

Sandra's father always said that you never get a second chance to make a good first impression; she was just hoping that providing everything she possibly could would negate some of the bad that came from her first meeting with the Gnomes. And if it worked, she wasn't above using the same "gifting" tactic with the other races.

Chapter 30

Fortunately for them all, everyone except for Violet knew the band or "track" system on the Haulers fairly well. They were frequently called upon to replace worn or broken segments of the track, so they were able to describe and partially draw what they looked like. It took a bit of trial and error, but they all breathed a sigh of relief when Sandra was finally able to make a piece that looked exactly like what they needed. The fact that it was made out of pure steel of dungeon-loot-quality meant that it was less likely to need repairs in the future; from her limited knowledge of their construction, Violet didn't think the precious resource had ever been used for Hauler tracks. They were usually made from iron, which had a greater tendency to crack and break than steel would.

The amount of steel in the tracks alone amounted to nearly a year's worth of culling and harvesting the resource from the nearby forest. Unless they were desperate for more machines to haul things in the capital, Violet thought they would probably cannibalize this creation for its parts.

For the most part, she stayed out of the conversation and arguments over how it was supposed to look and how it was put together, as she didn't really work with Haulers like that. Instead of listening to them describe what the pins that would connect the track pieces together looked like in detail, she rested in the corner to recharge some of her Spirit elemental energy for the upcoming enchantments she was going to be creating later. She still had plenty of Natural energy left, but the feedback system was entirely Spirit-based; the more complex machines required multiple elements to get them to work properly, which usually meant *at least* two Master Enchanters working on it together – *if* they each had access to three or more different elements.

That was rare, however, so the most common number that used to work on those feedback systems were four. That was the main reason her people were in trouble, actually; while there were some retired Master Enchanters still alive to teach what they knew, they couldn't teach using a hands-on approach – because there weren't even enough of them to create even a single War Machine. With some help from the Journeymen Enchanters they could get by, but it would take longer – and then they wouldn't have time to teach. There was no simple solution other than to train as many that had the aptitude as they could and hope for the best.

Which was why Violet had been both reluctant and eager to work with Sandra, if only for the chance of changing that. She wasn't really looking forward to teaching and learning from the same entity that practically orchestrated the destruction of Glimmerton, but she resolved to see it through in the off chance that some good could come from it. She didn't think she'd ever be able to *forget* what happened, but over time she thought she might be able to *forgive* her. Maybe...the verdict was still out on that one.

And supplying all of the material she could see stacked up along the corner wall to them for free, as well as allowing them to return home, would go a long way toward that forgiveness.

At some point during the construction of the Hauler, Violet fell asleep. The enchanting she had done on those strange "Repository" pillars had fairly wiped her out with the sheer size of the enchantments, as it took a lot more out of her than she was expecting. She hadn't wanted to admit it at the time, but that last one nearly depleted every drop of Spirit elemental energy she had in her body. It would come back with rest, she knew, which was probably why she had been so tired – and had been able to sleep even through all of the arguments and loud noises as the machine was put together.

When she woke up later, only the squeak of springs echoed through the room as some of the metal apes finished loading the transports with supplies. She was surprised to see that there were now *three* of the wagons that she had seen being constructed earlier, and all but the last were heavily laden with all types of precious materials. Violet got up and walked over to one of the full ones, using a little ladder permanently attached to the end to look inside.

Bars of different types of metals, with steel in the greatest quantity, were evenly distributed on the wagon – along with a myriad of other materials from high-quality wooden boards to skeins of thread – and held in place by additional wooden boards that crossed the bed of the wagon. They were all loose and not packed in small crates like she usually saw, but that was fine; she just had to make sure that they were covered with something to prevent any from flying out later while on the move.

*Don't worry, I'm planning on sealing it all up once it's all ready to go, as well as providing a place for everyone to sit. *

Sandra's voice in her head startled her for just a moment, but she recovered before she lost her grip on the side of the wagon and fell off. "This...is a lot. Are you sure we can just take all of this?" Now that she had a chance to see it all loaded up on the wagons, it was a literal treasure trove of material the likes of which she had never seen before.

*Absolutely, it's not really a hardship to create all of this for you, and I want you all to succeed. As contrary as it sounds coming from a Dungeon Core, I really do want you to thrive and fight back against the dungeons that are surrounding your people. If this all works out, I'm hoping this will establish a relationship between us that will benefit us both greatly. *

That last statement gave Violet pause as she hopped down from the back of the wagon. "How would we benefit you, especially when you can do all—" she waved her hands at everything in the room— "this by yourself?"

*For one, I would love to learn more about the way you enchant your machines, as it is almost entirely unfamiliar to me. I told you I have a passion for crafting, and learning as much as I can from various sources such as yourself feeds that passion. And, two, well...I'm hoping that – in the future – helping you now to get a handle on your dungeon monster problem will free you up to help the other races around here. It's not just the Gnomes that are in danger of being wiped out over the next few decades or centuries; the Elves, Orcs, and Dwarves are threatened as well. *

"Why should we help them when they didn't help us?" Violet demanded, as her people's prejudices against the nearby races were instilled into her from a young age. She was never told specifics of why they didn't deal with the other races anymore, but it had obviously been significant enough to warrant instructions not to have any contact with any of them.

*If they are abandoned to their fate, which will happen sooner or later if nothing is done to help them, then it won't be long before the Cores there will turn their attention to your people.

*I'm not asking for anything now, especially since you are all still in danger of being wiped out yourselves, but I have a feeling every race will have to work together to stop themselves from being annihilated. ***

Violet was incredulous. *Work together? Impossible.* She didn't think that was ever likely, but she was willing to humor the possibility if it allowed her people – and her friends that were in the dungeon with her – to survive. Thinking of those trapped in the dungeon along with her made her look around for any sight of them. "Where are Jortor and the others?" she asked, changing the subject.

* They are asleep down below; they worked hard to help finish the Hauler while you were sleeping. *

The mention of the entire point of her presence in the room made her feel guilty for sleeping while the others worked. However, one sight at the machine made her forget feeling guilty; instead, she felt pride at what her people had accomplished – because, as uniform and unadorned as it was, the Hauler was a work of art.

The tracks along the box were brand-new pure shining steel, perfectly placed along the gears that would allow them to turn. The spikes that were usually attached to the outside of the tracks were reduced down to numerous nubs instead; there were more of them than usual, but they also appeared as if they would work even better – and likely not tear up the ground like Haulers usually did. The Pilot Carriage was a perfectly sealed wooden box with no seams that she could see, with a thick steel undercarriage that was connected to the track axles. There was a portion of the Carriage that was cut out, where someone could stand and turn the two steering wheels that were attached to the sides of the cut-out portion. The steering wheels themselves looked to be made of a solid piece of lightweight wood, which would help whoever was controlling it turn the wheels without getting too tired. There was also a heavy-duty-looking hitch connected to the steel undercarriage, which looked plenty sturdy enough to connect to the wagons it was slated to pull.

Now all she had to do was make sure it worked.

Are you sure you're up for this? Do you need to rest more to recharge your energy?

It still felt a little strange hearing a dungeon asking about her energy and well-being; it was quite different from the normal impression she got from dungeons being hungry, murderous entities. Everyone knew they were "alive" in a sense, but she didn't think anyone knew the exact extent of their actual natures. If Sandra could be believed, of course.

"I'm as recovered from earlier as I can be. Let me see what I can do," she responded with only a little bit of false confidence. Violet knew what she was doing, at least in theory if not with much practice, so she was pretty sure she would succeed. How long it would take to achieve that success was another matter.

All in all, she was going to have to create three different enchantments – for each steering wheel. Fortunately, they were much smaller enchantments than the Stasis Fields she had created that morning – *or was it the day before by that point?* – so they wouldn't take as much energy to construct, but they were a bit more complex. One enchantment would go on the steering wheel, another on the gear below that would turn the tracks, and the last would connect the two together. The hardest part of all of it, however, was that she had to hold all three rune sequences together before she let it go, otherwise it would fail and fall apart.

Violet mentally prepared herself by going over the runes she needed to form, which had been drilled into her repeatedly when she was younger. She had also had the opportunity to repair or strengthen many of the runes on the village's War Machines, so the right pattern was fairly imprinted in her mind. Without giving herself a chance to psych herself out, she climbed up on the back of the Hauler and looked at the left steering wheel; using both hands this time, she willed her Spirit elemental energy out to two index fingertips – one on each hand – and started drawing the rune sequences she needed.

She took her time, because she didn't want to make a mistake. Strangely enough, she could *almost* feel a physical presence intently watching her work, and she stiffened up and stopped for a moment; soon enough, though, she realized that it was probably just Sandra learning from her – which was confirmed a moment later.

* Sorry about that; I just learned that I can sort of "lean" on the Visitor Bond to connect to your movements a little more. It's entirely observational, however, so there's nothing to worry about. *

Whenever someone said there was nothing to worry about, that usually meant that there was. Unfortunately, there was nothing she could do at that point but to continue her enchantments; she had already gone that far, so she might as well finish. Three different-sized concentric circles made of her Spirit energy floated over the steering wheel, and from that point she added smaller runes inside the circles; one rune looked like a tight spiral, another looked like six horns stuck together at the same point, and a third looked like little lightning bolts. They all had technical names, of course, but that was how she always thought of them.

The tight spiral – or "Rotational" – runes was fairly obvious in its purpose; it designated that a turning or rotation of the object being enchanted was a factor in its purpose. The six-horned – or "Adherence" – runes told the enchantment that it was to stay attached only to what was designated by the concentric circles she created earlier. Lastly, the little lightning bolt – or "Power" – runes were essential in the piloting process, as it designated how much power was needed to turn the steering wheels and have it mirrored by the gears below. It didn't make a whole lot of sense for it to be a one-to-one ratio; the Hauler pilot would quickly grow tired if they had to make a full rotation of the wheel to get the gear to rotate a single time.

Holding the rune sequence in place with her mind when it was finished, she jumped down and walked to the front left gear and started the process over again. The gear itself was almost as tall as she was, so it took a little longer to complete than the steering wheel, but she got it done, matching it up perfectly – though larger – to the one she did before. The strain of keeping both enchantment rune sequences was starting to make itself felt in her body, as her hands began to shake just a little.

Clamping down on the shakes with a firm resolve, Violet drew the simple linking runes – a series of "Transference" runes that looked like sideways ladders filled with various basic symbols – connecting the two rune sequences together, running it along the outside of the Pilot Carriage. Her hands were beginning to shake a little more by the time she was done, but she managed to complete the final rune without making any mistakes. As soon as she finished, she allowed the entire enchantment to complete – and took a few steps back at the same time. She had never attempted to create anything that complex before – small-scale models didn't count – and she worried that she hadn't done it correctly.

Incorrect runes could be harmless and just fade away if they weren't complete; on the other hand, though, they could and did tend to explode with a release of elemental energy if something was set up wrong. Normally, smaller-scale enchantments would just sting or make your hand or whatever was touching the failed enchantment numb for a few minutes. Larger enchantments like what she just completed, however, could do significantly more damage to both herself and the Hauler if she had done it wrong.

Violet waited...and waited...and waited... And nothing happened.

Violet breathed a sigh of relief as it appeared as though the enchantment had been completed correctly; when there was no explosion or any other indication that something had gone wrong, the fatigue of holding the rune sequences for so long faded, only to be replaced by elation. *I did it! Mom would be so proud...* She had always been the one to encourage Violet in her studies, though it wasn't like her father didn't care – he was just rarely there. She couldn't blame him, though, especially since he had been in charge of running the entire ELA.

Looking at the nearly invisible Spirit energy lines running between the two rune circles, it appeared as though her

324

shakiness towards the end of its creation hadn't ruined it one bit. In short, it was perfect, and Violet was extraordinarily proud. Jumping back up to the Pilot's area along the back of the Carriage, she turned the steering wheel quickly forwards and had to catch her balance as the Hauler jerked initially. She laughed to see how successful she had been and was eager to do the other side.

*Nice job, Violet! That was work worthy of a master there! Your control while holding all of those runes suspended was excell—uh, what is it doing? *

The Hauler had stopped when Violet stopped turning the steering wheel, but she could feel a tremendous build-up of energy for some reason. She looked at the runes on the wheel near her but couldn't see anything wrong; jumping off the back, she traced the linking runes and saw that they all appeared normal as well. It was when she got to the gear hooked into the track that she saw the runes she had placed there glowing brighter and brighter, pulsing like some sort of heartbeat. She was confused at first...before she saw the mistake.

"Oh, no – I forgot to reverse the Power rune—"

There was a brilliant flash of light and Violet felt herself being flung backwards at high speed...and then all was darkness.

Chapter 31

Sandra got the gist of what Violet was talking about before the entire rune sequence exploded with brilliant force, flinging her backwards until she hit the wall – hard. The Gnome woman slid down the wall to collapse in a broken puddle of arms and legs; she feared the worst, but after a quick check she saw that her little form was somehow still breathing. She acted quickly and brought three Repair Drones from across the hallway in the upper VATS chamber and immediately set them upon the Gnome for healing. One of her Ironclad Apes had to untangle her semi-jellied limbs so that they *could* be healed, unfortunately; Sandra was just glad that she was unconscious, because she couldn't imagine being awake feeling the pain that was likely infusing her entire body.

All in all, it took nearly 15 minutes of constant healing from three of her Repair Drones to repair all of the damage Violet had sustained – but she was alive. She didn't wake up after she was completely healed, but for some reason it didn't look like the same unconsciousness that Kelerim, Felbar, and Echo had or were still suffering from. It looked more like normal sleep, to be honest, so Sandra left her alone to sleep off the trauma of a near death as she surveyed the rest of the damage left by the explosion.

The Hauler was made of sterner stuff than the squishy body of a Gnome, fortunately, but that didn't mean there wasn't damage. In fact, the entire Pilot's Carriage had been essentially completely destroyed; it would be relatively easy to rebuild it, however, as it was made of wood that her Apes could put together and Sandra could seal it up. The track on the right side of the Hauler appeared almost unscathed, other than a few scratches here and there; the other track, however, was half gone. Looking around, Sandra saw a few pieces of the Steel track embedded in the ceiling almost 40 feet above the Hauler, as well as a few chunks peppering the nearby wall.

Luckily, none of that shrapnel had shot backwards to hit the wagons, nor did any strike Violet during the explosion – otherwise the little Gnome likely wouldn't have survived. Equally as lucky, since she had already helped to build the track – after hours of arguing between the other Gnomes that were still sleeping down below – she was able to rebuild it along with the gear and the Pilot's Carriage. A small portion of the undercarriage was damaged, but that was easily fixed by absorbing the damaged section, creating a length of Steel that would replace it, and then having her Apes hold it in place while she used her Core abilities to "weld" it back into place.

That didn't take more than an hour, at least, though most of that time was spent with her Apes hammering large pins into place with their fists; the way the track fit together with the pins was ingenious, as it allowed the "band" to stay connected while being flexible at the same time. It was unlike anything she had ever seen before, and she could only imagine the possibilities for new crafts using that same technique in the future. It was a pain getting it all into place, but once it was on the gear, it appeared to work perfectly.

With everyone essentially asleep for the night – at least, she hoped Violet was just sleeping at that point – Sandra had an opportunity to finish some more of her crafting. After checking on her Jute stalks, she found that the retting process had progressed far enough for the outside bark to be easy enough to strip off, leaving the fibers underneath usable for making into thread – or, more accurately, twine. Therefore, using the same technique she used for the Flax plants and Linen Thread, she extracted the fibers and dried them in her Leatherworking shop. After a couple of hours, they were dried enough to bundle up and feed into the next stage of the process, which combined the fibers together so that they could be spun into a relatively thick twine-like thread.

New Monster Seed and Origination Material found!

Jute Twine
While Jute Twine can be directly used as a Monster Seed, it can also be used as a material for use in the dungeon or other purposes.

You now have access to:
Tiny Jute Twine Bobbin
Origination Raw Material Cost: 5
Origination Mana Cost: 5
Monster Min. Mana: 5
Monster Max. Mana: 5

It was possible to make it thinner, but it wasn't nearly as durable and tended to fall apart easily if it was made any smaller. The twisting of the fibers together made it fairly strong as a result, which was why Jute twine was used in the making of ropes and other similar products. That, and it was fairly inexpensive to make, which was also reflected in the costs associated with them as a Monster Seed. It took barely a minute to acquire enough Mana and Raw Materials – obtained from absorbing the broken pieces of the Hauler from earlier – to unlock the rest of the Jute Twine-based Monster Seeds, and that finished that part of the crafting process.

That, of course, wasn't the end of it; she wanted to make cloth out of her new thread-type acquisitions. She had already started weaving cotton using a warp-weighted loom, so she continued that, as well as starting a Linen and a Burlap weave on separate looms. With a reed that she was able to make out of wood that would help condense the weave, her three weaving Apes were able to work fairly rapidly without tiring on the new crafting project. She even took control of one of them for a while to get used to the motions of feeding the shuttle pick through the weaves but left most of the process to them. Normally, crafting took a bit of her own personal attention to complete, but once they were started her constructs were able to repeat the same motions over and over and over without much supervision.

Within a couple of hours, they had all finished a large length of cloth 4 feet wide and 12 feet long, and Sandra was able to easily cut them off the looms by eating away at the thread or twine. The hardest part was tying off the warp thread ends, actually, because her Apes didn't quite have the finger dexterity for something like that; strangely enough, she ended up having to use two of her Tiny Automatons working in tandem to tie the thin strings together with some complicated maneuvers. And then, when she was done, she hoped and prayed that she had made enough and with enough quality to count as a material she could use for the future – and then she absorbed all of them at the same time.

New Origination Materials found!

Finely Woven Burlap Cloth
Finely Woven Linen Cloth
Finely Woven Cotton Cloth

While these Cloths cannot be directly used as a Monster Seed, they can be used as a material for use in the dungeon or other purposes.

Success! While the three different cloths couldn't be used as a Monster Seed, the fact that she could reproduce them for use in making sacks and bags, clothes, and other crafts was exciting. As soon as she unlocked the other types of fibrous-plant seeds using her new skill, she would add to the repertoire of available cloth-like materials, but for now she was just happy to have finished yet another crafting project – at least for the time being. She also briefly wondered why Leather hadn't been unlocked in the same manner for use as a material, but she realized it was probably because they technically weren't "finished"; there was a reason the Leather she had made already was starting to rot and decompose. She was missing some vital components to make them last.

While she didn't know when Violet would wake up, she guessed that there was still at least 5-6 hours before the other Gnomes awakened for the morning. *Plenty of time to get some more done.*

During the night, when she hadn't needed to use the Mana for fixing the Hauler or for her crafting, she had been feeding her excess intake into the requirements for some of the fruit-producing trees. As soon as she unlocked one, she filled up a plot with them and started to grow that particular tree in a long line. By the time the morning roamed around, in addition to the Orange trees that she left there, she now had Apple, Pear, and Peach trees filling up more than half the room with fruit. She would've unlocked more, but there wasn't enough time.

The reason Sandra did all that was because she wanted to have a larger variety of foodstuffs to give the Gnomes on their journey home; cooked Bearling meat and oranges would only go so far and would likely be repetitive without a little bit of choice thrown in there. Eventually, she wanted to look into acquiring some sort of vegetables or even wheat so she could make some bread, but that would have to wait until it was a little safer outside – and when she had more time.

Without more time to start something new, Sandra finished off the wagons for the ride ahead of them. Her Apes had already loaded all the supplies Sandra had stockpiled, though that stockpile was quickly filling up again against the wall as the Mana kept rolling in from her AMANS outside. If – no, *when* – the Gnomes came back for more, they would have plenty to take back with them.

Now all she needed to do was close up the tops of the wagons, keeping everything inside safe and secure. Using the same technique that she had used earlier and cheating the process a little, Sandra created large wooden boards that were laid across the tops of the evenly packed wagons and then she sealed them to the sides using the same ability she had used before to "weld" them flawlessly together. Then, on top of that platform on the frontmost wagon, she created some small wooden chairs with arms that would allow the Gnomes not piloting the Hauler to sit and enjoy the – likely bumpy – ride. To help block some of the hot sun – especially in the wastelands – she even extended a canopy of her new Finely Woven Cotton Cloth over the top of the wagon using long poles that were bent in an upside-down U-shape.

And then, when she was done with that, all the Gnomes woke up – all except for Felbar, of course.

Chapter 32

"What...happened?" Violet asked groggily as she sat up.

Sandra watched her quickly come fully awake as her eyes opened wide in surprise, before feeling over parts of her body, checking for damage. She sighed heavily in relief as nothing seemed to be wrong, especially after looking up at the Hauler, which had been fully rebuilt and repaired, looking as complete as it had before it partially blew up.

"That must've been all a dream then..."

Not quite – you blew yourself up. Fortunately, my Repair Drones were able to fix your broken body...but it was close. As for the Hauler, I took the liberty of repairing it while everyone was still asleep.

The Gnome looked incredulous, as if she couldn't believe that she was still alive. "I...think I remember some of that. There was a big flash of light and then...nothing until I woke up a few seconds ago. The parts before that are a little fuzzy, though," Violet added.

You created the enchantment linking the left steering wheel and gear, but something went wrong when you tried to use it.

Right before it exploded, you mentioned something about forgetting to reverse the 'Power' rune, I think. *

Violet thought about that for a second with her brow furrowed in concentration. "Okay, I'm starting to remember a little bit more of that, now. I can't believe I forgot to reverse that rune; it essentially captured all of the energy in the entire linked rune sequence and started to amplify it – catastrophically. I'm actually shocked that I'm still alive – that must've been one heck of an explosion."

* *It...was. However, everything is all patched up now – including you; do you think you have it in you to redo the enchantment? The others are already awake and heading up as we speak, and they're bringing food for you with them.* *

There was absolutely no hesitation on Violet's part as she picked herself up – which was fairly miraculous to see given that her body had been a broken mess the night before – and headed over to the Hauler. "I know what I did wrong now, so there shouldn't be any problems this time," the Gnome said while climbing up on the back of the machine. Sandra watched her immediately get to work re-creating the enchantment on the steering wheel before hopping down and working on the one for the gear below.

This time, the little lightning bolt rune she included in the sequence inside the concentric circles was both flipped upside-down and inverted, like it was a strange mirror image of the original. Violet did all of the enchanting faster than she had the day before, with more confident movements and almost no hesitation; toward the end, the obvious strain of holding it all together was evident, but she finished the linking runes without issue and let the entire sequence complete.

Despite her confidence and lack of hesitation, she still stepped back a few paces – just in case, apparently.

There was no explosion, nor any indication that anything was wrong – but the previous enchantment hadn't either until she tried it out. Now the hesitation showed in Violet's demeanor, as she looked up at the steering wheel and appeared to be psyching herself up to test it out. Before she did, however, the seven other Gnomes arrived in happy spirits.

"Violet! I see you finally decided to wake up," Jortor commented good-naturedly when he saw her looking at the Hauler. "How's the enchanting going?"

Sandra hadn't told any of the others what had happened; there really hadn't been a point, honestly, and she also felt that it should be up to Violet if she wanted to share.

"It's...going fine. I made a bit of a mistake on my first try, but I *think* I did it right this time," Violet responded with that same hesitation in her voice that she had shown just seconds earlier in her body language. Before she could stop him, Lankas

– who was reportedly going to be piloting the Hauler (at least initially) on their way back – jumped up and immediately started turning both of the steering wheels. Nothing happened with the right one, of course, since it wasn't enchanted yet, but the left one jerked once and then started to turn to the right smoothly after that.

Sandra and Violet held their breaths – Sandra only figuratively, of course – as they waited to see if it would explode...and nothing happened. Violet had done it flawlessly this time.

"Only one of them is done? Let's get that other enchantment set up and then we can get out of here and back home," Lankas said, jumping down to start looking at the wagons -- and what Sandra had done to finish them off.

"I need something to eat first, then I'll be able to knock it out fairly quickly," Violet told him, expressing that same confidence she had expressed earlier. Sandra was happy the Gnome had jumped right back into the enchanting; the Dungeon Core wasn't sure that she would've had the same drive and enthusiasm Violet displayed after being almost killed from the last one.

Jortor looked guilty as he handed over some cooked Bearling meat and orange slices to Violet – slightly less than what he had arrived with. Violet took it and practically scarfed it down without protest, before getting back to work. She completed the other enchantment even faster than the previous one, though she looked a bit drained afterwards; she didn't appear to be as wiped out like when she had created the "Stasis Field" enchantments in Sandra's Enchantment Repository, but fairly close, nonetheless.

As she sat down against the wall and finished eating a half an orange she had saved from earlier, Lankas and the others practiced controlling the Hauler around the Assembly and Storage room, which worked perfectly. Sandra overheard them saying how smoothly it moved, and how durable-looking the tracks were compared to the other ones they had worked on in the past. The Dungeon Core felt her own sense of pride in her crafting ability, even if she didn't physically "create" them using the same skills a normal crafter would. It still counted in her book.

It didn't take long for them to be satisfied and ready to go. Sandra had earlier had her constructs in the growing room pick some of the newest fruit for them as a surprise farewell gift, wrapping it up in a burlap sack for them to transport the food. She had also been cooking more Bearling meat for their journey since before they had gotten up, and then sliced it into very thin strips; utilizing her drying racks in her Leatherworking shop, she was able to remove much of the moisture in them, creating a kind of jerky suitable for travel. After they were dried, she packed the strips in four thin stone boxes filled with crushed-up Salt cubes to help preserve them for longer. It was an easy solution that didn't require Violet to create another Stasis Field enchantment on them, which she didn't think the little Gnome had in her at the moment.

They might not last the entire journey, but Sandra was hoping that the combination of meat and the variety of fruit would at least get them most of the way there. It was actually more than she thought they could eat, but she wasn't sure how far the capital was away from the village they had been living in before it was destroyed. If needed, Violet could always create a Stasis Field enchantment along the road to preserve things for longer.

"Are these apples? And pears? And...peaches? Where did you get these?" Jortor asked incredulously when he opened the large sacks (well, large for Gnomes, at least) of fruit Sandra's Apes were loading onto the Cotton-Cloth-covered wagon.

* Well, I don't need to sleep, so I was quite busy while you were napping. I unlocked the ability to grow these other fruits, though I ran out of time to do any of the others. *

"Others?" Jortor asked with great interest. His apparent love of food was obvious as he took a bite out of an apple and almost groaned in pleasure as juice ran down his chin.

"Hey, those are for our journey home, don't eat them all," Lankas slapped Jortor's hand away when he came to inspect what the other Gnome was looking at.

Jortor looked offended. "I was just taste-testing them; had to make sure they were going to be safe, after all."

*To answer your question, I can also unlock Plums, Apricots, Lemons, Limes, Coconuts, Elderfruit, and Ambrosia— *

"You can grow Ambrosia?" Jortor asked with awe evident in his voice.

*Well...not quite yet. It will take a while to unlock it and it'll need some unknown components to do it, but eventually I'll be able to. Why? Do you know what makes it so special? *

"Uh, yeah I do. It's supposed to be the most delicious fruit in the world, that's why it's so special," Jortor responded with a faraway look in his eye. "Oh, and I guess it also temporarily boosts the amount of elemental energy you can hold in your body, if you're into that kind of thing." He added that last part as if it were of no consequence.

Ambrosia allows a person to hold more elemental energy? Sandra had never heard of anything like that before.

"Hey guys? Maybe I can just stay here while you all go back, so that I can, you know, be here for when the dungeon makes the first Ambrosia. Someone needs to test it out, after all," the food-obsessed Gnome said to the others.

*You're entirely welcome to stay, but it could take years or even decades to unlock access to it. *

Jortor visibly warred with himself as he thought about that. "Well, maybe I can just visit in a year or two to see if you can grow it yet."

Sandra was secretly thankful, as she had visions of constantly having to use her Mana to keep the Gnome's bottomless pit of a stomach satisfied. As the rest of the food was stowed on board the covered wagon in designated areas, she looked at the Gnomes that were eager to leave – and then decided to ask for help one more time.

*Before you leave, I was wondering – has anyone given any thought to helping me contact the Elves? It would hopefully only take about a half hour or less, and it would assure them that I haven't stolen away their friend for nefarious purposes. I really don't want to be destroyed because of a misunderstanding. *

The Gnomes all looked at each other without saying anything, before turning away as if ashamed. Sandra couldn't blame them; going into another people's land when you couldn't communicate with them was inherently dangerous. She wasn't going to force any of them, of course, but she was hoping that someone would volunteer—

"I'll do it."

Sandra was surprised by the volunteer; Junipar was the only other Gnome woman in the bunch and she had rarely said more than a word at a time for the entire length of her stay in Sandra's dungeon. In fact, most times the Dungeon Core even forgot that she was there, as she tended to like to blend into the background – almost as if she wanted to be left alone.

"Juni, are you sure you want to do that? It'll be extremely dangerous," Violet asked from the side of the room. The others chimed in and suggested against it, but the small Gnome was steadfast.

"I think it's only fair that we help the dungeon when it has done so much for us. Despite what most of you think – I've heard your conversations when you thought you were being quiet – I don't believe this dungeon...Sandra...meant for everything to happen in Glimmerton like it did. She didn't have to save us from certain death from that massive lizard, she didn't have to heal Felbar, she didn't have to provide us with food and shelter, *and* she didn't have to create all of these supplies for us to bring back with us. Now, if *that* isn't worth at least trying to speak to the Elves, then I don't know what would be," Junipar continued, making that the most words she'd put together in the last day and a half.

The others looked shamefaced at her statement as they looked away, though Sandra noticed that none of them jumped in to volunteer for the young Gnome woman. A Mechanical Wolf came in from outside, the sound of its metal footsteps loud against the stone floor in the near-silent room. Junipar headed over to it and was about to climb on the back of Sandra's construct, when Violet spoke up.

"You're right, Juni – we owe Sandra at least this much for her help, but as the most-senior one here, it should be me. Actually, it should be Felbar, but from what I know he's still unconscious," the Apprentice Enchanter stated.

"You're too drained from your enchanting to go, Violet. I'll do it," Lankas said, which prompted a flood of volunteers from the rest.

* If Junipar wants to do it, I'd love for her to go for me. Unless you all want to go? *

"Uh...I think only one of us should go if we're doing this thing," Jortor said, to which everyone agreed. And then they argued for another few minutes on who should go, before Junipar just jumped on the back of Sandra's construct.

"I said that I'm going – just be ready to head out when I get back," the young Gnome said from Wolf-back. Before things could progress into another argument, Sandra had the construct start forward gently until Junipar was able to adjust her balance – and then it raced out of the tunnel that emerged in the Bearlings' old lair and out into the wastelands.

"You better not let anything happen to her," Violet said, trying but failing to sound menacing when she was now quite exhausted. Sandra thought that she was more drained from just the expenditure of Spirit elemental energy; the healing must've had at least a temporary effect on her overall health. That made sense – the Repair Drones could only repair what was there, and it was more than likely that something had been consumed in the process. She didn't think it was permanent, however – though it might also explain why those that were horribly injured during the bonding process tended to stay unconscious for a while, giving their bodies a chance to recover fully.

* Don't worry, I'm not planning on it; she'll be back here as soon as I can manage it and then you all can go home. I promise. *

Violet nodded, apparently satisfied with her response. Now all Sandra had to do was keep that promise.

Chapter 33

Sandra watched the Mechanical Wolf holding Junipar the entire way to the Elven village. It was only a few hours after sunrise and most of the Dungeon Monster hunters that she had seen frequently leaving the village had already gone out for the day, all except for the male Elf that had ended up finding Echo's bow outside of Sandra's Dungeon. She hadn't been able to hear whatever conversation he had with the leader of the village when he returned the day before – as her Shears couldn't get close enough – but there were grim expressions on everyone's faces all throughout that day.

From what little she observed that morning, the grim atmosphere hadn't changed much. And luck would have it, the same Elf that had discovered Echo's disappearance just happened to be the first that encountered Junipar on her Mechanical Wolf.

Afterward, Sandra regretted not thinking the entire operation through; the appearance of one of her constructs – despite it having a Gnome on its back – sent the male Elf into a rage. Junipar tried to call out a greeting, but as she spoke Gnomish, it likely sounded like gibberish to the other race. Instead, the Elf screamed insults directed toward her Wolf and basically ignored the small form on its back – and she found out why moments later.

"...not only did you kill my friend, but somehow you're now working with goblins, those filthy monsters! I can't wait until the Elites get here to wipe out your entire dungeon...too bad you won't be there to see it!" he said, before swiftly nocking an arrow, casting some sort of spell using Earth elemental energy, and then sending it hurtling towards Junipar.

Sandra reacted entirely too slow, as everything happened way too fast for her to comprehend, and since the arrow wasn't aimed at her construct, it didn't think to move; she jerked it to the side at the very last moment, which allowed the Gnome to avoid an arrow straight through her eye. Instead, it impacted her shoulder and slid deep inside her body, the tremendous force behind the arrow tearing through flesh, muscle, and bone like it was nothing. She cried out in pain after the shock of the injury wore off, before the blood in her pierced lung cut it off.

Sandra immediately stopped her Wolf and turned it around, heading straight back to her dungeon running full speed. The Elf tried to fire again as it retreated, but Sandra was ready for the arrow and was able to completely dodge it as it came screaming by. By the time he could fire again, they were already out of range, which was a good thing – because Junipar lost consciousness and tumbled to the ground as she lost her grip.

She had her construct lift her gently up in its jaws and run back with her impaled and bleeding body hanging limply to either side of its mouth. The sharp teeth of the Wolf probably didn't help matters, but by that time the additional wounds it inflicted were inconsequential – if she didn't get help soon, she was going to die.

Sandra had dispatched a literal army of constructs out of her first room as soon as she was injured, fortunately, which included four Repair Drones that were being transported faster than they could normally travel. Within minutes of frantic racing in approaching directions, they met up and her Repair Drones were able to get to work. She was still bleeding profusely, so she was thankfully still alive – but just barely.

How come everyone in or near my dungeon keeps ending up horribly injured and unconscious?

"You're just lucky, I guess," Winxa said as the Dungeon Fairy broke into her thoughts as she responded to Sandra's internal comment. It was only after silence from the before-talkative bunch in her Assembly and Storage Room that the Dungeon Core realized she had broadcasted those thoughts to everyone who was bonded to her.

"What happened?" Lankas demanded.

* The Elves weren't quite as...receptive as I had hoped. Junipar was injured pretty badly, but my Repair Drones are healing her right now. Soon enough she'll be back and good as new. *

"What?! You said that you'd make sure nothing happened to her!" Lankas continued, righteous anger in his voice. Sandra had to admit he had a point, she *had* promised that nothing would happen to her, but she in no way was prepared for what had happened.

*I apologize profusely. I didn't think they would mistake her for a goblin, so I wasn't able to protect her the way I promised. However, she's alive and headed back right now, in fact. *

Sandra's four Repair Drones had worked miracles on the nearly dead body of Junipar; as one, they pumped Holy elemental energy into her that amazingly sped up her recovery faster than the Core had seen before. The arrow practically pushed itself out the Gnome's body and plopped onto the ground, and the wound it exited from quickly sealed itself up. She couldn't see the internal damage being repaired, of course, but within seconds her Repair Drones had finished and put their pads and arms away.

One of the Apes that had come with her little army of rescue constructs picked up the unconscious Gnome and started to run back to Sandra's dungeon; halfway there, though, Junipar woke up screaming for a few seconds before she registered where she was.

I'm sorry about that, Junipar; you're safe now and you've been completely healed, though you may be inordinately tired for a couple of days. My Ape is bringing you back to my dungeon, where you and the rest can depart on your journey.

*I appreciate what you tried to do for me, and I apologize again for what happened. I just didn't think they would attack you outright like that; though, from what he was saying, I think he believed you were a goblin for some reason. ***

"Stupid, racist, too-tall Elves," Junipar responded weakly but with fervor. "That's one of the reasons my parents told me we don't deal with their kind anymore; they think anyone smaller than them are monsters or goblins," she added with a little sadness in her voice. "And I'm sorry, too, that I couldn't help more, but I think it's time we all get back home."

*I agree; by the time you get back, the rest should be ready to go. You can join them as soon as **you** are ready, and I would suggest sleeping along the way if you can until you regain all of your strength. Again, I apologize, but I do appreciate you trying.
**

"I'd say 'any time', but that wouldn't really be true." Junipar smiled weakly as she responded, and by that time they were already approaching the new entrance through the

Bearlings' old lair. Sandra had already told the others to start preparing for their journey, so they were ready to go as soon as she arrived.

Junipar and Violet are going to need a little rest, but they'll be fine after a day or two. As for the rest of you, I want to thank you all for your help providing my new Enchantment Repository examples of your runes; I am hoping to expand it someday soon and teach others how to use runes just as effectively as you all do naturally. Though, I have to admit, I am in awe of your natural ability – I've never seen anything like it.

I'm going to send a force of my constructs with you as far as they can roam past your village, but after that you're all on your own. Have a safe journey, and may the Creator watch over you.
*

Sandra added that last part in hopes that the Creator was listening – since it seemed as though she was some sort of pet project – and that they would be protected on their way back to their capital. She doubted that the Creator could actually do anything, but it didn't hurt to try.

Junipar was a little weak, but she was able to climb on board one of the wagons without needing any help. The others got into their places – with Lankas piloting the Hauler – and double-checked that everything was secure. Jortor turned to

Violet, who was still leaning up against the far wall and said, "Let's go, Violet – we're all here except for you!"

"I'm...not going," Violet responded with thinly veiled reluctance.

"What?! Why?" Lankas asked, shocked and confused.

"Have you forgotten who else is still here? Felbar can't be moved, apparently, and I'm not leaving him here all by himself. If – no, *when* – he wakes up, I want to make sure there is a friendly face near or otherwise he might make a fool of himself trying to tear up the dungeon," Violet added with a smile.

"Yeah, I can see him doing that," Jortor added, nodding along with his words. "But why does it have to be you that stays? One of us..." he said as he looked around, and none of the other Gnomes met his eyes. "Okay...maybe not."

"No, you all go home, and we'll follow as soon as we're able to leave. Get those supplies back to our people – they're going to need it."

Most of the Gnomes looked like they were going to protest further, but none of them said anything. Instead, they said their goodbyes and took off before Violet could convince any of them to stay; the Hauler worked beautifully, even when it was pulling three heavy wagons full of supplies. Within a couple of minutes, they were outside of the Bearlings' old lair entrance and the large complement of Ironclad Apes, Mechanical Wolves and Jaguars, and even a half-dozen Steel Pythons were accompanying them toward the Gnome lands. It would take them a couple hours to get there, unfortunately, because extremely rough terrain required that they take quite a few detours, but they would get there eventually.

"So...just us, I guess?" Violet said to one of the Apes that were still inside the Assembly and Storage room.

*For now; I'm hoping Felbar will wake up soon, as well as Echo. I'm worried about the Elven Elites coming here, but there's nothing that I can think of to do that hasn't been done already. I guess only time will tell. *

"I guess so... What should I do now?"

*If I were you, I'd get some rest before you fall down where you're standing. I don't think your body has recovered quite yet from the trauma of the...accident...last night, and I don't want you to overdo it. *

"Yeah, that's probably a good idea. But what will you be doing?" Violet asked.

*Something that I've been putting off for a little bit. I may not be available for a couple of days, but I'll make sure you've got plenty of food to eat. You can always visit the growing room and pick as many fruit off of the trees there as you want – just don't

351

*go past the Enchantment Repository. I'll have some extremely deadly traps set up below that to protect my Core while I'm undergoing...improvements. *

Violet agreed that she wouldn't and headed downstairs to Kelerim's old room, which Sandra decided to rename Violet's Room, as she was going to be staying there for a little while. She was happy that the Gnome had decided to stay, even if it was for someone else's sake; Sandra figured there was even more that she could learn from the Apprentice Enchanter if she dug far enough.

And, hopefully, with an additional Core Size Upgrade, she'd finally be able to take advantage of that knowledge.

Chapter 34

Violet got a little bit more to eat before crashing in her room, where she looked ready to sleep for the rest of the day, if not more than that. As for Sandra, she worked on replacing the constructs that had left her dungeon to escort the other Gnomes to the border of the wasteland and slightly beyond – just in case. Her Shears that were keeping an eye near the destroyed Gnome village of Glimmerton hadn't seen even a single lizard or other reptile since the two Ancient Saurians had retreated almost two days ago. That didn't mean they weren't just hiding in the forest waiting for someone to walk by, however.

Her own Area of Influence only reached a small distance into the trees, so her flying construct couldn't see anything dangerous near the forest border. Sandra knew the other Dungeon Core was out there, but she didn't know in what precise direction and how deep it was in the trees. As a result, she couldn't accurately predict when or if the Core would attack again, but she estimated that the party of Gnomes had until the end of the day to get out of range.

It took nearly five hours for the Hauler and the three wagons to navigate its way the just over four miles to the border of the wastelands, and by that time Sandra had been able to replace almost every construct that went with them inside her dungeon. Once they were on flatter, less-destroyed land, they were able to move much swifter and quickly reached the point where they couldn't travel any farther. When they suddenly stopped, Sandra spoke to them all.

That's it, everyone – my constructs can't go any farther. Good luck and I hope to see you all again sometime!

They said their goodbyes and departed, moving a bit faster than they were previously as their protective escort was no longer with them. She couldn't blame them – sometimes speed was its own defense.

Sandra directed her constructs back to her dungeon, where they would act as a sort of reserve force inside her Assembly and Storage room, as their replacements were already in place. They raced back in a fraction of the time it took them to travel with the Gnomes, and when they arrived Sandra started to seal almost everything up. She closed all of the access to the VATS, waited for her Mana to refill a bit before she set up her flame traps meant to destroy anyone entering her Home, and then cooked and salted some more Bearling meat for Violet when she woke up. Of course, she made a whole lot more than the little Gnome could likely eat in a month, but it was necessary on the off chance that Felbar – or even Echo – woke up before Sandra was done with her Upgrade.

She honestly hoped that Echo didn't wake up when Sandra wasn't there to speak to her, because she doubted she would be any more accommodating toward Violet and Felbar than the Elven villagers were towards Junipar. As much as it sounded counter-intuitive, she *wanted* those two to stay unconscious – at least for now.

For herself, she set up her little sphere of Singing Blademasters around her Core again, though she added a few Small Animated Shears to add some variety. When everything was as ready as she thought it was going to get, Sandra asked Winxa if she was ready.

"Of course I am! I'm actually very excited for you to Upgrade to Size 20 and finally unlock your Advancement system; it's been a long time since I've been around a Core for this long, and since...Wester...that I've been near a Core that knows about the special Advancements they can choose," the Dungeon Fairy said happily. "And hopefully you'll find some way to stop the Elves from wanting to destroy you," she added, with a faint hint of worry in her voice.

Well, I'm excited, too – but probably for different reasons than you. I can just see the potential for crafting that will come from it...

And with that, Sandra confirmed her decision to Upgrade her Core Size – and her awareness shrank down to just a small portion of her Home room. It was as boring and mind-numbing as ever, but the potential rewards for reaching Size 20 – along with Winxa's conversation and Sandra's flying constructs – made the experience not as horrible as she remembered. Either that, or she was getting used to it enough to not freak out every time she was trapped within her Core.

> **Core Size Upgrade Stage complete!**
> **12/12 Completed**
>
> **Your Core has grown!**
> **Current Size: 20**
>
> *Mana Capacity increased!*
> *Raw Material Capacity increased!*
>
> **New Advancement Options Available!** *(Unlocked)*

I did it! Finally, Sandra had done it; getting to Core Size 20 seemed like an insurmountable challenge when she first learned about the Advancement system, but she had reached it within only a few months. It helped that she had quite a bit of Mana coming into her Core from her AMANS up above her dungeon, but she was actually most proud of the fact that she survived the helplessness she always felt when she upgraded. It reminded her a little of when she was alive as a Human; her deformed hands had made many "normal" activities difficult to manage, and she'd felt like she couldn't do anything – or at least anything *right*.

"Approximately 52 hours, give or take a few minutes," Winxa said unprompted. "I figured you'd ask how long you were out, like you usually do," she continued with a smirk.

*Thank you, Winxa – I **was** just about to ask you that*, she sent towards the Fairy with amusement in her voice.

She didn't have time to talk anymore, because she was taking in all of the new sensations her Area of Influence was giving her. Not only had it expanded again – significantly – but she was aware of some...voids underground. Nothing had changed about what she could perceive aboveground – which was essentially nothing without a visual from one of her constructs – but under the ground was entirely different. She couldn't accurately measure the distance she could now reach, but she wouldn't have been surprised to know that it was six miles or more in every direction.

And those voids (some of which were quite significant) worried her; there hadn't ever been anything that was hidden from her before – at least underground – so she wasn't sure what it was.

"Those are the other Cores nearest you...well, their dungeons, at least," Winxa responded after Sandra asked about them.

How come I can't see inside their dungeons?

"You can't see inside theirs, and they can't see inside yours; it's apparently a rule that applies even to you without your contract. If you have one of your Dungeon Monsters enter inside one of those dungeons, then you should be able to see it through their eyes – or whatever they have that allows them to see," the Dungeon Fairy said, looking at one of Sandra's Small Animated Shears nearby.

*How do you know they can't see inside **my** dungeon?*

357

"That's simple; if the reptile-based Core had seen all of the traps inside your dungeon beforehand, I highly doubt it would've even tried to invade with the weaker monsters it sent against you. Think of a foreign dungeon like the area aboveground; you can't see it unless you have a construct up there, and the same applies to a dungeon as well."

Makes sense, I guess. Now that she knew what she was looking at, Sandra could identify the outlines of rooms and tunnels connecting them whenever she worked her way around the voids. All in all, she could detect eight distinct "voids" or dungeons within her Area of Influence – two per stretch of forest separating the different races. They almost appeared as if they were deliberately set so that each race would have to face two dungeons close to them that could reach *near* the closest villages, but not get anywhere near another race's village. When she thought about who placed them there – the Creator – she figured that was indeed the case.

Most of them were actually larger than her own dungeon, but when she "felt" her way around their Areas of Influence, they were much, much smaller than her own. What Winxa had said earlier about her ability to access all of the elements reflecting on how much she expanded must've been correct, because she couldn't think of another reason for such a difference. As they hadn't been able to access her own Area of Influence through that loophole that the reptile Core had taken advantage of, she reasoned that they were likely the same or a higher Core Size than her own.

But now she needed to check if that was still the case. Looking through the senses of her Shears hovering over each of the villages, she quickly zipped them through the air and had them locate each of the dungeons aboveground; it was fairly easy to find them since she knew where the voids were, though they apparently took pains to camouflage themselves. Three of the eight had their main entrances hidden in the trunk of large trees, two of them were partially hidden beneath some hanging foliage covering a hole in the side of a small hill, two others were camouflaged at the bottom of some overgrown pits, and the last was literally a hole in the ground.

With so much ground to cover, however, Sandra enlisted the help of another two dozen Shears from her AMANS to help with the searching; she didn't want to miss an attack from one dungeon while she was checking out another. She spent about 30 frantic minutes looking everywhere she could throughout the forests, finding that she could range even farther than she had initially thought. Her Area of Influence now covered a significant portion of the other Cores' Areas, with some being entirely swallowed up by her larger one.

She saw plenty of Dungeon Monsters – or at least she assumed they were by the way they walked aimlessly around – but nothing alarming. There were beasts like boars and bears and even some real-life Jaguars (as opposed to her constructs) from one of the dungeons nearest the Elves and slimes that oozed through the forest from the other; near the Dwarves were interesting-looking dirt and stone golems that reminded Sandra of her own constructs from one Core, as well as some various-sized goblins that were quite ugly and disgusting (but she had to reluctantly admit that, in the right light, some were about the same size as a Gnome) from the other.

The Orcs were hemmed in by small and large red-eyed Unicorns with sharp spiraling horns mixed with little white weasel-looking creatures on one side, and all sorts of deadly – and annoying – birds on the other. Only one of the Shears that she had sent in near the avian-based Core came out "alive", as the birds didn't take kindly to intruders invading their territory; the worst part was that she barely saw them before her Shears were attacked and basically snapped in half by the powerful beaks of the birds.

As for the Gnomes, there was fortunately little sign that the reptiles had started to move anywhere except for around the nearby forest. Though, alarmingly, the Area of Influence from the reptile Core was much larger than it had been before; it now reached all the way to the Gnome village all by itself, whereas before it had only reached there because of Sandra's own expansive Area. Worse than that, it had grown so large by that point that it was in danger of reaching through the forest it was in and finding the Elves on the opposite side.

Luckily, they weren't there quite yet, and the other Dungeon Core on the opposite side of the village was still small – and full of various undead. Sandra saw walking skeletons, decaying zombie-like forms, and even a few mist-like figures that floated above the forest floor. Those last caused her to get her Shears out of there, as they appeared to spot her construct – she didn't want to lose any more unnecessarily.

Everywhere – except for the Gnomes, of course – there were teams of people hunting down the Dungeon Monsters as a matter of course; they performed their culling that the villages were theoretically all there for, bringing back the dungeon loot that the monsters dropped when they were killed. And other than the reptiles staying relatively near the Core in the Gnomes' territory, everything looked...normal. There were no swarms of Monsters gathering and heading towards one of the villages, nor was there any indication that it would soon happen.

In fact, the only Core that really worried Sandra was the reptilian-based one, as it was an anomaly that was different from the rest.

How did they expand so quickly?

Winxa answered, even though Sandra hadn't technically been asking her. "It's likely that it stored up most of the Mana it had acquired from killing the Gnomes and upgraded more than once. Its upgrade time was likely still less than yours, and it might've been able to complete two of them since it first appeared that upgrading was what it was doing."

That seems like...a lot. With the appearance of those Ancient Saurians, I doubt they would've had enough to do that; not only that, but if I think what is happening is true, then it appears as if it is doing it again.

The Fairy thought about it for a few moments before responding. "You're right, that doesn't seem possible—wait a minute! Didn't you say that the Core looted things from the Gnome village?"

*Yes, but what does that have to do with—oh. If the Gnomes had been gathering "dungeon loot" for a while – from **two** different dungeons, probably – and hadn't shipped any away to the capital, then that village was probably like finding a treasure trove of Mana and Raw Materials. This could be very bad.*

"I agree – but what are you going to do about it?"

Sandra...had no idea. *I have no clue, Winxa. Give me a little bit to think that over; they are no danger to anyone right now, fortunately, so I think I have some time.*

With everything else looking as normal as could be expected, though, Sandra finally turned back to herself and her dungeon. Looking around her rooms, everything appeared just the way she left it, though Violet was down adding her own enchantments to the RRPs in the Enchantment Repository. The Gnome looked like she was going to be there for a little while, so Sandra opened up her new Advancement menus with anticipation...

362

Chapter 35

Sandra first opened up her Classification Menu and saw
that she had...89 Advancement Points! *How did I get that
many?* She didn't have to wonder long, as she brought up
another menu that described in detail where she had gotten
them.

Advancement Points (AP)				
Source	Criteria	Point Value	Lifetime Earned Points	Lifetime Spent Points
Core Size	Receive AP upon Core Size upgrade (does not count for Core Size 1 nor upgrade stages)	1 per Core Size upgrade	19 AP (19X Core Size Upgrades)	0 AP
Number of Rooms	Receive AP for each distinct dungeon room at least 4,000 cubic feet in size (20ftx20ftx10ft minimum)	1 AP per qualified room	25 AP (25X Qualifying Rooms)	0 AP
Unique Dungeon Fixtures	Receive AP for each never-before-seen fixture in your dungeon	2 AP per fixture	26 AP (13X Crafting Stations)	0 AP
Creature Eradication	Eradicate sources of nearby creatures (i.e. lairs and spawning areas)	3 AP per eradication	6 AP (1X Territory Ant Colony, 1X Bearling Lair)	0 AP
Sentient Race Elimination	Eliminate members of sentient races	1 AP per 10 eliminations	8 AP (12X Orc, 71X Gnome)	0 AP
Sentient Race Bonding	Form a new Dungeon Visitor Bond with a member of a sentient race	1 AP per 2 Bonds	5 AP (1X Orc/Dwarf, 1X Elf, 9X Gnome)	0 AP
?????	N/A	N/A	N/A	N/A
?????	N/A	N/A	N/A	N/A
(?????) Denotes an unknown, unique Source of Advancement Points. Perform this unknown action to unlock more information.				

Essentially, she received 19 AP from her Core Size being
at 20, 25 AP for having 25 distinct dungeon room, 26 AP from
having 13 unique Dungeon Fixtures which included all of her
different crafting stations (apparently her VATS didn't count, as

it was essentially just a series of traps without actual fixtures), and 6 AP from eliminating the Territory Ants and the Bearlings (even if she hadn't done it all herself). Sentient Race Bonding – the newest Advancement criteria that she discovered when she had bonded Kelerim – also gave her 1 AP for every 2 Bonds she made with members of a sentient race, meaning she ended up gaining 5 AP from those.

What made her sad and confused to look at was the 8 AP she had gained from the deaths of people; she only gained 1 AP for every 10 members of sentient races that she "eliminated", and the numbers didn't really add up.

Winxa, why does it say I "eliminated"...71 Gnomes!? And not only that, but it says I also killed 12 Orcs, but I distinctly remember there only being 9 of them that invaded my dungeon – and Razochek was technically killed by Kelerim.

"Hmm...I think that those numbers are tallied by every time you absorb the Mana that is dropped by them upon their deaths. Even if you didn't kill them, you absorbed their Mana." Winxa shrugged apologetically.

That makes sense with the Orcs, I suppose, but I didn't absorb anything from the Gnomes—

"Lest you forget, you shared that Mana with the other Core when *they* absorbed it, so that apparently still counts."

Sandra didn't like seeing that number; she was already being crushed by guilt over the deaths of the Gnomes and her involuntary absorption of the Mana they left behind. But now it appeared as though she was profiting in other ways from their deaths she hadn't been counting on. Unfortunately, there was no way to tell the system that it was wrong and that she hadn't actually "eliminated" them, nor would she want to risk the ire of the Creator.

What's done is done and I can't do anything about it; if I can keep that number where it is from now on, I'll have to consider that a victory. Now, to see what I can spend those Advancement Points on, even if a few of them are rather ill-begotten.

Advancement Options	
Current Advancement Points	89
Advancement:	**Cost:**
*Choose **1** Dungeon Monster from another available Classification (Repeatable)*	5
Give your Dungeon Monsters the option of having a chosen accessible elemental attribute in addition to their base element – Cost increases with each purchase (only works on Monsters capable of using/applying their element) (Repeatable)	10
Reduce the Mana cost of Dungeon Seeds by 15% – Cost increases with each purchase (Advancement 0/4)	15
Reduce the Mana cost of Dungeon Monsters by 15% – Cost increases with each purchase (Advancement 0/4)	15
Reduce the Raw Material cost of Dungeon Seeds by 15% – Cost increases with each purchase (Advancement 0/4)	15
Reduce the Mana cost of Dungeon Traps by 15% – Cost increases with each purchase (Advancement 0/4)	15
Extend your Area of Influence by 10% – Cost increases with each purchase (Advancement 0/10)	50
*Advance a current Classification **1** level to acquire access to stronger and larger Dungeon Monsters – this also includes any "Advancement Unlocked" Monsters – Cost increases with each purchase (Advancement 0/3)*	75
Select a second available Classification to hybridize your Core (This option is only available once)	150

Even if she knew what she wanted, she didn't have nearly enough AP to select a second Classification, so she was going to have to find something else to spend her points on. The one thing she had been thinking about, however, was the first, least expensive option: choosing a Dungeon Monster from another classification. With a mental selection of that option, she focused on it and another menu popped up and overwhelmed her with the choices she could select from. After about 15 minutes of perusing them and eliminating the ones that she didn't think would have any hope of achieving what she wanted, she narrowed down the list to a few base options.

Dungeon Monster Selection (Base)			
Bipedal (Fire/Natural)			
Jumping Springhare	Deranged Quokka	Boxing Kangaroo	Stealthy Chimpanzee
Barking Gnoll*	Silent Kobold*	Armored Troll**	Horrendous Ogre***
Giants (Earth/Fire)			
Baby Stone Giant	Juvenile Hill Giant	Young Cinder Giant	Young Ettin
Adult Ember Giant*	Adult Cyclops*	Mature Flame Giant**	Elder Guardian Giant***
Fey (Spirit)			
Playful Pixie	Sorrowful Sprite	Fiendish Fairy	Baleful Brownie
Naughty Nymph*	Destructive Dryad*	Spiteful Satyr**	Cruel Faerie Dragon***
Goblinoids (Spirit/Fire)			
Goblin Worker	Goblin Archer	Goblin Warrior	Armored Goblin
Shadow Goblin*	Hobgoblin*	Goblin Mage**	Bugbear***
Primordial (All)			
Diaphanous Spider	Mutated Sandwalker	Amorphous Ooze	Primal Wurm
Crystal Golem*	Unstable Shapeshifter*	Elemental Hydra**	Chaos Titan***
*Requires Advanced Classification Level 1	** Requires larger Core Size and Advanced Classification Level 2		*** Requires larger Core Size and Advanced Classification Level 3

She had hoped that the Bipedal (Fire/Natural) Dungeon Monsters would be the way to go for something that would be able to both craft and use their inherent elemental energy to enchant; however, looking at the list under that Classification, the only ones that she could select at the moment were apparently creatures that walked on two legs but didn't really have the manual dexterity she was hoping for. The Stealthy Chimpanzee was definitely an option, but Sandra didn't think that it would be too much different than her Ironclad Apes. While they would be able to use their elemental energy to enchant something, it still didn't quite have the manual dexterity she was looking for in the crafting process. If nothing else worked out, she would try it; she had quite a few Advancement Points, so she could get more than one Dungeon Monster if she needed them.

The Giants (Earth/Fire) were also another possibility because they looked generally "person-like", but they were likely too large to craft successfully; unless she scaled up all of her crafting rooms and workshops to accommodate even the youngest and smallest of them, she doubted they would be effective. And while they could probably craft larger enchantments, most of the smaller work might be beyond them – not to mention that bigger enchantment runes required a whole lot more elemental energy, which they may or may not even possess. It was too hard to tell based on what little information she had about them.

Therefore, she eventually decided to forgo making things large-scale and looked small-scale with the next option: Fey (Spirit). The options included Pixies, Sprites, Brownies, and even Fairies – though nothing like the Dungeon Fairy race Winxa was. Since they were much smaller than the other Dungeon Monsters on the list, the size difference was something she had to consider carefully; while they probably had more than enough dexterity to do even the smallest of detail work, it was quite possible that they would have the same problem as the Giants, with not enough elemental energy to create more than the smallest of enchantments. Added to that, it was limited to only Spirit as an elemental option, which would severely limit what could be enchanted. Still, the Fey Monsters she could choose from would likely be really adept at things like jewelry making, and even gem-cutting, as that required a very fine hand at the work.

Next up was the Goblinoids (Spirit/Fire) Classification, with Goblins of all sorts, including different combat-oriented types, but those ones didn't particularly interest her. What interested her the most was the Goblin Worker, which sounded ideal for what she needed – something that was used to the manual labor involved with crafting. And – as much as the Gnomes didn't want to acknowledge the similarity – the goblins that she had seen to the northeast near the Dwarfs really *did* look nearly identical in size and shape. Of course, the Dungeon Monsters she had seen up there were greenish-brown in

coloring, quite ugly, and probably had major hygiene problems –
but that was something she could live with. Whether or not
they had the same type of natural dexterity and attunement to
creating runic enchantments was something else entirely.

Sandra also looked at the other "all-element" option:
Primordial. She was disappointed to see only a Spider, an Ooze,
a Wurm, and something called a Sandwalker – none of which
sounded like something that could craft, let alone have the
ability to enchant successfully. There were other options in the
Classification that looked promising, as well as the other ones
she had narrowed down, but that was another problem – they
required her to "Advance" her Classification in order to use
them.

There were Gnolls and Kobolds, Nymphs and Dryads,
Shadow Goblins and Hobgoblins, and even larger Giants that
were accessible if she were to Advance her Classification;
however, what interested her the most was the Unstable
Shapeshifter under the Primordial option.

Do you have any idea what that is? Sandra asked Winxa
about it, hoping she would have some sort of insight into it. It
was a significant investment of Advancement Points if she were
to go that route (80 total AP), and if the Monster turned out to
be useless, she would only have one more she could unlock
before she was out of Points. With a little time and effort, she
knew it was only a matter of time before she received more
Points, but she wanted to be smart on what she spent her AP on.

"None of those – just like with your constructs – are anything that I've heard of before. I can only take a guess, but even that is likely to be ultimately wrong, so your best bet is to go with your gut – or intuition, since you don't really have a body anymore," the Dungeon Fairy replied apologetically.

Sandra decided that she wasn't prepared to spend all those points quite yet, even if it helped her original Constructs Classification. First, she wanted to test out the Advancement System to see if it was working; since it was untested by her and rarely used by the other Dungeon Cores in the world, she chose something safe that she thought would have an excellent chance of working: Goblin Worker.

Selecting the Goblin Worker from the Dungeon Monster Selection Menu was as easy as most other things in the Dungeon Core menus; all she had to do was concentrate on what she wanted to choose and the name on the menu blacked out as if it were no longer an option. A slight shift of something in her Core that felt strange but not uncomfortable was the only indication that it worked – at least she hoped; looking at her current AP on another menu screen showed that she was down to only 84 now. Nothing else happened for another few seconds, until—

New Dungeon Monster unlocked through Advancement!

Goblinoids (Spirit/Fire):
Goblin Worker now available!

Goblin Worker
Mana Cost: 50 Mana

370

50 Mana? That didn't sound so bad to Sandra, who didn't really have too much experience with how much non-construct Monsters cost. If it was the same size – or at least close to – the same size as the goblins she saw earlier, then 50 Mana was a steal; when she considered that her Segmented Centipede cost 100 Mana and was much, much smaller, then the ability for the reptile-based Core to make the Ancient Saurians made more sense.

"I've noticed that the flesh-and-blood Dungeon Monsters – that almost every other type of Core can create – are much less expensive than your constructs. I'm not sure if it has to do with the material or what, but I have to warn you: they are more...fragile than what you're used to," Winxa broke into Sandra's thoughts as the Dungeon Core was thinking about the disparity between the two types of Monsters.

Fragile? I'm not too concerned about that; I'm not sending this Goblin Worker into battle, after all. All she wanted it to do was use it to craft and enchant with – not help defend her dungeon; she had plenty that could do that already.

In order to find her new Dungeon Monster, though, she had to visit someplace new on her Core Selection Menu.

Core Selection Menu	
Dungeon Classification:	Constructs
Core Size:	20
Available Mana:	3550/19558
Ambient Mana Absorption:	10/hour
Available Raw Material (RM):	30500/49930
Convert Raw Material to Mana?	30500 RM -- > 1220 Mana
Current Dungeon Monsters:	14735
Constructs Creation Options:	17
Advancement Creation Options:	1
Monster Seed Schematics:	148 (6)
Current Traps:	36
Trap Construction Options:	All
Core-specific Skills:	5
Current Visitors:	4

Under the Advancement Creation Options, Sandra found a new menu that listed the Goblin Worker that looked almost identical to her construct-based one. Just like the notification had told her, the new Monster was only 50 Mana, so Sandra quickly created an Average Copper Orb to act as a Monster Seed, and then selected the Goblin Worker...

To say she was underwhelmed would be an understatement.

Chapter 36

"I've always hated the look – and, of course, *smell* – of those things; they just seemed like some sort of reject of the other races, like they were a...a...*mistake*, or something. I know that seems cruel, but then again, you don't have a nose," Winxa said, pinching up her nose at the sight of the disgusting creature on the ground underneath her Core – even though she had to be at least 50 feet away.

The appearance of a Goblin Worker didn't inspire much confidence that it could do much of anything. Although it was indeed about the size of a Gnome, that was where the similarities ended. It had a sickly-green complexion, warts and boils all over its body, a hunched-over back, and it almost appeared starved and desiccated – even though she knew from a prior conversation with her Dungeon Fairy that Dungeon Monsters didn't really have to eat...or sleep...or any of the other normal requirements that "living" creatures needed. Its stick-like arms appeared barely able to lift themselves let alone anything else, and she could easily see almost every bone in its chest and along its spine. It was wearing a dirty loincloth stained with...something she didn't want to contemplate – and that was it; the Goblin Worker was otherwise naked.

She was very glad that she couldn't smell anything, because she could *almost* see waves of putrid stench emanating from off of the Worker, and she had to agree with Winxa – it was disgusting and a bit vile. However, if it worked for her purposes (i.e. crafting and enchanting), then she didn't care overly much what it looked – or smelled – like.

Sandra took down the flame trap she had protecting her Home entrances and sent the Goblin Worker to her small Dragon Glass forge in the next room. A quick look showed Violet still up in the Enchantment Repository working on adding some small enchantments to various RRPs, so she didn't want to bother her quite yet. As soon as she discovered whether or not her Goblin would be an effective crafter/enchanter, she would see about working the Gnome to get some awesome enchanting done.

Taking a Steel bar and turning it into a simple knife was the first test of her Goblin, and after Sandra created the material she "entered" the body and mind of the new Dungeon Monster for the first time. The sensations she felt while controlling the Worker was almost euphoric; she could feel the cool air of the room on its skin, taste the slightly metallic tinge from the forge in that same air, and smell the slightly burnt odor lingering in the room. Her constructs didn't experience those same sensations, so to have *normal* senses again felt incredible. She hadn't felt so alive since...well...when she was Human, actually.

Of course, along with those sensations, she could also smell herself – or at least the body she was controlling. The horrid stench coming off of the Goblin made her choke and dry heave, before she was forced to exit its awareness to escape the smell. As soon as she left it, the muted sensations of her Core existence crashed back into her immediately, and all sense of smell was eliminated. She was equal parts disappointed and glad about her "normal" existence; on the one hand, she relished the sensations that only a flesh-and-blood being could experience – on the other, she was happy she didn't have to live with the smell of flesh-and-blood monsters.

She couldn't imagine having Goblins with their putrid-smelling forms as her only Dungeon Monsters, and she was doubly glad she hadn't chosen them for her original Classification. She imagined that, over time, she might get used to the smell, but it wasn't something that she was able to do at that time. For now, she was able to pull back her control of the Goblin Worker just enough to direct its precise movements the way she wanted to, though it wasn't quite the same as physically doing it herself. That made it a bit disappointing, as that was why she enjoyed the freedom of crafting as a Dungeon Core; it was something she couldn't do while she was Human – and it felt like she wasn't really crafting anything herself. Instead it was as if she was just...watching...like she had been forced to do for years when she was a merchant.

Nevertheless, the Goblin's agile fingers – despite the fragile and weak-looking body of the Worker – were able to manipulate the blacksmithing tools perfectly, better even than her Ironclad Apes. It was easily able to place the bar inside the

Dragon Glass forge to heat up and while it did, Sandra had it practice swinging a hammer, which it was able to do – but without much force or strength behind it. That made sense based on its appearance, but it was also a bit disheartening; it really was as weak as it looked, which didn't bode well for the blacksmithing trade – but perhaps it would do better in other areas.

That it wasn't cut out for blacksmithing was patently obvious when she directed it to retrieve the now-heated metal from the forge. As soon as it approached the super-heated Dragon Glass forge – which was extremely hot in order to soften the Steel – it literally burst into flames; the smelly and putrid oil that covered the Goblin Worker was apparently highly flammable, and even though no sparks or embers emerged from the fire, the heat rolling off the forge was enough to ignite the Worker on fire.

Strangely enough, even though she had pulled her awareness back from her new Dungeon Monster, she could very faintly feel the excruciating pain it experienced as it quickly burnt into a pile of ash and then disappeared, leaving behind the Average Copper Orb it had been created from.

I can feel its pain? Why would that even be a function of a Core?

"You've actually been very lucky up to this point, as your constructs obviously aren't capable of feeling pain. Over time, the other Dungeon Cores get used to the feeling of their

Monsters dying; either that, or their minds are so far gone that they barely even notice it anymore," Winxa answered.

So...when I killed all of those reptiles at the Gnome village and then here in my dungeon, the other Core could feel their deaths?

"Well...yes, but the Core had likely felt thousands or tens of thousands of its Monsters dying before that, so it probably wasn't a big deal to it. I've even heard – though never actually seen it myself – that some dungeons actually *enjoy* the pain they feel and even like to experience it firsthand, because it makes them feel more alive."

At first, Sandra thought that was just more evidence that the other Dungeon Cores were quite insane; after a moment of thought, though, she realized that she could understand wanting to feel more alive. Just a few minutes ago, she had reveled in the euphoric feeling of experiencing the sensations of the Goblin Worker – minus the horrendous stench – and she wanted more of that. Over time, she figured that anything that made her feel more alive would be welcome, though she didn't think she would go so far as to want to experience the first-hand pain of dying over and over. *That* was something that she thought might make her insane.

So, instead of attempting to craft something first and then enchant it, she instead fetched an already-finished Steel knife from her Display/Armory room with one of her other constructs and brought it to the forge room. While that was happening, she recreated another Goblin Worker and had it travel to where the previous one had died, waiting for the knife to arrive. When everything was in place, she got down to the business of enchanting.

Just like she had done with her construct in an attempt to enchant something – which failed spectacularly – she took over the Goblin Worker completely and worked on figuring out how to access its elemental energy. Choking through the horrific smell was a little easier since now she was at least expecting it, and after a while she was able to block it out if she concentrated enough – though that left less concentration for the entire enchanting process. Fortunately, she had become fairly adept at dividing up her mind through practice as a Dungeon Core, so it wasn't that much of an obstacle.

Using the Goblin Worker, she picked up the Steel knife and even the weight of the small weapon was significant to the Monster's muscles – or lack thereof. Regardless, she was able to hold it well enough that she thought she could enchant it without any problems. Sandra took a page from the Core book and "reached" inside the Goblin's body, grabbing hold of the inherent elemental energy inside its body—

Goblin Worker

Current Elemental Energy:
Spirit – 25 energy
Fire – 25 energy

The quick blip of a screen that popped up in her vision was a surprise. It seemed as though she could see how much elemental energy the Goblin Worker possessed; it had Spirit and Fire energy, which corresponded to its base Classification of Goblinoids. However, the 25 in each type was confusing, until she realized that the entire cost of the Worker was 50 Mana; if she considered that it was split in half, then it made sense in a way.

She also saw a "Special Ability", which she hadn't even known existed for Dungeon Monsters. A quick question to Winxa revealed that almost all Monsters that Cores had access to had some sort of Special Ability that used their inherent elemental energy, though like she had explained to Sandra before, her constructs couldn't *use* any energy – and therefore didn't have any. That was interesting news, and it was something she might try out later, but for now it didn't really matter to her too much.

Concentrating on the elemental energy, she started to siphon it out though the Goblin's finger like she had seen Violet do, which seemed the best way to try it out; she had seen enchanters use different implements to help with precise rune-carving, but it wasn't going to be needed in this instance. The enchantment she wanted to create was a simple yet effective one, which wouldn't need any fancy equipment.

Lifeburn was a useful enchantment for weapons, and it just happened to use the two elements that the Goblin had access to. Using her Worker's right finger to trace small runes that looked like a series of hashmarks with a line running through them onto the blade near the sharp edge, she watched as a red light emerged from her fingertip and seemed to float in place before settling loosely on one side of the knife. Keeping the Fire-based enchantment in place with a little more concentration, she flipped the knife over and used the same finger to create a series of swirls that were connected together.

When she was done – but before she let the enchantment finish – she looked at her handiwork. The shape of the runes was extremely sloppy, but the main form was there; she also saw that a few sections were thicker than others, meaning she had accidentally kept her finger there too long as she hesitated. There were a few other minor mistakes that she noticed, but she didn't think it would prevent the enchantment from completing; it would likely not be as effective as it would be if she had done it perfectly, but for a first attempt, it was crude but not horrible. Kind of like the first knife she had ever made in her forge.

Enchanting is much harder than I thought it would be. The masters I learned from made it seem so easy, but I guess that's why they were masters. I'm going to have to practice quite a bit to get to that level.

Before the enchantment was complete, it needed a catalyst; just like her dual-element traps Sandra had made in her dungeon, it needed something to connect them together to make them work. In the case of **Lifeburn**, it was an enchantment that temporarily heated the edge of the Steel knife up when it came into contact with something "alive" – which included Dungeon Monsters; therefore, the best catalyst to use was just a tiny drop of blood to signify how it would be activated. Using the tip of the knife, Sandra poked the fingertip of her Goblin's left thumb and felt the jab of pain that accompanied it.

Ignoring the pain, she smeared the tiny drop of greenish-colored blood – that somehow smelled even worse than the outside of the Goblin – along each edge of the blade in a very thin coating. It didn't require a lot, and that one drop of blood appeared to do the trick, because when Sandra let the enchantment complete, she felt the elemental energy flow out of her Goblin's body and fill the runes she had made.

I did it! I enchanted something! I can't wait—

The energy didn't stop flowing, however; the runes only appeared to be about halfway filled when the Goblin Worker's energy bottomed out...and then her connection with it was instantly severed as it dissolved into nothing and left behind its Monster Seed. Using her awareness of her dungeon, though, she was able to see the results of the failed enchantment on the knife that was now lying on the floor.

With the runes only just over half-powered, the resulting enchantment fizzled for a second before collapsing in on itself, which caused a minor explosion that shattered the Steel knife into three pieces. Fortunately, no damage was done to anything else in the room, as the explosion was fairly limited in scope; if her Goblin Worker was still there, however, it probably would've been killed outright or at least fatally wounded and wouldn't last long afterward.

Why...?

"I've never heard of a Dungeon Core even attempting to enchant something before, so I don't have any prior experience to pull from; however, based on what I overheard you thinking about its elemental energy, I believe it is directly tied to the Mana you spent on creating it. Unlike a member of a sentient race – for instance, Violet – when it pulled all of that energy out of its body, it didn't have anything to sustain it anymore; as a result, it essentially killed itself when it ran out of energy. I'm not sure what enchantment you were trying to do, but it must've required more energy than it could supply," the Dungeon Fairy answered her internal question.

*That makes sense, though now I'm really worried. That was one of the least-complicated enchantments I know that utilizes both elements; there are some that I could try that are even easier that only use one or the other, but that just means I am **severely** limited in what I can enchant. And even if it does work, will it recover that elemental energy on its own? I know* *that rest and sleep usually recovers it – at least in Humans and Gnomes – but would that work the same in a Dungeon Monster?*

"That is something I *can* answer with certainty: Yes, but very, very slowly. I know for a fact that when a Dungeon Monster uses a Special Ability, that energy is used up and can take weeks, months, or even years to recover – depending upon how much energy is used. For instance, that Ancient Saurian probably used its Special Ability to move much faster during that battle at the Gnome village, but for something of that size to use it so sparingly meant that it could take years for it to be able to do that again."

That was bad news to Sandra, as all her hopes of being able to enchant whatever she wanted disappeared as quickly as her Goblin Worker had when all its energy had been sucked out from it. True, the Worker was relatively cheap to produce, but if it could only do extremely basic and simple rune enchantments, then it was extremely limited in its usefulness. One or two enchantments before it was essentially useless made the whole enchanting process one of using up the Goblin and then just throwing it away like garbage; as much as she was disgusted and repulsed by the Monster, it seemed wrong to use the "living" creature that way. Sandra's constructs felt different to her, as they were like machines and weren't really "alive" to her way of thinking – so she didn't feel the same way about them.

It looks like I've got to rethink this whole enchanting situation. If the Mana spent to create the Dungeon Monster affects how much elemental energy it has, then I'm going to

need something that requires quite a bit of Mana to create. And

that probably means I'm going to have to end up spending quite

a bit of AP to get those Monsters.

"You've got to spend money to make money," was something her father used to say all the time. Of course, he was referring to paying for merchandise in one place to sell somewhere else for a markup, but she supposed it applied in her current situation. With a sigh, she turned back to the Advancement options she had...

Chapter 37

Obviously, to get what she wanted – no, *needed* – Sandra was going to have to Advance her Classification.

"I'm not sure exactly what it will do to your existing construct options, but I do know that in the future it will provide you with more selection when you upgrade your Core Size. In the past, advancing your Classification meant that you'd have access to Monsters that wouldn't normally be something you'd see, and they only get better the more advanced it is," Winxa explained when Sandra asked more about it. "Though, with what you're looking for, I doubt that any changes to your current Monsters will matter to you, as they likely still won't be able to enchant anything."

Regardless of what it did to her current Classification, Sandra decided that it needed to be done to get access to other Dungeon Monsters that *would* be what she was looking for. Therefore, with just a few moments of hesitation, she spent the 75 AP on advancing her Classification one level; the Advancement Option menu showed the Classification advancement option change from costing 75 AP to 750 AP, which meant it would be quite a while before she upped it again. She felt the same internal shifting of something inside her Core as it did when she spent 5 AP on acquiring the Goblin Worker, but it was much stronger.

It was so intense, in fact, that she...blacked out...for a second and her mind came to a screeching halt. It wasn't the same as being in the featureless grey void of death or the limited awareness of her Core Size upgrades. Those existences at least allowed her to think; her blacked-out state wouldn't allow her to do even that, which was probably good because she couldn't even worry or freak out about it. Sandra had no way of telling how long it took – mainly because she couldn't think enough about it to care – and when she came back to awareness it was with a sudden jolt; one second she was carelessly floating in a black void without direction or thought, the next she was back in her Core with menus scrambling for her attention.

Congratulations on your Classification Advancement!
Current Classification: Constructs (Advancement Level 1)

Your current Constructs Creation Options have been upgraded!
Your current Advancement Creation Options have been upgraded!
(Attention! Your existing Dungeon Monsters will not be automatically upgraded. Upgrades will only take place when a new Dungeon Monster is created. Mana requirements may have increased as a result of this advancement.)

You can now purchase Advancement Level 1 Dungeon Monsters from the Advancement Options Menu.

Constructs Creation Options	
Name:	Mana Cost:
Clockwork Tarantula	25
Reinforced Animated Shears	50
Hyper Automaton	100
Dividing Rolling Force	125
Lengthy Segmented Millipede	500

Iron-banded Articulated Clockwork Golem	750
Roaring Blademaster	1500
Large Armored Sentinel	2000
Mechanical Jaguar Queen	4000
Mechanical Dire Wolf	5000
Martial Totem	8000
Automated Sharp-bladed Digger	10000
Multi-access Repair Drone	16000
Steelclad Ape Warrior	24000
Titanium Anaconda	32000
Steel-plated Behemoth	40000
Gravitational Devastation Sphere*	15000

Advancement Creation Options	
Name:	Mana Cost:
Goblin Foreman	80

Uh…what just happened? Being bombarded by all of that information right when she came back to awareness was unexpected, but not as unexpected as the Mana Cost of her constructs being *four to five times what they were before*! The Goblin Worker – now Goblin Foreman – was only increased by a little bit, which was strange—

"There you are! It's been almost a week since you started that advancement to your Classification, and I was starting to get worried!" Sandra heard Winxa's anxious voice and looked around to see her hovering nearby with an equally anxious look on her face.

I'm sorry, I didn't know it would do that – why didn't you warn me?

The anxious look didn't disappear from the Fairy's face; in fact, it looked to be even worse than it was when Sandra had first seen her. "From the little I remember, it wasn't supposed to do that. It should've been like a super-quick upgrade that wouldn't have lasted more than a few minutes – not an entire week!" she exclaimed. "But that's not everything – you've got a visitor."

Huh? What visitor? Experimenting quickly by trying to eat at a nearby wall, Sandra found that she was still able to do it – which meant it wasn't an intruder, at least. Winxa sensed her confusion and pointed down below her, so she switched her attention to the floor beneath her Core. Violet stood there looking up at Sandra both in wonder and consternation, if such a thing were possible. She looked very impatient and appeared to have been there for a while.

* *Violet? What are you doing here? And how did you get past my trap— *

Sandra realized before she even finished the thought how that had happened; she had taken down the trap while she was experimenting with the Goblin Worker and enchanting and hadn't even considered setting it back up before she had advanced her Classification.

"You're back! I've been trying to communicate with you forever, it seems; I thought you said you were only going to be gone for a few days at most," the Gnome said with her hands on her hips as if she was trying to admonish Sandra for her lack of communication.

*I'm sorry about that; something unexpected happened and it took much longer than I had known it would. Are you ok? Did you run out of food? *

"No, I'm fine – but I finished setting up the Stasis Fields on those enchantment pillars you have in that room above and there wasn't really anything else for me to do. Felbar and that Elf are still unconscious, though I've at least seen Felbar shifting around a little. I came to see if something had happened to you and whether you can tell if one of the others will be waking up soon," Violet responded.

A quick look at the Enchantment Repository showed that Violet had indeed finished setting up the Fields on Sandra's RRPs, and that another twenty or so smaller enchantments had been added here and there, which was likely a good portion of what the Gnome had knowledge of. She was glad to see that the Gnome had kept herself busy, though she couldn't blame her for wanting to explore and find out what happened to Sandra – she was also glad that the flame wall trap had been taken down, otherwise there was a good chance Violet would've gotten burnt to ashes within seconds.

389

Another look at Felbar and Echo showed no outward change in them, but Sandra had a distinct feeling that they wouldn't stay that way for long. Especially since it had only been about two weeks before Kelerim had woken up, and if she added the time she was blacked out to her upgrade, then—

Wait a minute, Winxa – did you say I was down a week?

"Yes, and quite a boring week it was, too. I didn't leave for fear that you would come back when I was gone, and I wanted to make sure I was here—"

Sandra blocked out the rest of what the Dungeon Fairy was saying as she sent her awareness out to the borders of her Area of Influence, connecting with the Small Animated Shears she had out keeping watch on all of the villages and dungeons (where they were hiding in safe spots and weren't in a position to be attacked by some of the flight-capable Dungeon Monsters). She mentally exhaled a giant sigh of relief as nothing seemed too much out of the ordinary. Even paying special attention to the Elven village – and the area around it – didn't show any signs of the Elites that were coming to destroy her; she still wasn't sure what she was going to do about them, though she had thought she was going to have some more time to come up with something. *I guess I'll just have to hope that they stay away until Echo wakes up.*

Other than their visit looming over her head like an axe poised to strike her figurative head off, the only thing that worried her was the new Area of Influence that Sandra could perceive from the reptilian-based Core. It had expanded significantly since she had last seen it, until it extended just past the edge of the forest nearest the Elves. It wasn't yet a significant danger to them, fortunately, but it was something that could potentially be a problem in the future.

Pulling her attention back to her Home room, she realized that both Violet and Winxa had been trying to talk to her.

*I didn't hear anything of what you were saying; I was checking the borders of my Area of Influence, making sure that none of the villages nearest the wastelands were in danger. Being gone so long made me worried for their welfare from the other Dungeon Cores, especially the reptile one that attacked **your** village, Violet.*

She communicated that to both of them, trying to apologize for ignoring them but explaining that it was for a better cause. Winxa understood right away, of course, but Violet looked confused.

"What do you mean the...reptile one? It already destroyed my village and it is way too far away from the nearest town deep inside Gnomeria," the Gnome stated, which was actually the first time Sandra had heard what their land was named.

* To be blunt, I'm not too concerned about...Gnomeria for the moment. It's the Elves that are in danger; the Core that attacked your village gained a lot of resources and expanded where it could reach quite a bit since then and is almost able to reach the nearby Elven village. They can't reach it yet, but it might only be a matter of time. If they were to expand again – which could take anywhere from a few months to a few years – then they could wipe out that village just as quickly. And if that were to happen, they would gain even more resources to expand again and again, until they could finally reach far enough into your land to attack another town. Do you understand why I'm worried, now? *

Violet looked horrified at Sandra's explanation, which was honestly mirrored by the Dungeon Core herself.

* Hopefully, we have a while until that happens; given enough time, I can help the nearby villages enough through crafting or other support until they can adequately defend themselves. Of course, I need to survive that long – which I may not if those Elites arrive and try to kill me. *

Everyone was silent as they considered Sandra's words. Finally, Violet broke the silence. "If you want, I can try talking to them."

Sandra immediately shut that idea down – she had almost lost Junipar to the unprovoked attack by that Elven man that found Echo's bow, and she didn't believe that another visit would be any more effective. Nothing had really changed since she first learned about the pending attack; she still had the same barriers to communication that she had previously, with no real solution to prevent it from happening.

The only hope she had, unfortunately, was if there was something in her Advancement Options that would help. A Gnoll, Kobold, Ember Giant, Cyclops, Nymph, Dryad, Shadow Goblin, Hobgoblin, and even a Crystal Golem were all available now, but none of them seemed any more suited for communicating and stopping the impending attack than anything else she had considered. However, that didn't mean they were useless for crafting purposes and enchanting, which was what she'd wanted when she decided to advance her Classification – but they weren't what she *needed* now.

There was only one new option that – *might* – fulfill that role: Unstable Shapeshifter.

Chapter 38

Violet was tired of looking at stone walls and eating fruit and dried meat – as delicious as it was. She missed the sun, missed feeling the wind blowing through her hair, and also missed the company of others; the last nine days or so had been extremely boring with just herself as company – the "constructs" that Sandra had that just stood there and ignored her didn't really count as another person. They were Dungeon Monsters, after all, and not really ones for conversations.

So, she spent most of her days in the Enchantment Repository, using her rather meager skills at enchanting to continue the work that Sandra had wanted help with. She didn't really have anything better to do, and as much as she enjoyed looking at the different crafting workstations around the dungeon, none of it interested her in the slightest. If she really thought about it, Violet had to admit that the Repository idea of keeping every enchantment known in one place that could be used as a place of learning really appealed to her. If something like it had existed before now, maybe her parents wouldn't have been so caught up in running or teaching at the ELA that they might still be alive.

That didn't help the fact that it wouldn't and couldn't work, however. Already, the Stasis Fields she had enchanted that first day were starting to lose energy; within another few days, the Fields would fail and the temporary enchantments that the others had placed upon them would likely fade before she could establish another Field. While there were ways to enforce and recharge most other enchantment runes, Stasis Fields – due to their nature of frozen entropy – couldn't be maintained and recharged once they were established. Even though she knew that from her learning, she did at least *try* to recharge it – to no more success than she expected.

She had lots of practice recharging and repairing enchantment runes – that was essentially her job back in Glimmerton, after all. The runes on the War Machines would get damaged or start to fade after a while as the energy was used up in their use, and it had been her job to fix and recharge them. Which was why she thought it was a shame that the Fields in the Repository couldn't be done the same way. Regardless, she still did what enchanting she could and established more Stasis Fields over the rest in the room, finding as she did so that she could enchant four large fields before she was wiped for the day, as opposed to the three she was initially able to do. That meant that her capacity had increased quite a bit in even the short time she was practicing her enchantments in the dungeon, which only made sense; the more energy-intensive enchantments she did, the more energy she would be able to hold and use for even more enchantments.

It was more than tiring, though; such constant and intense enchanting was frowned upon usually, mainly because it frequently harmed the body with so much energy passing through it – unless you already had a larger capacity and your body was used to it. Violet's body was definitely not used to it, but the presence of Sandra's strange "repair" monster was able to fix all of the damage she did to herself after expending so much elemental energy. It was a fabulous training program that could revolutionize how quickly she could become stronger, though she would've easily traded it to have someone to talk to.

Which was the main reason she had gone looking for the reason for Sandra's silence. Even though the Dungeon Core wasn't actually "present" for her to talk to, even a voice in her head would've been preferable to the silence that permeated the dungeon. After a while it was starting to feel like some sort of prison that she could wander around in but never leave, and that was another reason why she had dared to go against Sandra's instructions and venture lower than the Enchantment Repository and adjacent storage room.

Any moment she thought she might be killed by some trap that was set up to stop her, but to her relief nothing did. She ventured lower and lower, until she came to a room that was much larger than the others nearby; in fact, in some ways it was larger than the room up above that they had used to assemble the Hauler and wagons. A large clear spherical object she guessed was about the size of her head was suspended in the middle of the room, glowing brightly as it shone down on a myriad of different small Dungeon Monsters slowly wandering around both on the ground and in the air.

There was a large tunnel leading off somewhere to the right and a smaller tunnel leading somewhere else on the opposite side of the room, though she couldn't see where either of them led from her vantage. She wasn't really interested in where they went, however, as all her attention had been on the glowing crystal-like ball in the middle of the air.

I'm assuming that's...Sandra's Dungeon Core?

She had heard about what they looked like from stories, but the descriptions just didn't give the Cores justice; instead of being some sort of menacing orb of evil, Sandra's Core looked...beautiful. She walked forward until she was standing staring straight up at it for who knows how long before Sandra finally spoke to her.

The revelation that the other races – including the Elves, who thought of most Gnomes as just slightly prettier goblins – were in danger really worried her; *not* necessarily because she was worried about the others, but because if they were killed the Core would become more powerful and spread its influence to engulf more of Gnomeria. The dungeons farther inside her homeland – that had expanded practically out of control – were already stretching their War Machines to their breaking point even by keeping them at a stalemate; if this one suddenly started reaching out and attacking from an unexpected direction, that could prove disastrous for her people.

As much as she still didn't completely relish the idea of working with Sandra because of her role – however accidental it was – in the deaths of her friends and destruction of Glimmerton, Violet was starting to realize that the strange dungeon might be their only option for survival. That was one of the reasons she had volunteered to go try speaking with the Elves, as Sandra's death would remove any possibility of help from the dungeon. The other reason was semi-selfish – she didn't think she could lift Felbar to move him away before the dungeon collapsed after Sandra's destruction if he didn't wake up from his (hopefully) temporary coma.

When that was shot down, she was partly relieved because she didn't want to be filled with arrows. The other part was at a loss of what to do, until Sandra surprised her with a potential solution.

I may have something that might work, but I'm not sure exactly what it is yet. If it doesn't work, there aren't many other things I can think of that might, so I'm crossing my non-existent fingers that it's a success. Now, don't be alarmed by what you might see.

Sandra's warning was barely enough to keep her from screaming as a large figure materialized out of thin air 10 feet away from her. It was as tall as an Elf but much wider; it wasn't even vaguely person-like in shape, however. Instead, it looked like a large solidified slime in a rainbow of swirled colors, with bright sparkles emanating from it like the night sky. It was strangely intriguing and almost hypnotizing at the same time, because when she looked at it the colors moved around in an unending downward cascade of ribboned colors.

Suddenly, it moved; what she could only categorize as an arm reached out from it and touched one of the metal "constructs" walking along the ground. Both paused for a moment, before the little metal monster resumed its original path.

Apparently, my shapeshifter cannot copy the shape of inorganic material – or at least that's the notification that I received. Do you mind if it touches you?

Violet took an involuntary step away from the strange monster. "Uh, why? Will it hurt?"

I...don't think so. I'm not really sure, because this is the first time I've had a chance to use this monster; I just unlocked it through a special Advancement system, and I'm kind of just going on instinct here. When I'm directing it, I get the feeling that it needs to touch something in order to acquire its form – though how that exactly works I'm not sure...

She hesitated for another few moments as she stared at the multi-colored monstrosity, but after seeing that it did no harm to the little metal construct, she shrugged and nodded her acceptance. The monster didn't even move from where it was; it just extended its arm until it was a long, thin sparkly spike that moved towards her left arm slowly. Violet flinched as it touched her skin, before a small – and very brief – jolt of pain ran through her entire arm that caused her to yelp, but that was all. The multi-colored arm retracted quickly back into the large form of the monster, before disappearing completely.

Violet briefly looked at her arm where she felt the little jolt of pain and saw a tiny drop of blood from an equally small puncture wound. By the time she wiped away the blood to see if any more damage had been done, the bleeding had already stopped. *That's not too bad.*

She looked back up at the strange monster and saw that the colors had frozen in their cascading effect; that didn't last long, however, as the effect returned – but much faster than it was before. The cascade became so fast that it was like a blur, and it was distracting enough that it took a moment for her to realize that the entire monster was shrinking, almost condensing in on itself. Within a few seconds, it was approximately the same size as Violet...and then the same shape...and then the colors evened out until it matched her skin tone, hair, and even her eyes exactly. It was almost like looking in a mirror – except for the fact that the form in the "mirror" was naked.

Violet covered her own self up in an automatic reflex, as if that could somehow cover the naked body in front of her. She felt herself blushing profusely as the other "her" blinked and started to move around as if testing its limbs.

Wow! That worked better than I thought it would! Why are you—oh, dang it! I guess this Shapeshifter can't copy clothes – good to know.

A sheet of beige-colored linen fell from above her twin with a slit cut into the middle of it, and the Shapeshifter managed to pull it over...her?...head so that it was draped over her like some strange poncho-looking article of clothing. It wasn't really any type of clothing by any stretch of the imagination, of course, but it at least made Violet feel a little better not having to stare at her own naked body. "What...what just happened?" she asked, still a little shocked and confused over what was going on.

This is my new Shapeshifter Dungeon Monster that I just acquired. I'm hoping that it will allow me to craft, enchant, and hopefully even talk to the Elves so that I can convince them not to attack. I probably should've warned you, but I was too excited to test it out to think how strange it must be to see something that looks like you appear before your eyes. I apologize...but isn't it neat?

Neat is not the word I would use...creepy, maybe? Disturbing... distressing... alarming... upsetting... frightening... those are much better words. She didn't say anything to that effect, though, as all she could do was stare in shocked surprise as the other Violet opened her mouth to talk – and a noise that sounded like some horrific combination of every beast she had ever heard before talking at the same time came out, startling both of them. She took a step back as the mouth opened and closed multiple times and the same horrifying noise came out, making her even more frightened.

* *Dang it! Of course it couldn't be that easy! I guess that verbal communication is out of the question for now. I wonder if it would be any different as an Elf—oh! I'm sorry if I frightened you! I had no idea it would sound like that; here, let me have the Shapeshifter change back to its normal shape because I can see that it's making you uncomfortable.* *

The other her suddenly lost its normal color and practically disappeared before her eyes as the form rapidly expanded, tearing the hole in the sheet even wider as it extended upward and outward. In less than two seconds, it was looking as it had before it had touched her, and she had to admit that as strange as it was, she did prefer it to be in that form as opposed to her naked twin.

"Uh...please don't do that again. That was just too strange," she said to the floating crystal sphere above her. She heard another apology from Sandra and then a promise that she wouldn't do it again. "Thank you...but if the monster there can't talk, what good will it do?"

*Oh, there is plenty that it can do; unfortunately, like you said, I can't use it to talk to the elves, but there are other useful things I can think of it being able to do – crafting and enchanting, for instance. *

"How will that help?"

*Oh, it probably won't, but we'll see. Meanwhile, I'll keep looking for a solution to the communication problem. *

Violet sincerely hoped that she found another solution, because what she had just presented was liable to make the Elves want to destroy Sandra's Core even more.

Chapter 39

Although she was severely disappointed that the Unstable Shapeshifter was unable to talk – at least as a Gnome – Sandra was still looking forward to seeing if she would have any more luck with enchanting than she did with the Goblin Worker from before. Given that the new Dungeon Monster she had purchased for 5 AP cost a whopping 16,000 Mana to create (and had to use her last Large Steel Orb as its Monster Seed), she had been hoping that it had much more elemental energy to work with. Fortunately, she was right.

Unstable Shapeshifter

Current Form: Base

Current Elemental Energy:
Air – 2000 energy
Earth – 2000 energy
Fire – 2000 energy
Water – 2000 energy
Nether – 2000 energy
Holy – 2000 energy
Natural – 2000 energy
Spirit – 2000 energy

Natural Ability:
Shapeshift: 0 energy

Special Ability:
None – adopts the special ability of whatever form it Shapeshifts into (if applicable)

Not only did the Shapeshifter have energy from *every* element, but when it changed into a copy of Violet, Sandra was able to look at it intently again and found that the elemental energy actually changed from what it was before.

Unstable Shapeshifter

Current Form: Gnome Female

Current Elemental Energy:
Natural – 8000 energy
Spirit – 8000 energy

Natural Ability:
Shapeshift: 0 energy

Special Ability:
None – adopts the special ability of whatever form it Shapeshifts into (if applicable)

Sandra had a feeling that the base form of the Shapeshifter had all the elements equally divided up based on its total, and then when it shifted into something else it would convert all that energy into whatever was able to be used by the form. She also figured if she were to use some of that energy while in a certain form, the remainder would be equally divided up again. The only question now was whether she *needed* to shift in the first place in order to enchant something.

Instead of going and getting another knife to enchant like she did with the Goblin Worker, she instead just created a flat piece of Steel that would work well enough for a basic enchantment and had it lie on the floor. Thinking of the simplest enchantment rune she could remember, Sandra concentrated on bringing forth a little Earth-based elemental energy and...found that she didn't really have any appendages to direct the energy. Taking full control of the Unstable Shapeshifter to better direct the flow, the creation of an arm, and at least a single finger revealed – at least in part – why it was called "unstable".

First, directly controlling the new Dungeon Monster felt like she was dizzily spinning around and around until she started to feel like she was getting a headache (or *mind*ache). Second, whenever she deliberately tried to create some sort of appendage – when she could focus enough to do so – the arm (or whatever you wanted to call it) would stay solid for about five seconds before it dissolved back into the mass of multi-colored solid goo that comprised the Shapeshifter. Third, when she quickly tried to call forth Earth elemental energy before her arm went away, what came out instead was a strange mixture of Air, Nether, and Spirit – no Earth at all.

She gave up after about 10 minutes of trying, because it was too frustrating and no amount of concentration she could summon would keep things stable enough to actually get anything done. Violet was still watching her struggle with the enchanting and looked amused, which was a step up from the frightened appearance she had earlier. Sandra felt bad about not even thinking about what kind of mental trauma seeing a copy of oneself would have on someone — but didn't know how to make it up to her.

Maybe if I Shapeshift into Felbar she'll feel better about it—

She immediately cut off that private thought, because she thought that the same type of mental trauma of seeing a friend copied would still apply. Echo, on the other hand, was probably fair game — being an unfamiliar Elf and all that.

* I'm going up to see if I can shift into Echo — the Elf — up above; did you want to come with me? *

"Um…no thanks, I've had more than enough of all that for one day. I'll probably get something to eat and head to bed early. I'm hoping that tomorrow is the day when Felbar wakes up, so I want to make sure I'm good and rested for what is sure to be…interesting," Violet said, excusing herself and running off.

"I can't say I blame her — that must've been quite a shock," a voice near her Core said. Sandra looked at Winxa and saw her frowning in the direction the Gnome retreated towards.

That was a big mistake on my part, I admit. I'll try not to be "wearing" Echo's form when she wakes up; I can't even imagine what will happen then.

Winxa stared at her Core for a minute with a strange look on her face, before busting out laughing. "As much as that would traumatize the poor Elf, I would actually love to see that," the Dungeon Fairy said as soon as she was able to speak again.

Yes, well, I'm still not going to do that. I need her help to prevent my destruction, if you remember, and I think that wouldn't inspire the greatest confidence in my assertions that I'm not there to kill everyone and take over the world.

"Yeah, you're probably right," Winxa said as she wiped a tear from her eye from laughing so much. "That does seem more important than my amusement...but maybe you can do that to Felbar?" she asked pleadingly.

Sandra didn't even bother to reply, as she was sure Winxa already knew what her answer would be.

While she still had at least nominal control over the functions of the Unstable Shapeshifter she had created, she tried to make it walk but only managed to shift a part of its form a few inches before it stopped. Sandra had more success before she had full control getting it to stretch its arm out to touch Violet, so she assumed that the best way to move the new Dungeon Monster was to just give it orders and wait for it to accomplish them whatever way it could.

As she was pulling out of it, something out of the corner of the Shapeshifter's slightly distorted vision caught her attention. Sandra immediately re-entered the Monster to see what it was; despite the "mindache" she almost immediately experienced, she was able to easily pinpoint the anomaly that caught her eye.

Peering almost straight up, she could see a strange floating "cage" of runes that hovered just barely above her Core. At first, she thought it might be some sort of enchantment that was keeping her floating in place in the middle of the room, or even what was keeping her trapped in the Core in the first place; upon further analyzation of the specific runes she was seeing, however, she started to get an idea of what it actually was.

She was seeing the inner workings of the Dungeon Core system that absorbed and funneled ambient Mana into her Core.

Sandra stared at it in shock and wonder for probably 10 minutes before the splitting mindache forced her to retreat from the Shapeshifter's form. When she tried looking at her Core with any of her constructs – knowing what she was looking for – she couldn't see it, unfortunately. There was something about the Unstable Shapeshifter that allowed her to see the strange but wonderful enchantment, and she thought about what she had seen.

There were long chains of repeating runes, most of which she didn't recognize at all, but those she did recognize were what tipped her off: **Absorb**, **Convert**, and **Strengthen**. **Absorb** was a simple rune that many Humans who had access to Water elemental energy could use to absorb almost any liquid, condense it, and then turn it into a solid, which made those with Water energy very popular in transporting water over long distances – as well as making those with a servant/cleaning-type bent to their profession very popular in keeping things clean.

Convert was a popular Spirit-energy rune among armor enchanters, as it helped to convert the energy of a strike into something else; the most basic use of it was in combination with the **Reflection** enchanting rune, which converted a blow to the armor into an equally strong repelling action, sending the energy converted from the strike back into the paw/tail/claws making the blow. It was a powerful enchantment and usually ran out of energy quite quickly, but it had reportedly saved more than one life that she had heard of.

The last, **Strengthen**, was the most intriguing as part of the enchantment. Normally, the Earth-energy rune was used to strengthen something Earth-based to keep it from breaking as easily – like a sword, some armor pieces, or even a clay pot. It was a very simple rune, which was why she was trying to use it earlier with her Shapeshifter on the flat piece of Steel she had created, but again, that didn't turn out so well.

It was intriguing in the enchantment around her Core, however, because it was *inverted* – something she hadn't ever seen before. Logically, she thought that would've meant the opposite of its intended purpose, like it was trying to "weaken" everything. Instead, it looked like it was doing something else, something vitally important that had extremely far-reaching implications and potential uses; instead of *weakening* the enchantment, it was using a portion of the incoming Mana to *strengthen* the very enchantment it was a part of.

Sandra could see no other purpose for it being there; with the inverted **Strengthen** rune – along with some other important parts, of course – it was essentially a self-sustaining enchantment that used the Mana it absorbed to recharge and maintain the enchantment...indefinitely. That made sense, though, because a Dungeon Core could potentially be operating for decades or centuries; very few enchantments Sandra knew of could last even a fraction of that long, especially those that were in constant use like this one seemed to be.

What made the enchantment even more unique, however, was that instead of separate elements for every rune – or even dual or triple combinations – each rune seemed to be made up of *every* element, which Sandra would've said was impossible if she wasn't seeing it herself. And since only those who could access a certain element could see enchantments and the runes they were made up of, that explained why no one had ever seen them before. It also explained why she hadn't seen it with her constructs; while they were technically creations utilizing all of the elements, they couldn't access any of them themselves.

That was probably unneedfully confirmed when she tried to analyze her constructs the same way she could the Goblin Worker or her Unstable Shapeshifter – nothing came up. It was almost like she was looking at a special moving object instead of a Dungeon Monster, for all that whatever granted her the information on the other Classification's monsters was concerned. She briefly looked at a foreign Core's Dungeon Monsters through her Shears aboveground and found that they were hidden from her analyzation as well, so it only seemed to work on her own.

Regardless, after taking another brief glance at her Core and the surrounding enchantment through its vision, Sandra instructed the Shapeshifter to travel up to the Kitchen where Echo and Felbar were still lying unconscious on the floor. She would've put them in a bed somewhere if she thought it would matter, but as they were essentially in comas she didn't think they particularly cared; besides, the nearby Repair Drone was keeping any type of injury they were sustaining from lying on the relatively cold stone floor healed the entire time.

It's time to practice and eventually put some of this new knowledge to work.

Chapter 40

Sandra soon discovered the other reason her new Dungeon Monster was considered "unstable".

The Shapeshifter could move remarkably fast as it flowed forward like some sort of semi-solid slime (when she wasn't directly controlling it, at least), and it wasn't long before it was in the kitchen and taking a little sample of Echo's blood. It was interesting to know that was all it took for her new Monster to shift into another form; not only that, but she also discovered after analyzing it again afterwards that it still had the capability of shifting to Violet's double. It was almost as if the Shapeshifter had a memory of sorts that filed away the forms of those it had taken a sample of, and it could pull those out at any time. Something also told her that if her new Monster died, any future ones she made wouldn't remember those samples.

After acquiring Echo's form, she took control of the Elf form and immediately ran to the VATS so that she could get up to the Assembly and Storage room. She had decided that she would use the room for enchanting practice since it was far away from her Core – she still remembered the minor explosion caused by the half-complete enchantment made by her Goblin Worker. She was planning on using a lot more elemental energy in the future, though, so if something went wrong, any resulting explosions would likely be quite a bit more...destructive.

The feeling of controlling a body that was very, very similar to her old Human one was interesting. There was a bit of a height difference (the Elf being at least a foot taller), but everything else felt refreshingly familiar; it was the first time since she had been made into a Dungeon Core that she felt almost free and like she could live the life she had wanted for so long – a life where she didn't have deformed hands. Echo's hands were delicate-yet-strong, as well as being calloused in places that indicated she was quite adept at using the bow she had carried; in short, they were perfect for her to do some crafting and enchanting.

The Shapeshifter's form was also naked, but since it was just herself and the cold stone didn't really affect her like it would normally – some sort of side-effect of being a Shifter, she thought – she stayed naked for the moment. She hadn't wanted to spend the time making clothes and the sheet that she created for Violet's twin was a bit cumbersome and would hinder her movements.

The enchanting practice – on a variety of materials – went much better than the first time with her Goblin, though she still had to practice quite a bit to have even passable enchantment runes. She only had access to Holy and Air elemental energy through Echo's form, but there were plenty of enchantments that she could create – and she had 8,000 of each type of energy to play with.

Using Holy elemental energy, Sandra practiced creating a **Minor Mending** enchantment rune on some scraps of cotton cloth. The enchantment was perfect for bandages or even clothing, though the last was a bit hit-or-miss; **Minor Mending** slowly healed wounds near where the cloth was pressed up against, and sometimes the runes would get sliced apart when they were on clothing, making them essentially ineffective. Despite having seen the enchantment done dozens of times over the years when she was human, she was having trouble getting it right.

First, she found that the thickness of her rune lines actually did affect the quality of the enchantment, despite thinking otherwise. When she was able to actually complete the rune, she could see it flare up when the energy from her body was pulled out and infused the enchantment; however, if the lines weren't perfectly formed, she could visibly see that the rune was extremely faint – which signaled to her that it wouldn't perform its functions very well or even just sporadically.

Second, if she started the enchantment from the wrong section of the rune, it fizzled and disappeared when she completed it, wasting the energy used in its creation. Fortunately, she only made that mistake once when she started it just slightly off from where she should have; after that, she made sure to start it in the exact place she was taught. She was just glad that **Minor Mending** was a relatively inexpensive enchantment to create – at least in the small size she was making it – as it only cost 15 Holy elemental energy per enchantment.

And third, expending so much elemental energy within a short period of time was literally draining. She didn't think her Dungeon Monsters could get "tired", but it turned out that she was wrong – at least when it came to using up its energy. Sandra figured that it was very similar to how she felt momentarily drained in her Core when she expended a large amount of Mana, though it was magnified exponentially when it came to her Shapeshifter.

In all, in just over 45 minutes of practice with the **Minor Mending** enchantment, Sandra had used exactly 3,000 Holy elemental energy – but it had paid off dividends. The last few that she was able to make were as near perfect as she could get; not exactly master-quality, but with the simple enchantment rune she was making it couldn't be improved too much even by a master. The form of Echo that her Shapeshifter had acquired was tired – and so was Sandra by extension – but she was happy with her progress. Of course, the enchantment she had been creating was so basic that it was actually recorded in some books that she had seen when she was learning as a Human; for the more-complex, three-dimensional enchantment runes and strings she knew, that practice was barely more than scratching the surface.

Still, it was a good foundation to prepare for that type of work. Next, she was planning to practice a little more complex Air-energy enchantment—

Sandra felt her connection to Echo's double waver for a moment and she paused in her actions. When nothing else happened after a few seconds, she started to make the first line for the **Hover** enchantment, when the wavering came back stronger and interrupted her concentration. The enchantment fizzled out without harm, fortunately, but the wavering didn't stop; after another few moments, Sandra felt Echo's form start to rapidly expand and lose its shape, until – after another second or so – she was back to having a mindache as the larger-sized Unstable Shapeshifter.

Confused, she tried to Shift the Monster again into Echo...but she was rebuffed.

Warning!

Due to its unstable nature, the Unstable Shapeshifter has temporarily lost the ability to Shapeshift.
Shapeshift Cooldown remaining: 59 minutes, 55 seconds

So, obviously there are some issues there that I need to consider. Sandra was annoyed that her new Monster had another drawback, because she thought that the inability to communicate (she tried again when she copied Echo's form and had the same problem) and enchant anything in its base form was bad enough. Still, the fact that she could finally enchant was a positive, and if that meant that she had to wait an hour after each use of the Shapeshifter's Shifting ability (hopefully the down-time wouldn't increase), then that was an easy price to pay – and might even be solved with another solution.

While she was enchanting, she had only spent a little of her incoming Mana on creating materials, so she had acquired enough to unlock a Monster Seed that would easily hold another Unstable Shapeshifter: Small Faceted Sapphire Sphere. It cost 7,000 Mana in addition to 2 Tiny Faceted Sapphire Spheres (which she fortunately had created and placed in her treasury a short time ago), but she needed it if she was going to be able to make another of her new Dungeon Monsters cheaply – because the Raw Materials needed to create another Large Steel Orb (at 32,000) was extremely expensive. She wasn't worried about Mana too much anymore, so if she could get away with something that cost more Mana but a third less RM (at 24,000) to create, then that was the way she was going to go.

Her thought was that if she had two of the Shapeshifters, then when one was on cooldown, the other would be able to work – if she timed them right. She still had to wait for her Mana to recover from the expense before she could do that, unfortunately, but she estimated that it would only take about a half hour or so before she was to that point. In the meantime, she was going to use that time to think more about the interesting enchantment "cage" around her Core. In fact, while its Shifting was inaccessible, she might even bring her Shapeshifter back down to look at it again and—

Something changed...somewhere. Sandra wasn't sure what it was that caught her attention, and a quick perusal of her dungeon and surrounding area showed nothing out of the ordinary; Violet was already asleep (or at least close to it) despite it only being late afternoon, the area around her dungeon aboveground was clear of anything that she could see with her AMANS and Mechanical Wolves and Jaguars keeping watch, and nothing appeared to her mind with a warning screen or anything. Everything looked as normal as it could.

When she expanded her awareness to her entire Area of Influence, she checked on all of the villages to make sure they weren't suddenly under attack – all of them appeared fine. Even checking what she could of the aboveground part of the Cores and the Dungeon Monsters they controlled showed nothing. *So, what was it—*

Then she saw it – the Area of Influence (AOI) for the reptile dungeon had increased again, and this time it easily enveloped the Elven village to the west. The Dungeon Core had obviously just finished another upgrade of its Core Size and had its AOI expanded again. Sandra could only hope – as strange as it sounded – that the Core would go through another upgrade again, but within a minute her Small Animated Shears above the dungeon entrance saw dozens of small-but-quick lizards pouring out and scattering in all directions.

Sandra instinctively knew what the Core was doing; since it had the same limitations she did when it came to seeing things aboveground, the only way it could explore its new, much-larger AOI was to physically have its Dungeon Monsters scatter and discover what was out there. Earlier, when it had acquired access to Sandra's AOI, it knew that the Gnome village was near based on the culling that they were doing, if not the exact placement of it. However, it probably didn't know where the Elves were at all; it knew they existed due to seeing Echo, but not *where* – which was why it was exploring using fast but likely-inexpensive Dungeon Monsters.

And once they found the Elves – which was almost a certainty – then another army of reptiles would march forth from the dungeon and attack the village. Simple yet effective.

Winxa – we've got a major problem. Sandra explained what she was seeing, and the Dungeon Fairy agreed with her.

"You're right about what the other Dungeon Core is doing. I'm going to assume when it upgraded its Core size that it no longer has access to your Area of Influence, so it's exploring what it now has within its own Area," Winxa said matter-of-factly. "So, what are you going to do about it?"

Sandra had to stop and think about it for a moment before she answered. The way she saw it, there were three options she needed to consider. The easiest one – and which may or may not solve her impending problem with the Elites coming to destroy her – was to do nothing. The other Core

420

would find the Elven village and attack it, killing all of the villagers and probably leaving an obvious trail back to its dungeon. When the Elites arrived, Sandra guessed they would either track down the reptile Core's dungeon and destroy it, or else leave and go back home right away, knowing that there was no point in risking themselves if there were no people left to save.

Sandra immediately dismissed that option; there was no way she was leaving the Elves to die at the hands (or claws and teeth, or whatever) of the other Core. Not only was she morally opposed to that, but their deaths would just be another thing that she would be responsible for – even if it was completely unintentional to begin with. And, selfishly, she didn't know if the Elites would go home even if they destroyed the reptile-based Core – they might just end up finishing their original purpose for coming there and give her dungeon a visit.

The second option was to defend the village the same way she had the Gnome village, though this time she would be prepared. She could send her constructs in beforehand to get in place before the reptile army even arrived, and perhaps even ambush them on their way through the forest. It would be easy enough to track their movements via her Shears and be prepared for their attack. The Ancient Saurians – if they attacked – would still be a bit of an issue, but since they were a lot slower, she knew she would have some time to plan for their arrival.

It was quite possible that some of her new "advanced" constructs that she could create now were capable of really damaging the Saurians, though her most powerful constructs were a bit out of her price range now that they had increased in cost. Still, Sandra thought it was quite possible that something might be effective, as the names of them appeared to make them quite deadly. Whether or not that was true was something that she'd have to explore later.

There were two problems that she could see with that option, however. One, she didn't think she would receive the same reception from the Elves as she did from the Gnome village. In the case of the Gnomes, her constructs were a complete unknown and in some way were related to the large War Machines that they operated, so they weren't completely foreign. For the Elves, though, they already knew about her constructs – at least in general terms, even if their perception of them was skewed – and believed that she was a danger to them. Not only that, but she had "captured/killed" one of their own, so they probably wouldn't take kindly to her Dungeon Monsters being so close by. In fact, looking at the situation from their perspective, she could imagine them seeing her forces killing the reptiles as some sort of power play over "food" or whatnot.

Two, even if she was able to beat the reptiles back and kill them all, she had no idea when – or if – the attacks would stop. From what Winxa had told her and her own experience with the reptile dungeon, she imagined that the assault on the

Elven village would be constant, and she would have to be on her toes every minute in case something slipped through her defense. It would theoretically never end, and she hesitated to think what would happen if she wanted to do something that would take her away from the action – like upgrading her Core Size. To add to all that, the defensive option still probably wouldn't sway their opinion of her dungeon and the Elites would likely still come looking for her.

Therefore, that left option three. And with that option, Sandra would make the choice to defend the people with the same lesson she learned from when the Territory Ants attacked her Core. Sometimes the best defense was a proper offense, just like the only way to halt the assaults was to destroy the source. And the source in this case was probably going to be just as difficult to get to.

Winxa, I think I know what I have to do.

"And what, pray to the Creator, is that?" she asked.

*The only thing I **can** do in this situation...destroy that other Core before it can kill again.*

The Dungeon Fairy smiled, which was not the reaction Sandra was expecting. "I was hoping you'd say that," Winxa said, weirdly giving her a thumbs-up.

You're strange, you know that?

"Oh, believe me – I know."

Chapter 41

Sandra wasn't taking any half-measures in her assault of the other Core's dungeon. She was going to send the majority of her larger constructs, as well as half of her AMANS with them; she was a little worried about depleting her dungeon of its main defenders, but almost all of her smaller defenders that couldn't travel quickly were still there, along with her bevy of traps to defend her Core.

From what she could see, there wasn't any sign of the Elven Elites, and it was closely approaching evening; even if they arrived within the next few hours it was doubtful they would try to attack her dungeon until at least morning. By that time, Sandra was hoping to replace what she could (within her budget) of her defenders with her more powerful "advanced" constructs, so she didn't think it would be too bad. If she were lucky, the Elites wouldn't even arrive that day or even that night, and she hoped that she would be done and gone from the other dungeon before they even showed up.

In all, her army consisted of 14 Steel Pythons, 22 Ironclad Apes, 14 Basher Totems, 15 Mechanical Wolves, 16 Mechanical Jaguars, 45 Singing Blademasters, and – last, but not least – 5,012 Small Animated Shears from her AMANS. She didn't bring any Repair Drones or anything smaller than them because they weren't fast enough to keep up with the others, and speed was becoming more essential by the moment. Sandra was barely able to track the quick little lizards that practically streaked through the forest on their exploration, but the ones she followed with one pair of her Shears were already three-quarters of the way to the edge of the forest near the Elven village. She gave them about 10 minutes before they were discovered – 15 if they were lucky.

As for her own construct force, she estimated that it would take almost 45 minutes to arrive at the dungeon as a whole; her Shears could make it there in a fraction of the time, of course, but she didn't want to go in just with them in case there was something that could stop them easily inside. She had never actually been in a dungeon before (hers didn't count), so she only had some vague stories of what they looked like to go on; the Heroes back in Muriel rarely needed to actually destroy a dungeon – because they culled them fairly regularly – so it wasn't often that new descriptions of them emerged.

As soon as they departed, Sandra started the process of replacing them for her dungeon with the Mana she had already accumulated and was still accumulating – though the amount she was receiving from aboveground slowly declined from the initial surge when all her constructs left the dungeon as they traveled farther away. With the increased cost of her constructs since her advancement, the just under 300 Mana per minute she had been receiving almost didn't seem like enough anymore – and when that number dropped down to just over 200 as the miles separating her dungeon and her Core-hunting force grew, it felt rather insufficient.

For instance, although she used some of the Mana that she already had to create it, the Martial Totem (the "advanced" version of the Basher Totem) took almost an additional 10 minutes for her to accumulate enough to afford its new 8,000 Mana price tag. Starting from almost empty, it was going to take almost an hour to be able to create another one based on those numbers – but she did have to say that (once she was able to see it) the increase in cost was worth it.

The Martial Totem appeared to be made completely out of Iron as opposed to the relatively softer undefined metal of the Basher Totem; this made it much more durable and should withstand more powerful attacks – as well as having some serious weight behind its own attacks. In addition, the pair of powerful arms it had before were joined by two other pairs along the "totem" part of the construct, facing in different directions and different heights so that it had basically every angle of approach to it covered. Not only that, but each pair of arms appeared to be able to independently swivel around in any direction, though it didn't look like they could rotate quickly – so no massive "Singing *fist*master" was in store any time soon.

Once it was in place up in the uppermost room, she had it move outside for a moment and practice attacking the surrounding wasteland's rock formations – she didn't want to expend any Mana to fix any damage it did to her dungeon. The results were spectacular; stone was practically pulverized into dust with each hit the Martial Totem performed on the rocks, and the damage to its own fists was fairly minimal. She was sure if it kept up the abuse it would get just as damaged as the old one used to, but for a test it performed amazingly. In her opinion, it was just as deadly as five (or more) of the original Basher Totems, which definitely made up for the increased cost.

While she was waiting for her Mana to accumulate so she could create some more, Sandra briefly contemplated converting some of her treasury into Mana and Raw Materials so that she could complete the reinforcements faster, but she ultimately decided to hold off until she was desperate. There was no specific need to rush at the moment, as she was still accumulating more than enough to create what she required to replenish her forces – it was just going to take a bit longer than she was used to. She just needed to have patience and it would eventually come to her – her treasury was for emergencies, and she wasn't *quite* at that point yet.

Now, if her constructs completely failed in their objective and were wiped out to the last...then she would panic and dive into her emergency fund. Until something like that happened, though, the smart approach was to keep on like she was doing. What she did decide to do, however, was use the Monster Seeds in the treasury to create the reinforcements so she wouldn't have to waste her Mana to make new ones.

Using some of those Seeds, Sandra did make a couple of the less-expensive constructs that had ended up leaving for the other dungeon, just in case she needed to change up the defense of anything. To start, she created one of the new Reinforced Animated Shears – and was surprised at how large it was compared to the older version. At about three times the length (approximately 9 inches), it was a lot deadlier-looking – especially since it was made of stronger metal than the last. It wasn't Iron or anything that solid, but when she rammed it into a nearby stone wall at high speed it only bent a little bit compared being completely destroyed like the original one would've been.

The new Roaring Blademaster was slightly longer than its predecessor (at about 2 and a half feet compared to 2 feet), but it was thicker around and had larger blades attached to the spinning pole. Not only did they look like sturdier bronze blades instead of the flimsier metal from before, but they were also thicker – which deepened the higher-pitched whirring "singing" from before and turned it into a lower-pitched "roaring". She didn't want to unnecessarily damage anything – including itself – so she didn't have it attack anything, but she could sense that it was a higher-quality construct well worth the additional cost to create.

She was just about to see what the Mechanical Jaguar Queen (at 4,000 Mana) looked like, but then her Shears keeping an eye on things near the reptile dungeon saw the moment when the Elves were discovered. The little lizard climbed up a tree on the edge of the forest and sat there staring at the Elven village a little over a mile in the distance. Along some of the other trees, her Shears could see a couple other lizards arrive and do the same thing, until there was at least a dozen of them all along the forest's edge. Less than a minute later, the pair of Shears floating above the reptile Core's dungeon watched as a flood of larger lizards, giant turtles, and crocodiles flowed out of the dungeon entrance – and headed straight towards where the Elven village was located.

The other Core must've learned something from the previous experience at the Gnome village – and the defense that Sandra had contributed to it – because instead of streaming ahead leaving the slower Dungeon Monsters behind, they stayed as a group and only advanced as fast as their slowest members, which was still fairly fast. Strangely, they began to slow soon after leaving the dungeon, and around 200 feet past the entrance they suddenly stopped.

A large hole in the ground was revealed when some vines and underbrush were ripped away, and the two massive heads of the Ancient Saurians that Sandra had seen before emerged from hiding – or guarding. They were still slow, but they moved with determination towards the Elven village with steady steps. At the rate they were moving and the distance they needed to travel, Sandra guessed that they would arrive at the edge of the forest in approximately five hours.

Her own Dungeon Monsters arrived at the edge of the forest a few minutes later, and they quickly ran/flew through without pausing, searching for the dungeon entrance. It was deeper through the trees, however, and moving through the trees was a little more difficult than passing through the wastelands – as strange as that sounded. A couple of times her Steel Pythons got stuck underneath some exposed tree roots, and in some places the trees had grown so close together that it was difficult for her Basher Totems to pass through and had to go around, delaying them even further.

While they were navigating their way through, Sandra finally accumulated enough Mana to check out her new Mechanical Jaguar Queen – and she was definitely impressed. The old Jaguar had been maybe five feet in length from nose to tail and no more than three feet tall; the Queen, on the other hand, was easily twice that – and made from heavy Iron. Despite the size and weight differences, it could still move as fluidly and deftly as a big cat and could easily outdistance all but her Steel Pythons in a race. Its jaws looked wicked enough to pick up and crush a Gnome whole (which she had no desire to do – just an observation). Due to its size, she placed it to guard the Assembly and Storage room up top, as it would make a good door guard for the time being.

That was about all she could do as her constructs finally arrived at the dungeon. Remembering what Winxa had said about some dungeons leaving an open tunnel towards their core so that their larger Dungeon Monsters could pass through, she had one of the Shears that came with the group fly over to the hole that the Saurians exited and checked it out.

After about a minute of exploration, however – and despite the hole going very deep underground, the end was sealed off completely. Sandra could see where the opening to what she assumed was the other Dungeon's Core Room was closed off, as there was a distinct outline of dirt that was subtly different from the surrounding earth everywhere else in the hole. It wasn't covered in stone, at least, but then she wasn't sure how deep the dirt went, either; her constructs could potentially dig a hole, but if it was 50 feet or more to get there that would take entirely too long. She used her Area of Influence to check it out and was instantly discouraged from pursuing that path; the thickness of the filled-in portion of the wall was currently at 30 feet – and growing.

With that avenue closed to her, Sandra directed her force to go through the main entrance. As soon as the first sacrificial pair of Shears passed over the threshold, her connection to it was severely narrowed. *What's going on?*

After Sandra quickly explained what was happening to the Dungeon Fairy, Winxa answered worriedly. "Remember when the reptiles attacked your dungeon? And how single-minded they were and didn't even try to deliberately avoid any of your traps? I thought it might be different for you due to your unique circumstances, but it seems that the limitation affects you as well. While your constructs are inside another dungeon, the influence of the other Core sort of mutes your control over them."

What does that mean, exactly?

"I'm not *exactly* sure, but I assume it means that you at least can't control them directly. It might also limit how much you can actually order them to do other than very basic actions like 'go forward down the tunnel' and 'attack'. You'll have to play around with it to see what you can and can't do."

Sandra didn't have too much time to do that, however, as she was on a bit of a time constraint – because the other thing that happened when her construct passed over the threshold was a complete halt to the reptile army heading towards the Elven village. Her Shears were watching as half of the lizards, crocodiles, and turtles turned around and headed back very quickly towards its dungeon, while the others (including the Ancient Saurians) kept their plodding pace. *The other Core obviously thinks its defenses in the dungeon are enough for me.* Either that, or it didn't exactly know what Sandra had to bring against it.

With a quick experimentation, because she didn't have a lot of time, Sandra gave orders to her pair of Shears that had entered first...and found that it was delayed by nearly ten seconds. After that, though, the construct flew down the tunnel at a quick pace, crossing into the first room (which looked fairly plain with dirt walls and crudely carved-out angles) – where it was immediately shot with a powerful jet of water. The force was so great that her Shears actually bent at the impact with the water and was flung against the surprisingly firm dirt wall, cracking fatally and her connection to it was lost.

She didn't even really see where the jet of water came from; all she knew was that – at least in the first room – there were no obvious defending Dungeon Monsters to contend with. Knowing that her larger constructs were currently more valuable to her, she sent another dozen pairs of Small Animated Shears inside the dungeon to "test the waters" again, and they survived long enough to see that the water jets were coming out from various holes in both side walls – and that there were at least three dozen holes that she could see. The only other thing that she noted was that the Tiny Copper Orb that the first pair of Shears had dropped upon its destruction was already gone – absorbed by the Dungeon Core.

I guess we're going to have to do this the hard way.

Chapter 42

Sandra's orders to her constructs were almost useless, as they didn't know how to avoid traps that well; they were more suited to going up against other creatures, people, or even other Dungeon Monsters – not testing their wits against dungeon traps. Fortunately, she found that the holes blasting out strong jets of water were stationary and couldn't move to target her constructs, so the best alternative was to have everything move through the room as close to floor height as possible. The jets missed most of the Shears when they did that, and the Steel Pythons made it through without even getting wet, but the others took a few dents and a crack in their metal shells here and there. The jets were powerful, but they couldn't shift something such as her Ironclad Apes more than an inch or two when they were blasted.

She lost another dozen Shears in the process with some unlucky movements of her constructs, but overall they came through rather unscathed. She could only imagine what those jets would feel like if her constructs were flesh-and-blood; if they were powerful enough to crumple metal – granted, it was a softer metal – then against skin or even clothing it would probably feel like an extremely powerful punch.

The next room was through a long downward-sloping tunnel, which emerged into a huge room that had two very large tunnels on opposite sides across from each other. A very slow-moving stream was exiting from the short tunnel on the left and flowing across a gradual slope of smooth rocks that led to the other large tunnel. There wasn't anything else in the room, and by looking outside of the dungeon with her AOI view, she could see that the way leading to the next large void was heading to the right.

This room was obviously supposed to be filled with Dungeon Monsters, otherwise it wouldn't be this easy. Wary of sneaky traps, she sent a dozen of her Shears forward and had them spread out throughout the room, hoping to trigger the trap – if there indeed was one. Nothing happened, so she sent them down the large tunnel on the right. Still nothing happened as they flew down the passageway, until they came to a sharp left turn that led a short way to the next room. Without any obvious danger, she sent the rest of her force forward into the right tunnel so that they could progress to the next room.

Halfway down the passageway, she heard a loud roaring sound behind her constructs. One of her Apes was just turning the corner to the next room when it managed to look behind the rest of Sandra's construct army; a huge wall of water was emerging from the short left-hand tunnel in the previous room, heading straight for Sandra's forces. She tried to get all of them to run quickly into the next room, but the delay between her command and their action was entirely too slow.

435

The rushing wall of water slammed into the back of her forces and the sheer power of it flung her constructs around like they were made of wood and not metal. Thousands of her Small Animated Shears were picked up and slammed against the tunnel wall leading to the next room and were instantly destroyed, along with more than half of her Singing Blademasters. She lost two of her Basher Totems as they were smashed top-first into the wall and crumpled like an accordion, and six of her Ironclad Apes slammed up against each other in succession, their heavy weight doing most of the damage to themselves – and doing enough to damage them so much that they couldn't move.

Her Mechanical Wolves and Jaguars were mostly okay after the wall of water hit them, as a lot of the water just passed through them and only carried them along the wave instead of smashing them apart. A handful were damaged fatally when they impacted other constructs – like an Ironclad Ape or two – but overall they came out relatively unscathed.

The only constructs that didn't sustain any damage at all were her Steel Pythons. They were picked up and flung away, of course, but their Steel bodies were more than a match for the impact that destroyed so many others.

In all – if she considered her vast quantity of Shears as part of her force – she had already lost over 75% of her constructs...and she had only progressed through *two rooms!* Sandra wasn't sure what she could do to be more careful to avoid a disaster like that, but she knew she had to destroy the Core at the end of the dungeon so that it wouldn't harm any more people. Thankfully, the majority of her remaining constructs were fairly powerful, and she still had over 1,000 Shears that had made it around the corner and slightly into the next room before the wave had hit them. Using them as more sacrificial pieces, she sent them into the smaller third room and saw them freeze halfway across to the exit. A barely visible frost covered them at first before expanding quickly, and soon enough she could see that a column of frigid moisture was filling up a square middle portion of the room.

The frozen water adhered to her constructs and froze them so solid they couldn't move; within 15 seconds, they were practically covered with ice – and then Sandra heard a series of cracks as the ice apparently contracted and snapped her constructs apart. As soon as they disappeared, the trap deactivated and their Monster Seeds dropped to the floor, only to be absorbed just like the thousands that had dropped a few moments ago from her destroyed constructs. Actually, when she turned to look at the Monster Seeds that had dropped from the results of the big wall of water trap, they were still being "consumed"; she knew from experience that she could only absorb them so quickly, and the amount that was there was quite a meal.

Avoiding the trap in the third room was blessedly easy after she knew about it, so she was able to direct the remainder of her constructs around it. The fourth room was almost as easy, as there were more water jets similar to the first room that needed to be avoided – though there were more of them (and more powerful) in this long, hallway-like room. She lost another two-dozen Shears when one of the jets appeared to be able to shoot downwards to the floor where her constructs were trying to sneak by, but only a few dents and cracks were evident on the rest of her larger forces.

The fifth room required her to sacrifice another half of her Singing Blademasters, as the trap inside the room was a line of unending sharp icicles that would shoot straight down from the ceiling, impaling anything that crossed the line. Even her Apes with their Iron shells weren't immune, and she lost one when an icicle slipped through a gap in its body and shot straight into its internal power source, killing it instantly. The only solution she could come up with to get the rest of her constructs through was to have some of her Blademasters spin and impact the icicles, throwing them out of line. The act, of course, was too much for her spinning constructs and damaged many of them beyond repair, but it was worth it to get the rest through relatively unscathed.

The sixth room was filled with a foot of water that didn't seem that dangerous, and after a little bit of investigation she couldn't trigger any traps. Sandra then used one of her Mechanical Jaguars to wade through the water and test everything out to the exit; when nothing seemed to happen, she ordered the rest to enter the room and make their way across the mine-lake of water in the long, 100-foot-plus room. Of course, that was when the reptiles that had turned back from the advancing army headed toward the Elven village arrived at the dungeon and immediately rushed inside. She couldn't see where they went after that, but they were near her constructs' location within a minute and coming through a hidden passageway in the tunnel they had just passed through, so she was forced to fight them on the reptiles' home turf.

Fortunately, the order to attack was given in plenty of time, and her constructs didn't need any further instruction. Like she had thought before, it was obvious that they knew exactly what to do against an enemy they could see – it was just the hidden traps that tripped them up so much.

It wasn't quite the slaughter she was expecting it to be – like when they met outside of the Gnome village. Instead, the crocodiles used the water extremely well, and even the giant turtles and lizards were able to dive under the water to attack from below; her Blademasters and Shears were next to useless because the water fouled up either their speed of impact or their spinning. Legs were ripped off of her Apes as two or even three crocodiles latched on and pulled them apart; her Basher Totems had trouble hitting the quickly moving reptiles through the water, which also softened most of the blows they were able to land. Her Mechanical Jaguars and Wolves actually had the best luck in fighting back, as the water didn't hinder them as much as the others and they were able to quickly maneuver around to get the attackers before they could strike at the other constructs.

Despite being in hostile territory and literally in the reptiles' element, her constructs still prevailed. She ended up losing 7 more Ironclad Apes – bringing her remaining total to 8 – and 5 more Basher Totems – bringing them down to 7 – but the rest of her constructs fared much better. Although she lost over 100 Small Animated Shears during the fight, she only lost 3 Singing Blademasters and one each of her Mechanical animals. With a dozen of those, 15 Blademasters, and just under 900 Shears, she was still well equipped to take on the rest of the dungeon. She was just glad that the entire reptile army hadn't turned back; otherwise she wasn't sure she would've had many survive an encounter like that with more opponents.

From what Sandra could tell by looking at the outside dungeon void, she looked to be over halfway done with the rooms before her constructs would arrive at the final Core Room – where she assumed and hoped the other Core was located. Five more rooms separated her forces from the target, and she was determined to get there before they were all destroyed.

It was when they entered the seventh room that the first sign of a defender made an appearance; Sandra assumed that the other Core was making good use of all the Monster Seeds that had dropped from all of her constructs' destruction and the fight in the sixth room. That's what *she* would've done, after all

– use whatever resources were available to replenish the defenders. Fortunately, it was just a few giant turtles that greeted her constructs, which were no match for the might of all her constructs combined together.

What *was* a match for them, however, was the trap in the room; there were rope-like whips of water that extended out from the walls and snatched up a few of her constructs up as they solidified around them. Three more of her Basher Totems were lifted into the air and smashed into the ground, completely demolishing them within five or six hits. Fortunately (or unfortunately – she wasn't quite sure), her other constructs completely ignored the traps and hurried to the exit, though one of the Apes got snatched...and was held in place because it was too heavy to lift. Sandra daren't try to free it with another construct, because the other "whips" were done with their Basher beatdown and were liable to snatch something else up.

Therefore, she left it there to struggle trying to free itself, and Sandra could only hope that the Mana used to establish the trap would eventually run out – at least temporarily, until it recharged – and free her construct at some point. She felt a little bad about leaving it there, but she had an objective to complete and couldn't afford to lose any more than she already had.

Her constructs entered the eighth room and Sandra paused as something nagged at her. She looked around the room filled with cascading waterfalls, large pools of water, and nearly a dozen crocodiles emerging from those pools – and couldn't see what felt off. She sent her constructs in to attack while a few dozen Shears flew in different directions, looking for any type of trap that could potentially spell disaster. They found a trap near the center of the room that made the waterfalls increase their flow, which also made the pools overflow into the rest of the room. Soon enough, the room started to completely fill with water, until all of her constructs were entirely underwater.

Luckily for them, they had already taken care of the crocodiles – losing another Ape in the process when it was ambushed – and they didn't need to breathe. It was easy enough for them to travel underwater to the exit, though getting through it was a bit more difficult; it was far above where the grounded constructs could reach, though her Blademasters and Shears were easily able to make it through. She also learned that her Basher Totems – in addition to hovering over the ground when they moved – could also hover sideways up walls...and she assumed even ceilings, though she didn't try that.

For her Mechanical animals and her Apes, however, they were forced to dig and tear into the reinforced dirt wall to make handholds that they could climb up, which consumed valuable time that they didn't have. While they were doing that, Sandra checked on the progress of the reptile army towards the Elves and found that the force was nearly where she thought they would be – and still about 4 hours out from the edge of the forest. She turned her attention to the other villages around the wasteland, finding that the Dwarves were just shutting down for the day as the light started to wane, and the Orcs were finishing for the day as well.

When she checked the Elves, however, she discovered what had been nagging at her. Just entering the village was a group of five Elves decked out in impressive-looking armor and moving very quickly. Sandra brought her Shears down closer to try to hear what was being said, as there was obviously a commotion in the village going on.

"...surely you don't want to go tonight? It's late and it'll likely be fully dark by the time you get there," the woman that seemed to be in charge of the village was saying to the newcomers.

A male Elf sporting what appeared to be – at least to her crafting senses – masterwork Platinum semi-plate armor, with basic-looking faded enchanting runes all over the outside spoke up. "We deliberately didn't stop for the night on the road because of the urgency of the situation. For every hour we delay, that dungeon in the wastelands is getting stronger; we're going in tonight, despite the late hour. Besides, the dark of the night doesn't really matter once you're inside the dungeon, so there's no point in putting it off. We need to ensure this area is safe before we get back to the capital – there's a lull in the pushes from the nearby dungeon's Monsters right now, but it probably won't last long."

The others with him, two women and two men with hard-looking faces and a no-nonsense attitude to them nodded their head in agreement but didn't deign to say anything. An Elf that Sandra instantly recognized as the one that had found Echo's bow and almost killed Junipar interrupted the conversation between those in charge.

"I can show you exactly where the dungeon is; that blasted evil scourge took Echo almost a week and a half ago, and I aim to get my revenge," he said with obvious pleasure.

"We'll take the help finding it, but you're staying out of there. *We* know what we're doing – *you* do not. We can't afford to protect you, and in all likelihood you'll set off a trap that will get us all killed," the leader of the Elites said.

"But—"

"There is no discussion here. You can agree to show us where the dungeon entrance is and then leave, or you can stay here, and we'll find it ourselves. It'll take a little bit longer, but I assure you we'll find it eventually – this isn't our first dungeon, as I'm sure you're aware," the dangerous leader said with so much authority in his voice that Sandra was practically convinced by his words alone. Fortunately, she didn't have to listen to him and wasn't about to let herself be walked over – like the village Elf obviously was currently allowing.

"Fine, I'll show you where the dungeon is located and then head back here," he said sullenly.

They left the village at a slow jog, heading unerringly for Sandra's dungeon in the distance. By the rate they were moving – not quite a walk, but not a run either – it would take them about an hour to arrive. That didn't give her a lot of time.

And lest she forget, she still had a Core to destroy herself.

Chapter 43

I think this qualifies as an emergency, Sandra couldn't help but think. Therefore, she started to liquidate her treasury, which somehow almost hurt her to do. Something about her former life as a merchant must've bled through to her current existence because it felt like she was pulling all her life savings out from the bank. Regardless, she wasn't going to enjoy the experience of accumulating more if she didn't survive the next hour or so; the wealth of Monster Seeds she'd created when she had plenty of Mana was imperative to that survival.

She couldn't replace everything she'd originally had in her dungeon rooms because of the cost difference; the Ironclad Apes and Steel Pythons – in their new advanced forms – were much too expensive. Instead, she made do with Martial Totems for where her Ironclad Apes had been and a plethora of Lengthy Segmented Millipedes to replace the Steel Pythons. The Totems were actually a good replacement for the Apes; even if they weren't as agile, they actually provided more attacking power in comparison.

The Lengthy Segmented Millipedes were a poor substitute for the Pythons, however. They couldn't move quite as fast and although they had 250 segments to them compared to the original 25 on the Centipede, they were still small and wouldn't provide much of a threat by themselves. Still, they seemed to be made of stronger metal and were quite formidable when in large groups, so for every Steel Python she was replacing, she created 10 to 15 Millipedes.

Sandra didn't have time or the available Mana to change or improve any of her existing traps – with the constructs being so expensive – so she left them alone. There also wasn't enough time to carve out any additional rooms or set any other new defenses, so she was basically stuck with what she had at the moment. She just hoped that they were enough to keep the Elites away from her Core; she didn't *want* to kill them, but if they were aiming to destroy her, she didn't want her defenses to hold back any of their lethality.

By the time she was done with replacing all of the absent constructs, her treasury was almost bare. She had a handful of random metal orbs in different sizes left in there as Monster Seeds, though they were joined by big blocks of various (non-Seed) material including Dragon Glass, raw Sapphire, and Steel. The Raw Materials she received from absorbing the hundreds of seeds filled up her capacity rapidly, and only a portion of it needed to be used to create the Monster Seeds she actually needed; as a result, she used a little bit of the Mana she received from that absorption to turn the excess RM into non-Seed blocks of different materials that required a lot of raw Materials to produce.

While she was doing all of that, she was forced to split her concentration between reinforcing her own dungeon and progressing through the reptile Core's dungeon. She quickly considered and then dismissed just having her constructs wait for the situation with the Elites to be resolved before she advanced any further down the foreign dungeon; waiting would only allow the other Core to build its defenses up more with additional defenders as it accumulated Mana, while hers would stay the same. It was entirely possible that waiting an hour or two to keep attacking could mean the difference between success and failure.

And if the Elites took a long time to get through her dungeon, then the risk that the Ancient Saurians and their smaller brethren would reach the Elven village would only increase. Therefore, she surged ahead, doing her best to keep her constructs moving through the other dungeon while filling up her own with more Dungeon Monsters. The process of creating constructs was fairly simple by that point, fortunately, so it was easy to make it almost automatic, which freed up the rest of her mind to tackle the harder task at hand.

The rest of the dungeon rooms her Core-hunting construct force had to fight their way through were difficult...yet easy at the same time. She remembered Winxa saying that most Dungeon Cores weren't as creative with their use of traps as Sandra was, and that definitely showed in the Water-element-based reptile dungeon. The traps in the remaining rooms were just slight variations of the rooms before, though they were set up differently; more powerful water jets in different formations, icicles that shot from the wall instead of the ceiling, more water whips, and a freezing band of moisture that was more spread-out than the first. Fortunately for Sandra, there wasn't a repeat of the massive wall of water that had demolished many of her constructs, but the navigation through the traps – and defending Dungeon Monsters – that *were* there severely cut down on her constructs on their way down to the Core Room.

Entering the final room, her constructs were greeted by a massive room that was around 200 feet in length and width, and about half that tall. There was a very large tunnel that led farther down on the opposite side of the room, and there were no other exits that Sandra could see either inside the room or from without using her Area of Influence. All in all, it looked remarkably empty of any fixtures or possible places for traps, but the room was far from empty; instead, it was half-filled with a Monster that, frankly, seemed like an impossibility.

Six massive snakes – each approximately 80 feet long and 8 to 9 feet wide – were undulating upright above her constructs, all connected together at their tails in some sort of merging of their bodies. The merge created another body that was longer than it was wide, though it was huge; Sandra couldn't estimate its length, however, because most of it was blocking the exit into the Core Room. It was just barely wide enough to allow it to pass through the exit tunnel, which was how it likely got to the room in the first place – but it wasn't going to be letting anything else through. There wasn't even enough of a gap around its body to slide one of her Shears through, and she couldn't see any other way to get past the massive Monster.

How in the Creator's name did this thing come about?

"It sounds like some sort of hydra variant, though I've never heard of one like this before. It must be some sort of special Dungeon Monster granted to the Core – sort of like your Core-specific skills you have – or it could be that it upgraded its Size enough to unlock the ability to create it," Winxa answered, after Sandra described it to her.

Sandra had no idea how to get past it, however, as her construct forces were a mere fraction of what it had been when they first entered. She had 6 Pythons, 3 Apes, 5 Wolves, 4 Jaguars, 6 Blademasters, and exactly 250 Shears left from her original small army, and it didn't look like she was getting any further with what she had. She was just glad that the massive Dungeon Monster was so large that it wouldn't fit out that access tunnel where the Ancient Saurians exited earlier, unless it was widened quite a bit beforehand. Then again, if it had exited with them, it probably wouldn't be there protecting the Core from her constructs.

She paused while she was trying to figure out what to do; fortunately, the hydra variant monster didn't move from where it was, and it was too far away to attack her constructs. It was always possible that she could try to draw it out from the tunnel, which would allow her to slip through some of her faster

450

constructs to destroy the Core – but she doubted it would be deliberately drawn out like that. Sandra had to find another way to—

The Elven Elites chose that moment to enter her dungeon, and most of her control over her dungeon was muted. Luckily, the connection to her constructs facing the massive multi-headed snake monster was still operational and unchanged, but she left them for the moment with simple orders to attack anything that attacked them – and to not attack the hydra-thing.

"…hope this dungeon isn't that fully-developed yet," Sandra heard one of the Elf women say as the Elite group strolled unconcerned through her entrance. She was dressed in unassuming-looking white-and-red robes that were cinched tight against her lithe form. "The rush here drained me a little, and I would love some rest."

"We *always* need rest, Alanthia," the leader said back to her as he – naturally – took the lead. "But with so few of us left, there's just too much work to be done to rest for long. The journey here was enough of a vacation for us compared to the fighting we usually have to do that you should be thankful for it."

"You're right – it was nice not having to watch my back every second of the day like the forests—hold up, Porthel. I can *feel* the Nether energy coming from the room ahead; let me negate it and we can pass through," the woman she assumed was named Alanthia told the leader, which Sandra now knew was called Porthel.

The white light of Holy energy illuminated her hands for a moment before shooting forward into the room, hovering in the center for a moment. A few seconds later, it shot unerringly for the trap's activation trigger near the entrance, smothering it in Holy energy.

"We've got about a minute before that negation spell wears off, so go do your thing, fearless leader," Alanthia said, with a playful wave of her hand at Porthel's face.

He returned a mock salute back at her and stepped inside the room with his beautifully crafted Titanium sword at the ready – where he was immediately descended on by the eight Martial Totems she had stationed on either side of the entranceway. Sandra saw his entire form briefly illuminate with a pale-yellow Air elemental energy before he became almost a blur, moving so quickly that he avoided every attack and circled around to the farthest Totem away from him. Another small expenditure of the brown energy of Earth surrounded his sword and he swung away at her construct, slicing easily through the iron shell of it like it was nothing. In less than a second, one of her defending Dungeon Monsters was destroyed – and the others soon followed.

Sandra kept expecting her Nether strands to come out and grab ahold of him, but nothing happened. Apparently, whatever spell the woman in white and red had cast using her Holy energy had deactivated the trap – at least temporarily.

How is she doing that?

"What? Who is doing what?" Winxa asked, confused. Sandra hadn't even had a chance to pass on what was happening to her because it all happened so fast, and by the time she explained it to her, the Elite group of Elves was already heading to the next room.

"I told you that the Elves are masters at manipulating the elements in which they have access to, didn't I? Apparently, that also extends to being able to somehow sense other elements and be able to counter them. I...think you might be in a little trouble here," the Dungeon Fairy said sadly.

I couldn't agree more. The first room caused exactly zero damage to the Elves and they appeared to not even consider it much of a threat. With the trap completely out of play, the Martial Totems had no chance against the leader; the Air energy he controlled sped him up so fast that they couldn't touch him, and the Earth energy had strengthened and likely sharpened his sword to the point where it could cut through even Iron without any issues.

Porthel didn't have any outward signs of what his elements were, but if she went by the colors that the others were wearing, they had every element covered – and then some. In addition to Alanthia in white and red, the other woman was dressed identically but the robes were colored black and green. The two other men were dressed in leathers and carried masterfully crafted bows; subtle accents of grey, blue, green, and white were easily seen on their leather armor, which meant – if she was correct in her assumption – they had every single element covered between them.

This wasn't a specialized Nether-Core-destroying Elite group that Winxa had theorized might come to try and kill her. No, this appeared to be a group that specialized in destroying dungeons...period. With what she had seen so far, she wondered how powerful the dungeons surrounding the capital had to be to not have been wiped out from them already.

"...seen anything like those monsters before? From what I saw, they appeared to be made entirely of metal," the other woman – whose name Sandra hadn't caught yet – asked the others as they paused in the tunnel leading to the second room.

"No, I've never seen anything like them in all my 453 years – but this is the wastelands, after all, so I guess anything is possible. It's a little worrisome, but if my sword can cut a stone golem apart, it shouldn't have any problem with the metal monsters in this dungeon," Porthel remarked, before forging on ahead.

"I thought you said this was supposed to be a Nether dungeon, Por," said the woman wearing black and green. "But I *feel* Holy energy ahead."

Alanthia was nodding her head as well, confirming the sense of the energy as well. "I feel it too, Clovera – but I guess that just makes this a dual-element dungeon, but that's fairly common. I've never heard of a Nether and Holy combination before, however, so that might explain the strange metal monsters," she added.

"Well, whatever it is, we have a job to do. Clovera, I guess you're up," the leader called back to her.

Sandra watched as the other woman, Clovera, copied almost the exact same spell as Alanthia had in the room before – using her Nether energy, of course. The trap triggers were smothered again and Porthel went to work dismantling her Roaring Blademasters in the room, though he didn't even bother activating his Air-based speed spell. The sixteen spinning constructs were picked apart with the dancing blade of the Elite leader and natural agility of his race.

"Show off," one of the other men remarked with a smile when Porthel was finished with the room's defenders. None of the others had done anything to help him, but he didn't appear to even need it.

"Whatever – I'm just conserving energy, because we don't know what's in store for us in here. I have an odd feeling that we haven't seen even a fraction of what this dungeon is capable of. Especially since these were likely the weakest of the monsters at the beginning; this might be a little more difficult than we were expecting, but I think we can handle it. It's a good thing that those villagers didn't try to assault this place, at least

– they would've been slaughtered in the first room, if not the second," Porthel remarked as they entered the tunnel ahead.

Halfway down, the man with the blue accents on his leather armor and Alanthia both said at the same time, "There's Water energy up ahead."

"What? Are you telling me this is a triple-element dungeon?"

The two that had sensed the elemental energy from Sandra's Water-based trap in the third room nodded their heads slowly, with their eyes wide in worry.

"I've only seen two other dungeons with three elements in all my years...and the only one I've heard of with more than that is the reason why this place is a wasteland even now. It's a good thing we rushed here, because we can't allow the same thing to happen again; we're ill-equipped to stop as powerful of a dungeon as that one was, so it'll be better if this one here is wiped out while it's still in its infancy."

Did that Elf just call me a baby?

"Well, technically, you're still way less than a year old. So, by all accounts, you could be considered an infant," Winxa added unhelpfully.

Sandra watched in mounting fear as the Elves negated her trap, tore through the Small Armored Sentinels wielding Steel swords (the weapons of which actually seemed to have a bit better defense against the Earth-spelled Titanium sword of the leader), and discovered that the next room was filled with a

Fire-based trap. Their faces grew grim as the realization of what they were facing set in.

"There's no turning back – we *must* destroy this dungeon, now, or the world is doomed to suffer untold death and destruction. If one of us falls, we have to keep going – we can't allow this dungeon to grow any more powerful."

Sandra couldn't help but think that Razochek had said approximately the same thing when he discovered the multi-element capabilities of her dungeon. She just wished she was able to communicate with the Elves and try to explain that she wasn't a danger to anyone. But, try as she might, she couldn't think of a way that wouldn't end in her own destruction or the death of Violet, the only other person in her dungeon—

A plan started to hatch in her mind when she thought of the Gnome, though it was going to take the right kind of circumstances to achieve – and more than a little luck.

Chapter 44

Instead of watching while the Elite Elves were slowly but steadily destroying everything within their path on their way to destroy her Core, Sandra concentrated most of her attention on her constructs that were miles away in another Core's dungeon. There was nothing she could think of that could stop them, and unless they suddenly ran out of their innate elemental energy, they didn't appear like they'd have any issues from the rest of her rooms. She realized that she had relied entirely too much on her traps to stop anyone or anything from progressing through her dungeons, and not enough on creating *physical* barriers. And, as much as she hated to admit it, many of her setups involving her constructs were practically useless without the traps to accompany them.

That wasn't to say that none of them were successful, however; it was her smaller constructs that managed to actually do some damage. Her Lengthy Segmented Millipedes, for example, were quite numerous and more difficult to kill because of their ability to continue even when most of their bodies were smashed apart. Two of the Elves that usually hung back while the leader did the fighting were injured as they were swarmed by the millipedes, in fact; it wasn't more than superficial, however, because they were destroyed by a frenzy of elemental spells that practically obliterated them. Any wounds were quickly healed by Alanthia with her Holy energy anyways, but the fact that they weren't invulnerable was good to know.

She also noticed that they took special care to reserve as much energy as they could while delving deeper into her dungeon; their teamwork and attention to detail was superb as well, though she couldn't help but notice whenever she checked on their progress that not everyone was pulling their weight. Other than a few times when they were forced to defend themselves or be overwhelmed by numerous constructs, most of the work was being done by Porthel with his quick movements and his excellent weapon. It wasn't necessarily the fault of the others, though – it was just that all of them specialized in manipulating their elemental energy in the form of spells, many of which wouldn't work well against her constructs.

Using Natural energy to poison a monster? Her constructs didn't have blood to poison.

Trying to burn them with Fire energy? Unless it was superheated to dangerous levels, it wouldn't do much.

Drowning them with Water? Her constructs didn't breathe.

Slicing them up with blades of hardened Air? Mere scratches on their hard bodies for the most part.

The only things that tended to work against them were projectiles like rocks made with Earth energy or restraining them with concentrated masses of elemental energy, though that took a bit to do for anything large enough to be a real threat. Sandra was sure that there were other things they could try – she wasn't an expert on manipulating energy in that manner, after all – they held off for the most part because their leader was doing just fine.

Except that, after a while, she could see that even he was starting to look ragged, after having essentially destroyed 95% of Sandra's constructs by himself. Sandra thought that he was probably going to run out of elemental energy at any time – but he just kept going, regardless.

But as that really wasn't her focus, she only periodically checked on their progress on their way down to her Core. Instead, she was embroiled in her own fight against a six-headed monstrosity that wouldn't move out of her way.

Sandra first attempted to get it to shift out from the exit tunnel – on the off chance that it actually worked – but the only thing that she accomplished was learning that the snakes could strike much faster than she could believe something that large could move. She was expecting them to be relatively slow like the Saurian she had fought outside the Gnome village; on the contrary, each snake head could dart forward and snatch up one of her Shears in less than a second, before rearing back into position. They only had four teeth – two fangs on the top and two on the bottom that dripped with a clear venom – that slid in and out of an internal pocket in their jaws, so her Shears weren't so much "bitten" as "crushed" in its mouth.

As she had figured, no amount of baiting could get the hydra-adjacent monster to move more than an inch or two; however, she did notice what seemed to be its drawback – when it did move, the body moved *very* slowly, which indicated that it couldn't travel very quickly. It was quite possible that it could drag itself with its snake heads by grabbing onto something ahead, but if it were in an open field, it could probably only move a mile every day or two.

Sandra managed to maneuver one of her equally fast Steel Pythons up to its side and a little underneath it, somehow avoiding a dozen strikes by the snake heads and hiding protectively underneath the bulk of the Dungeon Monster. She hoped to be able to bite into the side of the creature and find a way inside of it like what had happened when she killed the Ancient Saurian, but all her Python's bites did was scratch the surface of the hydra-thing's extremely tough skin. After about a minute of that, she was starting to make some progress as some chunks were being ripped away, but then the entire bulk shifted without warning and flattened her own metal snake like a piece of copper in a press. The enormous weight of the monstrous snake was, to put it bluntly, impossibly unreal – but the same could be said considering some of her own constructs, she supposed.

Sandra and her constructs were running out of time. While she was doing all of those tests to see if there was an easy way past, her waiting constructs had been attacked by a small force of reptiles that emerged from somewhere behind them. It was a small force, thankfully, but she did manage to lose another Mechanical Wolf to a crocodile; if she didn't hurry, her force would continue to be whittled down until there was nothing left. While the Core could easily provide unending waves of reinforcements, she couldn't quite do the same at the moment.

Therefore, it was decision time; should she attack all out and hope to be able to do enough damage to kill the massive monster, or should she keep trying out different scenarios to see if there was one that might end up being more effective? As she looked back in her dungeon to see that the Elves had just passed through the thirteenth room in her dungeon with only four more to go before they arrived at her Home room, she chose to go with option one – because she didn't think she'd have enough time before it was too late to matter.

The simple order to attack was the only one she needed to give as her constructs rushed forward, though she did try to get her Shears to aim for vulnerable spots like the snakes' eyes and even their open mouths when they attacked. Either they were extremely unlucky, or the order didn't really translate well, because all 246 of Sandra's remaining Small Animated Shears impacted the same place on the lower "body" of the hydra-creature. Most of them bounced off harmlessly like they did against a turtle shell, when all of them hit the exact same spot at full speed – which even the snakes couldn't match to try to

462

snatch them up – they actually made a sizable hole through its tough outer skin. Greenish blood slowly spilled out of the wound, but on the whole it looked fairly superficial.

And, unfortunately, she couldn't communicate fast enough with her constructs to try to take advantage of the wound. She thought it would be perfect if one of her Pythons were able to crawl inside and wreak havoc on the hydra-creature's internal organs, but they instead just slithered toward the body and tried to eat their way in from below. All but one of them was snatched up by the snake heads, crunched a few times, and then flung away to impact and get further destroyed by the nearby hardened dirt wall.

Her Blademasters were snatched up next and discarded just as quickly as they were bent out of shape, disappearing into their Monster Seeds even before they hit the ground. Her Wolves and Jaguars managed to reach the body and climb up on its back, where they attempted to bite their way through the tough lower portions of the actual snake bodies – Sandra assumed it was in the hope that it would be like cutting its head off. With all of them managing to gather around the same spot, they went to work biting and clawing through the skin and were making some impressive progress – before they started to get snatched up as well. Before long, they too were crushed and sent to join their fellow constructs who had been destroyed before.

Her Apes, on the other hand...didn't have much luck, either. While their hard and heavy Iron bodies resisted being crushed and tossed everywhere, they could at least be marginally picked up and released to bounce and slide away to the other side of the room. After most of them had been picked up and shoved away, they were looking quite beat-up and even missing limbs. Sandra despaired as almost all of her constructs were destroyed, though she did notice that her last remaining Python had managed to circle around the side of the large bulk of the hydra-thing's body. From what she could see, it was wedged into a small crack in the wall where it was in no danger of being crushed or picked up by the snake heads, though the bites it was inflicting still weren't doing a lot of damage.

Given an hour or more, though...

She highly doubted it would be left alone for an hour, but it was at least a shot. Her remaining Apes struggled to attack again, even bent all out of shape, and were picked up and flung away another time. However, something unexpected happened; when one of the snake heads bit down on one of her Apes, its right fangs must've hit the hard Iron wrong, because they snapped off and flew away across the room, ending up near the room's entrance.

The Ironclad Ape that inadvertently caused the damage was flung away with impressive strength from the snake, where it was crushed and destroyed as it impacted the far wall with tremendous force. She was down to only two Apes now – and the hiding/biting Python, of course – and yet she began to see a glimmer of hope.

A few minutes before, while the all-out attack was just starting, the trap that had grabbed her Ape up above finally ran out of Mana and collapsed, releasing her Ape that Sandra had been forced to abandon. She had been working it down through the dungeon, which was a whole lot easier now that there were no defending Monsters in the way, and she knew where all the traps were. The Ape still managed to take some superficial damage from those traps that couldn't be avoided, but overall it was largely undamaged.

She hadn't even known that it would be released until *after* she started her attack, so she didn't factor it into her plans. Now it was going to be an integral part of a new plan; as the other damaged Apes attacked again and Sandra forced the Python out of hiding in order to provide a distraction, her undamaged Ape ran into the room from the tunnel and picked up the large upper fang that had snapped off. Without pausing for more than a moment, it ran full-out towards the distracted hydra-variant; while the snake heads were flinging her other Apes away trying to catch her quick Python, the Ape managed to get close enough to the monstrous Dungeon Monster...and jumped.

It came down with the venomous tooth clutched tightly in its hands, plunging the sharp fang directly into the still-bleeding hole made by her Shears earlier. The snake heads seemed to go berserk after that, knocking the Ape off its body with a snake headbutt and finally catching hold of her Python – which didn't survive long. The two previously damaged Apes were flung away so viciously that they were destroyed upon impact when they hit the ground, rolled, and smashed into the wall.

Sandra watched through her now-slightly-damaged remaining Ape as the snake heads on the hydra continued to flail about crazily in all directions. Fortunately for her, her last construct was flung far enough away that the heads couldn't reach it, though they certainly tried. After a minute, the berserk flailing slowed dramatically until the heads finally stilled for about five seconds – and then they dropped to the floor, dead. A few seconds later, the giant Dungeon Monster dissolved into a Monster Seed, which appeared to be some sort of large Sapphire – much bigger than the one that the Ancient Saurian had dropped.

Instead of celebrating, Sandra immediately had her Ape on the move. Its left arm was damaged enough that it wasn't going to be winning too many fights with it, but she hoped that wasn't going to matter. As her construct passed into the tunnel, it picked up speed and ran as fast as it could into the Core Room. When it got there, she could see that it was another huge room – which only made sense if Monsters like the hydra-thing were created there. Of course, that also meant that the shining blue

Core she was trying to destroy was floating at least 50 or 60 feet off the ground in the middle of the room.

If she had even one pair of Shears left, it would've been easy to reach the Core and hit it – and hopefully hit it hard enough to destroy the shining crystal. As it was, she had a slightly-damaged Ape that couldn't leap more than a dozen feet in the air – if it were lucky. Looking around the rest of the room, however, she realized that even if her Ape could get close enough it probably wouldn't survive long enough to try jumping that high.

Dozens of crocodiles and giant turtles were surrounding her Ape, cutting off the exit back to the rest of the dungeon as well. It looked like the end, so she gave the only order she could to her Ape, knowing that there was no hope for it – but she thought she'd try anyway.

Destroy that Dungeon Core.

The delay between when her order hit the Ape and when it was attacked by the reptiles surrounding it felt like an eternity, but her construct at least fought back on its own at first without needing instruction. First, it picked up a crocodile that tried to snap at its leg by the jaws and used it to smash into another crocodile sneaking up from behind; when those two were stunned by the sudden defense of her Ape, it kicked out and turned over a snapping giant turtle that sought to take a chunk out of the construct's foot. Then it punched out at another crocodile that was getting too close, before kicking out again and crushing the skull of a second crocodile.

She could see when her order hit her Ape, as it paused for a half-second and then jumped over to the over-turned turtle on its back. That half-second allowed the other reptiles to close in, unfortunately, and her construct was in danger of being overwhelmed. However, its orders took precedence over its instinctual need to defend itself and it picked up the giant turtle in its hands – and began to spin around in a circle.

Crocodiles and giant turtles snapped at her Ape's legs but couldn't find purchase, luckily, which allowed her construct to pick up speed. It spun around and around so fast that the Core Room became a blur through the eyes of her construct, until she saw its hands let go of the turtle's shell. Less than a second after the Ape released the giant turtle at high speed like a massive discus, it was swarmed by the reptiles surrounding it.

As it collapsed under their weight, it kept its vision trained on the Core high up above – so Sandra was able to see the shell of its own Dungeon Monster impact and shatter the Core just as her construct was destroyed.

Chapter 45

I did it! I destroyed the other Core!

Her celebration was abruptly cut off as her Shears above the advancing reptile army – including the two massive Ancient Saurians – showed no change.

Uh...Winxa? Aren't they supposed to, like, disappear or something?

"Do you mean the Dungeon Monsters from the other Core? Why would you think that?" the Dungeon Fairy asked.

You know, because I destroyed the Core...I thought they were tied to it and would cease to exist when it was no longer there.

"Not exactly; they are still Mana-formed creations, and technically exist independently of the Core – though they are essentially mindless without a will of their own. What the Core does is absorb the Mana that is funneled to them from the Dungeon Monsters, it also allows them to have control over them. When that control is gone, the Monsters – in this case, the reptiles – will continue to follow their last order until they either succeed or are killed. If they succeed in their order, they will immediately stop and cease to do anything afterwards."

So...the village is still in danger of being destroyed? I did all of that for nothing?

Before Winxa could respond, a notification surprised Sandra.

> **Congratulations!**
>
> *You have discovered another Advancement Source!*
>
> **Dungeon Core Destruction:**
> *Receive AP for eliminating another Dungeon Core*
> *30 AP per Dungeon Core destroyed*
> **Current AP Earned:** 30 AP (1X Reptile Classification Core)

Wait a minute – I can earn AP from destroying Dungeon Cores? Sure enough, when she checked out the screen for her Advancement Point breakdown, it was right there at the bottom. There was still an unknown Source that had yet to be discovered, but that wasn't really a concern of hers right now.

"What? You got some AP from destroying another Core? I've never heard about that before," Winxa said, shocked.

If that isn't a bald-faced admission from the Creator of what I should be doing, then I don't know what is. The two unknown Sources that she had discovered as part of the Advancement system plainly pointed her in a direction that would help the nearby races stave off annihilation: bonding with sentients and destroying other Dungeon Cores. Luckily, she was already inclined to help them – though she didn't know how she felt about targeting the nearby Cores.

Sandra didn't really have time to worry about that, though, because she had bigger problems to deal with – namely

470

the Elite Elves that were just entering the very last room with her Iron-plated Behemoths. Porthel was looking absolutely ragged by that point, drained to the point where he appeared to be pushing himself forward by pure will alone.

"Porthel, you need to rest for a while – maybe even take a small nap so that you can restore some of your elemental energy. You're going to get yourself killed, otherwise," Alanthia said concernedly to their leader.

"*No!* We have to keep going, no matter if it kills me or not," the drained Elf hoarsely replied with ragged breaths. "You've all seen what this dungeon is capable of, and if we let a little something like my life get in the way of destroying the heart of the dungeon, then *everyone* is in danger of being killed by a dungeon that has access to *all the elements!* We've gotten this far, and it can't be much farther – I can feel it." Porthel stumbled forward with misguided determination in his step.

The other Elves just looked at each other in helplessness and followed after him. Porthel pulled out some more of his waning Earth energy and nullified the Air trap that Sandra had placed in the room, which wasn't surprising by that point – but they were about to face something they hadn't seen in the dungeon before: Sandra's Iron-plated Behemoths. The other constructs they had encountered were pale shadows in comparison to the massive Monsters she had in the final room – and this time their main member that could easily kill them was on his last legs.

The Elves stopped in surprise when they saw the Behemoth – all except Porthel; the leader stumbled forward drunkenly and activated what appeared to be the last of both types of his elemental energy. That boost was all he needed to pick him up as he dashed forward, avoided one of the flailing tails, and then jumped up into the air, crashing down sword-first onto the back of the Behemoth. The Earth-energy enhanced Titanium sword cut almost completely through her construct, though in the last couple of inches it stopped, the energy from the Elite leader's sword spell having run out.

Looking at it in surprise, Porthel tried to pull it out of the cut, but the blade snapped in half when he yanked on it the wrong way; fortunately for him, the damage he had done to the Behemoth was enough to destroy it, which meant that it dissolved seconds later, leaving behind a broken blade and a Tiny Dragon Glass Flake. The Elven leader looked at his half-a-sword in shock for a second, before collapsing to his knees in exhaustion.

"I'm...done. I've got nothing left – you must...finish this without me," he said breathily, before pitching forward onto his face as the continuous expenditure of elemental energy finally drained all of his strength. Alanthia rushed to his side and rolled him over, ensuring that he was still alive. Holy-based elemental energy poured out of her and enveloped his entire body, flowing through his armor and settling into his skin; Sandra assumed it was some sort of healing spell. There was no change in him, of course – the exhaustion created from using too much energy too quickly wasn't something that could be healed by anything but a good night's sleep.

"What do we do?" one of the men asked; Sandra still hadn't found out their names, so she could only designate him as the one who had grey and green accents on his leather armor.

The others were silent for almost a minute as they stared at Porthel on the ground, partially asleep but not full-on unconscious or in a coma like Sandra's other visitors. Finally, Alanthia got to her feet and turned to the rest. "We go on, just like he said; we can't fail now when we're so close."

"But…how?"

The Elf in white and red looked at the passageway leading to the next section where the Behemoths were in long hallways, eager to trample whatever invaded their domain.

"We hold nothing back, that's how. Use everything you have to get through; like Porthel said, if one of us falls, the rest have to go on even if it kills us all. One of us has to survive long enough to destroy the heart of the dungeon, even if it means using all of our energy to do it," Alanthia said with determination and a scary look on her face, before heading immediately towards the passageway, a red glow enveloping her left fist and a white glow enveloping her right. The others followed afterward with equally determined looks on their faces.

Based on what happened next, Sandra easily understood why they were so confident in their dungeon-destroying job –

because they were *frightening.* The first behemoth that charged them got a beam of super-hot flames boosted with a swirl of white Holy light, which was more than enough to carve a line through her construct as the Iron covering its outer shell literally *melted off.* It was destroyed within seconds, but not without a cost to Alanthia; she fell to her knees and panted heavily. She waved the others on as she said, "Go on, I just need to catch my breath after that...I'll catch up."

In the next hallway, the leather-clad archer with the grey and green accents on his armor stepped up to the plate and used a spell on his arrow before he released. The sheer amount of energy used in the greyish-green spell was so bright that Sandra couldn't even look at it before it was released; as it left the Elf's bow, however, the glow faded a bit and she could see massive vines expand out from the arrow, which fully enveloped the charging Behemoth. Her construct crashed to the ground as it was tripped up and the vines began to tighten, making the Iron plates of the Behemoth start to screech in protest. But even that didn't actually kill her construct – it just immobilized it.

The man didn't fall to his knees, but he did bend over like he wanted to throw up. "I'm fine – let's get going," he said, following – slowly – after the others as they easily climbed the feebly struggling construct all wrapped up in nature's rope. Looking back at the previous hallway, Sandra could see Alanthia had recovered somewhat and got back up, though she didn't rush forward. By the time she caught up with the others,

Clovera – the other woman in black-and-green robes – was just finishing up flinging a roiling green-and-black spell that rapidly aged the Iron metal of the Behemoth heading their way, until it rusted and fell apart. Just as the others had been affected, so too was Clovera; she fell to her knees but ended up on her side as her strength momentarily gave out. The others looked at her in concern, but she waved them on as well, stating that she'd be along in a moment.

The archer who hadn't attacked yet led the way into the final section of the room where five behemoths awaited them. Without pausing, the man who could control Water and Holy energy charged the arrow he pulled back on his bow with a spinning vortex of blue and white. Sandra could see him shaking from the strain of putting so much energy into it, and he sighed in relief – and likely more than a bit of exhaustion – as he released the arrow into the closest construct. As soon as it left his bow a massive glowing icicle essentially enveloped his arrow and it spun around so quickly it was a blur as it impacted the Behemoth like a giant drill. Sandra's construct rapidly had a hole five feet wide drilled through it, which made it collapse and disappear in less than a second afterward.

There were still four of the Behemoths, however, and they immediately attacked following the destruction of the first. What followed was a chaotic maelstrom of spells being flung at the constructs from the three Elves, as they worked together to destroy them one after another. Clovera joined in after a few seconds and added her flagging energy to the fight, which helped them destroy three more in rapid succession. Sandra couldn't help but notice that all of their subsequent spells were only a fraction of what they had initially started with, and by the time the third Behemoth went down they were all practically lying on the floor.

The very last construct, the final obstacle in between the Elves and Sandra's Core bore down on the worn-out figures without pause. The Elite group was able to struggle to their knees at least, where they threw everything they had at the Behemoth; a large icicle "arrow" impacted its side, breaking apart a small chunk of the Iron-plating but ultimately not doing fatal damage; another arrow landed on the stone floor in front of the construct, and two sharp tree trunks sprouted pointing in the direction of the charging Behemoth – but were destroyed when they were crushed under the weight of the metal monstrosity; bands of black and green twined together wrapped around the construct's two "front" legs, which caused them to rapidly rust and lock up – but then the Behemoth just turned itself around and kept moving using its back legs as its new front legs, dragging the stiff and locked-up rusted legs behind it; finally, Alanthia pulled deep from her reserves of energy and blasted out another super-heated beam of Fire and Holy energy, which severed the front-facing flail-tail – but ultimately ended up doing nothing to stop the construct.

All of them fell down afterwards, too weak from the rapid expenditure of elemental energy to fight their impending doom. They weren't unconscious or half-asleep like Porthel still was in the other room – which may or may not be a bad thing for them; if Sandra was in their place, she wouldn't want to see her death coming. A few more minor spells shot out from the prone forms but ultimately did no damage to the Behemoth, as it was too durable for the minor uses of energy that would've likely killed something flesh-and-blood.

The metal nature of Sandra's constructs was ultimately the Elves' downfall; while they could've theoretically helped throughout the rest of the dungeon – freeing their leader up from having to expend all of his elemental energy to tear through her Dungeon Monsters – only the strongest (and therefore the most expensive energy-wise) of their spells could have any type of lasting effect or end up damaging them. Sandra could well see how effective they would be working as a team in any other dungeon, but she still couldn't help but think that there was still something lacking with their setup, nonetheless.

With them essentially out of elemental energy – or so depleted that most of their spells didn't really do anything effective – the Elite Elves could only wait for their doom. Sandra's Behemoth dragged itself forward and raised its massively heavy Iron-plated foot above the prone form of Alanthia and stomped down—

"STOP!" a voice shouted from the exit leading to Sandra's Home room.

And with that simple word, the foot of the Behemoth stopped an inch away from making an Elven pancake.

Chapter 46

Violet woke up with a jolt and sat up in her smelly-yet-comfortable bed and blinked away sleep. She had gone from what felt like a dead sleep to fully awake – and she couldn't figure out why. *Was it a bad dream?* She couldn't remember dreaming about *anything*, in fact – it was like she was so tired she didn't have any energy left to dream with.

Violet? Oh good, you're up! I need your help with something.

So that's what it was – mystery solved. She rubbed the sleep out of her eyes and immediately wished that she had slept longer, but she had at least gotten enough to feel relatively rested. More importantly, however, was that her elemental energy reserves were at least mostly recovered.

"What's so important that you had to wake me up?" she asked, slightly irritated – but who wouldn't be after being woken up so abruptly?

Sorry about that, but it's a bit of an emergency. The Elite Elves arrived already and are attacking my dungeon with the intent to kill me.

"What? I thought you said they weren't due for at least a couple of days?" Violet said, throwing herself off the bed and steadying herself before she fell on her face – because she wasn't fully coordinated yet. If Sandra's dungeon really was under attack, then she could be in danger herself – not to mention Felbar.

* They apparently decided that I was quite the threat and quickened their pace to reach here ahead of schedule – and then didn't have the decency to wait until morning. It's not going so well, by the way. *

Now **that** didn't sound good. "Why? I've seen your...constructs...and they seem quite formidable to me." If the Elves were able to easily tear through Sandra's monsters as it seemed they were, then that didn't bode well for Violet's own safety.

* Well...about that... *

Sandra proceeded to tell her what had happened with the dungeon that had attacked and destroyed her own village, how it had expanded enough to find the Elves, and then what she did to try to stop them. Violet actually agreed with her decision to destroy the other Core, as she didn't want the same

480

thing to happen to the Elven village as what happened to Glimmerton; unfortunately, many of the monsters that Sandra could've used to defend the dungeon were no longer present to do their jobs as a result.

"As much as I applaud your efforts, it sounds like you've dug yourself a hole here. I've come to appreciate your decisions to help save us, but it looks like I need to take Felbar and get out of here. No disrespect intended, but if you're going down, I don't want to be brought down with you," she said with slight regret. She really did appreciate all that Sandra had done to save their lives and provide them with supplies, but she still couldn't quite forgive the dungeon for the role she played in the deaths of her friend. Nevertheless, things didn't sound good for Sandra's survival.

*Hold on – don't give up on me yet. I have an idea that might work to prevent them from destroying me, but I'm going to need your help. I promise that if things are looking bad, I'll get you out safely. In fact, I've already moved Felbar up to the Assembly and Storage room up above, with one of my constructs there to help get him to safety if things don't work out. *

Violet thought about that for a few seconds. *If Felbar is at least safe, then all I have to do is worry about myself. I've trusted Sandra this far, so I might as well see what this is all about.* She had stayed behind out of an obligation to make sure

Felbar was taken care of; with him assured of safety – if the dungeon was to be believed – then she thought it was worth the risk to herself to see what Sandra had in mind.

"Fine, but if it looks like we're all going to die, I'm out of here. Where do you want me to go?" she asked, finally interested in what was actually happening instead of just wanting to escape.

* Just head back down to where you saw my Core and I'll explain it upon the way. *

So, that's what Violet did; she stopped off by where the trees had been grown and pulled off an orange for a little late-night snack – because it was apparently still night-time, according to Sandra. She couldn't tell that herself, of course, because she hadn't seen the sky in nearly two weeks.

* So, I realized that I was going about this situation with the Elves, and perhaps every other race, all wrong. I was thinking of everything going on – and reasonably so, given my current form – in terms of Dungeon Cores and Dungeon Monsters versus Heroes or Elites or Warbands or Warmasters; I was so worried about trying to prove that I wasn't going to harm them and I only wanted to help that it blinded me to other avenues. What I should've been concentrating on all along was my background,

482

my knowledge of crafting, and, above all, the one thing I have the most actual experience in. *

"And what is that?" Violet asked, interested in spite of the situation about where Sandra was going with all of this.

* *My parents were merchants most of their lives, so naturally I joined the family business. It may not have been my choice of professions, necessarily, but to say I didn't learn from them would be a lie. It was only when I looked at this situation from that perspective, using the knowledge I learned from my father from a young age, that I came up with a solution. Tell me, what would be the biggest obstacle keeping you from becoming a Master Enchanter – if, say, you were given the knowledge you needed?* *

"Well...if I had the knowledge I needed, then I'd say that the biggest issue would be having enough elemental energy to even attempt some of the master-level enchantments and rune sequences," Violet answered. "Even if I had the knowledge of how to do it perfectly *right now*, most of them would require more energy to enchant than I currently have access to." She was more than halfway down to the bottom where Sandra's strange-looking crystal body floated in the middle of the room – but she was also *fully* confused at where the Core was going with her questions.

* And what is preventing you from acquiring more elemental energy reserves? *

She had to think about that for a moment. Everyone knew that killing a dungeon's monsters was the fastest way to increase your available pool of elemental energy; there was something about killing them that released some sort of *power* that was absorbed by anyone nearby. However, her people had also learned over centuries of testing that you could also hone your energy use by months of endless repetition and increase your actual energy reserves by using vast quantities of energy over a short period of time.

This was dangerous, however, as it could potentially damage your ability to manipulate the energy if you consistently "bottomed-out" – which meant essentially using every last drop of your supply. You usually passed out before that happened if you did it *too* fast, though, but it was possible to push through and do it. It was still extremely dangerous.

She had heard a rumor that the other races could get stronger like that as well, though they rarely – or never – used their elemental energy to create enchantments. They used them in different ways, which was fine for them; Violet was much more inclined to trust in enchantments than by flinging dangerous elements around willy-nilly like the Elves or enhance her body like the Orcs reportedly did.

"Time and ability, mostly. I don't have time to repeatedly create one enchantment over and over, honing my skills in enchanting and *maybe* increasing my energy reserves by a small fraction. And I don't have the ability to take on and kill monsters, which would help but would still take a while. That, and draining myself completely is way too dangerous, because we're not meant to live for long without some sort of elemental energy in our body," she finally replied honestly. That was the main reason people either damaged their ability to manipulate elemental energy or even *died* when pushing themselves too hard; the energy was a vital part of your body and being without it was akin to being severely dehydrated or starved for days on end.

It was a shame that the only way to fill it up again was to rest and sleep; if there were some other way to fill it up quickly, she would do almost anything to find it.

What if there was a way to regenerate that energy without having to sleep? *

Is she reading my mind? Violet wouldn't have put it past the Core, given that the Gnome didn't know exactly what the strange "bond" she had agreed to actually did. Then the import of what Sandra said hit her and she stopped in her tracks. "You've got to be kidding...that's what this is about? Everyone knows that it can't be done; other than a few fruits and other edible items like that impossibly rare Ambrosia you and Jortor were talking about — that can temporarily boost your energy reserve — there is nothing that has ever been found that can actually *restore* energy other than rest and sleep."

*Ah, but what if there was? How valuable would something like that be? *

"I don't think you'd even be able to put a price on something like that—wait a minute, you're serious, aren't you?"

*Absolutely. Which is why I need your help. I'm still not quite practiced enough to do as intricate an enchantment as I need, so I need you to do it for me. *

Violet couldn't believe what she was hearing, but she picked up her pace in her descent towards Sandra's room — just in case it wasn't too good to be true. Sandra wouldn't explain any more until the Gnome got there. When she finally arrived, she found that the room was partially filled with about two dozen of Sandra's larger constructs, though they were congregated near the other, larger entrance. She asked about it earlier and was told that it led to the actual defensive dungeon rooms, so she assumed that they were gathered there as some sort of final defense of the Core.

Directly below the glowing crystal that was Sandra was her old friend the crazy multi-colored shapeshifter. And near that was a pile of colored orbs that looked awfully familiar. As she moved towards them, she heard the sounds of metal banging around and other unfamiliar noises coming from the tunnel leading to the defensive dungeon rooms.

We're going to have to hurry – they are almost here. Though, I'm going to have to change my plans with them a little bit; don't worry, though, I think it will be for the better.

Violet had no idea what Sandra was talking about, but that didn't matter because she had finally recognized the colored orbs in a haphazard pile. They were representative of all of the elements and what had been used to bond with the Core nearly two weeks ago – and the grey and green ones still called to her.

She looked over at the shapeshifter to see that it wasn't there anymore; instead she was looking at a copy of her naked self again.

I apologize, but this will only be temporary until I can show you the enchantments I need.

She bit back her anger at the appearance of her naked copy as she watched the shapeshifter make some complicated and not-so-complicated runes in the air, though no energy was sent into them. Which was a good thing, as they likely would've exploded with how poorly they were executed.

She recognized some of the runes, but she could sort of understand what the other ones were; regardless, she soon started to divine what she was looking at.

"That's...that's...genius! But do you think it will work?"

*Honestly, I have no idea – but at this point I don't think it will hurt to try. Now, excuse my poor enchanting skills – I've only been technically doing it for less than a day, you know – but this is how I **think** they should be strung together... *

Chapter 47

When Sandra looked back on that last half-hour when the group of Elite Elves were tearing through her dungeon like it was a leisurely stroll through the streets of their capital, she honestly thought that she was going to be on the defensive side of the upcoming negotiation. Fortunately – for Sandra, at least – the sheer ferocity, mass, and defense of her Iron-plated Behemoths turned the tide.

She was just glad that she had been prepared for any eventuality.

If they had broken through her massive constructs and made it to her Home, she had some reinforcements that she had managed to scramble together from the constructs that had been destroyed on the Elves' descent through her dungeon. One strange thing she noted – and asked Winxa about – was that she couldn't absorb any of the Monster Seeds while the Elves were still in the room.

"It allows the sentient races to collect them if they wish to, though these intruders have something other than acquiring 'loot' in mind, as you call it. As for why the other Core was able to absorb it almost instantly when you attacked its dungeon, it's because Dungeon Monsters aren't classified as sentient intruders, so the restriction was negated." As strange as that sounded, it made sense. Otherwise there would be no reason to enter a dungeon – from the people's perspective – unless they were there to destroy the Core.

Just minutes before the Elves entered the final section of the last defensive room, Violet had finally succeeded in enchanting what Sandra was thinking would be her ticket to survival. And, she secretly hoped, another step in the goal she had made for herself; even though it now felt like it was being pushed on her by the Creator, she still personally desired to help all of the sentient races nearby. Whether it was through destroying nearby Cores or through her crafting, there were multiple avenues to success that she could see.

She just had to share that vision with those she was hoping to save.

The issue she had been having before with trying to convince the Elves that she wasn't a danger – and that she was only trying to help – had one major flaw that she only just recognized through her experience as a merchant. Very few people (or Dungeon Cores, for that matter) did things for free – it was as simple as that.

Sure, there were good Samaritans out there that genuinely helped people that needed help, asking for nothing in return. But even most of them – but not all, of course (she did believe that some *were* actually entirely altruistic) – basked in the feeling that helping other people gave them, or the fame that came with it, or just secretly hoped that what they were doing would come around again and benefit them somehow in the future. This couldn't be truer of the merchants she and her father had associated with over the years.

She wanted to help the people for multiple reasons, and not all of them were altruistic. For one, she felt somehow guilty by being associated with the other Dungeon Cores that murdered and slaughtered hundreds or thousands of the races every year. Two, she wanted to be left alone to do her crafting, and the best way to do that would be to eliminate the threat of the nearby dungeons so that they wouldn't try to attack her. Three, she wanted her crafting to *make a difference* – and all the feelings that went along with that. And four (and probably the most selfish reason), was that she wanted to be looked on with appreciation and perhaps even a little envy from those around her – which were two traits she had rarely experienced when she was Human.

But nobody else needed to know those reasons, as they may or may not understand them. What most people understood, however, were the reasons most people did what they did – at least back in Muriel: to make life better. It could be accumulating money that made life better, or building a larger house, or eating delicious foods; in the case of those lands surrounding her wastelands, it was *safety*. Safety against the nearby Dungeon Monster attacks, safety for their family, safety for their people – it was essentially all the same.

Therefore, Sandra was going to start selling that safety.

Selling wasn't quite the right word, as she didn't necessarily need anything they could provide – except maybe some rare materials. Other than that, what Sandra really needed was their *Cooperation*.

Violet had done a superb job, but even when she was done with the enchantment, Sandra could see some improvements that could be made. Regardless, the glowing Elemental orb of Spirit Mana was a sight to behold – *and it worked!*

Using the nearly invisible "cage" surrounding her Core as inspiration, Sandra had devised a way to apply parts of that enchantment to create something that would act in a similar manner – but basically in reverse. Whereas the enchantment and rune sequences on the "cage" around her were designed to absorb both the ambient Mana and the Mana from the deaths of living beings that were funneled to her, the much smaller enchantment "cage" on the Large Spirit Elemental Orb Violet was holding did the opposite.

By inverting the most important runes she had identified, **Absorb** and **Convert**, instead of absorbing and converting ambient Mana, it would *absorb* Mana from the Elemental Orb and *convert* it to elemental energy. By inserting another rune in the sequence, **Transfer**, it would transfer that energy to anything that came into contact with it – which was exactly what had happened to Violet when she held it after the enchantment was complete.

492

Sandra hadn't needed her to say anything; the look of wonder on her face had been enough to prove that it was working. And with that glorious piece done, proven, and working exactly how she had imagined it would, the last piece of the puzzle was complete.

"STOP!" Violet yelled out as she stood on the edge of the tunnel leading to the last defensive room. It was entirely unnecessary, of course, because Sandra completely controlled her constructs, but it hopefully gave Violet a little more authority in the eyes of the Elves. Since Sandra couldn't communicate with them, she had to hope that at least one of the exhausted Elites could speak at least a little bit of Gnome.

"Is that...a goblin? What's a goblin...doing in here?" the archer in grey and green wheezed out.

"No, that's not a goblin, that's a Gnome," Clovera spoke up from the ground as she struggled to rise.

Alanthia had even gained a little strength back by that time and was able to scramble on all fours out of the way of the stopped Behemoth foot that was hovering over her body like a death sentence. "She's right – don't any of you speak Gnomish? I clearly heard her say 'Stop', despite the fact that I haven't heard it spoken in many, many years," the white-and-red-robed Elf remarked.

Sandra and Violet were in luck. She translated that last part for the Gnome to indicate that Alanthia was the one to talk to but avoided mentioning anything about goblins – there was no need to make her annoyed at that point. Then she fed to Violet what she wanted her to say, though she left it up to the Gnome in how she wanted to go about it.

"Do you yield?" Violet asked Alanthia, walking up confidently even though Sandra knew the Gnome was fairly intimidated by the Elite Elf. Fortunately, she was still holding onto the...*hmm, what to call it...*Mana Converter? Elemental Energy Recharger? Miracle Energy Source? Regardless of the name, Violet gained a bit of confidence from the enchanted Elemental Orb as she siphoned off the Mana inside of it. The conversion process from Mana to the energy that she – or any other sentient – could use wasn't instantaneous; it slowly refilled the Gnome's energy over time instead of all at once, but it was still a whole heck of a lot faster than refilling it while sleeping.

And it didn't appear to be a 1-to-1 ratio, either; while she couldn't see exactly how much energy Violet was gaining from the enchanted item, she *could* vaguely sense the Mana level in the Orb had only fallen by a small amount. She thought about a way to possibly recharge the Orb through the ambient Mana around it sort of like how her own Core functioned, but for the moment that wasn't part of the enchantment; as a result, it was finite, but hopefully it would last a while before the Mana ran out.

"Yield?" Alanthia spoke back to her in stilted Gnomish as she struggled to get to her feet – and failed. The Elf was too

494

drained from her energy expenditure to get past her knees. "What are you talking about? And what is a Gnome doing in a dungeon?"

Sandra was glad she didn't have to translate, otherwise the delay in the conversation would eventually get annoying. "I'm speaking for the Core of this dungeon and she has an offer for you."

"She? Offer? I have no idea what you're talking about, but even the Gnomes have to know about the danger a dungeon like this would impose on us all." The Elite Elf looked confused, and so did the others; obviously none of them spoke Gnomish, so they didn't know what the conversation was about.

"As hard as it is to believe, Sandra – the dungeon here – isn't a threat to any of you. In fact, it's just the opposite – she wants to help. It sounds crazy, I know, but as far as I can tell it's true," Violet continued, to Sandra's consternation. *Crazy?*

"I don't believe you – the dungeon must have done something to your mind to make you think that way. I've seen entirely too many of my friends die over the years from a dungeon's monsters or traps to know better," Alanthia retorted grimly.

"Believe me or not, it doesn't really matter to me. What matters is that you were about to die before the monsters of this dungeon were stopped – or do you believe you would've lived another minute or two? It appears as though you've used almost all of your elemental energy reserve to get even this far."

The Elf appeared as though she wanted to protest – but she literally didn't have a leg to stand on. "You...may have a point. If I had just a little more energy, I would've torn through this last metal monster and then would've destroyed the heart of this dungeon."

Sandra ushered in her constructs she had created as reinforcements through the tunnel, and their appearance made the faces of all the Elves drop in resignation – and a little fear. That wasn't exactly her plan, as it was just to show that fighting would prove fruitless, but it served her purposes – for the negotiation, at least. And this was a negotiation, even if the Elves – and Violet – didn't realize it yet.

"Okay...so maybe not. So, what is it that this dungeon wants?" Alanthia asked bitterly.

"Like I said, she wants to help. But she also needs something in return."

"What could we possibly have that a dungeon could want?" The Elf looked both confused and wary.

"She needs to...*bond* with you. As well as agreeing to help in the future in a joint project of cooperation between the different races?" Violet said, a questioning tone in her own voice as she repeated what Sandra was telling her.

"I won't be some sort of slave to a dungeon!" Alanthia practically shouted – or as much of a shout as she could with her exhaustion.

"It's not any sort of slave bond, it's something else entirely. First, it will allow Sandra to talk to you—"

"And control my mind, apparently," Alanthia rudely interrupted her. Sandra could see Violet starting to lose any intimidation she felt from the Elves and was starting to get a little angry.

"Fine, believe what you will. If it were up to me, I'd have let you all die here, because I'm pretty sure you all thought I was a goblin when you first saw me, didn't you?" Alanthia didn't have the presence of mind to mask her guilty expression. "That's what I thought. But the fact of the matter is, your people need you, and I don't want another innocent village to be destroyed."

The Elite Elf tensed up at that. "Are you telling me this dungeon will destroy our village if we don't agree with this 'bond' thing?"

"No, not at all. In fact, Sandra saved some of us from a full-scale attack against our own village by an army of monster lizards and crocodiles and turtles. And while she ended up very recently destroying the dungeon responsible for it, there is another army of them headed for your people's village right now." Sandra was glad Violet didn't mention *how* the reptiles had been able to attack them in the first place.

"What?" Alanthia asked, shocked. "That's impossible!"

"Again, believe what you will. I'm sure your people need your help, because if it was anything like what attacked us, they won't survive for long. And since you destroyed most of Sandra's monsters, there's no army of constructs to help defend them – if your people even allowed them to."

Alanthia was silent for almost a minute before she finally translated all that was said in Gnomish to the other Elves. Their expressions ran the gamut between confusion, anger, and finally fear – though it was obviously fear for the villagers, and not necessarily themselves. Sandra was glad to see that they cared for their people that way; from what she could tell, they didn't enjoy delving through dungeons and destroying their Cores – it was only done to ensure the safety of their people.

Silence reigned over the room for a few minutes before, finally, she saw resignation on all of the Elves' faces. "I hope we don't regret it, but if what you say is true – and we can't afford to lose any more of our people – then we...agree to this bond. But even if you let us leave, we're essentially all out of energy. We won't be much use in defending the village."

"And that's where the help Sandra said would come in. She has developed something...unique and wonderful...to help you with your problem." Sandra told her which one of the archers to go to, as it wasn't completely obvious which one would be the most receptive. As she approached the man, she held out her hand with the enchanted Elemental Orb.

"I...can feel something within that thing...what is it?" the archer said, getting to his knees from his previous semi-prone position.

"It's something called a...Spirit Energy Orb, and it will help," Violet said, naming the enchanted Orb. Sandra thought it was a good name, as it was simple and fairly described what it functionally was. With obvious reluctance, she passed it to the archer and instantly Sandra could see a change pass over him.

"I can feel my Spirit energy returning! How is this possible?" he exclaimed in wonder as he held onto the Spirit Energy Orb. Some of the color that Sandra didn't even realize had faded from his skin started to return, like he was quickly recovering from some kind of convalescence. And, in general, that's pretty much what the rapid expenditure of elemental energy was.

"It's something that the dungeon came up with just recently, and she has plans to give you all one once you've bonded with her. It's a relatively slow recharge to your elemental energy, but by the time we're done here and get you back to the village, I imagine you'll be ready to put the hurt on those massive lizards. The only problem, however, is that in order to create one of these Energy Orbs for each of the elements, Sandra needs to do something...strange," Violet told them hesitatingly.

"Strange how?" Alanthia said.

Her question was answered when Sandra had her Unstable Shapeshifter enter the room in all its multi-colored glory.

"Don't worry, it's only a little blood," the Gnome said, smiling innocently.

Chapter 48

The next hour was a whirlwind of activity. Sandra acquired a sample of each of the Elves' blood – including their fallen leader's in the earlier part of the room – and then retreated with her Shapeshifter back to her Home room while the others stayed where they were. Not that they could move much from where they were, other than the archer that was holding onto the Spirit Energy Orb and looked to have no intention of letting it go. The Elf archer had already recovered enough to stand up and, although he wasn't quite back into fighting shape, he was much better than just a short time ago.

Now that she had seen the complete enchantment with its rune sequence, Sandra was able to copy it using the copies of each Elf with their specific elements. She previously reasoned that the "unstable" part of the Shapeshifter – where it was impossible to shift for a period of time – only kicked in after a set amount of total time in Shifted forms passed; she worked it out when she had originally copied Violet and then Echo earlier in the day. Even given that, she had to work very quickly to finish with all of the Elemental Orbs before it kicked in.

Fortunately, the energy cost of the enchantment was very small – probably both in relation to its actual size and the fact that it didn't do anything really...*flashy*. Most of the runes were basic utility enchantments, and those rarely cost a lot of energy to produce — at least from the information she had learned while she was still Human. That low energy cost was a good thing, because the first two Sandra tried to make failed miserably — but at least there wasn't an explosion. The rune sequences weren't even fully-developed, so it didn't even pull any energy from the Shapeshifter before they just fizzled away.

When she finally completed one, however, she was elated. Of course, it was fairly crude compared to the one Violet had made, but it would work; how well, she wasn't sure, but it was better than nothing. Subsequent enchantments were marginally better, however, so she knew she *could* improve — it would just take time.

While she was doing that, she was also using some of her smaller constructs to deliver normal Elemental Orbs to the Elves to start the bonding process. As hesitant as they were, they all still agreed to it, and the process used only twice the amount of resources as it did with the Gnomes. *Obviously, it's based on size or some other metric I don't understand.*

Before she bonded with Porthel, however, she made sure the Elven Elite leader had possession of the Earth and Air Energy Orbs to help restore his energy levels a little — enough to wake him up. The others had to be there to calm him down, though even when they did he was against the whole bonding process — until he really looked at the Energy Orbs he was holding. Eventually, with the others already bonded to Sandra — and the "gift" of the Orbs already in his possession – he agreed to it reluctantly.

"But what about the Elf that was captured and killed by you? Are we supposed to forget that?" he asked, still unsure about everything that had been decided without his knowledge.

*Echo is fine. She was bitten by a deadly venomous snake that came from the other dungeon and I had to pull her inside to bond and then heal her. I'm not sure how long she's going to be out still but bonding with someone while they're unconscious tends to send them into some sort of coma. My Repair Drone is keeping her alive right now, so that's why she hasn't been released yet. *

"What are your plans with her?" Alanthia asked.

*I didn't really have **any** plans with her, other than to save her. But now that we've brokered an agreement here, I'd like to keep her near as a sort of Elven...liaison. It will make it easier to communicate with the village if there is a need in the future. *

"I...understand. Speaking of the village, we need to get back if this lizard army is as close as you say," Alanthia remarked hurriedly.

Instead of having them travel back up through the dangerous parts of the dungeon – there weren't any constructs, but the traps were technically still active – Sandra had them travel through her Home room so that they could reach her VATS to the surface. She still didn't completely trust them, so she made sure to keep them "under guard" from her constructs as they passed through; they were anxious to get back to the village, however, and still consumed with wonder at the Energy Orbs they were carrying in their now-bronze-gear-tattooed hands from the Visitor Bond.

Before they went too far, though, she instructed Porthel to grab a new sword from the "Armory" nearby, as his sword had been destroyed. Of course, she only had high-quality Steel swords for him instead of his Titanium one, but he was happy with it, nonetheless.

"You...crafted all of these?" he asked in shock as he took in all of the weapons and random pieces of armor that she had been storing there.

*Yes, it's something I enjoy doing. I'm a crafter's dungeon at heart, after all. *

Porthel was silent as he selected one of the thinner, yet strong and durable, Steel longswords Sandra had lovingly crafted; she had to admit that it was one of her better ones, which just went to show that the Elf had a very discerning eye. "I will freely admit that I don't fully trust you, being what you are, but...you're also unlike any other dungeon I've ever seen or

504

heard about. The verdict is still out on whether what you're doing has alternative motives, and only time will tell. Regardless, I thank you for these gifts and for sparing our lives when you could've ended us quite easily," he said sincerely, before his voice turned harsh. "Of course, if you are deceiving us about anything – including this lizard army that is purportedly heading for the village – then you can be assured we'll be back."

*Fair enough. Let's just consider this more of a business deal rather than...an alliance. If you hold to your end of the bargain, I'll hold to mine. *

He nodded in acceptance without saying anything more, before he joined the others in traveling up to the top of the dungeon using Sandra's VATS rooms. They were barely fazed by the fact that they were being shot straight up with an Air-based trap, but they also had other things on their minds. Not to mention the "miracle" Energy Orbs they still held in their hands.

Sandra's Mechanical Jaguar Queen was still in the Assembly and Storage room; she hadn't sent it against the Elves after it was obvious that it likely wouldn't have been much good – and it was also set up there to ferry Felbar away if Sandra were to be destroyed. Since that didn't look like it would happen, Felbar was moved back to safety – now in Violet's bedroom down below – and the Jaguar was free; it was also more than strong and large enough to transport all of the Elves on its back to get to the village faster than they otherwise would've arrived.

As they left, Sandra couldn't help but be proud of what she had accomplished – with the help of Violet, of course. She had created something new through crafting that had never been seen before, and thoughts of how to improve upon it and expand its capabilities came to her in waves. Not only that, but she had survived when all had been almost lost, she had *bonded* the Elite Elves, and she had established a...business relationship with them.

Father would be so proud.

*   *   *

Sandra was right about the capabilities of the Elven Elites against "normal" monsters. With the help of the villagers who had at least 20 minutes of warning before the reptile army arrived, they set up an impromptu defense that worked remarkably well.

When they were originally sighted coming out of the trees (aided by torches lit at the forest's edge and spaced all over the valley leading to the village, since it was still dark out), the smaller reptiles were keeping pace with the two Ancient Saurians; when the village came within view, however, the smaller reptiles must have had orders to attack as soon as they could because they streamed forward, leaving the massive lizards behind. With forewarning of the attack, the villagers were easily able to use their bows at a distance – many with similar elemental energy manipulations as the Elite archer who had invaded Sandra's dungeon, thereby making them deadlier – to wipe out more than half of them before they got within a hundred feet. The rest were taken out by the Elites, with fireblasts, shards of ice, dark Nether-y tendrils, sharp thorns, and even hardened slices of Air assaulting them from all sides. They only held back their energy use a little, because it started to refill from their Energy Orbs almost immediately. It was a little awkward for them to hold while they were attacking, she noticed, and she immediately thought about crafting some sort of necklace to hold it close to their skin. Maybe even enchant the necklace as well...and then add some gemstones with even more enchantments...

She was lost in the crafting possibilities as she watched all the Elves wait for the massive lizards to get closer, as they were still quite a bit slower than the smaller reptiles had been. The Elites even passed around their Energy Orbs to the villagers to help restore some of their energy, though to Sandra it almost looked like they were reluctantly handing over their first-born children. By the time the Saurians were within range, most had been able to restore at least a small amount of their energy before the Elites collected the Orbs again.

It was a time-consuming slaughter, but a slaughter, nonetheless. Arrows enhanced with elemental energy rained down on both Saurians, followed up by shards of ice, stone, hardened air, fireballs, poison gas, and all matter of manipulated elemental energy attacks from afar. Even the toughened skin of the massive lizards couldn't stand up to that, and their wounds mounted until one fell while it was still 50 feet out from the village. The second must've activated whatever special ability it had to speed up, as it stumbled quickly forward, bleeding, burnt, poisoned, and barely alive.

Porthel took the initiative and sped himself up, enhanced the strength and power behind his new Steel sword from Sandra, and proceeded to hack at its neck a couple of times while dodging attempted bites from the Saurian. It wasn't long until even the less-powerful Steel sword was able to cut through its neck and it fell dead, only feet from reaching the village.

Nice job, Porthel. Congratulations are in order. Just don't forget our agreement.

The Elite leader looked up into the night sky and somehow pinpointed her Shears watching from above. "Don't worry, I've not forgotten. But I think we're going to need more of these Energy Orbs; they are extremely valuable in a fight, and I can see these villagers eyeing ours."

*I will be crafting some more soon, especially since those that you have are finite. I'm not sure exactly how long they'll last, but they will run out eventually. *

The Elite leader looked surprised as he held up one of his Energy Orbs. "These will run out of energy? You didn't tell us that!"

*It's all part of the package, I'm afraid. I guess I'm in the consumable trade now – I've got to keep you coming back for more, after all. *

"You're more devious than I gave you credit for. Though, even if that's the worst of it, you're still the strangest dungeon heart I've ever heard of."

*Thanks...I think. *

As the Elves celebrated that night, Violet went back to bed – she was still tired despite all of the activity – though the Gnome crafted another Spirit Energy Orb and even a Natural Energy Orb for herself by copying what Sandra had her create earlier, and then slept with them curled in her arms like two little babies. Sandra did the same for herself – not the sleeping, but the crafting – and found that the Orbs actually replenished the elemental energy in her Shapeshifter, which was extremely handy. Then she spent the next day replacing most of her constructs that had been destroyed, while also devising plans for the future.

Sandra still hadn't had any contact with the Dwarves (Kelerim as a half-Dwarf didn't count), so that was something she'd need to do soon. She also had to figure out what was going on with the Orcs, and whether Kelerim had succeeded in finding his father. The Gnomes she had saved and had left her dungeon were probably still on the road, but eventually Gnomeria would learn about her existence.

Most importantly, however, was the large influx of materials she had gained access to either through natural means or through her Transmutation Core-specific ability. With the ability to enchant now – though she *really* needed to practice – and those new materials, there was so much crafting to be done…

Felbar and Echo woke up within an hour of each other approximately a day and a half after the Elite Elves had saved their village from destruction. Felbar was understandably confused, shocked, angry, and – at the same time – *intrigued* by the dungeon and the development of the Energy Orbs. Fortunately, Violet was there to calm him down and answer any of his most pertinent questions, though Sandra chipped in whatever information he requested when he started asking specifics.

He may be a gruff, grizzled-looking warrior on the outside, but there's obviously a shrewd mind underneath that exterior.

She had to leave Violet to get him acquainted with the dungeon and get him some sustenance as well; he woke up just as hungry and thirsty as Kelerim had all those weeks ago. Echo didn't have someone familiar there to get her accustomed to her surroundings and to explain everything the way Violet had for Felbar – so that job was left to her.

Sandra briefly thought about using her Shapeshifter to become one of the Elite Elves, but with all of the other projects she had going on, she hadn't quite yet had time to craft any clothes; she didn't think that having one of them dressed in a sheet with a hole cut out would be the best first impression. That, and if her Shapeshifter ended up reverting back to its normal form while talking to the likely-confused Elf after she woke up, the strangeness and deception probably wouldn't go over well. Besides, she still couldn't actually "talk" out of the Shifted forms, so it was ultimately a poor idea.

Therefore, when Echo woke up – inside a little room branching off from the growing room down below that Sandra made and moved her to, with just a Repair Drone nearby – Sandra was there to greet her...via her mind.

*   *   *

Echo struggled awake, a strange nightmare bombarding her mind with thoughts of strange metallic undead monsters and snakes – *oh, how I **hate** snakes.* Finally, she was able to open her eyes and did so abruptly, staring at a stone ceiling above her. It definitely didn't look like an arborent, and her people rarely built with stone, so she must be—

She quickly sat upright and saw she was in a small room, with an exit leading...somewhere – where that somewhere was, however, was a mystery. A moment after sitting up, she held her head in her hands as the room started to spin, the act of sitting up making her dizzy. She immediately noticed that she was practically starving and likely dehydrated; the lack of food and water probably had a big part in her dizziness.

"Wha—? Where—?" she asked the room when she finally got a chance to look around, before scooting away (more like flailing because of how weak she was) from one of the white cylindrical monsters she recognized in the corner. She waited for a moment to see if it was going to attack her, but when it didn't even move she started to relax a little...until a voice that sounded like it was in her head spoke to her—

* *Hello, Echo. I apologize for the sparse accommodations, but I haven't had the chance to build you a bed quite yet.* *

"Who are you? *Where* are you? Am I a prisoner?" The questions just rolled off her tongue as she began to panic.

*Oh, no – not at all. But quite a lot has happened since I had to heal you from that snake bite. Now, let me explain exactly who I am... *

End of Book 2

Author's Note

Thank you for reading The Crafter's Defense!

Sandra made a lot of improvements to her dungeon in this book, not the least of which being the creation of her AMANS above her dungeon. I wanted to be able to speed up her progress without making her too overpowered, which was what the increase in incoming Mana was able to achieve. Even with plentiful Mana, the one thing she *didn't* have enough of was...time. Time until she was attacked by Elves, the time needed to upgrade, the time stolen away by her Classification advancement – they all hindered her in some way, but that also led to some interesting developments.

In the third book, I'm planning on including more enchanting, more crafting, and the introduction of the Dwarves nearby. Eventually, Sandra would like to collaborate with all of the races to help defend themselves, but only time will tell if she ends up getting what she wants.

Again, thank you for reading and I implore you to consider leaving a review – I love 4 and 5-star ones! Reviews make it more likely that others will pick up a good book and read it!

If you enjoy dungeon core, dungeon corps, dungeon master, dungeon lord, dungeonlit or any other type of dungeon-themed stories and content, check out the Dungeon Corps Facebook group where you can find all sorts of dungeon content.

If you would like to learn more about the GameLit genre, please join the GameLit Society Facebook group.

LitRPG is a growing subgenre of GameLit – if you are fond of LitRPG, Fantasy, Space Opera, and the Cyberpunk styles of books, please join the LitRPG Books Facebook group.

For another great Facebook group, visit LitRPG Rebels as well.

If you would like to contact me with any questions, comments, or suggestions for future books you would like to see, you can reach me at jonathanbrooksauthor@gmail.com.

Visit my Patreon page at https://www.patreon.com/jonathanbrooksauthor and become a patron for as little as $2 a month! As a patron, you have access to my current works of progress, which I update with (unedited) chapters every Friday. So, if you can't wait to find out what happens next in one of my series, this is the place for you!

I will try to keep my blog updated on any new developments, which you can find on my Author Page on Amazon.

To sign up for my mailing list, please visit: http://eepurl.com/dI0bK5

To learn more about LitRPG, talk to authors including myself, and just have an awesome time, please join the LitRPG Group.

Books by Jonathan Brooks

Glendaria Awakens Trilogy

Dungeon Player (Audiobook available)

Dungeon Crisis

Dungeon Guild

Glendaria Awakens Trilogy Compilation w/bonus material

Uniworld Online Trilogy

The Song Maiden (Audiobook available)

The Song Mistress

The Song Matron

Uniworld Online Trilogy Compilation

Station Cores Series

The Station Core (Audiobook available)

The Quizard Mountains (Audiobook available)

The Guardian Guild (Audiobook available soon)

The Kingdom Rises

The Other Core

Spirit Cores Series

Core of Fear

Dungeon World Series

Dungeon World (Audiobook available)

Dungeon World 2 (Audiobook available)

Dungeon World 3 (Audiobook available soon)

Dungeon Crafting

The Crafter's Dungeon (Audiobook available)

The Crafter's Defense

Made in the USA
Monee, IL
29 October 2020

46297464R00300